THE LAST OFFENDER

By

NOAH NICHOLS

To Tamara, who had/has the patience of a million monks to deal with me and my literary crazy.

Thank you kindly…

Life is confusing and people are insane.
-Langhorne Slim

Contents

FIRST STRIKE

Sometime in 2028…

INSIDE: The Detainee

Johnny Helks, who'd been sprawled out for a multitude of hours, was fast asleep on cold concrete. Inside the dank cell he so dolefully called home, his living quarters consisted of confining bars and defining scars.

"HOLY! WHAT IN THE…" A massive, life-altering explosion occurred suddenly just outside the prison where Johnny had been toiling away for nearly ten years, promptly jarring him awake with what seemed to be some sort of earthquake. The deafening shock wave shook the penitentiary, rattling all fortified sides of the holding pen as though they were flimsy window drapes.

That loud blast…what was that? And why am I on the floor instead of my bed?

The currently-in-the-dark prisoner's confusion caused him to create a million and one different scenarios, fluctuating haphazardly until a certain scenario sprung to mind. Mentally jumping to a tragic—and conceivably premature—conclusion based solely on his own conjured fear, the detainee's mind raced through a gamut of *what-if*s and *oh-no*s.

Maybe some bomb just went off.

Johnny always knew that it was a possibility for a thing like that to occur, but never did he think it was something that could turn into a harsh reality.

"Don't get ahead of yourself. Still don't know what's happening here…"

Clearing the cobwebs from his solid stupor, the thirty-nine-year-old was oblivious to what was really going on. Or what he was about to be put up against.

"Hello?"

His scratchy rasp echoed down the lengthy corridor, carrying all the way to the end and back with no reciprocation from anyone.

"*Seriously*, guys. Answer me! What the hell happened out there??"

The second strike of nothing. Not a single sound. Johnny could've heard a pin drop from the prison yard blacktop—if someone were actually there to toss it up in the air. No one answered him. No footsteps. No acknowledgment of any kind or signs of life ascertained.

Just him and only him—quarantined.

Looking down at what was written on his shirt for the first time since awakening added even more confusion to his situation. "Double zeroes?? What is this? Where's the top of my uniform?" Outfitted in a freshly pressed white tee and the bottom half of his mandatory orange jumpsuit, Johnny was momentarily perplexed as to who would want to switch shirts on him.

Don't get the numbers thing at all. Double zeroes? What's the significance?

"Whatever; a shirt's a shirt, I guess."

My God, if this is some form of sick joke they're playing on me because I disgust them…

Shivering and twitching like a sewer rat, the malcontent of a male was definitively stuck in a rut. Trapped with no discernible sounds inside or outside except for the extraordinary explosion that had occurred seconds earlier, he had few options left at his disposal.

There's one thing I could try to do…but let's just wait a little bit longer until I'm sure I can…

"Is anybody around? Come *on*! What was that crash?"

Three strikes of utter silence now. It began to seep deep into Johnny's psychosis that something was wrong, off. He'd been apprehended years ago for committing two shameful crimes, and although Johnny was used to being the odd man out, this wasn't the normal type of shunning at play—not in the least.

What if everyone's dead? What if I'm the only one left? NO; stop jumping to conclusions!

"Well, where *is* everybody, then?!"

The state prison continued to creak and crack in the background as if it were one giant ghost eerily floating about, haunting the jittery convict with spooks to spare. This wasn't an elaborate scheme hatched by other mean-spirited cellmates—this was something else entirely.

This has gotta be something messed up; this has gotta be something awful.

"HELLO?!" the terrified man shouted. "ANSWER!!"

Again, no answer to his plea. Just one isolated voice, bouncing around like a ping-pong ball rich with pain and panic. Mulling over the catastrophic alienation for minutes had unexpectedly transitioned into deliberating for hours—a thing that Johnny Helks had grown accustomed to while serving hard time. Drawing blanks inside his head, Johnny finally recalled what his original plan had entailed.

It's my only shot at getting any answers. I have to do it. No other way around it unless I wanna die in here!

Johnny scrambled over to his bed, retrieving a few rusted tools that he had crafted over several months—with high hopes that the stopgap gadgets could eventually lead him out of the enclosed mess and allow him to find out what was truly happening.

Not gonna get anywhere behind these bars. Never did and never will. I need to see what that blast was!

"Wait a second..." the bewildered man said irritably, as if he were a DMV employee. "Why in the world's everyone gone? Even if some bomb did pop off, how come there are no inmates around? That doesn't make any sense. Am I the only one left?" he questioned by his lonesome. "I just *don't* understand. WHAT IS GOING ON?? PLEASE...SOMEONE...ANYONE!!"

Once more, his desperate plea was met unceremoniously with nothing at all as Johnny's bellowing traveled down the penitentiary hallway with the distinct fluidity of a ballerina. With his frightened voice disintegrating, he felt more alone than he had ever felt before.

All right; you win! I'm scared now. You happy, God? Do I deserve this? Am I honestly that horrible? Left here to wither away...left here to suffer...left here to...

His original idea hit him over the head again like some souped-up car in the Daytona 500 smacking a wall. "Hey, I don't have to die! I can get out...I KNOW I can..."

Just like Clint did in that old movie, Escape from Alcatraz!

Taking his tools and making his way to the one spot he knew he'd spend eons focusing on, Johnny suddenly felt the sprout of a faraway hope being instilled. It reassured him that it'd undoubtedly be worth it, that the reward would pay dividends once he finally broke through...and once he'd *finally* be able to see the light of day.

CLANK. CLANK. CLANK.

The first laborious thirty minutes were set to a feverish pace, with his hands working at more of a sprint on the track than a walk in the park. An hour elapsed. And then two. Beads of sweat dripped to the concrete floor at steady intervals. Johnny cursed like a sailor whenever the salty moisture entered his eyes, always wiping the pesky perspiration from his reddening canvas of a face with shaky frustration. For the entirety of an arduous stretch, he barely made a dent into the small crevice of his desired escape route. The wall had been modified aesthetically, but it was nowhere near the stage he'd like it to be.

Gotta keep clanging and banging, even if it takes me forever…

CLANK. CLANK. CLANK. CLANK. CLANK. CLANK.

Two hours of strenuous labor became several, quickly transitioning into one full day gone before Johnny Helks even knew what had happened. His hands started to feel like a pair of heavy bricks; his scarred body and mind were ready to give out, just a dehydrated man prepared to lie down and die. Insanely exhausted, he stopped chipping away at his unattainable master plan.

"Guess this is it for me. And what a way to go out: kicking the bucket in prison."

Without getting an answer to this mystery…

BANG. BANG! BANG!!

Johnny's dry lips cracked open from the sudden noise down the corridor. "What the hell?"

Once his whisper met the musty air, the trio of strange crashing sounds completely vanished. Utter silence after. Nothing—and no one—seemed to exist alongside Johnny in the big house. Hopelessness filled the dreary atmosphere with the certainty of a suicide hotline operator.

"Should I just throw in the towel? Call it quits? Curl up into a ball and wait for death?"

Well, there's nothing left to do. I'm finished in here. No water, no food, no chance…

"Might as well get myself up so I can die like a man, though…tuck myself into that cot over yonder. That'll give the guards an easy job," Johnny said with a sly grin. "If there **are** any anymore."

Willing himself up one overworked joint at a time, the prisoner took a look around the cell in a rare show of calm. Once vertical, spaghetti legs were born. Failing to keep upright for long, Johnny tripped awkwardly over nothing. Reaching out to break the fall instinctively, both of his worn hands grasped the ice-cold steel bars in a desperate attempt to seek support. But the beams surprisingly gave way, flying open and see-sawing back and forth. The cell block door was now unexpectedly ajar, and Johnny Helks could not contain his excitement—nor a growing amusement toward what he had just witnessed.

"I'll be damned…" he guffawed.

After the tumble forward granted a wonderful discovery of impending freedom, the glint of a metallic object caught his eye, snapping him out of a drawn-out, fascinated trance. Beside the bars that he'd previously thought were enclosing him lay a silver key on the ground, mysteriously available.

Someone unlocked this cell! Why, though? Who in their right mind would allow me to just walk outta here??

"Who cares why it's happened? I don't have to be stuck. I don't have to rot away; I don't have to live this vapid existence anymore! I'M FREE! I can do whatever the HELL I want!!"

BOOM. BOOM. CRACK. CRACK.

Four sounds came out of nowhere, much louder than his clanks to the cemented surface.

What's all that?!

"Who's down there??" Johnny asked shakily.

No answer. Only the sound of a faucet running in the distance.

I didn't hear that before…not even a drop…

"HELLO?! Stop playing with me!"

His receding echoes ricocheted off the paint-chipped walls.

"Look, the fun and games are over…because I'm coming out of my cell now…so drop these shenanigans and tell me exactly what's going on here!!"

Met with silence once again, all he could do was sigh. Even the water refrained from cascading out of its faucet. Officially spooked, the fragile-minded prisoner cautiously set foot outside his cell to assess the situation.

AM I DEAD? IS THIS MY OWN VERSION OF HELL?

His thoughts continued to scream inside, yet on the outside, he remained quiet while walking down the corridors in timidness. Every cell checked was empty, yet electricity still ran through the prison as though everything was still running smoothly. But not a single person, dead or alive or comatose, was in any area of the prison. And with each nervous footstep taken, Johnny Helks became more and more frightened of the unknown circling around him.

This can't be. Everybody can't really be gone. Can they? Who's manning the power?! Why're all these rooms still lit up?

"That 'splosion shoulda caused a blackout…" Johnny discerned.

As each second passed, the prisoner kept swimming in a sea of possibilities and theories. Yet none of them added up to make a lick of sense. In all the years of his lackluster life, this unexplained phenomenon had taken the cake when it came to outright alienation.

Oddly enough, nothing had been tampered with in any room visited. No matter which floor he meticulously patrolled, each small cell inspected only added to Johnny's rising confusion. Beds were perfectly tucked in; reading materials were placed neatly by the pillows. It was like everybody had been plucked away, right out of thin air—like a brand-new penitentiary had just been built.

Even smells new around here now…

Surveying the abandoned areas, Johnny pondered a preposterous scenario. "Was everyone snatched up like in that HBO show *The Leftovers?* And that's why it smells better? No more musky man-scents to endure? But those sounds…what were they? I can't be alone, can I?!"

In a fit of rage curated by loneliness, a sweaty Johnny Helks lifted one particularly stained mattress and its metal frame over his head, throwing them down to the floor in ire. When the frame was done rattling about, an unforgiving silence introduced itself once more.

Somebody…anybody…come out and say this is just all a gag…please…

"I **can't** be alone in this damn place. Either I'm going crazy or there's definitely someone in here with me! And I'm thinking I ain't no loon! I know what I heard. It's not in my head, you sons of bitches…COME OUT!!"

Nothing yet again. No response to his urgent demand.

Just the echoes of a madman's bellows.

After some time spent aimlessly slumming around, Johnny accepted his new reality. "All right, everybody. Have a laugh. 'Cause I'm biting. You got me. I MUST BE THE ONLY ONE LEFT! Just me. JUST JOHNNY! Might as well head on out, then. I've already scoured this godforsaken establishment for everything it's worth, right? After all, I'm pretty much a free man—and the *last* man, seemingly! Sounds great. I can go outside, be in peace. No gruff guards hovering, no burly prisoners trying to shank me or tattooing my neck! BEAUTIFUL; simply…*beautiful.*"

More talking, more vital energy wasted. Johnny had exhibited a fierce determination in his vocal capabilities, but he hadn't a strong enough will embodied within to keep on moving. And if any other person could see him in this brittle state, the writing was on the wall. Delirium and exhaustion had set in snugly. Water began to go through the mind of the dehydrated man as he continued to patrol the drab halls in despair. Rapidly running out of strength to push on, the prisoner's mindset wasn't firing on all cylinders.

"I'd suck a dick for an ounce of water right now…" he said tiredly.

Wait a moment. I don't have to perform fellatio on a fellow! Things are different now. That faucet was running…

"OF COURSE!"

Slightly off-kilter, a nearly broken Johnny Helks remembered an important factoid. Water—that precious giver of life—had been all around him every step of the way. Like traffic in Los Angeles: omnipresent and widespread. Whether it be through the dingy sinks or the cafeteria where grizzled employees used to serve each prisoner slabs of slop for sustenance, it made no difference. The world-famous H_2O wasn't hard to find. He just had to go over to the tap. Any tap. Simple as that.

I'm not confined anymore. I now have what I've craved for so long.

"I can do this; hell…I can do anything I want…"

First destination: the faucets. Any which one would do, but Johnny arrived at the one that had been streaming just moments prior. Eyeing the dilapidated silver hook as if it were a woman's breast, he grasped the nozzle with mouth-watering anticipation. Tilting his head to the left, the parched prisoner turned the knob and opened his kisser. However, what instantly met his lips wasn't a refreshing stream of water, but instead a disgusting cough-up of rusted, discolored liquid.

"Shit!" he yelled, yanking his head out of the sink. "No clean tap water, even??"

Just check more; check 'em all, check every single one! This doesn't mean anything.

After coming to find that another five faucets weren't working, Johnny lacked the motivation to continue plodding along—and the energy for it, more importantly. The scarcity of drinkable water was a buzzkill, and his valuable energy was dwindling by the second.

I'm going to lose my mind.

Rather quickly, things spiraled downward. The mentally pummeled male began to physically let loose. Several tumultuous years of holed-in frustration and pent-up aggression all came to the forefront of an abandoned slammer. No spectators were present for the anger, just a pissed-off person blowing off steam.

Beds were overturned. Bars were punched. Screams were released.

"Therapeutic…" he murmured in the aftermath of his conniption fit. "But I gotta get out of here…I've gotta drink…HEY, what's that buzzing sound?"

A faint whirr could be heard near the right side of the prisoner's ear.

Am I hearing random things now outta paranoia?

Dizzy from dehydration, giddy from desperation, and reeling from a slaphappy hysteria, Johnny collapsed onto the hard concrete of an empty cell. The backbreaking work of trying to claw his way out a day before had depleted him.

He had nothing left to expend.

And like so many times before while imprisoned, he gazed up to the ceiling in subservience. But this time was much different, for he no longer wanted to keep going. In fact, after living through so many hardships as well as creating so many of them for others, he wanted to die. The lids of Johnny's heavily bagged eyes slowly shut as blaring, droning defeat welcomed him…

Peaceful darkness, greeting his final conscious moments, ushered in what he instinctively thought right then and there to be a decorous death.

INSIDE: The Selected

Lizzie Janis awoke to the perplexing sight of a school bus's interior. Every glass window lining the left and right sides of the public transport had been blacked out by shutters, rejecting any possible hope of an outside view. Strapped into a semi-ripped seat, she looked on in complete horror as five other girls near her age came to in a daze. All of them were in the same exact predicament, and all had numbers on their plain white tees that resembled jerseys.

My head…it's pounding like a freaking jackhammer…

"Why're we trapped in here??" one of the younger-looking girls in glasses asked, crying quietly. "And WHY do I have the number two on me?!"

"I don't know. Mine says three. Try and stay calm so we can figure out what's going on," another girl at the front of the bus responded kindly.

Due to an eclipsing shock taking over, Lizzie formally introduced herself to the other captives. "I'm Lizzie. Sixteen. From Columbus, Ohio. And if any of you are wondering what number I've been given, it's one."

The teen in front scoffed at the straightforwardness. "Um, yeah, hi, Liz! Are you for real right now? Who cares about our names, our ages, the numbers, or where we're from?"

"Well, *I* care…and I'm sure the others do, too. So…I'm Chelsea, everyone. From Michigan, born and raised. I would say that it's a pleasure to meet all of you, but I'd be lying if I did."

"Shut da hell up. That ain't even funny! Look at us, look at dis sitch! Don't really think it's time for a lame joke…" an African American teenager added.

Chelsea cracked a smile. "And what's *your* name, sunshine?"

"Tamika Wilson. From da Bronx. And I am number four. Satisfied?!"

"Very. You're a book now, by the way."

"I'm a WHAT??" Tamika hollered.

"Listen, I've got a great idea. Don't be snarky with each other, okay? Let's try to recall how we got here and retrace our steps, since we might learn a thing or two about why this has happened to us…" Lizzie suggested.

"Yeah, yeah; good plan," Tamika said. "So, um…what's da last thing any uh you chicks 'member?"

The girl who had scoffed rudely at Lizzie spoke up immediately. "I remember singing that vintage Coldplay song 'Fix You' in my car. You guys remember them?"

Every tied-up teen said no.

"Oh, it's pretty. You should listen to it sometime!"

Chelsea laughed. "I'll definitely check it out—if we ever get outta here."

"Right; *sorry*. Anyway, lemme retrace. I recall driving back home from seeing a movie with my boyfriend. He had to work later on in the night, so we caught a chick flick, *I Am Just for You*. Y'know, with Derek Andrew? It was a special fifteenth anniversary re-release of the film and I knew he didn't wanna see it, but that's how much he lov— cares for me. I'll admit, though, I was upset he couldn't call off work. We could've had a LOT more fun…"

"And why were you so sad, girl? You one of those needy bitches who can't be alone fo' mo than ten secs?" Tamika snapped.

"Lay off…I'm simply telling my story. It's pointless to throw shade, especially now. We're all in this together. Oh yeah, and just in case ya care, I'm Riley. From Utah."

"See? It *does* matter what our names are. 'Cause now I don't have to look at you as that one girl who thought it was stupid to say who we were and where we're from anymore!" Lizzie joked.

"I suppose you're right…guess I was just thrown for a loop there at the beginning. Still am, actually," Riley said.

"Don't blame ya one bit; it's nuts!" Chelsea agreed.

"Hey, what do ya'll think of those two girls ova dare? You think they number five? And who da hell wrote *HELP US* on dat back window?!"

"Not a clue. None of us did, that's for sure. Strange how they're seated beside each other, and we're all spread apart. But it could be nothing, Tamika," Lizzie opined. "Maybe they are five; we don't even know what these assigned numbers mean!"

"True, true. Weird dat bofe of em' haven't said a word, doe. Notta peep!"

Chelsea tried her best to stare at the two silent girls. "I could be wrong, but they kinda look like they may be conjoined? By the way they're moving and their head placement, it seems like that's a possibility. Since they're near the back, it's hard to tell…"

"No way; that's not even a thing. Is it?" Riley wondered.

"Uh, *yeah*, it is. You haven't seen them people on TV who have it n' shit? It's def real. But dey muteness is weirding me out, I'll say dat much," Tamika said.

"This situation's weird in general," Lizzie followed up. "We just have to keep talking about what we remember and figure it out…"

"Sounds good. You're up, then!" Riley exclaimed.

"Okay. Hmm, where to start…"

"How about ya start at da end?" Tamika offered snidely.

"'Course. Um, let's see…I was in my room, scrolling on my phone, checking social media—the usual for me."

"Riveting," Chelsea said sarcastically. "That used to be the usual for *all* teens—obviously back when the Internet was affordable and not government-dictated like it is now."

"Yeah; no doubt. Only reason we have it is 'cause my grandma— whom I live with—is even more addicted than me. After that crazy blackout hit, she freaked. But then when it came back, she couldn't live without it…splurged her life savings on an annual plan. But you're not missing much; it's not that great now, since it's so monitored and neutered. Anyway, I can't remember anything else after being in my room. Like at all. But you know what? I *do* kind of remember feeling sick at dinner."

"Hunh," Riley blurted.

"What?" every girl asked, except for the twins.

"I remember being nauseous as well…"

Tamika rolled her eyes. "So what? My stomach be swimmin' too; don't mean nothin'. And even if it *did*, how da hell does that help us in here?"

"*Any* information regarding our final waking memories is helpful right now. What *isn't* helpful is your attitude, so why don't you just chill and contribute?" Lizzie said bossily.

"I agree. If the four of us were feeling queasy, that HAS to mean something. It's not a coincidence. I mean, it *can't* be!" Chelsea said.

"Definitely; it could all correlate. But I have a confession to make…I may have been drunk before taking off from the theater. Not too much, though! Don't judge me," Riley requested.

"You a damn trip, ya know that? Drinking underage n' driving intoxicated? What's wrong wit yo pale white ass?" Tamika demanded.

"My boyfriend and I were loosening up, all right? He was heading out for a twelve-hour shift and wanted to drink—as did I. Guy works hard—for pennies, essentially. So we drank while watching the movie. Snuck in some gin. He was having me drink more than usual, but it doesn't even matter! I bet *you're* one to talk, Tamika. High and mighty, my ass. Bet you've downed some malt liquor in your day!! Some forties probably…"

"Fuck me, that's racist."

"Tamika, I know what she said is ridiculous, but don't elevate. It's not worth it. And it'll only lead to more bickering between you two…" Lizzie advised.

Chelsea, preferring to avoid further confrontation, changed the subject in an attempt to attain more information. "So we got a head count, we got the names, the states, but we didn't exactly say how old we all are…and I think we should."

"Damn, does it matter? We *young.* Pristine teens, yo! So I honestly don't need ta know. Stupid worryin' 'bout dat shallow shit, anyway!" Tamika said.

"Well, whatever…I'm seventeen—just turned it. Only four years to go until I can LEGALLY drink! Sorry for letting you down, Tamika," Riley quipped. "I've been known to rebel."

"Kiss my beautiful black ass."

"Okay, I'll sincerely do that, but *only* after you say your age and we manage to untie ourselves!"

"I'm fourteen, you bitch."

Riley laughed at the smugness. "Ooh, quite the mouth for such a young one!"

"Once again, kiss my beau—"

"Girls, girls," Lizzie verbally stepped in. "We aren't getting anywhere doing this. You dislike each other; we get it! Move on. Chelsea, what do *you* remember?"

"Oh, it's on me now?"

"Why the hell not…wouldn't hurt," Riley said.

"I—uh, well…I know this'll sound incredibly boring, but I recall wanting to get in an afternoon nap. I'd just finished reading *Beauty Queens* by Libba Bray. Which is an absolutely **awesome** book if you're wondering."

"Ugh, get on with it! Nobody reads novels anymo. You goofy fo' doin' so!" Tamika insulted impatiently.

Chelsea continued, not missing a beat. "When I was situating myself on the couch for nap time, my dad handed me some piping hot cocoa. It was so danged good. And after I drank some, I pretty much passed out. Although I did have an upset tummy before crashing…"

"Man, none of this adds up. Were we all drugged and then dragged in here?? What *is* this, you guys?" Lizzie wondered.

"Are we bein' held fo' ransom? Any y'all's parents loaded?" Tamika questioned the captives.

"Nope; I've been raised my whole life by a single mom who's a struggling actress-slash-waitress. Bio dad left when I was five…" Riley said.

"My mom's a bank teller and my dad's a mechanic!" Chelsea answered happily. "They say it's a basic, ho-hum existence, which leads to sporadic misery. But my parents are still together, surprisingly!"

"I didn't even get to *know* my parents. They divorced when I was young—the age of six—because of this really crazy thing that happened with a guy babysitting my sister and me."

No one spoke after Lizzie paused, which created an uncomfortable silence that filled the bus.

Feeling a strange need to continue, the blonde teen revealed more of her background. "He was a family friend, supposedly. And no, I don't wanna talk about it, so don't ask questions. I'll just say this: nothing happened to me personally. After that, my mom and dad were never the same, though…so they both kinda quit being parents. Dropped us off at my grandparents' one December weekend a little over ten years ago, and that was that. Been gone ever since…"

"Wow, I'm sorry, Lizzie. I don't know what to say," Riley said.

Tamika softened. "Yeah, me either. You've been through da ringer, girl. Heart goes out to ya…"

Chelsea sighed. "I'd give you a big ol' hug right now if I could!"

"It's all right. Thanks. I suppose I'll never know why they chose to vanish. Things were just bad for us growing up."

"Trauma wrecks certain people who can't deal with awful things. I'm sorry your parents seem to have fallen into that category!"

"Ain't that da truth, Riley…" Tamika said.

With a tear falling from her eye, Lizzie righted the ship. "So back to the age thing…how old are you, Chelsea? I believe you're the only one who hasn't said yet."

"Right! I'm twelve. Twelve and a half!"

Riley acted like a clipboard-carrying manager. "There ya have it, then. I'm the oldest at seventeen. Lizzie's sixteen. Tamika's fourteen. And last but not least, Chelsea's the youngest at twelve."

"AND A HALF!" Chelsea shouted.

"You forgot dem freaks in the back, doe!" Tamika said. "Those mutes are our ongoing mystery…"

Twelve and a half? Holy crap. That's the same age my sister was when everything changed for her, when she was taken advan—

Suddenly a howling pierced through the pitch-black windows of the yellow four-wheeler entrapping the girls. Panicked screaming inside nearly silenced the roaring of an unknown entity gliding nearby outside. But it was too loud to ignore as fear seeped into each and every girl aboard.

"Da fuck is that noise?!" Tamika shrieked. "My heart's in ma damn throat ry now! WHAT IS DAT??"

Before anyone could muster up anything, the school bus almost toppled over from the sheer force of one powerful—and currently invisible—monster. The veiled creature continuously rammed into each side with no relenting while the cries for help became deafening.

We're dead. We are so dead.

Lizzie shut her eyes in the midst of an uncontrollable chaos, clasped her hands together tightly, and prayed very passionately for it all to just go away.

<u>INSIDE: The Racket</u>

Akin to a bloated beached whale on a sandy seaside, Johnny was laid out on the prison floor.

For the second time in under twenty-four hours.

Unresponsive for a long spell, he remained motionless until a bucket of water splashed onto his face. The icy-cold water instantly caused a jolting revival of uncorked animation.

"*AH!* That's ridiculous!!" Johnny barked, wiping the wetness from his barely-there hair. "Was I only dreaming about being free? I'm still in this cell…"

But while he'd indeed been sleeping, he hadn't been dreaming. Upon gathering his senses after receiving such a shocking delivery of frigid water to the grill, Johnny Helks peered over to an open cell door. Everything was how it had been prior to his collapse. Not a sound emitting from anywhere, and not a person around the premises. Just like before.

Wasn't a dream after all.

"Who did that? Who throws a bucket of water onto someone's face and then runs away?? The whole point is to see the reaction!"

While steady in his thinking-out-loud reasoning, nothing was going as planned for the miffed, dripping man. Not even a splash to the face could bring him any reinvigoration. Without a doubt, conventional rise-and-fall actions and reactions weren't the norm anymore. For Johnny and Johnny alone, this was a topsy-turvy world that he now inhabited. And whoever taunted him was an enigma, both in motive and in malice. As bizarre as it was, the sad truth was that after having woken up so startled, Johnny would've loved nothing more than to see another human being sneering back at him. His mind had started to play tricks on him. In this environment, what was real and what wasn't? As confused as ever, the disturbed jailbird thoroughly questioned himself while dusting off and standing up.

Am I truly alone? Have I hallucinated all of this? Even the water? Is that it? Am I DEAD?

"Think, think, think!"

A head-scratching visual clue presented itself. After the shock of the splash had worn off, the prisoner noticed something rather peculiar on his right arm. It was a bandage—the kind of adhesive a person would have after having blood work—and it certainly hadn't been there before he fainted. On top of that discovery, Johnny felt completely rejuvenated physically—a far cry from the previously depleted, near-death quandary that he'd been so entangled in. Gone were the aches and pains of a man flirting with the ripe age of forty, and in its place was a two-liter of piss and vinegar. Adrenaline coursed through his veins, making him feel like he was a rowdy, know-it-all teenager again—fully ready to tackle life with reckless abandon.

Johnny then had an epiphany.

"Someone's helping here. Fucking hell, that is rich! Of all the people stuck in this oven, they'd pick ME? But why? Why me specifically..." he asked himself with genuine intrigue. "And who would *want* to??"

Going through a list of possible names and coming up terribly short, he became besieged by his own bewilderment. Wanting to know just why this could happen and imagining just who'd assist a perceived lowlife in such a strange way ate at him from the inside out. At a loss for what to do or where to go next, he went back to his old ways, unloading an arsenal of erratic behavior.

"WHAT IS THIS CRUELTY? HEY!" Johnny screamed at the top of his lungs. "ANSWER ME!!"

A response that he'd gotten quite used to over the span of a day then followed. Nada, nothing, zilch. Just his booming pleading. Again and again. Monotonous in its execution, it was beginning to seem futile. Momentarily, Johnny Helks believed that it was fruitless to keep pushing forward. What was the point of all the hemming and hawing if nobody were there to hem and haw right back?

Maybe I'm meant to rot. Maybe I shouldn't even move a muscle...just to see what happens!

"No, I can't stay. It's not my destiny to die in here," he said softly. "There's gotta be a reason I was injected with something. Hasn't killed me yet and I feel great...better than I've felt in years."

But why, WHY is someone wanting me to continue?

CRASH. POW. SPLAT.

The trifecta of surprising sounds—reminiscent of the campy, ancient Batman television series where its frequent fistfights flashed comic-book influenced exclamations across the screen—once again introduced themselves to a polarized Johnny Helks. Emanating from a floor below him, the bombastic crashes seemed to be luring the prisoner into something grave. Something dangerous. Temporarily fearless, he convinced himself to go and investigate.

"Fuck this sitting-duck syndrome."

Johnny marched down to the area that the sounds had originated from. Bypassing the cafeteria, he saw that chairs were all stacked neatly onto tabletops barren of any clutter. And the place was clean. Mostly empty. *Unusual, to say the least*, he thought as he kept walking past. *That area's ALWAYS messy…cracked tiles, stained walls…*

"Then again, everything's been unusual since I first woke up to this alarm clock of a nightmare!" Johnny stated.

As he rounded the corner of a prototypical penitentiary hallway, he saw that the coast was clear, devoid of any person who could've made those head-turning noises. But a small thing caught the eye of the disparate celldweller.

A lone notebook—opened perfectly symmetrically in the middle of the corridor—splayed six words in black sharpie across the left and right sides of its white pages. Three to each page respectively, the words heeded a warning:

SAVE THE YOUTH. SOON. OR ELSE…

"The hell? Save what youth?? This doesn't explain *anything*! It just hurts my brain even more, dammit!!"

In a display of frustration, Johnny tore the pieces of paper up, rolled them all into a ball, and threw them onto the ground defiantly.

"There's your 'OR ELSE' right there, you bastards!"

KNOCK-KNOCK, KNOCK-KNOCK.

From the door at the end of the hall, someone—or something—had started to knock on the other side in rapid succession. The knocking, gradually becoming louder and louder, spooked the prisoner into deer-in-the-headlights mode. Steady in its deliverance, the presumably nefarious knocks filled Johnny with a terror that he hadn't felt since he was a kid hiding under his covers from the boogeyman. Also known as his dad.

However, he was an adult now, and he needed to see what—or who—this was.

Who'd want to go to these lengths just to scare me?

As he cautiously neared the door, the knocking thundered on, each step only elevating the suffocating tension to greater heights. The consistent pounding initiated his ears into a tinnitus-based fraternity.

"This is it. No going back," Johnny said, the racket almost drowning out his clichéd, personal pep talk.

As he opened the door slowly, the knocking suddenly stopped.

With the door more than halfway ajar, he gaped, looking as dumbfounded as he was deteriorated when he computed what had caused the unruly noise.

It was a gargantuan boombox with Bumpboxx as its white-lettered label branding, now pumping at max volume once again.

"Wha…I don't underst—"

Cut off before completing his sentence, Johnny Helks was attacked from behind. Blindsided by a nightstick, his kneecaps were hobbled with a couple of vicious swats landing flush.

Pain swarmed over the prisoner's legs as he writhed on the ground like a feral animal caught in a net. When Johnny tried to turn himself around to see who had done this to him, a steel-toed boot placed itself on the back of his head, mushing his nose and lips into the cement floor with supreme force. He was entirely at the mercy of whoever was choosing to torture him.

While giving his absolute best effort to break free, Johnny felt the sting of a long needle being inserted into his sweaty neck. The fluid from it flooded in, warming the insides of his tensed body immediately.

"STOP! JUST TELL ME WHAT YOU WANT!!" he gurgled.

Within seconds of his begging for a halt to the ambiguous insanity, darkness took over Johnny's consciousness—as the retro-styled boombox, vibrating and distorting from such an earsplitting cacophony, had its volume hastily lowered to the point of zero. A shaky needle-carrying hand then lifted it up off the ground and walked away, distancing himself from the primary target: an out-for-the-count convict.

<u>INSIDE: The Agents</u>

"That was off the page, man. Seriously, I can't **believe** I just did that!"

"I know, I know. What a rush, right?"

"Yeah, it was. God, it *really* was! And that notebook idea you had on the fly? Pure genius on your part, I must admit. A quality mind-bottle!"

"Thank you; thank you very much."

"But…with that being said, what exactly do we do next?"

"We keep watching and listening. That's what we'll do."

"Are we safe, though?"

"Brent—now, see, that's where we're different."

"And just what do you mean by that?"

"Well, it's obvious…"

"WHAT IS?!"

"Hey, hey; simmer it down. He may wake up. Not likely, but still."

"Will you please tell me what's so obvious already?"

"Simple. You're a worrier, a stress-monkey. I don't get you sometimes. You signed up for this, so you knew *precisely* what you were getting into. Just like I did!"

"Thanks for the refresher, Captain Obvious."

"There's that word again. But I'm not the one who's so obvious."

"Oh yeah! I almost forgot! I have a tendency to overthink all the things that could go wrong here. Speaking of which, I'd be foolish not to say for like the thousandth time that a lot of what we're about to do to this dude could go super south super fast."

"You think I'm not aware of the dangers involved with this?"

"No; I'm not doubting your level of awareness, Simon. I'm doubting your outlook on the ordeal."

"Never doubt what I'm about. I am a professional. I've got this."

"Really? Something this ambitious has never been done before. It's unheard of."

"My ambition can easily match what lies ahead."

"But there are variables. He's not our only concern!"

"So what? Let it get batshit. I love a challenge. My whole life's been a damn test. Obstacle after obstacle! And you know what?"

"What?"

"I've hurdled up and over them all like it was nothing! To me, this is just another one to leap across. That's it. Nothing more, nothing less. So get with it, will ya?"

"I'll try. But it's a different kind of beast once you're out in the elements with a released freak."

"Listen; everything's going to be all right. I'm not gonna let anything happen to you, buddy. You've got a wife back home expecting."

"*Fuck*! Don't say that, okay?"

"What? What'd I do wrong?"

"Basically, you signed my death warrant by talking like that."

"HA HA! You're hilarious. You're kidding…right?"

"Sort of! I dunno, Simon; you shouldn't get too personal."

"Gotcha. Keep it strictly professional. Will do, sir."

"Good. Thank you."

"Welcome. So to recap, we got the jump on him earlier by sticking that needle into his jug…"

"Yes; I was there. It was pretty harrowing. Exhilarating, even."

"Look at you! What a smart city boy, using those big words."

"Uh-huh."

"I'm thinking we oughta move toward our scheduled post in five, so get ready. I'll meet up with you after I smoke this cigarette. I need a bit of fresh air. Been stuffed in all day at the prison."

"You sure ya wanna do that? Seems hazardous outside."

"Um, yes. Positive. Why wouldn't I?"

"Because…of the air itself??"

"*Brent*. We were cleared long ago! How many times have I explained it? You saw the lab results yourself."

"Doesn't mean they're right. Especially now that we're out here."

"Hogwash. The monitoring of the conditions was *exhaustively* thorough. The only side effects are temporary nosebleeds. We've been through this countless times. It's a waste of breath."

"Remember what I said about those variables…"

"The only variable here is human. It's not the weather around us. This chem climate is a non-factor. And I believe that I—sorry, *we*—can manage them both with no problems whatsoever."

"But what about the bus? That's a sensitive issue."

"It'll be handled with the utmost care. We're in complete control."

"I suppose we are. Those black shutters are locked in place. We triple-checked everything before leaving."

"Affirmative. They can't see us! Like I said, totally in control."

"If you say so. It's just that Helks is a loose cannon, you know."

"We wouldn't be here if he *weren't*. And that's why we have the guns."

"All I'm trying to have you realize is this: when you toy with the fragile emotions of a documented sociopath who has been diagnosed with an acute dissociative identity disorder AND is a sexual deviant who's also been charged with attempted manslaughter—in a setting like this, no less—it's not built to last. It won't end well. For anyone."

"See…right there, bro. That's the thing you don't get about this."

"What am I not getting? Please enlighten me."

"*I'm* the wild card in this. Not him."

"Possibly. We'll just have to see about that as it plugs along, huh?"

"Why don't you let your guard down for a moment? *Relax.*"

"That may be easy for you to do, but for me it isn't. This is hard."

"Come on. Get off your moral high horse! Don't you feel it?"

"Feel what?"

"That palpable energy. That…undeniable dynamite…"

"Not really sure I follow. Oh wait, you mean the jeopardy we're in?"

"We aren't in any type of jeopardy. Stop. *We* are not. *He* is."

"How can you honestly say that with a straight face?"

"Because we have an insurance policy. If things get iffy, we know what to do. We know what to unleash."

"That aspect slipped my mind. I've seen what you're referring to. It's unlike anything I've ever laid these eyes on. Truly an incredible accomplishment of manufactured terror."

"Wonderful; archive this. Something we finally agree on. *Great.* Our break's almost up! No time to go smoke now."

"Sorry for talking your ear off, boss. My fault. I'm in distress."

"When this is all over, you owe me a pack of Marlboros."

"Why? For being instrumental in you missing one measly cig?"

"Yeah, for making me miss a moment of that sweet cancer-stick goodness. Actually, you know something…make it two packs!"

"Tell you what. If we make it outta this crazy shit alive, I'll buy you *three*. If I am physically able to, that is."

"Deal! You know damn well I'm gonna hold you to that."

"Of course."

"As much as I'd like to keep chatting, we should go."

"Ready when you are."

"Cool; let's head on out, then. He'll be stirring soon."

"The agents are wearing off?"

"Correct."

"I figured they'd be fading shortly."

"That's funny to me."

"What is?"

"By the way you were acting when the handlers were hauling him off, I was thinking you believed that he was going to revive right then and there!"

"My nerves were shot. I've never been a part of something like this."

"Hell, I don't think *anyone* has. We're the first!"

"And that's why I'm having reservations about it now…"

"Don't be such a pussy. You're here for a purpose; you're good."

"I appreciate that. Same to you."

"It's just too bad we can't kill him. Is it not?"

"You're a sick pup, Simon. It's not about that at all. And it never has been. The plan's admittedly complicated, I'll give you that; but to murder the man? Not in the cards."

"It should be, though. He's a scary individual."

"Can't disagree with you there."

"The infamous Johnny Helks…boy, he has no *idea* what he's in for."

"I'd like to hope so. Or is it the other way around?"

"Shut up, Brent. That's four you owe me now."

"Crap."

"Let's go. Enough of this larking around. There's food still on the table."

"There is? I could've sworn I cleaned up after we were done eating."

"It was a figure of speech! I know you put the plates away, ya idiot!!"

"Sorry about that. Was briefly confused by your verbiage. My bad."

"Who would've thought you'd be such a dick with diction?"

"Guilty as charged. Ever since grade school."

"Well, you have my sincerest apologies for flustering you! Let me know if this is a better line…WE HAVE MORE WORK TO DO."

"Yes; actually, it is. Much improved. Black and white—I like it."

"Careful, underling. I'll go five packs on your ass."

"We still have to get out of this mess first, man."

"You have my word that we *will*, friend. Let's move out. Time's money and a set piece awaits…"

<u>INSIDE: The Defeat</u>

When Lizzie managed to refrain from trembling like a freezing hobo in the dead of winter, she opened her eyes to the sight and sound of an emotional withdrawal. The other girls—who were still entrapped in their respective restraints—sat in silence, waiting for yet another abrasive terrorization to begin. But the noisy force of nature, with its unclear intentions and ferocious attacks, had vanished from the vicinity. Hundreds of seconds passed by in a hushed unison, and only after hearing a throbbing, whirring buzz circulating around them, Lizzie chose to speak up.

"All right…just what is *that* now? You guys hear a fluttering as well?"

"Definitely do. Sounds sorta like one of those lawn sprinklers…"

"Man! I haven't seen one uh dem in a long-ass time, Ry!" Tamika said, scootching herself to the left in her strapped-down seat. "But I hear dat ish, too. Wonder what it be."

Searchingly, Chelsea listened to the light purring hanging over their heads. "Terrific; now it's stopped. 'Course it did. I don't know what that wickedness was outside, but I *really* don't want it to come back," she said with a slight stutter.

"You 'n me both, sister!" Tamika shouted.

"Worst. Predicament. Ever. I'd rather be dead than be locked away in here like some cattle primed and ready for butchery," Riley stated.

Lizzie sorrowed. "You may just get your wish. We could be killed at any moment. I don't think this was designed to be fun for us…"

"No shit, Sherlock!!" Tamika said facetiously.

"*Love* those books—and the BBC series," Chelsea blathered. "*Love* Sir Arthur Conan Doyle and Benedict Cumberbatch!"

"Shut yo stinkin' trap! We don't ca—"

Lizzie cleared her throat, interrupting the urban youth from getting revved up. "I have a theory I'd like to share. What if this is a test of some kind? Like for us to all pass together?"

"Well, if this *is* a test, we are currently failing it!" Riley scoffed.

"Hear me out…" Lizzie continued. "What if we're here for a reason? And not just to be picked off one by one, but to *learn* something."

"Like what?" Chelsea asked, half-baked and half-numb.

"Yeah, er, there's where I'm stumped."

"Miss Liz, this ain't some shitty team-building exercise fo' us ta work through. Whoeva set up dis *Saw*-like game ain't tryna betta our asses!" Tamika said with unbridled confidence.

Riley nodded. "This scenario certainly is torture-porn material. I feel like we're a bunch of hapless, disposable characters in a horror flick—about to be sliced and diced."

"Speak for yourself. I'm no airhead, okay? I read and write extensively and wouldn't *ever* run up the stairs if a masked killer were to chase me around my house," Chelsea claimed. "Hey! I *got* it. This could maybe be a slasher flick audition!! Albeit a bit unorthodox. Or—OOH, this'd make for a great book, too!"

"You only twelve! Whatchu know 'bout writing?" Tamika implored.

"*And a half*…gosh, why is someone's age always such a catalyst for knee-jerk judgment?"

"All right; with insight like that, she does seem pretty intelligent for her age," Lizzie pointed out.

"Thanks for your humble acknowledgment," Chelsea said sheepishly.

Tamika groaned in disapproval. "Big fuckin' whoop. So just 'cause Ms. Bookworm can string a sentence together, and just 'cause she younger than us, that means we should listen ta her theories on why we stranded here?"

"Since you seem to be so in-the-know and full of wisdom, Tamika, do *you* have any idea as to why we've been put in this position?" Riley asked.

"No, I don't. And if I did, I would've told all uh ya from da jump."

"Then shut up about it. In here, nobody's theory is off-limits. We're trapped as one. So let's be a unified front!"

"I agree with Riley. She's right; we have *got* to stop snapping at each other. What good does that even do? It's not gonna get us anywhere and it's a complete waste of time," Lizzie said.

"*Awesome.* Let's remain calm 'n see where it all leads! While somehow workin' together as we be constrained n' can't do ANYTHANG at all ta get outta dis shit!!" Tamika barked.

"Man…I'm guessing that whoever kidnapped you didn't have the chance to hear your grating, high-pitched babble. If they had, they would've had enough forethought to keep you off of this kooky clunker. For the sake of our own eardrums!" Riley said.

"Get bent, bitch. That's real classy. Sitting over there, making light of a kidnapping like it's whatever. Fuck outta here wit dat."

"No offense intended, Tamika, but the worst thing that we've had to deal with so far on this bus of bullshit is *your* ignorant ass."

"Enough. That goes for you, too, Tam. Just chill!" Chelsea pleaded.

"I'll be chill if she chills. But I ain't got time fo' her nastiness or her *HO*lier-than-thou attitude," Tamika said.

"Chilling commencing…now! No worries on this side," Riley pitched in.

"We all want the same thing. And that's to escape this. So let's not fight anymore, okay? It's not worth the effort," Lizzie suggested.

"We're chilled. Don't trip; no mo venom's comin' out unless Ry steps ta me with her white-girl superiority complex."

Riley sighed. "UGH, please spare me the race card! We've all heard it before!"

"Stop it, you two. We've gotta get on track or else we're gonna derail quickly. We have to think of a way outta here. Look around a little more; try to see if *anything* could possibly help us," Chelsea advised.

"Even if multiple pairs of scissors were on da damn flow allowing alla us ta cut our way out, it wouldn't really matter, 'cause—wait, why's dat again? Oh, right! I know why…'cause we can't MOVE!!" Tamika surmised obnoxiously.

"What?? I wasn't aware that I was tied up," Lizzie said.

"It's news to me, too! Wow, this *sucks*. Gee…I hope we all get out!" Chelsea joked, breaking the post-traumatic jitters with some comic relief.

Riley looked to the back of the bus as well as she could. After mumbling variations of the non-word *hmm*, she wondered aloud, "What if the key to our freedom is in one of those mute girls' bellies?"

"And what if it isn't? That's retarded. A key isn't needed here; we're tied in knots from the waist up with leather straps! A key's useless," Chelsea said.

"Not from where I'm seated…as you can clearly see, I am closest to the door," Riley informed. "And there's a padlock on it."

"But once again, why does it even matter if we can't physically move ta find ourselves da key?!" Tamika asked.

"Because it was probably put there for a reason. We can't quit. It's, like, gleaming and beckoning us to figure it out. We just have to think outside the box. Where would that key be and how can we get it?" Lizzie pondered.

Stretching to get a better look, Chelsea reasoned like a sleuth. "This is a major turning point. If that padlock weren't meant to be an important clue, then it wouldn't be there for us to solve. That door would be blocked off, impossibly black and void of hope, just like the windows are."

"Ding ding ding! And that monster—or *whatever* it was— didn't try to kill us like it so easily could've when it was smacking into the sides of the bus."

"It's great and all dat we still alive, Ry…" Tamika said, yawning loudly before continuing on, "but I'm getting pretty damned thirsty. Tired too. And I also wouldn't neglect a cheeseburg n' fries from Five Guys right about now…problem is dat we can't move, therefore we can't get out 'n we can't eat or drink somethin' ta survive!"

"I think that I can speak for everyone else trapped in their seats when I say that we all understand the brevity of this gloomy situation," Lizzie concurred.

"Don't exactly know what dat word 'brevity' means, but y'all ain't showing any urgency ta me!" Tamika hissed.

"And just what're we supposed to do? What would work for you? Cry and beg to whoever's watching us? Hope for hearty meals and bottled waters? Ask 'em to untie these straps off our bodies??" Riley asked angrily.

"It'd be a start!"

"Girls…*please*; you've gotta stop going for the thro—" Chelsea said, halting abruptly after hearing a few voices outside. "You hear that?"

"Yes," Lizzie confirmed quietly. "Don't say anything; just listen."

As if cast from the inside of a trash can, the subdued voices were close enough for the girls to detect that the vocals belonged to only two men, presumably in their mid- to late twenties.

"Should we attempt to attract their attention? Yell out like damsels in distress??" Riley interjected over the outside whispering. "They could help us!"

"Or dey could *hurt* us…" Tamika said fearfully.

Suddenly a boisterous knocking intruded the confines of the bus as hands pounded on its metallic exterior. Petrified and stationary, the girls remained reticent despite the constant cracks being delivered to each side of the yellow vehicle.

After a minute of knocks, a singular voice came forward with clarity. "Hello? Anyone in there? Based on this sign that says *HELP US*, it sure seems like a possibility. I'll be the first to introduce myself; I'm Gil. Please answer if you can. There's been a terrible, terrible accident. And the air's been compromised by it. But my brother Jack and I have survived by the grace of God," the faceless man said, breathing and coughing heavily after every other word.

"Keep quiet; this could be a trap!" Lizzie whispered cautiously.

"*Maybe*, but it could also be our release…" Riley countered.

"Regardless, we gots ta do **something**. They'll leave soon, and den we back ta square one…'n dat's not a good fuckin' square to be on," Tamika stressed, equally as cautious in her whispers.

"If you're scared, that's okay; we are as well. But there is something *monstrous* out here. Have you heard it? I think the creature was just circling this area. We barely got away from it about an hour ago. Please, if anybody's in there, let us in so we can hide with you for a while. There's NO protection outside right now, and that thing will tear us all apart if it comes back!" the frightened male warned.

"Holy shit; they've actually seen it? We only *felt* it! What accident's he talkin' 'bout? We NEED ta find out!!" Tamika urged.

"No; I'm *telling you*…they wanna gain our trust. This could be an elaborate scheme to trick us. For all we know, they could be our captors—not some saviors!" Lizzie asserted, shifting her eyes left and right as the men circled the perimeter of their enclosure.

"This is fucked up! I just wanna be rescued and see what's going on outside. We have to let our presence be known, or else—like Tamika said—they'll bolt! And we can't allow that to happen; we can't!!" Riley seethed.

"WE'RE IN HERE! SIX OF US ARE. N' WE'RE TRAPPED! HELP! PLEASE HURRY!!" Chelsea yelled out of nowhere, alarming everybody.

The unseen man named Gil seemed aghast by the impulsive announcement. "All right, all right; my brother and I will save you soon. Sit tight. The door to the bus is jammed—it's welded shut. We'll try to kick it in."

The two men attacked the door, cursing up a frenzy when failing and falling flat with each strike. Their swift kicks grew louder as both males continued to reassure the girls not to worry.

And then, miraculously, after it'd been doubted by all restrained within the public-school transportation's quarters, the front door of the broken-down bus was destroyed by a double-teamed kick.

Just as the men were about to be seen by the imprisoned girls, a myriad of gunfire exploded behind them—rapidly pinging the rusting, metallic sides of the yellow bus.

"Get back! You're not wanted 'round here, you piece of shit!" Jack bellowed, shooting his gun recklessly as they hopped off the four-wheeler in haste. "We told you to stay away!"

Throughout the screams of the teens trapped inside and the impromptu gunfight between strangers outside, Lizzie hyperventilated her way into a surreal daze.

Is this even happening right now?

Before another thought could tread the fluids of her swirling head, a stunning shotgun blast rocketed into the war-like atmosphere, catapulting one of the once-faceless men into the smoky air toward the steering wheel of the bus as if he were a mere lawn dart.

"NO! JACK!! YOU FUCKER!" Gil cried out.

Jack, slumped into the corner like a rag doll, wore a vile mask of clumped crimson on his gruesomely indistinguishable face. His chest presented to widening eyes a gaping hole of gore, while his gold necklace remained relatively clean. The near-catatonic girls collectively stabilized themselves into an utter shock as bullets kept whizzing by on the outside.

Gurgling pools of blood, the dying man tried to mouth some last words when an ominous howling encompassed the entire area. In an instant, Jack was yanked out by his twitching legs with an incredible swiftness and power. Only a trail of plasma was left in his wake. The predatory culprit—unseen but its fierceness certainly felt—had struck hard and fast.

Minutes passed as all the girls sat in wonder at the sightless spectacle happening on the outskirts of their school bus. Bullets slowly began to come few and far between. And after a heart-wrenching thud to the front hood, the howls and screams subsided. Silence filled the air as the apparent killing entity exited without doing any more damage. The girls sniffled in solidarity as the dust seemingly settled…

"Looks like we back ta square one," Tamika whimpered in defeat.

<u>INSIDE: The Help</u>

A flickering light hung above the passed-out prisoner while a continuous buzzing wafted across the now dark and decrepit hall. These were the only two things coexisting with a sleeping Johnny. The right side of his body lay prone on an unforgiving floor as his left arm was contorted into an uncomfortable position. This was his resting place for hours on end. But with the agents wearing off in his shocked system, he was set to wake up any moment—and once he was able to study the new surroundings, things wouldn't be the same for him again.

Ever so faintly, his crow's-feet-plagued eyes and his achingly sore joints began to plod about. Inch by inch, he moved his extremities, albeit with great difficulty. It was a night-and-day difference from the previous awakening. Johnny Helks had felt like a million bucks before—a rejuvenated man. But he'd been stuck with body-boosting narcotics then.

Now I feel like the regular me. Not a desirable person to be.

"Wait...why are most of the lights out now? Doesn't matter," Johnny said, disoriented and disillusioned. "Gotta get up. They want you to give in. They want weakness. I'm better than this. I will not die in here! Ya think it's going to be that easy to break my spirit?! It isn't!!"

Just him again. Alone and angry. No signs of life. But was he really alone in the prison?

Someone's still here, watching me. I feel it. I know it...

Paranoid to the max and back whenever any slight noise introduced itself, Johnny was convinced that someone had to be tracking his every move.

"I'm not giving in. DO YOU HEAR ME?! I AM NOT QUITTING!"

Silence. Nothing, laughing right in his afflicted face.

"I am going to kill you. So help me God, I'm killing you in the most *evilest* of ways. Whether it's one of you, two of you, or a whole ARMY of you—it doesn't matter to me at all. You're falling right at my feet. And I don't know what the hell's happening here on this insane train, but you better make sure to dismember me the next time we meet…because I won't stop until you're dead!! A needle ain't gonna cut it next go-round! Come try me again; see what happens!!"

Drip. Drip. Drip.

The faucet?

Running faucets—several of them at once—grabbed a perturbed Johnny's attention.

Somebody must've turned them back on just to fuck with me…

As he heard the faucets pouring endlessly, he could almost taste the water on his tongue. With lips cracked and a mouth as dry as cotton, the only thing Johnny wanted was to drink from every single faucet in the prison until he was hydrated and couldn't gulp up any more.

But when he tried to walk toward the alluring sounds of refreshing water, his knees gave out. The excruciating agony was a clear reminder: they'd been brutalized in a fevered blur by an unseen attacker wielding a nightstick.

"Like a coward, a damned weasel…not even man enough to come and face me now, are ya?! Son of a bitch, this hurts!"

Turning back to where he had originally gotten up, Johnny Helks discovered just where he'd been dropped off while unconscious. At the front gate of the penitentiary, a wincing Johnny made certain with a pinch to the shoulder that he wasn't dreaming. He was not.

In front of him stood a doorway to freedom—wide open. And a sealed six-pack of Fiji Natural Artesian Water was at the foot of it along with a burlap sack to store it all in and a fresh new shirt to wear.

Why's this stuff here? What's it matter? I'm not locked in and I'm able to leave whenever I please. AND I've got some clean water now? Can't believe I didn't see it beside me. Stop thinking and start drinking!

"This is unbelievable…this is unreal," Johnny gasped, stepping forward as he ripped the plastic off and downed bottle after bottle of the rustless, delicious water. "I am free."

Once outside, he noticed the air first. To look at it was a sublime mixture of dread and fascination. The sky was colored in a uniquely green-and-purple plume of experimentation. It was as ugly as anything Johnny had ever seen inside the prison walls. And he'd seen many unspeakable acts of depravity performed in there as well as having been a recipient of many such acts. The environmentally altered landscape around him was decimated; the barbed wire fence surrounding every side of the penitentiary was torn down and roads were fractured and faltering. Dead birds in droves lay mangled on the scorched soil. Cars had been set ablaze and stripped. But above all else, a particularly unsettling image took center stage.

"Good God. That is awful," the gawking convict observed. "It's like one big landfill for humans…"

In the middle of a field nearby lay a mound of bodies, all different shapes and sizes, severely charred to the bone and piled high atop each other like a hamper of dirty clothes. He threw up just from taking in the disgusting visual. Darkened beyond recognition, they almost looked like burn-victim test dummies. The stench of seared flesh overwhelmed him. He had to leave and find a less horrific setting, if he even could.

What has happened? I've never witnessed so much destruction.

"Is this the end of the world?" he asked himself, squinting toward something furry a hundred yards away. "A dog's over there? Is my mind playing tricks on me?"

I think it actually is a pooch!

In the foggy distance, a beautiful white Siberian husky with one blue eye and one brown eye ran up to Johnny excitedly, affirming that it wasn't a mirage of the mind. The freed prisoner pet the top of the animal's soft head as it wagged its tail happily. "Where'd you come from, big guy? You scouring this grisly land just like me? And where's your owner, hmm? They lookin' for ya right now or are they…"

The thick-coated, panting dog with triangular ears turned around suddenly, hearing something at a high frequency. "What is it, boy? What'd you hear??"

A second later, as if he'd been ordered to by his master, the alerted husky ran off—just as fast as he had run up to Johnny. "HEY! COME BACK!!"

Well, isn't that great. I could've at least had man's best friend by my side for some companionship and protection…but no…can't be so lucky.

"No time for crying…must keep moving…"

As far as Johnny could see, materials of all kinds were strewn about the voluminous wreckage. Bottles of empty alcoholic beverages littered the land, but one specific brand caught his eye.

Ciderboys?? Last time I had that it got me in trouble—deep trouble!

"Get outta town; that is the **craziest** coincidence. Donatos pizza, too?!"

Close by the bottles of booze were countless boxes, discovered to be empty upon Johnny's vigorous inspection. They were from Donatos, an Ohio-based pizzeria that was yet another reminder of a sour time.

Last time I had a slice of their pie it got me in trouble as well. Everything about that night back then was troublesome...

Compact discs, DVDs, 4K Blu-rays, books, various paperbacks and hardcovers alongside cases and cases of video games were all a part of the destroyed vistas. Snooping about the rubble, he plucked out an assortment of items.

Going through the CDs first, the artists didn't ring a bell for Johnny Helks. "Never heard of any of these guys..."

He glossed over each case, reading the artist names and album titles.

Astronoid - *Air*, Burial - *Untrue*, Brand New - *The Devil and God Are Raging Inside Me*, Edison Glass - *Time is Fiction*, Explosions In The Sky - *All of a Sudden I Miss Everyone*, Falling Up - *Fangs!*, Failure - *Fantastic Planet*, Godspeed You! Black Emperor - *Lift Your Skinny Fists Like Antennas to Heaven*, Hum - *Downward is Heavenward*, Jogger - *This Great Pressure*, Joseph Nothing - *Dreamland Idle Orchestra*, Last Days of April - *Angel Youth*, Longwave - *Secrets are Sinister*, Menomena - *Friend & Foe*, Russian Circles - *Enter*, and This Will Destroy You - *Another Language*.

"What kind of bands are these, anyway? Falling Up? This Will Destroy You?? Why can't there be some Converge or some Tony Danza Tapdance Extravaganza in this lot of garbage? I bet it all sucks!"

How would one really know if these albums sucked unless they actually listened to them? Maybe you shouldn't be so judgmental...

"Too bad CD players are practically extinct these days! I'd be lucky to find any lying around here…I'd be grateful to find ANYTHING useful!!"

Incensed by his dismal circumstances, Johnny threw the digipacks and jewel cases down to the ground violently. Inserts came loose and the plastic that housed some of the discs ruptured upon impact.

Up next was the eclectic selection of movies.

"Let's see; what do we have here?" Johnny asked, thumbing through the films. "*Super.* Don't really know any of these either—except for one! But I'm more of a TV guy."

The movies were from a wide range of genres.

Another Earth, Beyond the Black Rainbow, Breakdown, Cloverfield, Creep, Cube, Eagle Eye, Identity, It Follows, Lone Survivor, Moon, Oblivion, Series 7: The Contenders, Surveillance, The Cabin in the Woods, The Game, The House of the Devil, This is the End, V/H/S, and *You're Next.*

Quickly discarded and forgotten about, the books were next on the chopping block. Some were older, some newer, with even a few graphic novels wedged into the literary lot. Only a few were remembered by Johnny.

Alone Together by Sherry Turkle, *Channel Blue* by Jay Martel, *Cure for the Common Universe* by Christian McKay Heidicker, *Desperation* by Stephen King, *Freeway* by Mark Kalesniko, *Infinite Jest* by David Foster Wallace, *Here* by Richard McGuire, *Pines* by Blake Crouch, *Psycho* by Robert Bloch, *The Martian Chronicles* by Ray Bradbury, *The Shadow Girl* by Misty Mount, *Time Out of Joint* by Phillip K. Dick, *Tin Foil Hat* by Justin Bauer, *We All Looked Up* by Tommy Wallach, and *Yesterday's Gone* by Sean Platt & David Wright were what he skimmed through.

"I've seen Alfred Hitchcock's adaptation of *Psycho*, but I never got around to reading the book. Maybe I'll get to it now that I have ample time to do so…like in that *Twilight Zone* ep where the guy survived a nuclear holocaust and stacked a bunch of books to read. But unlike him, I don't NEED glasses to see." Johnny snickered. "As for the rest of these…back to the junk pile you go! Eh, on second thought, I'll take *Tin Foil Hat*; the cover's kinda cool."

What was the name of that classic TZ episode, anyway? Time Enough at Last? Was it that? I've watched 'em all; I should know.

The video games were the last to be looked at. However, not being much of a gamer in his teens and not showing any inkling of interest in his early twenties, Johnny didn't care to finger through too many of them. Swiping ten randomly from underneath the material shambles, he chuckled at the interactive entertainment's grandiose cover art.

Dead Space, Heavy Rain, L.A. Noire, Mad World, Metal Arms, Shadow of the Colossus, Skies of Arcadia, The Legend of Zelda: Breath of the Wild, The Last of Us, and *Watch Dogs.*

"We've certainly come a long way since *Galaga* and *Pac-Man*! I'm too old school for this next-gen stuff; it looks boring to me. Guess they aren't that 'next-gen,' though…they're older now!"

Beside the games were a cracked Playstation VR headset and a broken Nintendo Switch.

"Ah, I remember these things!" Johnny reminisced joyfully, picking the hardware off the ground. "I played 'em at a buddy's house before I was incarcerated!"

After having another laugh to himself, Johnny spotted disastrous implications up ahead. The downtown skyline was now on fire. Bristling with flames, blackening smoke plumes melded into the clouds like a fine-tuned machine as the air itself stank of gasoline and rotting carcasses.

Johnny stepped across the thousands of physical media items, cracking and snapping jewel cases as if they were tiny pistachio shells. No matter where he went, both of his feet were buried in the quicksand of crushed merchandise. Broken Bluetooth keyboards, empty coffee cups, loads of oddly clean clothes—but just for girls, and dirty Twinkie morsels rounded out the billowing landscape. Like a caveman, he scarfed down the fragments of cream-filled sponge cake as he continued to see items that ignited nostalgia. Both good and bad.

"A Corn Pops pile?!" the freed prisoner asked incredulously. "That cereal killed my childhood…I'm not even gonna check to see if there's any left."

As he walked away from the cereal boxes, another buried artifact from his cognizance burrowed back into his peripherals.

"Pallets of Pepsi…and not one can missing out of any twelve-pack? Why're all these here??"

Pepsi: the stuff my dad used to give me when he was sorry for being HIM. Plopping me in front of a screen, erasing my misery. Or doing his best to try to do so temporarily. But it never worked. It couldn't.

Johnny Helks moved past the chipboards and pop cans gleaning his haunting memories. "High-fructose corn syrup's awful enough for me to avoid them…even while in a situation like this. My water will do; it's all I need. All this body needs."

He kept walking and looking, already wiping clean the long-gone traumas orbiting his head.

Whoa; AlphaSmart Neos! I used those back in school…haven't seen one in forever…and Crimson Cup? Loved that place; wish I could be drinking some of their coffee right now. But this torched area won't allow such luxuries, I'm sure. Hell on wheels, my prison's in better shape!

The world seemed to be a lost cause—injured yet trying to heal, much like his assaulted knees.

"What the…" Johnny said, cupping his mouth in disbelief.

Half a mile away, something was destroying architecture. The lurking figure couldn't exactly be made out; just a silhouette of its humongous form was there to gawk at. Decimating building after building, the mysterious entity tore through any man-made structures still left standing on their hinges. The extravagant visual amazed Johnny.

"The fuck is that thing?" he marveled. "Looks like a force to be reckoned with."

Otherworldly howling overtook the ruination, scaring Johnny almost half to death. What could only be described as inhuman shattering sounds gave him heart palpitations as the being mowed down trees and flung debris. Apprehensive but stupidly curious about the cloaked monster, Johnny Helks decided to play it safe—for the time being.

"No way I'm going over there."

As the ruckus was escalating, its operator of rampage decreased the onslaught in a flash. And much like an aging man's libido, it had vanished. In its path of destruction, all that remained to the naked eye were more constructions deconstructed. Viewing the many buildings abolished and the smattering of trees knocked over, Johnny shook his head.

I have to be dead. That's all there is to it. This isn't real; it can't be.

"But if I've died, why am I in this sticky situation? I don't get it."

And that's when he looked inward, thinking long and hard about the despicable things he'd done in his life. Perhaps this whole thing was an eternal punishment, doled out in soul-crushing pieces to seek retribution against the awful acts that Johnny had previously committed.

Has to be a personal hell I'm being held in. This is just too supernatural and too weird for it to be anything else.

"Self-explanatory. I'm stuck—meant to suffer."

Dissolving himself of an absolution, Johnny mindlessly trekked forward. Through the nightmarish abyss of moot loot and burnt bodies, he cringed his way across an army of plunder.

No survivors. No screams for help. Nobody found along the fires. There was simply an eerie, smoky serenity. Despite the fact that no one seemed to be alive anymore, the convict commendably called out for any person in need of assistance while nursing his nagging injuries.

"Is anyone still alive? Anyone?? Lord knows I can't do this alone. I'm badly injured here."

Nothing but a response of crackling flames swarming over spoils.

Johnny Helks continued onward in hopes of extracting answers to the deeply darkening mystery. Feeling an overwhelming but natural desire to be in contact with another human, he began to sob like a teething baby.

This isn't fair. I'm sorry for what I did; really, I am.

Stricken with remorse for his past sins, the freed prisoner mentally retreated as he physically advanced to parts unknown.

"I deserve this death," Johnny grumbled, clearing tears away.

On the torched ground, he felt something under the sole of his foot. It was thick, solid. When he looked down, he saw that it was something that could be essential to utilize.

Either on himself or on someone else.

A gun. Loaded, too.

Jackpot. I could just end it all right now. Make it a whole lot easier on myself.

Johnny quavered as he stared fearlessly into the barrel of the gun, his heart thumping and skipping its quickened beats.

"Maybe I shouldn't even care anymore. Why should I? Shit, I'm a walking target anyway."

His fingertips were on the trigger, tapping it rhythmically like an acne-infested gamer would his controller.

"Squeeze it; all it takes is a single squeeze…" he urged tentatively.

Should I do it? Is this how I should go out?

Not able to give an immediate answer to his own life-searching questions, he sulked and lowered his head. And that's when he saw another possibly essential item to examine—not for use, but for clues.

It was a notebook—the second one that Johnny had come across.

And what was written on it was just as much a vague brain-twister as the blunt one that had preceded it.

It read in big, black caps along two pages side by side:

BOARD THE BUS TO BE THEIR HERO. OR ELSE…

"There's that 'or else' again. Or what?! What else is there that you could do to me? I *already* have a gun cocked and I'm prepared to off myself right here! So…what are YOU gonna do about that? Huh?? Show yourself!"

Fractions of a second after his pointed demand, some shouting erupted nearby. At first Johnny thought that he was the unlucky one being screamed at, but once his momentary confusion had disbanded, he made out exactly where the verbal chaos was coming from.

It's coming from down below that hill. Can't see anything from my vantage point. I have to get a better look…but my knees…

Without prolonging the journey any more than he had to, Johnny Helks limped forward painfully.

"God, how I wish I could sprint…"

As he neared the site of screams, Johnny tripped and fell rather roughly into yet another pile of damaged goods. But the silver lining in the tumble was a 24-pack of bottled water: another bundle of Fiji, unopened in its boxed-up cardboard casing.

"Hallelujah."

Johnny quickly downed two bottles and his thirst was quenched dramatically.

A loaded gun and now some MORE water? Somebody must be looking out for me. But why Fiji again?? There's gotta be a reas—

The piercingly evil howling that had scared him earlier returned, interrupting his theorizing. It could easily be heard from his position over the screams coming from the opposite direction.

"What the hell's that damned thing??" Johnny questioned, hiding unknowingly beside a portion of rank dog manure. "AH, so gross!"

Slithering his way up off his knees with delicacy as stabbing pains traversed in and out of his legs, he came up with a brilliant idea.

I'll roll down the hill like a log. Saves time and effort. That should work well…then I'll finally be able to see what's going on…

Johnny started rolling. Gaining speed as he slid downward toward something especially radical, he had no idea how to combat whatever it was once he saw it.

If he even *could* manage to get a shot off on the beastly thing.

Mid-roll, the distinct scream of an impassioned male rang out clearly.

"NO! JACK!! YOU FUCKER!" the man yelled, firing his gun in a frenzied fashion.

"Who's Jack?" Johnny wondered aloud, favoring his injured knees amidst the pulsating ammo clash.

Such a magnificent-sounding battleground.

A hailstorm of bullets and bellows followed until the increments of battle cries, howling from the monstrous atrocity, and intermittent gunpowder pops grew further apart. Before Johnny could make heads or tails, the war that was being waged with such fervor had ended anti-climatically. And although the prisoner's overall hearing wasn't as good as it used to be, he could've sworn that he'd heard what sounded like an object—or a person—smack against the side of a large vehicle.

Was that a bus?

He waited for more screaming, more shooting, more of anything to happen. But nothing was uttered after the thud.

"I can't wait any longer. I gotta go see what that was!"

Just then, an airplane came into view up above the tainted sky—dipping and diving across the smoke-filled air due to engine failure.

Coming in hot and spiralling outta control! Oh man, that plane's gonna crash right into one of those high-rise towers…

Immediately after completing his premonitory thoughts, the commercial-airline craft dovetailed out of sight, and moments later crashed into a building as bright orange flames engulfed the downtown skyline.

That was so cinematic! Shame, though. Whoever was piloting that bird could've explained what has happened here…but now they're probably deep-fried charcoal. No point in going on that fetch-quest.

Johnny, grimacing with each step forward and still agape from the glowing embers of the recent jet explosion, stumbled onto a wild scene of blood. Trails of red canvassed the obliterated area, and a yellow school bus with ghetto-looking graffiti outlined on its left side was lodged firmly into a section of separated, crumbling road.

Who's Noah Nichols? And why is he wack AF?

"So many mysteries in front of me…"

Newspaper remnants floated about the tarnished land as Johnny read what one emboldened header appeared to have foreshadowed:

NUKE TESTING WORRIES

That gives some credence to my first theory! Maybe this is a fallout.

"Or maybe it's just another red herring. This is weird…" the wandering and wondering man said, trying to read the whited-out article below its bold heading. "Misdirection. Like those sounds back at the prison were."

And if it had anything to do with nukes, where's the radiation?

Pulverized by the presence that had commanded it in the blusterous moments beforehand, the bus dead ahead of the freed prisoner wasn't in tip-top shape.

With strains of doubt in his voice, Johnny called out to see if anyone was still around. "Anybody here? Speak if you are, 'cause I'm about at the end of my rope!"

No one seemed to be around.

It was totally clear, devoid of any people or any telltale signs that someone alive had been there. Except for a huge white sheet draped over a turned-on-its-side car, which said:

BRB U 3 STAY PUT!!

Why are there claw marks slashed on the hood? What all am I dealing with, anyway?

The razed zone looked to be exhausted of existence, as only flames around Johnny filled his ears with a crackling steadiness.

Until a feminine voice cut through the crackle.

"Are you still there, whoever you are?" she asked, fearful.

The freed prisoner lit up with happiness. "Yes! Still here!!"

"We're trapped in this bus. Just…don't hurt us."

"Wouldn't even dream of it!" Johnny exclaimed sincerely. "How many of you are in there?"

"Six. We're all tied to our seats. The door's been kicked in; it's open. The two men who successfully broke through it were killed. We think. Please don't harm us!"

"It's a promise. Cross my heart. Don't be afraid; on my way to you now," he assured, hobbling in pain toward the ransacked bus. "It'll take a moment, though. I'm injured…"

"Take your time; we definitely aren't going anywhere," the girl replied meekly.

Even taking five steps forward depleted Johnny, as his calves and kneecaps were burning with a forest fire's worth of torment. It was close to being unbearable in its constant badgering. But he'd finally found people. And they didn't seem like they wanted to cause him any harm.

These are probably innocent people, confused and hurt just like me. Regardless of how bad I feel, this is too big to pass up.

After struggling to reach the entryway of the bullet-laced school bus for a while, he arrived at the threshold of one more mystery to be solved—as well as finding a conveniently placed knife by the foot of the steps.

Dark puddles of hot, congealed blood and slippery entrails splashed onto the faded soles of a gimpy Johnny as he stepped up and over the splatter matter. "Disgusting; absolutely horrible…" he proclaimed while his shoes squished the stripped guts.

When he reached the top, he quickly turned his head to the left to see six girls held captive. Their faces showed glimmers of suspicion and terror all at once, as the uneasiness and tension were ripe.

They have numbers on their shirts, too! Why?

Knowing that someone had to talk, Johnny initiated conversation with the numbered group.

"Hello there. Worry no longer. That…*whatever*…is gone now, so I'll gladly untie all of you—with this knife I found right outside. And if ya wanna get outta those jersey tees, I saw loads of clean clothes nearby. I won't look when y'all change," Johnny said, smiling with a frisky innocence. "Where are my manners? The name's J—"

"Look, I'm sorry…but can we please name-drop AFTER you get us da hell outta here, my man?" a black teen sassed.

"Of course; good thinking. We may not have time to waste, so it'd be smarter to move faster."

"Thank you. You're a godsend!" a nerdy-looking girl near the back wailed.

"Just trying to figure out this nightmare…same as you all are, I'm assuming. Are any of you hurt?"

"No," the girls informed simultaneously.

"That's good, then. At least that's one bright spot!" Johnny said. "None of you saw anything while tied up?"

"Other than seeing a grotesquely bloody guy yanked from where you're standing, we just *heard* things," Lizzie replied. "Gunshots, explosions, screams. Then it all stopped…"

"*Right*…what a dumb, dumb question to ask. How could you see anything? Between being tied down and these shutters keeping ya in the dark, it's impossible. But look at this BLOOD on the steps! I mean, cleanup on aisle four!!"

The assembled girls shook their heads, cringing blankly.

Well, I was only trying to lighten the mood.

"I also didn't see a thing, except for some plane crashing downtown, it looked like." The freed prisoner smartly switched gears.

"Though whoever was aboard can't possibly be among the living anymore. As for your situation, I came waddling toward this insane scene a bit too late, I believe. Didn't see anybody…no baddies! Oh well; things'll perk up now that I'm here to bail y'all out, won't they? Got this bag; it's full of bottled water. And I'm certain you're *probably* thirsty…"

The still-in-shock girls looked pleased.

"We REALLY appreciate the help. Just a few minutes ago, we all thought that we were gonna die! So…thanks," a tanned teen said kindly.

"Hey…don't mention it!" Johnny replied, knifing each one of the girls' leather straps with focus and thoughtfulness. "Because I'd like to assume that if *I* were strapped inside a school bus ridden with a boatload of bullets, you'd do the same thing for me."

Four of the girls smiled warmly, while the other two didn't. Or couldn't. They were both inherently mute and almost vegetable-like.

"What's wrong with those girls in the back?" he inquired.

"Don't know. They haven't said a word, they're conjoined, and they've been entranced like some ecstasy-takers at a rave," a rather white girl up in front commented plainly.

Just noticed that HELP US thing—who wrote that if they were restrained?

"Before you ask, none of us wrote on the window," the same girl answered, almost telepathic in her timing. "We don't know who did it. It's very weird."

"I see that…well, this whole fucking situation is weird!" Johnny winced, instantly regretting the coarse language used. "Sorry. I've been known to swear like a sailor."

"Dude, who *doesn't* swear? I fuckin' say fuck all the time," the black girl admitted with a witty disposition. "I'm Tamika, and it's sho' as shit nice ta meet you in da midst of such a damn mess."

An introverted girl who resembled a librarian's young daughter spoke with trust in her tone. "And I'm Chelsea! Thanks so much for saving us. It feels freaking great to get out of these constraints!!"

The pale female chimed in halfheartedly. "I'm Riley. Hi."

"Lizzie," the tanned teen revealed. "That's my name."

I cannot get over how beautiful Liz is; wow. Flawless skin and hair. Those soft lips. Just so innocent. So…blossoming in all the right places. And that name; why does it sound familiar?

"Now that we're outta these straps," the bronzed bombshell interrupted his internal lusting and lingering, "I think it's about time we learn your name as well as your motives…"

Johnny grinned widely, nodding in agreement at Lizzie's forthrightness. "You really wanna know that confidential information?"

"Sure we do," Riley encouraged. "I'm positive we'd all love to know the legal birth name of our hero."

The freed prisoner laughed, throwing their constrictors down onto the ground with a sense of victory.

Beaming with delight at his newfound purpose, he felt genuinely wanted for the first time in a long time.

"The name's Johnny Helks. And I'm here to help…"

SECOND STRIKE

Sometime in 2017, 1997, 2018, & 2028…

OUTSIDE: The Twentysomething

A dark and rainy night. Streetlights appeared only sporadically—yet were the main source of illumination. The rain faithfully continued its torrential downpour onto a busy-bee windshield alongside the humming flow of an original motion picture soundtrack to the film *Beyond the Black Rainbow*. Driving on the open road, the contemplative male was distraught over a nasty breakup that he'd seen coming for weeks. Ignoring an unending stream of his ex-girlfriend's texts and calls filtering in, he saw that she was hysterical, trying her best to make amends and start again.

Of course you're sorry…you won't have me around to enable your sleazy drug habit anymore!

"That's all you care about. It's all you ever cared about."

Frantically apologizing and explaining her side of the story through a barrage of sad-faced, heart-shaped emojis wore him out. He simply wanted no part of it. The games, the deceptions, the BS. Her ham-fisted insincerity had been embarrassingly exposed. He'd bent over backward for her on countless occasions—for nearly three years—and what was the thanks he got in return? A swift stab to the spinal column. That was it. Pain and paralysis. An ocean of anguish. He would never forgive himself for giving his soul away so easily to a trashy tweaker who couldn't care less.

"Yeah, you care *now*…" the upset man said, looking down at the glow of his smartphone. "I guess when you've been caught red-handed, it's real easy to cower and want a second chance!"

Getting himself worked up over good memories now forever tarnished, he threw his digital distraction onto the shotgun seat of his near-death Honda Civic. By the way he'd tossed it, it was clear that more damage had been intended. But knowing that a certain someone was paying a pretty penny for a monthly lease impeded his elevating aggression. When it came to addictive devices, tight financials always kept his temper in check.

If I wasn't being charged an arm and a leg—wait, my mom pays for it, anyway! This damned thing. All it does is cause trouble, and I hate it. I hate how I need it.

The texts from her were constant. Neither his phone's battery life nor his patience would last much longer. Singular sentences, coming in at a quick clip via voicemail and text, were pleading for a response—until they turned hostile due to being digitally and phonetically rejected.

Johnny…baby…please don't do this. Don't end us!! :(

I need you badly. There, happy now? I admit it

It was just a rly stupid ducking mistake okay

***fucking**

You HAVE to know that he didn't mean a thing to me!

I love you and only you. Please text or call back. Please.

I'll be up all night waiting. I'm not quitting just yet

FINE BE THIS WAY I DON'T EVEN CARE U ASS

YOU AREN'T WORTH THIS MUCH WORK YA KNOW

BTW HE'S MUCH BETTER IN BED!! JUST FYI

O YA AND HE ALSO HAS HIS OWN PLACE UNLIKE U :P

WELL GOODBYE FR THEN! HAVE A NICE LIFE. OR NOT.

"All women start off as angels only to end up as demons," Johnny pontificated, mystified by the opposite sex and his limited experiences with them.

Thinking of no possible way to reply with any kind of maturity given the infidelity enacted, he calmly set his phone into the cup holder by the car's stick shift.

Happy to be done with her. Good riddance…

As he continued to drive aimlessly and wander about in his own mind for a lengthy amount of time, the phone began to vibrate again.

Over and over.

"Will she STOP already? Take the hint!"

The smartphone vibrated incessantly atop a mini-heap of coins. Dimes and quarters jangled underneath it in harmony.

I can't handle that annoying sound! I'm answering. But I'm letting that two-timing harlot have it.

"Listen, Ericka…" he said rashly after swiping right. "We're done. This whole thing—it's over. You hear me?? And don't ever call me again. Go suck my best friend off!"

There was a hush on the other end, yet just enough breathing had been dispersed to signify that someone was still there.

When he checked his phone, he saw that it wasn't Ericka on the line.

It was actually his cougar-like neighbor from across the street, Mrs. Janis, a woman he'd known since he was a little boy.

What could she want? It can't be what I think it is…

Sweet, non-confrontational, and slightly sexy, she was the type of woman Johnny liked to keep interested—the type to keep on the side to pounce upon if her husband wasn't cutting it during times of horny need. And he had done just that until receiving payoff on a late September evening earlier in the year. A forbidden one-night stand was enjoyed by both parties. But that promiscuous night shared between them had turned out to be an isolated event. Afterward, Johnny had been snubbed.

Much to his dismay—since the kinky physicality was admittedly top-notch—Mrs. Janis had smartened up after her momentary lapse in judgment. She vehemently insisted that there was to be no more risky business, though she *had* gone on record as saying how much she'd loved their time together. But it was decided rather conclusively that nothing could ever come of it.

Too much for her to lose. A house, two kids, and a husband with hefty, ironclad benefits. What makes me so special? I have nothing to show for myself. And I'm almost thirty, living with my parents.

"Um…Johnny? Are you okay?" Mrs. Janis fretted, snapping him out of a dizzying state of self-reflection.

"Oh; hi there. Sorry, Mrs. Janis…I didn't know it was y—"

"Please don't talk to me like that. I'm not a teacher, am I?"

"No, you're not. Not at all."

"Exactly; so call me Vanessa. You've called me lots of other better names…especially on that one magnificent night…" she whispered deviously, as if to muzzle the words to prevent her spouse from potentially overhearing.

"Sorry again, then. Vanessa it is. Didn't mean to be so rude to you…but I'm just…NOT myself at the moment…"

"I know it wasn't directed toward me. From the sound of it, seems like you're having girl troubles. Did some broad break your heart?"

"You could say that," he replied, an air of indifference in his voice.

"Well, whatever she did to you…*listen*, I've known you for a long time, and you're a great guy. Your mom and I were classmates from first grade all the way to high school. She's raised you right, so you'll find the girl who's right. Believe me. She's out there…"

Johnny smiled at the compliments given, his condition improving. "Thanks for that, Vanessa. Your words are appreciated. It's been great being your neighbor for so long; thank you."

If only I'd gone to your house instead of that one guy's back when I escaped my father's vengeance…how different would things now be for me?

"Anytime. So look, I called you for a reason. I need a favor."

"Hmm, I see…is that what we're going to call it from now on?"

"Not that. Remember, I told you that that *can't* happen again."

"Fine, fine. I was kidding. Kinda," Johnny said sheepishly.

Mrs. Janis unveiled her agenda. "Plans have changed for tonight. I originally had a babysitter scheduled to watch the girls because Terry and I have to go to a banquet dinner. But she's flaked."

"*Terry*," he blurted in mocking fashion. "How's that dummy doing?"

"He's good; same as always…" Vanessa said, moving along. "So, I'm in a tight spot. No one's available on such short notice…"

"And you trust me enough to watch your kids…is that what you're getting at? Do I have that correct so far?"

"Mm-hmm; you've got it."

Johnny proceeded to fidget his fingers up and down the steering wheel, patting the top of an unraveling fake leather cover. While the rain kept slapping his windshield unmercifully, he thought about whether he should comply to being the last-ditch babysitter for a woman with whom he'd had a minor—although immensely steamy—affair.

"I don't know, Vanessa. It'd be a bit uncomfortable."

"I don't really see why you'd think that. How would it be?"

"For one, we've had *sex*…and it was damn good sex, even if it did only happen once," Johnny stated. "And two, I'm just not that guy. You know what I mean? I've never babysat before, and I have no idea what I'd do in that vulnerable position—if your kids were to go wacky on me. All things considered, I'm not the sort of dude to rule the roost! Any roost, mind you."

"While I understand your concerns—and they are duly noted—you won't even have to worry about much at all…"

"What do you mean by that, exactly?"

"You aren't really *watching* them…you're just standing guard, so to say. It'll be easy."

"How old are they? You never told me, since we kept our thing so low-pro."

"Lizzie's five and Markéta's twelve…"

"MARKÉTA? What kind of name is that??"

"It's Czech and Slovak for Margaret. My family heritage has its origins there—the Czech Republic—and I liked the sound of it, so I pushed for it…since I had to push her. Out of my southern area."

"I know how birthing works, thanks!" Johnny said, laughing.

"You're *welcome*. So that's it—that's the lay of the land. And oh, you won't have to worry about Lizzie whatsoever; she'd be sound asleep in her bed by the time you got here. What do you say, Johnny? Ball's in your court."

"Well, it doesn't seem like it'd be that stressful, but I'll be honest with ya…I dunno if I'd be able to handle a girl who goes by the super-special name of Markéta!"

"Will you give it a rest already? It's a wonderful name. In fact, in 2005—the year that she was born—it was the *eighteenth* most popular name for a baby girl in all the Czech Republic!"

"GET OUTTA TOWN!" Johnny exclaimed with a put-on disbelief.

"It's true, it's true. The name was used in that calendar year approximately six hundred and sixty-six times, even! Wait…uh-oh, I don't think that's a good thing…"

"No! It isn't! She's cursed. That's the number of the devil. Hey, Markéta *does* sorta sound like it'd be the name of a brutal metal band! Or maybe a ritzy grocery store…I can hear the commercial now…*come get manic at Markéta Organic…where healthy, grass-fed food is our MO!*"

"Funny. I'm busting a gut over here; sounds like that make-believe place would give Digest Nature or Fresh Thyme a run for their money! So do you wanna do it or not? I'll pay cash. A hundred bucks for around four or five hours of your time…"

"What about drinking? Can I bring alcohol?"

"I suppose…but what kind is it? Regular beer, hard liquor, what?"

"Just a variety pack of Ciderboys. I've had it in the trunk for the past three weeks. I was gonna drink all of it with Ericka, but you know—her cheating got in the way of those plans. Thankfully the consistently cold weather has been my refrigerator."

Since Daddy doesn't like to see me drinking, he thought randomly.

"Sure, if you're responsible with it. This goes without saying, but…don't give any to Markéta. She loves that cider stuff. I caught her drinking an Angry Orchard with a friend during the summer…"

"Damn, only twelve and she's already dabbling in drinking!"

"*And a half.*"

"I'm sorry?" Johnny asked.

"She always says that whenever I let her know she's still too young."

"Wait a sec…I didn't even think of this earlier, but if she's twelve and a half, why hire a babysitter in the first place? Wouldn't it be pretty acceptable to leave her there—put her in charge? You said she's only going to be lounging on her phone…"

"I'd usually agree with that, but she wants to go out with some questionable friends tonight—and I told her that she couldn't. Your main duty would be to make sure she doesn't try and skip out."

"So I'm like substitute parenting?"

"Yeah, if that's what you wanna call it! Just be mindful of her bratty attitude because of me saying no to her, okay? She's at that stage where she thinks she knows everything and then some…"

"'Course she does! I was the same way. Kids insist on acting older than they really are. It's cute, but awfully annoying."

"Couldn't have said it better myself. But anyway, you probably won't have to worry about her that much. She usually stays in her room, moping around, on her phone like every other girl her age these days…I'd only ask for you to check up on her every once in a while."

"Ten-four."

"So, are we good on this deal?" Vanessa asked enticingly.

"*Absolutely*. Why not? A hundred dollars and permission to drink for barely doing anything? Doesn't sound like a terrible gig!"

"Splendid, then. I trust that you'll do an adequate job, Johnny."

"I'll certainly try. See you in about an hour?"

"That's perfect. Take care and drive safe. The rain's been a bitch!"

Johnny sneered, shaking his head. "My ex-girlfriend's been more of a bitch than this rain. At least the downpour will end sooner or later! Ericka will always be trouble…"

"Are you positive that you're all right to do this?"

"Yes! I'm totally straight with doing it," Johnny confirmed.

A couple of polite goodbyes later, he hung up and drove toward the Janis household. In all actuality, he was only about five minutes away—ten at the most—but he'd intentionally said an hour to get a flask hit in to ease his nerves as well as to prepare himself for the daunting charade of acting responsible. He had to give off the impression that he was a reliable adult.

Once I down this shit, I'll be floating n' coasting before I arrive…

Johnny found a desolate parking lot, an ideal spot to lather his throat with some cheap scotch before posturing as Mr. Mom. A recurring bad habit; an everyday thing. The familiar burning sensation of the rigid-tasting alcohol traveled from his esophagus to his beer belly in-training.

"I feel like my problems aren't even problems anymore," he declared to an empty shopping center. "God, I am a **lightweight**."

Better hit the brakes on this private party. I need to get paid…I'm so broke right now…and my mom's too afraid of my ass of a dad to spot me any money.

With his drinking—and thinking—under control, Johnny wisely set out for the Janis estate. Not really knowing what to expect once he got there but not exactly caring all that much, he pulled into the driveway with the obtuse elegance of a drunken frat boy.

"Aw yeah; I'm here. Gotta get those drinks from the back! Keep it going all night…" he said, stumbling out of the car like a bumbling idiot.

Vanessa, witnessing his belligerence from her roofed-in porch, began to have second thoughts about her choice of a caretaker. Clearly he was in no condition to babysit. But from Vanessa's own description of the situation, it was an easy job. And when one's desperate to make an engagement on time, they'll try like hell to make it work—no matter what the circumstances could entail.

"Need some help?" she asked.

"With the cider? Nah, I got it handled! So many times I'd carry way more booze to Ericka's place…" he bragged, stopping himself once he brought up his ex. "Dammit."

"You okay? I'm a little worried," Vanessa admitted.

"I'm *completely* cool. Just gimme a moment and I'll be all right."

"You know…maybe we should forget about this whole thing…"

"Absolutely not; no way. What? Are you KIDDING me?!" he shrilled.

"If you can behave and get through this like a mature adult, I'll allow you in my house. Are you sure you can be here for hours without issues?"

"Positively sure about it, Vanessa. Swear on a stack of Bibles, even!"

"Then sober up fast, will you?"

"Yes, ma'am. Right away, Mrs. Janis!!" Johnny mocked childishly.

"I told you **not** to call me that! That's your last warning…"

"Never again. Promise, my dearest…sweetest…uh, what're we talking about again?"

"Oh my, you are hammered," Vanessa said with disapproval. "Better tone it down before Terry sees you. And my lord, your breath reeks of liquor! Here, have a mint or two…freshen your breeze.

Abstain yourself as best you can. Quick. He'll be down any minute now…"

"Terry! My boy!! He's cool. And hey, that's your husband, too."

"*Yes*…he is my husband, and you need to shape up quickly!"

"I'm good. Honest. Watch me nail this…like I nailed you!"

"SHUT UP. Don't be so obvious!!" Vanessa hissed.

"Sorry, honey. I'll behave like you'd like me to."

"Whatever; just don't talk much. We'll be out of your hair soon enough, so **maintain**…and sorry, but I have to do this."

"Do what??" Johnny asked, confused and teetering.

A hard slap across the face stunned him. Vanessa had indeed meant business.

"CRIPES, WOMAN!"

"That was for your own good. Snap out of it…he's coming!"

Terry came down the stairs straightening his tie, clueless to the slap heard 'round the porch. He smiled at Johnny like a coworker would flash a grin at another in the beginning of some blasé workday. Insincere, surface-level politeness to please the wife, with a handshake and a thank-you added for extra credit.

Johnny smiled right back after extracting his hand away from Terry's stronghold cranked on him. "Evening, Mr. Janis. How've you been, sir?"

"Just fine; just fine. And yourself?" the husband asked with an aura of disinterest.

"Well, my girlfriend and I broke up recently. And I've been in between jobs for the past year, but other than that, things are going GREAT for me."

"Ah, sorry to hear that. Don't let it deflate you, though…there are plenty of fish in the sea, as you know…" Terry said, putting his arm around Vanessa.

"Eh…that's the thing. See, I don't really wanna swim anymore."

"Clever. Real clever. But seriously, you'll get over her. That's always the case, especially when you're young."

"I guess so…but I kinda don't care about the games you have to play. It's too tiring. You have to deal with all the drama and the deception, and for what? To get some tail? And it's like…only for seconds—or if I'm having a good day, *minutes*—of pleasure…"

Terry laughed loudly. "Trust me, Johnny. You'll feel like death for a while, but then someone will come along to inject some life back into you. You'll forget all about…what's-her-face?"

"Ericka."

"Damn. You know something? I know an Ericka. She's a total floozy. You're better off, bud. Just gotta get outta your mama's basement to improve your chances! Women respect men who're independent."

Independence isn't free when you're six feet deep in poverty.

"Yes, sir. Don't I know it! In a bit of a hole right now, though."

An impatient and unnerved Vanessa intervened. "Babe, we should head out so we aren't late for the banquet."

"Suppose you're right. Traffic may be horrible since it's been raining like cats and dogs the whole night," Terry said.

"Yup yup, it's raining hard out there—uh, cats and dogs hard," Johnny quipped, slurring his words.

"Ya all right there, son?"

"We should *really* get going…" Vanessa urged, staring at the inebriated Johnny sternly.

"Whoa, that look could kill!"

"Huh? What look?" Terry asked, only half paying attention while scrolling through text messages maniacally.

"Nothing, dear. He's just being funny about my resting bitch face is all!"

"It's definitely prominent, Mrs. Janis. Especially right now!" Johnny joked. "I actually feel sorry for you having to see it every day, Mr. J…"

"Oh God; it's the *worst* in the morning!"

"Hey!! Thanks a lot!" Vanessa yelped.

"Kidding. You know I love you. And for the record, you don't have to call me Mr. J, Johnny…just say Terry!"

"Can do, Terry!!"

Vanessa steered the conversation once more. "Lizzie's already asleep, so you won't have to worry about her. On the off chance she wakes up, tell her that everything's okay and that we'll be home soon. If she's still crying, though, get Markéta. She'll know what to do in that crisis. Certain stuffed animals are the cure for situations like that…like her zebra…"

"Got it." Johnny nodded.

"And I'm sure Vanessa has told you about our other daughter's deal, but she honestly won't be *too* much trouble. I'll bet she doesn't even leave her room the entire night," Terry predicted, getting a pair of North Face coats from a rack near the front door. "Can't ever seem to pry her away from that phone of hers…"

"Kids these days…am I right?" Vanessa said, clearly wanting to leave.

"We've always had something to distract us from the things that truly matter. All that's different now is that better-quality screens are readily available to do the ignoring in. The Internet's a better babysitter than I could ever be…"

"Very insightful, Johnny. Can you imagine the reaction if we lose it one day? I shudder to think what would happen! Being without Ericka seems to have made you highly reflective!" Terry teased.

"Nah, I was still an insightful person when I was with her stupid ass…" Johnny pointed out. "Just was blind to her BS."

With a parting glance and a mouthing of warning words, Vanessa informed their new-hire babysitter, "We didn't have time to stock up on groceries this weekend, so our kitchen's pretty bare. But I've left forty dollars on the dining room table…in case you'd like to get some pizza and wings or something like that."

Bonus. That'd go nicely with my alcoholic beverages. My stomach is beginning to rumble…

"Thank you for the extra moolah. Have a great time tonight, guys!"

As Vanessa and Terry opened their car doors, they waved to Johnny before shutting them and departing. The moment the front door shut, Markéta stomped down the stairs in a scurry. Making a beeline for the kitchen, she didn't even bother to say hello to her supposed sitter—she only uttered nonchalance coalesced with a teen-centralized snottiness. "What up?" she asked passively.

"Hi, you must be the Markéta I've heard so much about…"

"Unless my parents have been hiding another twelve-year-old with the same name, then yes. That's me—I am her."

Johnny grinned at her dry wit. "They told me *not* to tell you about your evil twin sister…"

The tween ignored his attempt at a witty retort. "You must be Johnny, then, I take it."

"That's right to have taken it like that."

"Excuse me?"

"Nothing. Just being dru—I mean, *dumb*."

"You smell like alcohol, that unmistakable scent of scotch…"

"Shit; sorry about that. I didn't mean to breathe it on you. Your mom gave me mints to cover it up; apparently they didn't do the job."

Markéta giggled. "It's a good smell. And it fits some people perfectly. You're in that elite group."

"Oh, thanks a lot. I didn't ever strive to go for an alcoholic's aroma, but if it works, why not?"

"You're funny, Johnny. I'm glad that other stiff called off."

"Yeah? Not too exciting of a babysitter?"

"Not at all. A boring, goody-two-shoe lady who just needs to get laid."

"Okay, then!" Johnny started to feel uncomfortable. "So, I wasn't really prepared for interactions like this…your parents both claimed that you'd be holed up in your bedroom the whole night."

"That's what I usually do, but…honestly, I only came down here to get an IZZE and some steak stroganoff leftovers that I ordered from Noodles earlier today."

"Good soda. And a good fast-casual restaurant, too. What kind of IZZE do you like the most?"

"Blackberry. That's my shit," the tween said, suddenly snacking on a bag of chips.

"What are those? Trader Joe's?"

"Yep…they're yummy, man. Better—and healthier—than Doritos. Want some?"

"Thanks for offering, but I'm okay!" Johnny refused amiably.

"Are you?"

This girl's cute. Lively. Jet-black hair, a freckled face, and a body that'll be amazing in about three years. Well, it's already kind of amazing…shut up, Johnny. She's twelve, you total perv.

"And a half…" he said, not realizing what he said out loud until it had parted ways with his lips.

"What's that?" Markéta asked with a puzzled look.

"It's nothing! I was just thinking of—you know what, it's seriously *nothing.*"

"All right, fam. I'll scratch that one off to you being a little drunk."

Johnny nodded energetically. "That's all it is. I shouldn't even be here, to be honest with you. Your mom called me as a last-minute replacement…I've never babysat anyone in my life…"

"No way; *really?* I assumed that this was your paid profession!"

"False. Well, I lied. For a short period of time after I graduated from high school, I actually used to be the best damn babysitter going," Johnny joked. "It's just that I like to drink too much. That's majorly frowned upon when you're taking care of kids; I don't know why."

"Alcohol ruins a lot of things, that's for sure. But what are you, dude…how old, I mean…probably not even in your thirties yet? You'll be able to maintain."

"I'm twenty-eight, just on the cusp of thirty."

"You're on the cusp of *twenty-nine*, not thirty, but continue…" Markéta pointed out like a pretentious geek.

"So *anyway…*" Johnny said, ignoring her remark altogether. "I'll try to keep it under control. I don't wanna be all haggard and sweaty like my dad. I NEED to leave that hazardous environment soon. Ashamed that I still live there. But my mom would be in bad shape if I left. I'm all the love she has in her world."

"Oh yeah? He's a drunk, huh…"

"To put it lightly, *yes*. And he's a very mean one at that."

Piece-of-trash dad. Hope he dies soon. Ruined me and my mom. But it's good he's employed nowadays; that trucking job keeps him away from her and her away from his beatings. Still can't believe she stayed with him after what he di—

"Johnny? You all right?" Markéta pestered. "Earth to Johnny??"

"Sorry; I spaced out there for a moment. Just thinking about some stuff that happened in the past. No biggie."

"Yeah, I noticed. You went dark on me for a sec. Wanna talk about whatever you thought of when you blanked?"

"No, no; I'm cool! It's just some lame, whiny kid crap. The usual 'my daddy didn't love me enough' sorta stuff. I won't bore you with all of that," Johnny said, mustering up a half-smile.

"I'm not saying that we could relate to each other or anything as I don't know what you've been through, but my father isn't the greatest guy. I have my complaints."

"You should have *loads* of complaints! An amazing house, a sweet mother, a dad who's here for ya, and a little sister who probably loves you to death. Real taxing on your psyche, I bet."

Markéta sighed. "There it is. Like so many others, you only see the exterior and not the **interior**!"

"Blah, blah, blah be blah, you're using words that are somewhat intricate. And it's hurting my head…since I'm blitzed…"

"I'll keep that in mind," the tween said, her brightening smile eventually giving way to a batch of laughter.

"Just dumb it down is all I ask! Can ya do that?" Johnny challenged.

"Sure can, Sitter Man."

"Wonderful. As you were…"

Johnny kindly waved Markéta off as if giving her the express written permission to trek back upstairs.

Please take flight and never be seen or heard from again for the rest of my time spent here. That'd be easy.

And that would have made the night easier for him. More than anything else, it would've at least given him some peace of mind. No one to look after. He could have just sat and watched television or zombified himself into the welcoming glow of his smartphone. But the girl had shown an interest in being around him—a distinctively keen interest in getting to know more about the makeshift babysitter who was buzzed and who was also a little lenient by her calculations.

Their time together wouldn't last long, but their developing bond and its aftereffects would soon send ripples across the waves of both lives…

"I'd like to hang out with you tonight. I mean, if that's cool!" she said, tiptoeing her way around the chance of being rejected by him.

"Yeah…totally. I'd like the company, especially now. I've had it pretty rough recently. My girlfriend and I just broke up and I'm all sensitive about it. Like a girl during her per—well, you know. Ah! *Sorry*. I shouldn't even be talking like this."

"Why? I don't care, dude. I completely get it. This boy I like a lot—who actually *kinda* looks like a younger you—is at a party tonight, and I wanted to go so bad. But my mom had a stick up her ass and straight denied me. I just know that this one bitch I hate with all my heart is gonna be there, and she likes him almost as much as I do. So yeah, I feel left out…like I'm powerless to stop something from happening…"

Johnny met the adolescent's longing gaze, her facial expression explaining to him how much she'd wanted to be somewhere else cooler. And not right there with him talking about it.

He opted to go the middle-school route: the passing-of-the-paper, question-checkbox approach. "Who does this boy like more? Her or you?"

"I don't know yet. That's why I wish I could be there."

"You dunno who he likes more?? There's no *way* that's true. A girl always knows! And a guy always lets it be known…"

"Well…he hasn't…perhaps he's left a few hints here and there for me to analyze, but certainly nothing concrete."

"Bullshit! That's *total* bullshit, and you know it!" Johnny insisted.

"It's not, fam. I've had all of seventh grade to scope the situation!"

"Okay, so why worry about it now? What's so important about this night? How come you haven't flat-out asked him if he likes you or not?!"

Markéta raised her arms in a show of opposition. "It's not that easy. I really like Jonathan, all right? I can't be a dork about it and press him about who he wants more. It has to be natural…it has to feel *right*."

His name's Jonathan?? That explains a lot. I'm like her backup.

"Uh-huh; I see…" Johnny said snidely. "Was tonight the only time it'd feel right?"

"Yeah, it's all built up to this. That's why I'm extra bummed that I'm not there to make the move or to see if *he'll* make one on me…" the girl revealed, mining for sympathy.

"I see what you're trying to do. And just so you know, it's not gonna happen…"

"What? I'm not doing anything! Only talking to my awesome babysitter. That's it," Markéta said, lowering her head like she'd been scolded.

Johnny held his right hand up to the anxious tween's face as if for her to talk to it. "I wasn't born yesterday, Markéta! You're attempting to make me feel sorry for you so I'll start thinking of ways to help you get over there—without your parents knowing and without me getting in trouble. But here's the thing: I don't need to look even cooler than I already am…I'm really cool as is. So, is that it? Am I pretty spot-on?"

"Pretty much, yeah," she admitted shyly.

"I *knew* it. How predictable. You kids are all alike, I swear."

"Look, you don't even have to tell them! It'll only be for a few hours. You can drop me off a block or two away from the house and then pick me up at the same place!"

A block or two away…I remember when I used to think that'd make a difference…

"Damn; you have this all figured out, don't ya? It's an airtight plan, isn't it?" Johnny asked incredulously.

"All right; fine. Say no. It's cool," Markéta said, dejected.

"**No**. *There*. I said it! N-O, NO!" Johnny repeated.

The tween with a fresh complexion and commercial-worthy locks of black hair slumped onto a wooden stool beside the island counter in the kitchen. She resorted to the fabled puppy dog face: an unbeatable look utilized by only the most masterful of manipulators.

This girl's too cute. Why does she have to be so adorable?! And she could easily pull off being fifteen or sixteen, no problem…STOP. STOP NOW.

"Tell you what, Markéta. Your parents left me money for food. Why don't I order a pizza? I'll even get wings as well!"

"You sincerely think that some grub will magically fix everything and make me forget about what I'm missing?!"

Johnny concurred. "That's right, missy! It did for me when I was your age. Do you think I got my way all the time? *Hell* to the *no.* I was shut down more times than I can even remember…and might I add, much harsher than what you've probably had to endure in your short stay on this planet."

"Yeah, yeah, yeah. Blah, blah, blah be blah. If I wanted a lecture that sounded like it was lifted word for word from a crappy parenting book, I'd call my mom. Or my counselor."

"Hey, that's good. Really good, actually. And I like how you used the *blah* thing on me like I did on you a while ago. Do you write your own material? I like your pizzazz, your chutzpah to buck the system."

"Whatever, dude…" Markéta mumbled, standing up abruptly with her face permeating a boiling disappointment. "I guess I'll be going back upstairs to rot away while my friends and the boy I've liked this whole year have the time of their freaking lives!"

Johnny groaned at the tween's overt melodrama. "Trust me from a wealth of past experience, there will be many, *many* more times where it'll be the 'time of their freaking lives.' CAPICHE, little lady? It's not the end of the world for you tonight; there'll be more can't-miss parties down the line. I guarantee it."

"Right; because I'm supposed to take pointers from an alcoholic twenty-eight-year-old who's going through a breakup and still lives at home!"

"Stop and listen to me on this, okay? I'm just trying to make y—"

Markéta cut him off rudely. "NO; you know what? You don't have to *try* and do anything! You're like them—you're just like my parents. All you can do is deny, deny, deny! And to think that I thought you were cool."

Ouch. How can a kid make a person feel so old so fast? I'm not even thirty and yet I suddenly feel like I'm a fifty-five-year-old asshole father…plan B time!

"Come on, don't be like that…I *am* cool. Honest!" Johnny promised.

"I don't think you are; sorry. I'll see you around. It was nice talking to you—for the first ten minutes that I was down here."

"Every intuition I have is telling me not to do this, but I'll make you a deal, all right? I won't let you go out to see that boy tonight, but…I'll bend on something else…"

Don't do this, you idiot. Are you mentally handicapped?? She's **way** *too underage!*

"Go on. I'm listening!" Markéta said, crossing her arms like an entitled brat and tapping her left foot on the linoleum flooring.

"We will get the pizza, and we'll get some wings. But here's where I'll make you raise your eyebrow…and by the way…you seriously *cannot* tell your parents that I allowed this, okay? Like I mean it…for real!"

"Sure; cross my heart and hope to die."

"I brought a variety pack of Ciderboys with me and I was told in confidence that you tend to enjoy hard cider?" Johnny teased seductively.

The girl's hazel eyes lit up. "Um, *yeah*…hard cider's awesome. You'd actually let me drink some of those?!"

"Yes; against my better judgment, I would. But only if you give me your word—your firstborn in the future, your everything ethical circulating in your body right here and now—that you keep this shady shit strictly between us!"

"You have my word, Johnny. I wouldn't *ever* think of snitching you out."

"Okay…good. That's a relief. So I guess there's just one question to ask…"

"What's that, Mr. Sitter?" Markéta asked in a heightened anticipation. "Ask me anything!"

"Which flavor's your favorite? I've got Cranberry Road, First Press—which is their regular apple flavor—and, let's see here," Johnny said, rummaging through the clinking glass bottles in the variety pack's cardboard box, "…there's Mad Bark and Strawberry Magic! What'll it be?"

"Hmm, what's that Mad Bark? That's a sweet name for a drink."

"It's a combination of apple and cinnamon in hard cider heaven," Johnny answered blissfully, a magnetic smile etched on his face.

"That sounds lovely," the girl gushed. "I think I'll have that."

"You sure? Cranberry Road is exquisite."

Markéta looked temporarily tempted, then declined. "It's not Thanksgiving yet. That'd probably be better to try around that time, right?"

"Uh, maybe? It's not like you'll have the opportunity to give it a test run then or anything—unless you randomly decide to run away from home and come live with me across the street…" Johnny said, goofing around but strangely half-serious all at once.

"Perhaps that wouldn't be such a bad idea!" the tween said, flirting with a lick of her lips and a wink. "I'd like that."

This is wrong; this is so WRONG. But she's so cute…and innocent. What're you doing? What the hell is your problem right now? You're hitting on a girl who's not even out of junior high yet?! Stop!!

"Let's put them in the freezer to get 'em colder faster. They've been beside the living room couch for a while now, and I think we need them ice cold for this special occasion."

Markéta agreed with a high five and a come-hither type of smile. "Sounds great to me. In the meantime, I'll go get my cozy pillow and blanket to hang out on the couch with ya. Anything you wanna watch?"

Johnny hadn't thought that far ahead, since his mind wasn't focused on television. "Um, I don't know…maybe we could stream seasons on Hulu or StuQueue? I love watching TV; it helped me get through some rough patches of my yesteryears."

"What kind of shows are you watching right now?"

"Quite a lot. *Justified*, one hidden gem of a crime drama. *Fringe*, a noble science-fiction series. *Gravity Falls*, this mythologically driven cartoon that's for kids *and* adults. Also just finished up *Bates Motel*, which was a **mind-bender**. What about you? What're you into?" Johnny asked with actual interest.

"I'm really into *Stranger Things* and *The Walking Dead* these days."

"Hipster. Shocked you didn't say *Orange is the New Black*, too…"

"That's a good show as well! What's wrong with it?"

"Nothing…"

"*The Vampire Diaries* is my favorite show, though!" Markéta tipped off arbitrarily. "Love, love, love it! What's yours?"

"*LOST*. Now and forever. There is none higher. Ever seen it?"

"'Fraid not. But I've heard good things. Is it bingeable?"

"More than most! Epically epic is how I describe it."

"Ooh. It must be good then! Who's on that show? Anybody I know?" the intrigued tween inquired.

"Ian Somerhalder's in it! Isn't he one of the main characters on TVD?"

"Yeah! He was Damon Salvatore. Now I've gotta watch *LOST*!"

"Definitely do so. But it's much too involved to get into tonight. Ya wouldn't wanna stop…so let's shoot for something simpler. Have you ever watched *The Last Man on Earth?*"

"Thought I was the only one who liked that hilarious show! None of my friends dig it!"

You could stop this thing from leading to law-breaking. It's all up to you. Don't ruin your life over some petite girl who hasn't even scratched the surface of her teen years yet! Stop this; stop this now!!

"I can't, all right…I just ca—"

"Sorry?" Markéta interrupted, confused. "What are you talking about?"

Johnny inhaled and exhaled before responding. "I'm nervous about this. I don't want you to get the wrong idea. I'm only being nice here; I feel bad that you're missing out on a fun Friday night with your friends and that boy you like. I just don't wanna be a party pooper."

"I'm not missing out anymore. This is starting to turn into a much better night all around. And I'm beginning to think that you're *way* cooler than that boy is."

"Aw, shucks. Don't say that. I'll begin to blush. And I'm a grown man, so that'd be embarrassing to do in front of you."

"Seriously, though. You doing this for me—when it's such a high-risk situation—shows how awesome ya are, and I appreciate that. Plus it doesn't hurt to know that you dig dope shows!"

"Right on," Johnny said, bewildered by the way things had taken shape. "Well…uh, so I'll just order that pizza and the wings now, I guess."

"Word. Make it a large; extra cheese and pepperoni!" Markéta ordered, storming up the stairs giddily. "And garlic parm on the wings!"

What am I doing? This is nuts. It's insane…

Johnny whispered incessantly to himself. "It's nothing; it is absolutely nothing. You're not doing anything horrible. Yes…you're about to willingly supply a minor with alcohol. But big deal; big fucking deal! People have done much worse. I'm merely making this kid's life a little better, even if it's just for a brief moment in time! Hell, I should be awarded a medal for it. This is cool; it's completely *cool*. We'll eat the pizza, eat the wings, drink a few drinks, laugh at some of Will Forte's stupid hijinks…and then I am off the clock. Vanessa and Terry will come home and I'll be history."

He began to dial the number for the local pizzeria while footsteps slowly cascaded down the stairs, each creak emitted gaining more of his attention.

Why do I even want to see her right now? I saw her like a minute ago. I should be ordering the pizza and wings, not caring about seeing Markéta. She's TWELVE!!

As Johnny manically inner-argued with himself over his next set of possible actions, indecent thoughts poisoned his mind. The fresh-faced tween strolled into the kitchen wearing booty shorts that clung to her firm frame and a flimsy white tank top that left very little to the imagination. All of her silky white skin was on full display.

"That's not…that's not really…" Johnny stammered. "I don't—"

"What? It's not appropriate? You gonna chastise me? Make me go back up those stairs to change into something more acceptable?"

Who is this girl? She's tempting me and I feel ashamed by it. THEN STOP! You can still end this madness at any time.

"Man, oh man; you look supes cute."

"Thanks, Johnny. So do you…" Markéta smirked, twirling about like an exotic dancer.

"I feel like I'm already in a lot of trouble with this."

"Don't be silly. We're just gonna drink some ciders and watch *The Last Man on Earth*. What's so troubling in all of that? Don't be lame."

Johnny relaxed his overworked nerves. "When you put it like that, it's hard to see why I even worried in the first place!"

"Cool then! So, let's pop a few open and watch."

"Let's…"

The high-def TV in the posh living room zapped to life with a single push of a button as the faces of Markéta and Johnny were bathed in the sultry glow from the screen.

"Wanna start at the beginning?" the girl asked softly, seating herself beside the skittish sitter. "I'm in the middle of Season Three, but I've been wanting to go back—relive some things and catch up on others…"

"Whatever you want to do. It's your place; I'm just a guest," he replied.

"Incorrect. It's my parents' place, technically. But that doesn't mean you don't get to have an opinion on how we go about things here, Johnny!" Markéta squeaked like a mouse. "It's not gonna be one-sided tonight…"

"Well, with this specific show, I was all caught up—as I've been watching live since the series premiere, but it'd probably be nice to revisit everything again," he replied.

"So that's what we'll do!"

"The drinks should be cold enough soon. I'll get them after the first ep," Johnny stated, stretching his legs out to rest on the coffee table.

"'Alive in Tucson,' here we come…" the tween said with excitement.

"Huh?"

"That's the name of the first one."

"*Oh yeah*; right. Sorry, I'm a bit nervous to be chilling on this couch. It feels like I shouldn't be underneath a blanket with a girl your age."

"We're just sharing it! What's your deal, dude? Take a pill."

"No, we are not **just** sharing it. You're playing footsie with me!"

"Is that bad?" Markéta wondered, her use of puppy dog eyes melting him.

Get out. Get out while you can. You don't have to be her babysitter; she's old enough to watch herself. But the second you leave, she'll leave and go to that party…she doesn't care about her sleeping sister, and Vanessa will come after you with a hellish fury if you duck outta this!

"Fuck, fuck, fuck!!" Johnny wheezed.

"Language, sir. That's not an appropriate response to my question. And that kind of gratuitous, foul language is beneath you, I think…"

"You don't even know me, kid. How could you *possibly* know what's beneath me?!"

"Because I see it in your eyes. You're damaged. But I believe there's a lot of good in you, and I feel comfortable cuddling. You should too. So stop being such a baby and *chill* yourself."

Johnny obliged. "That I can do."

"Can you now?" the girl implored.

"Don't believe me…just watch…"

Markéta cracked up. "You're a moron."

After the first episode ended, the babysitter—who wasn't really acting like one—got up and went to the refrigerator. "Still want that Mad Bark, or have you changed your mind?" Johnny asked politely.

"Nope; I'd still like to try that one, please!" Markéta chirped, bubbling with an obvious eagerness.

"One MB coming right up, milady," he said, handing off the desired bottle of cider to the underage girl. "I've been hankering for a Cranberry Road."

"Looks like it'd be pretty good."

"Oh, it is. It's so good. Makes me think of Thanksgiving. Crap, that's why you didn't want one, wasn't it? 'Cause it's not Thanksgiving yet!"

"Okay, okay; so I sounded like an idiot with that…"

"Yeah, you kinda did."

"Maybe I'm just more of a cinnamon girl, you know?"

Johnny looked deeply into her eyes; and while he knew that it wasn't right to have such impure thoughts formulating, he felt like he could be himself around Markéta. Her innocence calmed him. It was like nothing else he'd ever felt. They stared at each other for a moment and then made a standard toast.

"Here's to this night. To us. And to *The Last Man on Earth* as well!" the girl announced cheerfully.

She's using me for this alcohol. That's all it is. Like Ericka used me for drugs. And I've fallen for it…hook, line, and sinker. End this now. Before it goes too far. Don't be a sucker.

"Want another Mad Bark?" Johnny asked after several minutes had passed. "I'll let you have the last two."

"Sure thing; I'm done with this one. Might as well go and get it. That is, if you don't mind…"

WHAT ARE YOU DOING?! ARE YOU EVEN LISTENING TO ME??

"Not at all. I was gonna head over to the fridge again anyway. Let me dispose of the evidence!"

Must throw the trash out before they get home later…

Johnny Helks, feeling irresponsible and reprehensible all at once, walked into the kitchen to get two more bottles of Ciderboys.

"So I'm aiding and abetting a tween drinking…in other words, I am committing a crime. This is low—even for me!" he admitted. "Stop, stop, stop…"

But you can't, can you? The temptation's much too strong. You're sick.

"Shut up; it's not and I'm not! I can reel it in at any time," Johnny informed his antagonizing inner thoughts. "Nothing crazy has happened yet."

Yet? You're already planning on something happening??

"What's taking you so long?? I'm in need of another drink—stat!" Markéta complained.

She's too needy; slip her a mickey. That'd put her to sleep…

"Be right there; calm yourself! You're lucky that I'm even allowing this!"

"You're the one who's lucky…" she retorted rebelliously.

"Am I?" Johnny asked.

"You are. I'm hot stuff."

Can't argue with that. She is.

Before the in-over-his-head babysitter moseyed back into the living room to down some more bottles of cider and cuddle up to a game Markéta, he realized how to remedy his climbing anxiety over the sensitive situation. Only one thing could turn the tide, and it set off a solace in Johnny's mind.

"Muscle relaxers," he verified, pleased pink at his remembrance. "That's it right there. I have a few left in my pocket…I'll just take those, swig from the flask, and all my worries'll wander away! Though it's a pity I don't have a mickey. For her, not me."

Wait, I may…

Without any further delay, the pills were popped and the scotch was dropped. Johnny felt the stinging rush of cheap, hard liquor roll down his throat. It was liberating for him to lose inhibitions. And he'd gladly done it many times before this fateful night—to mask the hurt and the rejection of a life that seemed to hold a grudge against him. Still, he wasn't proud of his liquid-courage dependency. In fact, Johnny was ashamed of it. With leanings of justification sprinkled in, he hyped himself up to head back into the clutches of an attractive, albeit severely underage girl. On a couch—close—together.

I've coped in the past, and this is how I'll deal with this fucked present. Sedate myself even more to get through it all.

"COME ON, ALREADY! MAD BARK ME!!"

"That pussy is pushy…" he grumbled under his breath, cracking himself up. "Coming, dear! Don't get your panties in a bunch…"

"I don't have any on," the girl revealed.

"There's an instant visual; thanks for the report!" Johnny said jokingly, handing off a frosty bottle to his couchmate as he plopped down beside her.

Markéta took it and began to fondle the shaft of the glass provocatively, staring right into his eyes as she did so. "Do you like me, Johnny?"

"'Course I do. What kinda question is that?" he asked, opting to be aloof and standoffish.

"It just seems like you don't wanna be around me. Like you're trying to avoid me, even if you are being super cool—which you have been, don't get me wrong—with letting me drink with your hazy ass."

"You're young, Markéta. Too young for me to be having any sort of sexual thoughts toward. You get that, right? It's not safe. All of this isn't."

"But are you attracted to me, Johnny?" she asked with her go-to puppy dog look. "Do you think I'm pretty?"

"Very much so; yes. You're a knockout…and you'll be *so* incredible once this body of yours blossoms…"

"Yeah, well, it's ready to be touched *now*. So please, I'd love to feel your hands on my soft skin."

Johnny tried to deflect the minor's advances. "Can't we drink and leave it at that? That's what the original plan was. Watch *The Last Man on Earth* together while I facilitate you getting a bit tipsy; have you momentarily forget about missing out on that dumb party. That was the plan in its entirety—that's what was supposed to happen, Markéta."

"But it can be so much more than that. I like you. There! I'll be up front about it. I like you—a lot. And not just because you've facilitated me with hard cider. It goes deeper than that."

"Why? I'm nothing special, okay? Just a twentysomething guy who lives across the street from you, and who only knows your mom from her being best friends with my mom—hence why I stupidly agreed to help out in a pinch. That's it."

"It's more than that, and you know it. You *have* to feel this thing we have; don't deny it. I sensed it the second I saw you."

"Listen, I know you're bummed and all about that boy being possibly poached by that girl tonight, but making moves on me isn't going to be the solution to your ongoing dramas. I think that you're looking for a knight in shining armor…and I'm here to tell ya—as unfortunate as it may be for you to understand this—I am most certainly *not* that knight. And I never will be. Not for you; not for anyone. Got it?"

"Johnny, you've underestimated how extraordinary you truly are. That ex of yours must've done a real number on you for you to think so little of yourself…"

What is this? Maybe it's time to take the gloves off. This girl's spent a scant twelve years on this planet and she's psychoanalyzing me??

"You have no idea what you're talking about!"

"I don't?"

"No, you don't. You know nothing about relationships. You're only twelve. So don't come at me with an illusion of knowledge. You have none yet. You're grossly inexperienced, and you should **stay** that way."

"The truth hurts, I see!" Markéta exclaimed, amused.

"What the hell do you mean?"

"It's *typical* for an adult to pull the ol' age card. Like you're so much better…what, because you're older? Give me a freaking break, Mr. Babysitter!"

Girl has a good point there. I'm definitely not any better than her…

"You're right; I'll admit that that was a weak card to pull. I shouldn't act like you can't have an opinion on my relationship woes just 'cause I'm sixteen years your elder," Johnny conceded, giving the tween an opening.

"I can tell that you're a little more chill now. That's a good thing; you needed to loosen up."

"Could be the muscle relaxers currently going through my system."

"*What*?? When did you find the time to take something like that?" Markéta interrogated. "I've been right here with you. And how come you didn't give me any? That's way rude, dude."

"Wow, greedy much? If you must know, I took a few when I was getting us the next round of booze. And secondly, the thought of giving you one of 'em never really crossed my mind. I'm already distributing alcohol to a minor; I don't need to be a drug pusher as well. Stop being so needy!"

"They say you always want what you can't have. I guess I'll forever be habitually unfulfilled," Markéta opined. "Sorry, not sorry."

"My head's much too dizzy for this. I'm floating quite nicely now…"

The tween laughed boisterously. "Me too; it's an awesome feeling. Two in and I feel like I'm a feather gliding in the wind."

"*Lightweight.*"

"And so what if I am?! Would you hold that against me?" the underage girl questioned flirtatiously.

"No; of course not. But if you drink one or two more of these ciders…you may be incapacitated," Johnny informed. "Perhaps you should go easy from here on out."

"This may be the only chance I have for a long, long time to feel like this. I'm not gonna quit now. We've just begun to have some fun!"

"You know, I'm sure if I were sober and grounded in reality, I'd argue with you more…but I'm pretty cross-faded at the moment. So, you win. Let's keep drinking. Still have half of it left!"

"Keep it going, definitely. 'Cause you know why? Yolo, bro. YOLO."

Johnny grunted his contempt for the overused acronym popularized by youth culture. "Please don't say that. And if you absolutely *have* to, at least say the phrase with the actual words that belong to it."

"Jeez, for claiming to be so stoned, you certainly have a beef with such a small aphorism!"

"How in the blue hell do you know what that word means, young lady? *I* don't even know what that means! But maybe I'm just too drunk to think straight. I know I can't **see** straight, so there's that to take into consideration."

"Actually…funny thing, I recently looked up the saying on Wikipedia when I was listening to that rap classic 'The Motto' by drizzy Drake. That's why I know the word *aphorism.*"

"Fascinating stuff. Thanks for sharing. Even though rap's crap, I remember that stupid song!"

"Hey! Rap isn't crap!!"

"I take that back. Not ALL of it is bad. I do enjoy some mainstream hip-hop, like Action Bronson and Childish Gambino. *Mr. Wonderful* and *Because the Internet* are awesome albums…but Drake's stupid. Sorry!"

"He's not stupid; *you're* stupid," Markéta said with certainty.

"I know I am—for allowing this illegal activity to continue…"

"That's not a stupid thing to do. It's *smart*."

Johnny shook his head in disagreement. "Nothing about this is intelligent in any way, shape, or form."

Markéta beamed, her teeth sparkling white in the television's projected light. "For allowing it, **you're** intelligent in EVERY way!"

"*Right.*"

"So…you gonna go and get me another one? Or do I have to get it myself? Come to think of it, maybe I should. You could see my cute booty shorts again. I wore them just for you…"

Johnny became aroused by the teasing nature of her sex-fueled, suggestive speak. Ashamed, he elected to be the one who'd get up— so as not to see any section of her creamy thighs. "That's okay. I'll go. It'd do some good to keep the blood circulating. Otherwise I'll zonk out if I stay put."

"Fair enough. Don't want that happening! I want you…*up*," Markéta said sexily.

It's gone too far. Fuck it, though. If we've both come to this point, might as well go all the way…she clearly wants it…and I'd be gentle with her. Wouldn't I?

"Stop, Johnny; stop. Give her one more and then tell her ass to head upstairs before Vanessa and Terry get home," he said, entering the dimly lit kitchen in a drunken shuffle.

"Another MB, please!" she requested from afar.

"I know…I was planning on giving you the last one!"

Just give her one more and call it off. It's tempting to keep it going, since she's TRYING to tantalize you, but you must kill this craziness…before it develops into something you'll regret. Have her go to her room; throw out the bottles, dispose of the evidence outside, and simply wait for those damned parents to return.

"Solid plan. But there's a problem. I have to have the willpower to go through with it…" Johnny answered himself with melancholy.

Bide your time, then proceed to casually end the flirting festivities. Let her down easy. And don't even think of leading her on some more—like you have been.

"Okay, okay. I'm going back in…and I will slowly end this thing…"

"What's the holdup?!" Markéta shouted impatiently. "I'm ready for round three!"

How about a round four and five to really leave you loopy?

"Coming! Have some manners, will ya? I mean…you're being waited on, for God's sake."

"So sorry, Mr. Sitter. I know I'm difficult to handle."

"You're fine. Just relax. I'm coming back," Johnny reassured.

"Aw, you think I'm fine…" the girl said, sighing like she'd just been swept off her feet.

"No, I didn't mean it like that…ugh, you *know* how I meant it! Like how a person says 'you're fine' when someone bumps into them while getting out of an elevator or whatever!"

"Chill; I was only kidding. Don't get your panties in a bunch over it."

"I don't have any on," the makeshift sitter countered cleverly, repeating Markéta's arousing line from earlier.

"You're a wily one, aren't you?"

"I try to be at times," Johnny replied tamely as he sat back down.

"Why don't you plant a kiss right on my strawberry-glossed lips?" Markéta urged, creeping ever so slightly onto his lap unsolicited.

"That probably wouldn't be such a good idea…"

"And why not?"

"Because you are *underage,* Markéta! You're twelve and I'm twenty-eight. Why am I even having to explain this to you again? It's against the law. I could go to jail…and I've heard that they don't take too kindly to sex offenders in there."

"No one has to know. You think I'm gonna go run to my parents and tell them that you molested me??"

"Absolutely not. I have no reason to believe you would. It's just that it's wrong. That's mostly what is stopping me, in all honesty."

LEAVE, MORON! GET UP AND GO!! They'll be home soon, anyway…

"I won't tell, Johnny. It can be our little secret. Our hot, steamy secret," Markéta went on, slithering her way closer and closer to his lips.

"You're drunk…and if we weren't at your house right now, I'd tell you to go home."

"So what if I am? It feels fantastic. I love how I feel; I love being here with you. Alone…ready and willing…come on…*live* with me!"

The tipsy, teeny tween closed her eyes, hoping for a heart-melting kiss to take place between them. But just as she leaned in, the doorbell rang.

Startled into their neutral corners of the couch, they both realized that it was probably the pizza delivery guy with their order.

"I'll go get that. You stay here," Johnny said.

"Yes, sir, Sitter sir!"

Opening the door, Johnny saw a scrawny, white-as-rice male—no bigger than five foot eight with a face as saturated as the pizza he had brought over.

"Hey, buddy…" the delivery boy greeted, monotone and disconnected. "How you doin' tonight? I have one large pep with extra cheese, and an order of twenty-five wings here for ya."

"How much I owe ya again?" Johnny asked the Donatos employee, fishing in his right pocket for the two bills.

"Thirty-three fifty, please."

"Cool, cool; you know what? I've got forty on me, so go ahead and take it off my hands!"

"Thanks a lot; have a good night!"

"You too…"

When the front door shut, Markéta jumped off the couch and rushed over to have a peek at the pizza and wings that were placed on the kitchen countertop. Johnny then went in the living room to grab his bottle of cider instead of plowing into the pie first.

She must be starving…and not only for me now, thank God. Distract her with the grub and kill time. I'll be outta here within an hour or so…

"Maybe. Who knows if they'll run late…with a five-year-old and a twelve-year-old to parent, I'm sure they don't get out that much," Johnny hypothesized, heading back into the kitchen.

"Holy freaking crap, this pizza's good, dude!!"

"Is it? Hope it's more enjoyable than their awful frozen food version my mom bought last weekend! Wow, it smells wonderful. Bet it tastes even better…"

"You have no idea…get your muscle-relaxing ass in here and eat!"

"Hook me up with a slice. And shoot me like five wings! I need to be sober—and fast…"

"This cheese is to die for; they didn't skimp at all!" Markéta marveled, gobbling up two of the tiny, delectable pieces. "Ya want some water?"

"Sure! That *would* help stave off this buzz a bit. Got VOSS?"

"Uh. No? I don't think so. We only have tap. What even is that?"

Her lack of bottled-water education was amusing to Johnny. "It's mineral water sourced from Norway; sorta expensive! I always get the ones that come in a huge glass bottle. That glass is so sturdy I'm sure you could kill someone with it if you had to!"

The tween balked while eating. "Whatever you say there. So would ya like a glass of our lowly tap water or not? Sorry we don't have what you want."

"No, thanks…I wouldn't be caught dead drinking that stuff. Or caught lying by a cup of it, I guess. Not 'cause I'm some pompous prick or anything—it's because of a personal experience. As a boy I saw a lot of nasty, rusty water comin' outta our kitchen faucet when I'd go in to sip."

"I see; sorry…well, just keep on drinkin' what you've got! And get this!" The underage girl handed a piece of pizza to the faux babysitter, and the crust's greasy bottom almost caused Johnny to fumble it clumsily.

"Saved in the nick of time. Drunk and with muscles relaxed, I can still avoid having my food hit the ground, baby!"

"What a man you are," she said with sarcasm.

"And what a woman you'll be…" he purred.

"Are you joking or are you serious?"

"I'm serious; dead serious."

Markéta grinned. "Make a woman outta me right now, then, won't you?"

"I could certainly try to…but I'm not sure if you'd be ready for what I'd be able to give ya…"

"You really are drunk, aren't you?"

Johnny proceeded to recite the alphabet backwards in order to prove his awareness to her, though he failed with a laughable effort. With a slew of scotch swimming in his stomach, he was in no condition to sound intelligent.

I'm nearing pass-out territory. Better sit down…

"Let's get in the living room. I'm tired of standing around," Johnny said.

"Me, too! It's a lot more comfortable on the couch."

"I'd rather be dizzy seated than dizzy standing! Want me to bring more drinks?"

Markéta laughed as if he were the funniest man alive. "For sure, yeah; bring it on…"

The two inebriated people—one legally and the other not—stumbled their way back to the couch, a comfy area that would soon be the incubator for a cocooning union.

And a soon-to-be slumbering union, due to Johnny sneaking an incapacitating agent into Markéta's drink.

Chloral hydrate, don't fail me now. Do what you do.

"I know it's wrong, and I know I've probably already said it to you, but I just want you to realize that…you look *really* adorable…and I'm glad you came down those stairs a few hours ago to get your leftovers."

"Aw, Johnny! That's so sweet of you to say. I'm glad I came down as well!"

"I mean it. This isn't the alcohol talking, or the relaxers doing their thing…this is me, telling it like it is. You're cute as a button."

"Come closer and show me how much you mean it…" Markéta insisted, guzzling down her fourth bottle of alcohol.

"Beg your pardon? May I ask how I should go about doing that, exactly? I'm the type of guy who likes specifics."

"First, you get over here…then, you unhook my bra and play with my hardened nipples while I moan in delight."

Johnny nodded deviously. "That *absolutely* classifies as specific. You're definitely not a prude. What else?"

"Then I trace my fingers around the zipper of your jeans and unzip it—to get my hands around your thick, pulsing cock..."

"You kiss your mother with that mouth? Just kidding. Go on. Please!"

"After I have your rod palmed, I'll stroke the shaft up and down until it can't possibly get any bigger, and then I'll guide your hand ever so sweetly to my happy trail."

"Your happy *what*??"

"You know, that primrose path that leads down to...my kitty..." Markéta said, hiccupping after her slurry and sultry sentence.

"Maybe this should be where we stop; let's stick with words and no action. I don't like what we're building to," Johnny suggested maturely.

"Nonsense; we're having a great time! Lemme put some mood music on...as we continue to get more comfortable with each other."

"Oh, God; mood music? Really? Are you gonna bring out candles and chocolates as well?" Johnny asked.

"You'll see...you may hate it, but I like the album a lot."

The tween drank from her fifth cider of the evening—the one with altered contents—then stumbled off the couch and turned on a little JVC boombox inside an entertainment center.

I hope my drink tampering pays off soon; it's the only way this can end without regret for me...and for her...

Markéta took the remote control for the television and within a moment, the living room was pitch-black—barring the blue hue emitting from the JVC's tiny LCD screen. Pleasing to the ear, the music filled the air with an easy-to-swallow auditory atmosphere.

"What is this? It sounds like someone I've heard before..."

Markéta frolicked back to Johnny, nuzzling up to his side. "It's Justin Timberlake! He's the freaking man. This album, *The 20/20 Experience*, is such a sexy classic. Smooth and nice...just like my skin will be on the tips of your fingers."

Johnny was uncomfortable with the sloshed girl's forwardness. "I don't think this is a good idea. To keep going like we are won't result in anything positive…"

"Well, I disagree…" she rebutted, removing her slip-on sneakers. "I believe it's going to result in something *really* positive. Take off your shoes; get loose!"

"Ugh, I'm too drunk to argue with you. I can barely keep my eyes open now," the makeshift sitter said as he drifted to the corner of the couch, situating pillows to rest his head on.

"But we're having fun! Aren't we?"

"It's been a lot of fun. Just have to wrap it up now."

"Come on; that's *lame*. I can't party alone!"

"Sorry. I don't know what to tell you. G'night, Markéta. You should probably go upstairs to your room; you've downed five bottles already. I don't want your mom and dad to get the wrong idea if they come in and see us like this."

Undeterred, the horny tween popped over to his side of the couch like a pet dog rushing toward a table for scraps.

"What the fuck are you doing??" Johnny questioned angrily. "You're pushing it. *Stop*. My head's swimming; I can't handle this."

"Yes, you can. You can handle me right here…" she said, guiding his left hand to her waist and then his right hand to her navel.

Oh my LORD. She feels so warm to the touch, and so good in my hands. No; you can't do this! Stop it right now! But I'm weak…I'm fucking weak…and I'm also immobilized…the only thing I can get up is my dick…

"Now…doesn't my body feel *ready*?" Markéta taunted.

"I'd say so," Johnny replied meekly. "But this is just…this is—"

"No more. It's time for us to stop wasting time. Come here…"

Justin Timberlake's boppy album opener, "Pusher Love Girl," played in the background as Markéta made her move. Nearly helpless to put an end to it, Johnny's equilibrium was completely out of whack, his judgment skewed by an overzealous consumption of alcohol as Markéta forced her tongue into his resisting mouth.

"Don't fight it. You taste good on my lips. Really good!"

Give in. It feels nice; it feels right. She wants you and you want her…

Irresponsibly green-lighting the illegal activity, Johnny reciprocated.

Twenty minutes of strongly placed kisses, furious fondling of each other's private parts over the pants, and exalted panting in ears all took over the two nestled on the couch.

"Fuck, you feel so great. Your body is per—" Johnny moaned as she finally grabbed his now-unsheathed piece of man meat. "Right there, *yeah*…aw shit…"

"Like that, Johnny?"

"Yes; keep going. I'm rock hard for you."

"I can tell…want more?"

"I want a LOT more," the sitter demanded, ripping off her shirt in one quick motion. "I want to be on top of you…I wanna be inside you."

Markéta opened her mouth wide and wrapped her moist lips around his stiffened penis. Diving in with no hesitation, she sucked Johnny like she was licking the most delicious Popsicle ever created.

"Yeah, suck my cock. Ahh, that's good. You're…amazing. Have you done this before?"

The twelve-year-old nodded as she kept sucking.

As the boppy song "Tunnel Vision" glided gracefully above the ecstasy taking place, the underage girl arched her back as Johnny inserted two fingers into her slippery genitalia.

"Like that?" he asked, repeating her question from a moment before.

"Mm-hmm, yes…*yes*…" she responded with a shortness of breath.

"You have a nice little ass," Johnny observed as she performed oral sex on him. "It's firm…"

"Thanks; I try to stay in shape!" Markéta exclaimed midstream on a lick to the top of his manhood.

Johnny laughed in disbelief. "You're only twelve; you don't *need* to work out."

That's right. She's TWELVE. Exactly what are you thinking? You're a monster.

"Just shut up, will you?!" he insisted to himself desperately.

"Everything okay up there?" the tween asked.

"Um, yeah, totally okay. I promise. Let's step it up a notch, shall we?"

You're going to burn in hell for this.

"Get on top of me, Johnny—right now."

"You must be a mind reader…because that's precisely what I was wanting to do."

"So do it!" Markéta urged in the heat of the moment.

The drunken babysitter jumped onto the underage girl's bones, sloppily kissing her and darting his mouth into hers like a professional pornographer. For minutes, they were squarely entwined in a game of groping. The girl's starry eyes—glazed over from way too much alcohol—revealed to Johnny that she was quickly approaching the runway of dreamland. Yet he didn't stop his orally charged assault on her small, tight body.

This is sinfully wonderful.

"Your skin's so silky, so incredible…I was getting hard just thinking about what it'd be like to touch it."

"Mm, baby. Give it to me…give it to….me, John—" she said, slipping away to a slumbering state. "I want you to be my first, I want y—"

"Markéta? Hello?" Johnny asked, poking and shaking her to rouse a response. "Earth to half-naked girl?"

She's out, Johnny. This is where it ends. Pick her up, take her to her room, and if you have to, finish yourself off later. But it's OVER…all right?

Gone. The tween was soundly asleep, courtesy of the tampered-with cider that had lulled her into an unexpected hibernation. No matter how many nudges the sauced male gave her, she was utterly unresponsive to his tried revivals.

"What do I do now, then? What's supposed to happen here?" he quizzed himself, still straddling her torso in a hot-to-trot readiness.

Easy. Get off of this poor girl and call it a night! That's why you spiked her drink: to have her go to sleep…and get outta this!!

"But she said that she wanted me to be her first…"

Are you nucking futs? Have you lost your mind?

"I'm drunk and high, sure…but I know I'm not crazy."

You must be to even consider having sex with a passed-out minor!

"She TOLD me she wanted it! So it's different; it's *way* different."

No, it isn't. You're the adult; act like it. Don't be a rapist.

"What?! It's not rape; it's not anything like that!" the sitter squawked.

Yeah, it is. She's not conscious of what's happening. Look at her! She's out like a light. And you're going to justify having sex with this girl? 'Cause she mumbled how she wanted you? How could you even think about doing such a thing?

Johnny sighed at his own thoughts repelling him from doing the dastardly act. "She *wants* me! Said so herself, dammit!"

You're sick if you go through with it. Truly sick.

Ignoring the inner workings of his torn psyche, Johnny again mounted the vulnerable Markéta, sliding his fingers around her hips. He began to kiss her rosy cheeks sweetly—closed eyes and all— tracing his left hand across the matted hair on her forehead.

Whispering into her pierced ear, Johnny assured the comatose tween of one thing. "I'll take care of you here. Trust me on that…"

A thrust and a grunt of pleasure then followed his creepily committed words—and not a single minute elapsed before he collapsed. He fell into a dizzying, sweaty oblivion beside the unconscious girl. Now fully relieved and relaxed, the smashed babysitter slunk by Markéta and spoke softly to her.

"You were *great*. Really. I mean it!" he confided hazily.

With his eyes slowly shutting and his mind wandering away, Johnny placed his right hand on the side of the girl's lifeless face.

"Thank you. Just…thanks. I needed this," the woozy sitter said, petting her hair until he dozed off.

***

An hour and a half later, a five-year-old girl stood silently by her sleeping sister, tugging on both of Markéta's earlobes like they were ornaments on a Christmas tree.

Johnny turned to his side as the sound of a door creaking open caused his body to reposition.

At the front door, Vanessa and Terry were devastated by what they saw.

The shock on both of their faces when they surveyed the sexually explicit scene said it all. Flabbergasted, the parents couldn't even eke out a single syllable to dignify what they'd unfortunately seen. Only blank expressions—each one horrified to the highest order of horrors.

Terry spoke first. And much to his wife's surprise, he spoke with a controlled tenor. "Take Lizzie bean upstairs now. I'll handle this myself."

"Okay; will do…" Vanessa said, still in total shock as she motioned for her youngest daughter to run toward her. "Honey, let's get you back into bed! I'll read you a story…"

"But Mama, why's my sea star look like she about to get in the shower?" the five-year-old asked. "And why she counting sheep beside this man I don't know?"

"Pay no mind, baby. Your sister's all right. Daddy will take care of it. Let's just go, okay? I've missed you so much," the mother imparted, smiling tenderly.

"Mommy, I missed you too! You so sweet!!"

"Sleep tight, Lizzie bean…everything's okay here, so head on up with your mother. I'll see you in the morning," the father said.

Vanessa took their oblivious daughter upstairs, but in mid-flight, Terry instructed her to do something distracting.

"Turn on some music in her room. And keep it relatively loud in there, will you?"

"Yes; of course, dear…I was already thinking of doing that," the wife replied timidly. "Please don't do something that'll land you in jail."

Lizzie perked up from the last word said. "JAIL?! Who's gonna go to the jail, Mama??"

"Nobody, honey. No one at all…" the mother assured immediately. "Keep those toes moving; I'm *right* behind you!"

"Okay, Mama!!"

Once the mother and daughter were out of sight and the father heard them scampering through the hall upstairs, an inflamed Terry looked at the two incapacitated individuals on his living room couch.

Pacing around the white carpet, the distraught father thought of the viable options in his precarious position.

How exactly do you react to seeing your twelve-year-old daughter passed out and three-fourths naked beside a man you allowed to babysit your children? Not to mention the fact that the man in question was three-fourths naked as well. The several empty bottles of alcohol were a startling reminder as to what had taken place between them.

After shaking his head in repulsion, the father raised his voice.

"Wake the fuck up, you party animals!"

Johnny was the first to stir.

But the moment he opened his eyes, a pair of hands clenched down on his throat with militaristic velocity.

Shit! What the hell?!

"What happened here? What'd you do to my daughter tonight??"

The soiled and spaced sitter was gobsmacked, not knowing what to say.

"SPEAK!!" Terry screamed, slapping him hard across the face with his right hand as he maintained a commanding grip with his left.

"AH, SHIT…THAT HURT, MAN!" Johnny yelped like a weakling.

"Good; it was *supposed* to. What'd you do to my baby? What did you fucking do?!"

"I don't know, all right…we had…we were drinking a couple of ciders. She was upset that she couldn't be at that party, and I felt bad for her."

The father wasn't happy with the explanation. "So you decided to make things better with a bit of alcohol, is that it? You made the decision to have sex with MY daughter??"

"Jeez, it's not…ah, sir…*please*, just gimme a minute. My head's spinning. I can't think straight."

"Soon you won't be able to think at all…because I'm going to kill you! I swear to my God above that I am gonna **murder** you for this!!"

"PLEASE, Terry…*calm down*…and lemme try to explain!!"

Markéta, previously sleeping her way through the chorus of screams, began to come to, rubbing her eyes in lethargic confusion.

"Dad? What's happening right now?"

"Baby, listen to me…I need you to go upstairs…and I need you to go into your room and lock your door. Can you do that for me?"

"I guess so…but why? I don't under—wait; oh, fuck…" the tween blurted out as the hazy memories became clearer.

Terry nodded with the kind of sternness you'd see from a cranky old man. "That's right. *Oh, fuck* is correct. Go up to your room, Markie. We will deal with you later…I assure you that we'll be talking about ALL of this soon enough."

"Yes, sir. I'm out of here…history," Markéta obeyed, slinking off the couch like a slug as she stared apathetically at the man who had stolen her virginity.

"As for you, Johnny…we aren't done by a long shot! You have a lot of explaining to do before I KILL YOU."

In the clutches of an irate father, the fried sitter grumbled. "If you intend to kill me right where I sit, then why even have me explain anything? You can put it together pretty easily, I think. You can *see* what has happened! It's not a mystery."

"You damned piece of shit, I just wanna make sure that I have *everything* documented for the authorities. 'Cause when they come asking invasive questions about your death, I have to be certain that I've got it all covered correctly."

"How thorough of you, Terry…" Johnny joked, still suffering the effects of an addiction untreated.

"Funny man, I see. But you know what's not so funny? Being six feet under…deep down in the dirt…removed from the world where you've harmed an innocent child. Gone forever, Johnny! Gone for *good*."

"That's pretty final sounding…" the twenty-eight-year old said, clearly not taking Terry seriously thanks to his inebriation.

"You don't think I mean it? You think I'm not a man of my word?"

"It's not that…I just don't think you'd go to *those* lengths…"

Terry smacked him across the face again—this time looping the stiff slap over the left ear of Johnny, deafening him momentarily. "I have guns everywhere in this house; you hear me? I'm gonna tie you up and put one right in your mouth, Johnny. I want to see your fear before you die."

"Okay…now I believe you're taking this a little TOO far, sir…" the sitter said with worry, finally realizing the dire situation he was in.

"Taking this too far?! You got my daughter drunk off her ass and then you molested her!! In my eyes, I'm not taking it far enough!!"

Johnny writhed in pain as Terry grabbed his head, jerking his neck back and forth.

Oh my God, he really may kill me. This may be my last night alive…

Without thinking intelligently, the endangered man said the first thing that came to mind in his defense. "It was consensual. She *wanted* to do it. I didn't molest her. I **swear** to you. I'd never do something like that!"

That angered Terry even more. "CONSENSUAL?! She's not an adult, Johnny! *You're* the adult…or at least I thought you were…"

"Look, I'll get locked up…I'll do whatever you want; just don't kill me! Please…I can't die—not before I hit thirty!"

"You don't deserve to live after what you've done. Because in my opinion, you're no good for no one now. That's reason enough for me to end your miserable existence!"

No good for no one…my own father used to say that to me all the time…back when he used to…

"ARE YOU LISTENING TO ME, YOU FUCKING LIVE-AT-HOME LOSER?!"

Johnny welled up with salty tears like those of a newborn and its spent mother. "I am…I—please, my ear…my neck…*stop*…"

"No; I won't stop. You're going to pay for this, my friend. And you're paying with your life!"

"How? What are you gonna do to me, Terry?"

"I already told you what I plan on doing…maybe once you sober up, it'll be easier to digest…"

"Not likely," Johnny said with a noticeable sadness.

"Stay right here. Seriously, do NOT move. Or else you'll be sorry you did," the father warned, loosening his death grip on the sex offender's reddened throat.

I have to do something. Think of how to escape this. THINK!

Terry, sweating and swearing like a man possessed, walked briskly over to a tall wooden cabinet located in the far corner of the living room. After tinkering with a combination to unlock it, its doors opened and revealed a fleet of heavy artillery. Guns of all shapes and sizes—handguns, machine guns, shotguns—flooded the interior of a sturdy cabinet. Busy unlocking the gun haven, Terry had stupidly kept his back turned to the man he intended to murder.

But the blitzed babysitter in hot water didn't dare stand or even move until he could hatch a plan. And in his mind, he had done just that.

I'll snatch one of the empty glass cider bottles, hide it under this pillow, and hit him when he gets close! So simple, yet so brilliant...

When the opportune time to strike came, Johnny would do so— to get out of this crazy mess with his life intact.

"You wouldn't..." the nearly naked man gasped, goading Terry into a false sense of security and superiority. "You won't really go through with this..."

"I would and I *will*!" the gun-toting father barked back.

"Then make it quick. Get it over with!!"

"Oh, you'd like that...wouldn't ya?" the maniacal male mused.

Johnny swallowed hard, worrying that the bright plan he'd devised in such short order may backfire. "Yeah, well, I think that it'd be for the best...",

"Hey, the faster you're outta here...the better for me and my family!"

"Exactly! So finish this. I *deserve* to be killed!!"

A searing anger masked Terry's logistical reasoning and his instinctual ability to spot an obvious trap. As the father took a silencer sidewinder-style to Johnny's jugular, Terry gloated over how much control he had over him. An alpha-male fantasy that would soon lead to a detrimental breakdown.

"Do what you have to do. Keep on squirming...beg for forgiveness...yell for redemption, whatever you need. It's ALL pointless!"

Johnny stretched his right hand to the empty bottle, reaching the tip of it while embroiled in the struggle of all struggles. With his fingers tightening together, he was astonished to feel the bottle in his grasp.

And it was ready to be swung at a cranium as hard as humanly possible. As the two men flailed about on the couch like wildlife enemies, Johnny knew that he needed to strike soon and escape this unholy mess. Preferably unscathed.

"You can't kill me, Terry! It's not right!! Please…stop…I'm *sorry*!!"

The enraged father hocked a loogie in Johnny's face as he screamed his rebuttal. "DON'T YOU TELL ME WHAT'S RIGHT AND WHAT ISN'T, YOU RAPIST MOTHERFUCKER!!"

"We can work something out…let cooler heads prevail; we ca—" the semi-seized sitter pleaded before being cut off.

"You're damn right we can work something out! It's about to be **permanently** worked out!!"

Welp…it's do-or-die time…gotta take a swing…or else I'm toast.

Clenching his fist around the circumference of the concealed bottle, Johnny Helks wasted no more of his soon-to-be-drained energy, as he struck Terry's right temple with savage intentions.

Glass shattered onto the side of the father's face as mass amounts of blood oozed out of his skin. Terry toppled up and over Johnny, making his way unceremoniously to the carpeted ground.

"You fuckin' psychopath!" the injured father of two howled.

Move, move, move. This is your chance. Your ONLY chance!!

The surly, discombobulated babysitter pushed and pried his body to a standing position.

"AHH!" Johnny bellowed in agony as he moved.

Still shaking off an inebriation and the true atrophy in progress, Johnny managed to stand up—with some doing—and his eyes were right on the front door.

"Don't ya dare leave this house, you bastard…don't you leave this situation like a coward. Face what you've done; face me!!" Terry demanded, flopping on the floor like a bird with clipped wings.

"So…stay here and get murdered? No thanks!" the sitter said as he stumbled around to find his footing as well as his clothing.

Just then, the anguished father grabbed hold of Johnny's ankle.

It was a tight and determined grip, firm like the one that Terry had had on his throat mere seconds earlier.

"Let me go!!" the twentysomething squealed desperately.

"**No**…you are *not* getting away from this…I won't letcha!"

"GET OFF!" Johnny insisted, kicking wildly at Terry's hands with his other foot.

If I weren't so messed up right now, I'd easily be able to break free!

As if someone were looking out for him, Johnny—in his frantic attempt to escape—tripped over the teal tennis shoes that had been left behind by Markéta, dropping a well-placed knee directly into the father's groin.

"SON OF A BITCHING SHIT!" Terry roared, nursing his nethers.

That works…now's my chance to run and never look back!

Sprinting toward the front door in what resembled more of a shambling waltz, the makeshift sitter had his bloodied, glass-plastered hand on the doorknob when Vanessa came barging down.

"What have you done to my husband?!" the panicking wife interrogated. "And what have you done to my daughter, you *horrible* man?!"

"Sorry, don't have time to talk…your husband's wanting to kill me!"

As a single tear cascaded down Vanessa's left cheek, the door to Johnny's freedom opened and he stumbled out to his car as fast as he could.

"COME BACK HERE! YOU CAN'T GET AWAY FROM THIS, NO MATTER WHAT YOU SAY OR DO TO TRY AND ERASE IT! JOHNNY…**JOHNNY**!! WHAT YOU'VE DONE TONIGHT…WILL HAUNT YOU FOR THE REST OF YOUR LIFE…"

Johnny pushed Vanessa away as she came at him like a hungry zombie. "I'm so sorry…I can't face this…I just *cannot*…"

Getting into his car, he revved the engine and hightailed it out of there like he was the wheelman for a bank robbery.

In the rearview mirror, Johnny saw Terry limping toward the residential street, arms waving frantically and many unclean words flying. The man's wife—and the mother of his children—sulked on the pavement as their youngest daughter comforted her while holding a stuffed zebra.

Seconds passed by and before Johnny knew it, the murderous husband and father of two was but a blip on the radar. Left to agonize and cry alongside his devastated wife and kids.

The twentysomething relaxed. "Free at long last."

But Johnny couldn't get Vanessa's grave warning out of his head.

Maybe she's right…what I've done tonight…it could haunt me. Forever.

"No way! I'll be okay…that girl wanted it; she TOLD me she did!"

That doesn't take away from the fact that it was a vulgar thing to do. It was fundamentally vulgar.

"It's all right," Johnny assured himself. "This will all blow over…"

In a heightened state of denial and delusion, he got back on the highway, driving aimlessly much like he'd done earlier while harping over his ex-girlfriend.

Back when he still had some sense of normalcy.

Before his entire life hadn't changed for the worse.

I should never have gone over there. I should've…I…

He wiped his tears away. "Like my dad used to say to me when I was a kid: *You're no good for no one, Johnny.* No fuckin' good for no one."

The dark road then swallowed him in a slew of bad memories relived.

<u>INSIDE: The Only Child</u>

An early morning and a start to the weekend. No school, no work. Except for an eight-year-old's mother, working a double at the diner downtown. She worked too hard and too much, but she had to provide for them. Because Lord knows her lazy husband wouldn't.

With one extended stretch, little Johnny woke up, anxious to get out of bed and play. A trip to the bathroom later, he was ready to roll.

The small-in-stature Midwestern house was quiet, while the wind outside swayed gently against its siding. During fall season, things had *felt* calm. Things felt good—when the boy kept in line and didn't make his dad mad by misbehaving like he so frequently did.

The young boy's stomach rumbled in hunger as he crept downstairs coyly in fear of disturbing his sleeping father. And he wouldn't dream of ever doing so; not if he'd like some peace on this sunny morning—or the next day, even.

I want Corn Pops. And that toy at the bottom of the box.

With each step that creaked, little Johnny cringed at the sounds made by his bare feet. The last thing he wanted was to wake his big and bad dad up.

Mommy isn't here to protect me if he wakes.

"Please don't wake, Daddy…" the blonde-haired boy whispered, looking over his shoulder as if he were being followed. "You just stay asleep. For a long time, too."

Fearfully and gingerly, the only child of a failing-at-life mother and a sailing-through-life father made his way downstairs without a hitch.

The kitchen cabinet's all mine. The fridge…all mine.

Climbing up the kitchen counter, little Johnny opened the cabinet door and yanked the box of Corn Pops down from its spot alongside the other boxes of artificially sweetened cereal.

"I've got you!" the bright-eyed boy declared to a cluttered kitchen.

The yellow box was still sealed—waiting to be ripped apart by two tiny hands, which would scour the insides of it like a raccoon digging through stinky trash.

Gotta get the milk, the bowl, and a spoon!

But there was no milk carton in the refrigerator. Only a jar of mayonnaise, a loaf of wheat bread, and a six-pack of Heineken.

Little Johnny sighed. "Come on, Mommy! You said you were gonna go to the store last night…cereal without milk is no good!!"

Being without wasn't as unexpected as the disappointed boy had projected; it was a common occurrence in the Helks household. Enjoying a bowl of cereal with some nice, cold milk was a rarity. But one thing was usually present in the fridge at all times: alcohol. Various brands, bottles, and cans.

Why can't there be more things in here? Eating it dry is crummy!

"Super-duper crummy. I hate it," the child bemoaned under his breath.

Hold up! Milk's the best, but it's not the only thing we have! I can use water!! That'll be better than having nothing.

Sitting at a lopsided, stained table, the child screeched out of his deteriorating dining chair and walked to the kitchen sink's faucet tap to extract.

The municipally supplied water ran for six seconds before it sputtered out and stopped, leaving little Johnny with a rusty seep to see—and drink.

EW. DISGUSTING. Got some of the yuck stuff in my mouth! Shouldn't have stuck my face underneath that tap!!

Caught in his upset thoughts over the faulty faucet's drought, he'd momentarily forgotten about the toy tucked inside the box of sweetened corn cereal. A prized, plastic-molded plaything awaited.

"Forget liquid. I'll dig in and see if there's a cool toy!"

With the messy quickness of a delirious Black Friday shopper, the boy tore open the foil-lined bag. His hands slipped deep below its puffy corn contents to fish out the toy. At last, he held the plastic throwaway in his palms.

THIS is it? Not too cool. Pogs?? At least it isn't a baby's toy.

Multiple pieces of the poppy goodness were splayed across the shoddy table as little Johnny sighed in disappointment.

They're still okay to eat, even if I don't have any milk or water with 'em...

Upstairs, a sudden stomping on the wooden floor occurred, frightening—and freezing—the young boy seated at the table.

Thanks to his perked ears, he knew that his father was coming to. Grumpily and loudly.

"Oh, no; please, no. I didn't wake Daddy, I didn't wake Daddy...I couldn't have! I just *couldn't* have..." Johnny repeated again and again, trying his hardest to convince himself.

"JOHNNY?! YOU DOWN THERE??" his father belted from above as he made his way down the stairs. "Jesus H! What's this clothes iron doing on the steps? Someone's bound to trip over it! *Johnny!!* Did you put this here?!"

Terrified, the only child didn't say a word back. He'd always been scared, ever since he was born into the world. One constant prevalent, his biological father had never failed to put the fear of God in him. It started with that booming voice, harshly threatening, which had been the culprit of traumatizing the eight-year-old into a submissive silence so many times before.

Worried that not speaking would hurt him even more than responding, little Johnny buckled and gave up his whereabouts. "Sorry, Daddy. I didn't hear what you said. Had my headphones on. I'm just at the kitchen table eating cereal. Sorry again, Daddy!" the quivering boy apologized profusely.

The father was already barreling right toward him when he replied. "CEREAL?! You didn't open up my box of Corn Pops, did you?? I hope to *hell* you didn't go and do that, boy...for your own well-being! That's MINE and mine ONLY...both you and your mother know very well that that's the one cereal I like to eat!!"

"I didn't mean to...I thought it'd be okay to get the toy, and I—"

"YOU FUCKING **KNOW** THAT'S THE ONE DAMN CEREAL I LIKE!"

Little Johnny started shaking. "I'm sorry. I wasn't trying to make you mad or anything like that. Really, all I wanted was the stup—"

The burly father interrupted. "What you did was get your grubby hands inside *my* Corn Pops! You WRECKED the whole box!"

Before the boy could explain himself further, his dad hurled the box across the kitchen and into the living room area. Screaming and carrying on like his car had just been stolen from a strip mall parking lot, the father stormed toward little Johnny with fire in his eyes.

"I didn't mean to make you so mad like this—honest."

"You're damned right I'm mad, boy! I had a shitty night last night, and all I wanted this morning was some cereal. And YOU had to ruin that, didn't you?"

"I—I guess that I just didn't think about it when I was doing it…I'm *sorry*."

"Yeah, you *are* sorry, all right. I swear…you are no good for no one, Johnny. Always have been, and probably always will be."

"Don't say that, please. It's *not* true. I'm a good kid; I'm not bad."

"YES, YOU ARE! YOU RUINED A PERFECTLY GOOD BOX OF CEREAL! ALL BECAUSE YOU WERE BEING GREEDY AND WEREN'T THINKING ABOUT OTHERS WHO MIGHT WANNA ENJOY A BOWL FOR THEMSELVES! LIKE ME!!"

Little Johnny's irate father grabbed him by the collar of his T-shirt, lifting him up with ease and pressing him against the kitchen sink. The young boy's back smashed against the elongated metal faucet, causing him great duress as his dad shook him like he was a vending machine that hadn't coughed up a bag of chips.

Why's he making such a big deal out of this? It's a box of cereal and besides, there's not even milk! Daddy didn't used to be this mean…he's gotten so much angrier…I wish he'd stop being angry!

"I said I was sorry and I really meant it. So, **please**…it's okay!" little Johnny insisted, thinking of a way to somehow smooth it over. "You can go to the grocery store and get another box! I promise I won't touch it. EVER!"

Without warning, the unconscionable father struck his child hard in the face with a closed fist. The young boy, who'd been laid out by the lashing, whimpered and whined until a tidal wave of tears began to well up and splash down onto the linoleum flooring.

"You hit me…why'd you *hit* me…I said I was sorry, so why—why'd you do that?" little Johnny asked in a sobbing shock.

"Because you deserved it! For saying something so outlandish like that. And you're lucky I don't beat on you more! As if I'm gonna go and get myself another box just 'cause *you* suggest it?? Get real. I'm too hung over to be going out in the wee hours of the morning, anyway."

A blubbering mess now, the physically abused child couldn't articulate an understandable sentence. Instead, he cried and cried until his face resembled a ripe tomato.

Ow, my nose hurts so bad. Is that blood trickling down my lips? Oh no; it is!

"Go clean yourself up…before your mother comes back from work and sees you like this," the father ordered, tossing a few paper towels to his son still on the floor. "She doesn't need to know about what's happened here—she's already stressed enough!"

He just wants me to keep my mouth shut…

"DID YOU HEAR ME?"

Little Johnny nodded quickly, trembling.

"Good. Now get up off that dirty floor and get yourself into the bathroom. Wash well! Make sure that blood's gone by the time I check!!"

"Okay, Daddy. I will," the only child mustered through his sniffling.

As the bloodied boy made his way into the lower-level bathroom, there was a rattling of the doorknob at the front of their house.

Is that Mommy? I better hurry before she sees me!

"Johnny, don't you dillydally! Pay no attention to who's at the door…I'll take care of whoever it is," the frustrated father said, an urgency noticeable in his voice. "SCRAM!"

But it was too late to comply. The door swung open. A frazzled mother with an apron full of grease stains was standing at the threshold, holding a gaggle of keys that were jangling and a purse that was swaying to the side of her hip. She'd arrived back home early—almost an hour earlier than expected.

"Babe!" Johnny's dad exclaimed. "How was work?"

The mother ignored her husband's question, eyeing her son's battered face. "What's happened to him? Why's he cowering in the corner??"

"See, now *that*…that I can explain! I was about to tell ya, I really was—but I wanted to know how your shift went first!"

"Spare me the fake interest in me waiting tables, Ed. What happened to Johnny? Why's he all quiet and scared?"

"He just fell down the stairs a few minutes ago! That's what happened, babe. See the clothes iron there? It was on the steps…and *still* is, to prove my point—since he tripped over it like the clumsy kid he is! It was a hard fall, as you can clearly tell!"

"That's not true! He's lying to you!! I wasn't even on the stairs when it happened!" little Johnny said, running toward the legs of his mother.

"When *what* happened, honey? You can tell me—don't be afraid to."

"You're seriously gonna believe a snot-nosed eight-year-old over the man you've been with for nearly fifteen years?"

The mother stared a hole into her antsy husband's eyes for five seconds until turning her undivided attention to her young son. "Sweetie, tell me what really happened while Mommy was away, okay? That's all I want to know: the truth."

"He—well, Daddy hit me…he punched me 'cause I was bad…after I opened up his Corn Pops without sharing them with him."

"WHAT A LIAR! THAT IS NOT TRUE, JANIE!!"

"Go on. Mama's listening…don't you worry about what Daddy's saying. Just keep looking at me and tell me more. I wanna know everything there is to know."

"That's it, Mommy. That's all there is to the story. I put my hands in the box to get the toy out, and Daddy didn't like that one bit because he wanted the cereal all to himself. He said I ruined the whole thing…I was greedy, and—and then he yelled a lot at me, and I couldn't even understand most of it. So that's why he hit me right in the face."

"Is that what you did, Ed? You hit our boy in the nose, just 'cause he 'ruined' a box of cereal?? Is that what ALL this is about? You had to go and strike my son—because he wanted a toy outta some stupid Corn Pops?!"

"Janie, he *knows* that that's the *only* cereal I like…he knew what he was doing when he was doing it! Johnny did it to spite me. I acted accordingly; I'm justified in my actions."

"What kind of man can justify hitting a defenseless child? Who are are you anymore, Ed? You're definitely not the mild-mannered man I met so long ago. That person's *gone*…"

"BABE! No, he isn't! He's right here, and he's never, ever left."

"That is not true…and it hasn't been true for a long time. You've changed, Ed. You're a drunk now—a jobless loser who uses me and torments Johnny…all because you're miserable; you are a miserable human being. And that's *your* fault. No one else is to blame for it."

"That's not fair. You know I got laid off from my job at the factory…this JOBLESS LOSER held down a well-paying job for almost two damned decades! And I supported your ass when you were pregnant with this little **pussy**!!"

"Yet again—here we go! Cue the sob story! Shit happens, Ed. You think I haven't been laid off before? Suck it up and get another job…just like the rest of us have to! So you lost your job—a job that you seemed to be quite good at—but that doesn't mean you can go around and run roughshod over a small, impressionable boy! God forbid Johnny grows up to be like you, thinking that drinking all day and all night's a normal sorta thing to do!! My son…*our* son…is no pussy; he's a brave and beautiful boy. So how dare you hit him! How DARE you strike him in the nose like you did!!"

"All right; okay, Janie. Maybe I flew off the handle there…I apologize…to you and to Johnny. I'm sorry! Happy?"

Janie scoffed at her husband's asinine attempt to make amends. "That's *real* sincere. How many times will you have to make these empty apologies?"

"As many times as I screw up, I guess."

"I can't take it anymore, Ed. I've tried to, for you and me…for Johnny…but I just can't keep doing it. Life isn't supposed to be this difficult. You've made everything so much worse."

"Sure, this is all *my* fault. Like always, right? Go ahead and put it ALL on me once again. Just 'cause I've been outta work for a handful of months and I enjoy drinking some beer every now and then, I've gotta be crucified for it—vilified—for simply being down in the dumps!!"

"A handful of months?? It's been THREE YEARS since you last worked…" Janie pointed out factually, still clutching her shivering son.

"And that severance package I received has gone a long way for us!"

"Where's your pride? Where's the shame in your day-in-and-day-out sulking around this house? Ed, things have to change drastically for me to even *consider* keeping this whole thing afloat."

The hungover husband scrunched his face into a ball of confusion. "What's that supposed to mean, Janie?"

"It means that I think we may finally be done. I'm tired of putting up with you—and I was *already* tired. But after seeing what you've done today…having the audacity to hit our little boy…to me, that's unacceptable."

"I said I was sorry, babe. You know I didn't mean to do it! I let things get a bit out of control is all. John-John knows I love him to death! He's a scruffy lil' bastard…and he understands Daddy has a few issues, but, well, deep down…he knows that Daddy loves him *dearly*…"

"No loving father would ever dream of punching their kid in the nose…over a freaking box of cereal!"

Ed motioned for his still-terrified son to come toward him. "My boy, I'm *sorry*, all right? You understand that? I was out of line; I was childish…it's just a box of cereal. And it was stupid of me to overreact like that. I'm sorry, Son. I *truly* am."

The only child couldn't look at his father.

"Tell ya what; I'll make a deal with you…how about I letcha stay up late tonight and we watch *The X-Files* together? I taped the most recent episode on the VCR, so we can skip all the commercials! How 'bout that, huh?"

Little Johnny kept his eyes on the ground, unreceptive.

"Hey…I'll even letcha have a Pepsi or two since it's the weekend! I know your mom doesn't like you watching scary stuff and drinking such sugary sweets, but shows and sodas like that are good for ya…they get your heart racin'…Son, I'm **sorry**, okay?"

Remaining in the arms of his caressing mother, the young boy didn't speak a single word to his apologizing abuser.

But Ed wouldn't waver in the face of silence. He continued admirably, bending down on one knee to invoke a peaceful solidarity. "So, c'mon, whaddaya say…how bout' ya give your ole dad a big hug and we'll just forget this even happened?"

Janie brushed tears away from the side of her son's watering eyes, nodding her approval to say what he wanted without any fear of being struck again. "Tell him, honey. It's *okay*. I won't let anything happen to you."

"No; I don't wanna give you a hug…and I don't wanna forget about you hitting me. I want you to be nice to Mommy and me. And if you can't do that, then I want you to go away so you can't hurt us ever again."

"Johnny, my boy…you don't *really* mean that, do ya?"

"I *do*, Daddy. I don't want to see you if you're like this—you scare me and have for a long time. Mommy tries her best and you don't; you don't care about my feelings. You don't care about them AT ALL!"

"No, no, no. Of *course* I care. I'm your father…your one and only daddy!" the shaken father said, breathing heavily as he rose up from his knees. "You have to know that I love you and your mommy *very* much."

"Gimme a break with that crap. You don't even love yourself. There's no way you can love both Johnny and me. It's impossible. You *hate* yourself…and you've let the world kill the good in you. The drive you once had is gone…and I've had to pick up the slack since your slow-burn mental breakdown. Also, you can't buy Johnny's love with caffeine and a TV series he really shouldn't be watching. Not anymore."

"Fuck you, Janie. You don't know what it's like to work a job for nearly twenty years just to have it taken away from you like it's *nothing*! Like YOU were nothing! You have no clue how it feels!!"

"Calm yourself before I have to call the cops. Because I *will* if I have to, Ed. I'm serious."

"You'd do that? After everything we've been through? All these years…just thrown away…because I've raised my voice to you and our son?!"

"Because you've *assaulted* him, you stupid son of a bitch!" Janie fired back.

"Don't talk to me like that; you're no better than me. So you've had a steady job and have been supporting us financially for the past three years! Congratulations; good for you!! I supported you for *years*, might I add, and with fucking ease—I handled all things moneywise during those nine treacherous months of your pregnancy!"

"Sure; make light of the situation. At least I was trying to better myself back then—going to community college, taking online classes, doing whatever I could to create a future for us. But now, look at you! You've fallen off the wagon, Ed…you're getting drunk each and every night; you don't lift a finger to help around the house…and now you've HIT my son."

"OUR son, Janie. He's not just yours. I helped make him, ya know."

"You may have done your part then, but you *aren't* doing it now."

The uneven father lunged right at his wife, as her dismissive way of writing him off had flipped the hostile switch in him. Janie didn't stand a snowball's chance in hell of moving before Ed was right there, but Johnny was much too young and much too nimble not to see the incoming attack. He'd actually anticipated it for several minutes—so luckily, little Johnny escaped the lunge.

Ed grabbed his wife by the throat, yelling directly into her ear to establish his dominant presence. "YOU BITCH! YOU FUCKING FORGETFUL BITCH! NO APPRECIATION AT ALL FOR ME!!"

With choking gasps of struggled breath in between, the seized mother urged her boy to run away. "Honey…head upstairs…lock the door…call nine-one-one…do it; DO IT NOW!"

"Yes, Mommy. I'm going!" the traumatized child promised.

"GO, BABY! GO!!" Janie ordered hurriedly.

"I'm going, I'm going!!" little Johnny reassured.

"Oh, no, you aren't…you ain't going *anywhere*!" the unhinged father said, shoving Janie into a wall and heading toward his son.

Half-concussed by the hard blow taken to the back of her head, Janie crawled shakily toward her maniac of a husband. "Don't you hurt a hair on his head! You hear me…you, you crazy bas—"

Before the injured mother could utter another word, she passed out on the hardwood floor—either from an overwhelming fear or from the head wound that she'd suffered courtesy of her mentally ill husband.

It was now down to Johnny, pitted against his extremely abusive father.

Man against child. Bear against cub.

Oh my God, Mommy. Don't leave me! I can't be alone with him…

The fight for his eight-year-old life was officially on.

Ed dove at little Johnny and wrapped his fingers around the ankle of the young boy as he tried to run upstairs. Yet he was no match for the strength of his father. The grasp tightened, both hands clamping down onto the two small ankles with a manly power.

"Let me go, Daddy! Just let GO!"

"Never! You and your mom are mine. You'll *always* belong to me!"

"No, we won't!! Get off of me…let go!!"

"You bastard, stop wiggling so much!!"

I gotta do something…hit him with something…but what?!

Struggling to see what he could find, he saw—just a few steps above him—a clothes iron: the same clothes iron that, just a day prior, he'd foolishly and lazily left on the stairs when he had been told to take it to the closet. Kicking and shooing his way from under the clutches of his determined father, little Johnny reached with all he had in him to retrieve the handheld metal appliance. His fingertips managed to touch the base of it, reaching closer and closer to achieve a full grip on what could become a decent defender.

*I'll use it as a weapon. I'll sock my bad daddy right in the face with it! And then I'll call 911 and this will be over for me and Mommy…it'll be fixed…**all** of it!!*

Little Johnny waffled his father's veiny forehead with every ounce of might inside his body. As it hit the intended target, it was as unexpected as it was painful. With both the father and son at the midway point up the stairs, the blow to the head sent Ed careening back down the steps, tumbling sideways in agony while screaming.

"Daddy…I'm sorry, I had to do it…*sorry*, I just had to!" the boy said as he began to run up the stairs, unharmed and in the clear.

"You're gonna pay dearly for that one! That could've killed me!!"

"I wanted you to leave me alone! And I want you to leave Mommy alone; don't hurt her anymore!!" Johnny pleaded.

The in-recovery-mode father, rubbing his head from below the top of the stairwell, spoke strained words. "Just come down here and help me up, would ya? I swear that I won't hurt you if you do…"

"And you won't hurt Mommy, either?"

"Of course I won't, Johnny. I won't even *think* of hurting her again. Please, will ya just stop all of this madness and help your good ole dad out? I love you, Son."

This is a trap; it has to be. He's never this nice to me. He wants to beat me up for beating him up…that's what it is! Well, I'm not falling for it.

"I love you, too, Daddy…but I can't come back down there. I don't trust you enough. You'll hurt me and yell at me for hitting you in the head!"

"Dammit, boy! You get down here right now or else you'll be REAL sorry you didn't!" the father bellowed, switching off his temporary sincerity in a heartbeat.

"*Sorry…*"

"Lemme tell ya something; you're gonna be sorry…you are going to be *supremely* sorry that you turned your back on me," Ed declared, scampering up the stairs as fast as he could given the head injury slowing him down. "As soon I get within arm's length of ya, I'm grabbing you by that lil' neck of yours, and I'm gonna rattle the shit outta you. Maybe that'll knock some sense into you!"

I've just gotta get to my room, then I've gotta lock the door behind me. Call 911 like Mommy told me to do…and they'll help us get away from meany-head Daddy once and for all!

Running through the hallway and not looking back as he did so—except for chucking a few pairs of shoes toward his pursuing father—little Johnny opened his door and promptly slammed it, locking it behind him. His head then swiveled around the room to find his emergency phone.

Mere seconds later, the amplified sound of his father's voice cut through the door.

"Johnny, I'm only going to say this once, okay? Open this door."

"No. I won't listen to what you say! I'm calling for help and you're gonna be in sooo much trouble pretty soon, mister!!"

"Open this door right *fucking* now or else I'm breaking it down…and you won't wanna know what happens after that!"

"I'm not afraid of you. I can't be; I have to be strong for my mommy."

"Your mommy *wants* you to open this door up for Daddy!"

"Does not! She wants me to call nine-one-one!!"

The father pounded on the flimsy wooden door while its foundation faltered with each powerful hit, instilling a deep-rooted fear in his son. "You don't wanna do that."

Maybe not, but I have to…I have to be brave for Mommy…

The cordless phone had been spotted sitting atop a pile of worn school clothes. The young boy snatched it up quickly and started to dial the easy-to-remember three digits when his line of concentration was broken by an intrusive interruption.

A loud crash at the entrance sent the stunned eight-year-old's door—and its shoddy hinges—flying across the room, landing at little Johnny's feet.

Holy crap; holy crap. He's in here now. I'm dead meat.

"Put that down…and come with me. I'm not playing around. This all ends here, you understand? So just DROP it…" Ed said, referring to the phone in his son's quivering hand.

What do I do, what do I do, what do I freaking do?!

"YOU HEAR ME, JOHNNY?? THIS THING'S DONE. AND IT'D BE SMART FOR YOU TO FORK THAT FUCKIN' PHONE OVER, OR ELSE I'M COMIN' TO GET IT—AND YOU WON'T LIKE ME WHEN I'M TRULY ANGRY!!"

In a split-second decision, little Johnny threw the cordless phone as hard as he could toward the threatening mouth of his destructive father, temporarily surprising him into shielding his face from the airborne object.

"STOP THROWING THINGS AT ME!"

Being much smarter than his age required, the only child of a very dysfunctional couple ran and slid beneath his father's stump-like legs, surprising the towering man even more than before.

Breaking free, he sprinted down the stairs in a panicked flurry as his heart beat faster than it would on an exhilarating roller coaster.

Once downstairs, the eight-year-old checked on his fallen mother in the living room. Janie was stirring a bit—even partly responsive to her son's concerns, but she wasn't altogether there. Yet the overprotective mother did know to tell her boy to leave the house—while he could still do so in one piece.

"Get outta here…find a neighbor, go across the street—to Vanessa's house. Have her call the police…she'll protect you…make me pro—"

And that's when she nodded off once more as the back of her head bled out.

"Mommy!! Wake up, please! Don't go to sleep!!"

As little Johnny tried shaking his mother back to consciousness, his father, full of white-hot anger, barreled down the stairs.

"JOHNNY! GET AWAY FROM YOUR MOTHER!! THERE'S NOTHING TO SEE!" the unemployed, unfeeling man shouted as he rounded the corner.

Not wanting to stick around to see what lifelong trauma would happen next, the nervous boy scurried up to his feet and bolted for the back door in the kitchen.

"GET BACK HERE!" the seething father demanded while leaning down to check on his wife.

"NO!! I'm getting help!"

A disobeyed Ed ran full speed at little Johnny but halted at the threshold of the back door, yelling obscenities and stomping the ground with his boots before returning to his nearly dead-to-the-world spouse.

I did it; I can't believe I did it! I got away from the monster; I escaped my big bad daddy. What'd Mommy say to do again? Oh yeah, go to a neighbor and get help from them! That's what I have to do…

Opting to travel a block down the blue-collar neighborhood street instead of heading toward the area his mother had told him to go, the child feverishly knocked on a red double door.

Going to Vanessa across the street is too close to him right now, so this is better. Mommy just said to find a neighbor. This'll be much safer.

"Hello in there?! Please open! My mommy's been hurt, and I've been hurt too!" he hollered on the stranger's porch. "We need help!!"

After waiting a while with his requests for help going unanswered, the boy slunk his head down in sadness and began to walk away—until the doors cracked open slightly.

It was a male in his mid-thirties with a healthy head of brown hair draped over his finely-tuned body—wearing only blue boxers to cover up anything that could be construed as inappropriate.

"Can I help you?" the nonplussed man asked rather kindly.

"Yes; yes…you can, a lot! My mommy and me, we were hurt…see my nose??"

"Ooh, yeah, I see that there. Looks positively awful. What happened?"

"Daddy got mad at me for getting into his box of Corn Pops, and—and he, then he…" Johnny trailed off, overwhelmingly upset over what had transpired.

"Just take your time with your words; I'm sure it was a horrible experience…" the friendly neighbor soothed.

"It was; it really was…but it's not even over! My mommy, she is *still* over there, right down the road, and she—she's in loads of danger, so we gotta call nine-one-one, we gotta do something!"

"'Course we will, boy…'course we will. How about you try to relax some and come inside? You can tell me everything there is to know…and then we'll make it all better, I promise you."

"Promise?" the young boy questioned hesitantly.

"Absolutely. We'll do it together."

Little Johnny smiled, entering the stranger's house willingly. "Thank you."

"My pleasure," the chiseled man replied, smiling back brightly.

As the eight-year-old walked into the neighbor's house, he noticed a hand placed onto the small of his back—a peculiar placement.

Is this a good guy or a bad guy?

When the front door shut, little Johnny got his answer to the internal question once he turned around to face him—as the man's blue briefs hit the floor, unveiling an unbelievable erection.

"Now then…what was it you were saying was troubling you again, cutie?" the neighbor fawned, locking the door and approaching the confused child meticulously. "I'd *love* to make you feel so much better if I could…"

INSIDE: The Scuffle

"Man, it's just, like, when you're the product of a hazardous environment…you're fair game to become as hazardous as that environment itself. Ya know what I'm trying to say or no?"

The bartender smirked, displaying his hundredth sly smile of the night while listening to Johnny go on and on drunkenly. "I guess I do, buddy. We've all had rough childhoods, though. At least you're still here—in good health, apparently—drinking and talking away."

Johnny's head swerved to the far left immediately after the barkeeper's spiritless reply—a clear sign that the many pints of alcohol he'd consumed had now taken control. The twentysomething male continued reminiscing ignorantly, like a typical loudmouth would at a dive bar on the outskirts of nowhere. "The thing about it is…I was a nice and carefree kid. I really was. But it was all yanked away from me—within one day. Because of two assholes…who had to go and fuck me up for life."

Wish they were dead. Wish I had the guts to kill them both. If I did, it'd be easy…since we all still live in the same neighborhood.

"My damn dad…he NEVER, EVER believed what happened to me—despite my constant insistence that it was true—so we never moved away. And we should've!"

I should actually do it someday—I should kill them.

"Friend, I'm just a bartender. The booze is supposed to be what erases your negativity, however momentarily—not me. That's why you're here…to drink away all the unhappy, right?"

"Righto, my kind and patient mixologist. Keep 'em coming, by the way…" Johnny requested as his head veered hard right. "Wowzers, I'm jacked!"

"Listen, next round's on me, buddy…but after that, you're cut off."

"And just why in the hell are you gonna deny me more liquor?"

"You've been drinking steadily for my entire shift tonight, guy, and your head's about to bow down on this counter…"

"Don't you worry your metrosexual ass about that; I can control my head movements like nobody's business, man. I've never hit a bar counter—not **ever**! I've been drinking people under the table in fine establishments such as this one right here since like…forever!"

"Try to keep it down and drink your last shot with a little dignity, will ya, bud? And as for your personal problems, it's a simple fix there: move forward with your life and stop worrying about the past. 'Cause it'll eat you up inside…"

It already has. God, if this preppy bartender only knew the things I've seen—and all the things I've done. Like that girl…what was I even thinking? Only twelve. Well, that's why I'm hiding out in dives.

Johnny ignored the barkeep's advice, focusing on the song playing over the PA system instead. "What's this tune sparkling in the background? It's pretty…"

"Song's 'So Here We Are' by a British band called Bloc Party— off their album *Silent Alarm*, which has been on repeat all night."

"Spiffy ditty! I like it lots. So…" Johnny stopped speaking and prefaced what he was about to say with a quick shot down the hatch, setting his glass on the counter with an authoritative swagger after. "Pour more, will ya?"

The bartender groaned audibly. "You're cut off. I told you."

"Oh, yeah; forgot about you killing my vibe a sec ago. Perhaps it's for the best. I'm hazy enough."

"Quite hazy, indeed. Just relax and let it roll off of you. Here's some ice water to help clean out the toxins. And a bag of pretzels to sop it up…my treat!"

Johnny gave a high five to the air beside the barkeeper's right hand in a show of tanked appreciation. "Ya know something, you're all right. Thanks for this salted snack!"

"No problem, bud. Take care of yourself, okay? Things'll get better."

Yeah, right. I don't think they ever can. I've dug myself a hole, climbed into it, and have somehow managed to shovel all the dirt over the top of me!

"You got it, my trusty barkeep!" Johnny said cheerily.

Another man saddled up on the stool beside Johnny, making his presence known as he sat with a deep sigh. "Hey there, Mr. Sitter. How're you doing on this dreary night?"

Johnny turned to the left, wondering if he'd just imagined what he had heard. "Terry?" he asked, wanting to be wrong due to his drunkenness.

"Yeah, it's me. *Terry!*" the winter-coat-wearing man confirmed jubilantly. "How's shit been?!"

The young drunkard was shocked as he leered into the face of a father who had finally found his prey. He'd done his best to stay hidden, and for months he had accomplished just that. But now, he was face-to-face with the man he'd escaped by the skin of his teeth—the father of a daughter he had taken advantage of.

How'd he find me?

Nearly speechless, Johnny blurted out a standardized reply. "Things are going fine, I guess…how…how're you doing tonight, Mr. Janis?"

"Ah, hell, I'm doing just *dandy*! Thanks for asking. But call me Terry! I've told you that you're more than welcome to in the past."

"Okay, then…Terry."

"You know, I've come a long way to see you again. So this is a special occasion for me—as I'm sure you most certainly know!"

Johnny had already grown uncomfortable with their conversing. He knew that he'd been found—tracked down like a deer in the woods by a beer-swigging, camouflage-sporting trapper. Realizing the position he was in, Johnny chose to go straight toward apologizing for his unjust actions. And in a strange way, being side by side with the father had done a lot to sober him up.

"Listen, Terry…I'm sorry for what I did. Don't think for an iota of a second that I don't think about what I did to your daughter. 'Cause I do. I do a lot. Now I know it may not *seem* like that…since I ran off that night and never came back home, but I mean it. I just hope we can move past this."

"It's that easy for ya, huh? I'm supposed to shake your hand, accept your apology with a smile, and go about my business? Let you be?"

"No, I…I'm not saying that it should be forgotten or even *forgiven*; I'm just saying that I hope my actions won't lead to some physical violence here! So, I'm calling for a truce…if at all possible…" Johnny offered feebly.

"A truce? A TRUCE?" Terry repeated, elevating his voice among the patrons' chatter around them. "You raped her, Johnny. You've taken a twelve-year-old's virginity…you've wrecked a young girl! DO YOU UNDERSTAND THAT?"

Hearing the father raise his voice to an upper-level roar, the suspicious bartender came over to their nook and interrogated them both. "Everything okay, gentlemen?"

Johnny answered dismissively. "Yeah. We're good. Just working the kinks outta our friendship's machinery…"

The bartender glared at Terry, not laying an eye on Johnny. "What about you, friend? What'll ya have?"

"Oh, *right*…I almost forgot where I was!" Markéta's father said, palming his forehead in a *d'oh* moment. "I believe I'll have a scotch on the rocks and a Kentucky Bourbon—if you have that on draft."

"We actually do," the barkeep revealed. "Anything else?"

"That ought to do it!" Terry said.

With another simmering stare toward the two men, the bartender grinned and headed toward the other dwellers seated nearby.

"What's your endgame?" Johnny questioned his stalker.

"Excuse me? What do you mean?"

"You know *exactly* what I mean…" the slurry male whispered close by the father's ear. "You come in here, pat me on the shoulder, act all chummy with me; but for what? Why didn't you just wait till I was outside?"

"Because I wanna see you sweat. I want you to know that I've got your number, Johnny. I've got you; you're mine. This scavenger hunt's done."

"What're ya gonna do? You can't haul me off without a fight. I may be pretty drunk right now, but I won't go down so easily."

"I've got my plan; don't worry about that, Mr. Sitter."

"Yeah? Well, what if I just get up from this stool and walk off? What the fuck would you do about that? Make a huge scene in front of all these people?"

"No, that'd be stupid…" Terry replied. "It's taken months to find you, Johnny. And I only found you because of a little birdy chirping."

"Who ratted me out? I was thinking you were just tailing me!"

"It's a secret! Not really all that important, but…ah, hell, why don't you ask your weak-in-the-knees mommy?"

Dammit! I knew that I shouldn't have texted her my hideout location!! Shouldn't have been texting anybody. Damned phones. They're only trouble…

"Oh, wait! You won't be able to ask your mother about the details of our deal now that I have you right here, since I'm not gonna give you up after all the tracking, planning, and sacrificing."

"Just stop, man. Spare me the speech," Johnny said, getting frustrated and feeling safer than he should. "So your daughter and I…we did some stuff. Won't ruin her life…it probably helped cultivate her maturity. Hell, I bet she's a lot wiser from the experience all around."

"Are you the most delusional man to ever live?? You have no clue about what happened, do you?"

"No clue whatsoever, hoss. How 'bout you connect the dots?"

"Johnny, you impregnated her. By deflowering a twelve-year-old—and not wearing a condom while doing so—you got my baby girl pregnant."

"No way that's true. *No*…that didn't happen. I would've heard something about that, even in hiding. That's bullshit."

"It isn't bullshit at all, you motherfucker," Terry said with hostility, wanting to raise his voice yet again but knowing they'd be paid another visit by the bartender or maybe even the cops. "We had to make the decision to…to abort the life that was growing inside her."

"Are you *seriously* for real right now? Am I in some nightmare?"

"You are…and it's one you created all on your own, Johnny."

"I still, I—I don't believe you. You're playing head games…to screw with my mind. That's what this is—that's what ALL of this is!"

"*Look* into my eyes. Do you think these eyes could lie? You think that I'd go out of my way to track you down…and notify you of my daughter's abortion…for the sake of a demented gag? Are you just a psychotic scourge to society?"

Johnny shook his head incessantly, as if he were a little boy trying to prevent the reality from existing. "No. I refuse to believe it. And you know something else? I'm getting outta here—right now."

"I wouldn't advise that, Johnny."

"Why's that? You gonna follow me out to the parking lot? Fight me to the death??"

"Something like that, yes."

"Then go RIGHT AHEAD, Terry! Let's do it. Mano a mano!"

"I'm ready; been ready ever since that night."

Johnny clapped exuberantly in Terry's face. "Great. I'm *so* glad that I'll be able to make your wish come true, then!"

"Can we at least wait until I finish my drinks? I just got them."

"Stay if you want…but me? I'm leaving this joint! Follow me now—or follow me later. I'm sure this isn't the end of whatever this is!"

"I intend it to be," Terry said chillingly.

"All right, man. Your move. I'll see you out there," Johnny rebutted. "I'm not running from this thing anymore. Let's settle it."

"Yes, let's…after you…"

The bartender stopped Johnny as he departed. "HEY! Your sad tales almost made me forget about your tab! Our card reader's out of service, so that means ya gotta pay with leafy green, and you owe me a grassy park's worth for your boozing tonight!!"

"Ah, come on, Jason! You know I'm good for it. I'll hit you up with the moolah next time," Johnny promised, stumbling a bit as he headed for the door. "Whether with a card or cash, I gotchu later."

"That's not how we do things; pay up!"

"I AIN'T GOT IT!!"

Terry stepped in, flashing six crisp fifty-dollar bills at the barkeeper. "Here. Will this be enough? Or do you need more?"

"Uh, no…that'll *definitely* be enough, I'd say. More than enough."

"Excellent. Much gratitude for the quick service. You've been a good tender."

Johnny scoffed at the saving gesture. "I'm done with all this. Hope you're happy, Jason! You just lost a regular! And another thing, the food sucks in this place!! Don't eat any of it, people…it's ass!"

The barkeep leaned in, asking Terry about the drunken disorderly. "Do you know this guy well?"

"Yeah, we go way back."

"Is he gonna be all right getting home? Or should I call a cab?"

"That's not necessary. I've got it under control," Terry said happily. "It'll be handled."

"Sure hope so. Dude has issues—lots of them."

"He really does…"

"Well, thanks for stopping in. Enjoy the rest of your night," Jason said with about the same passion as an automated phone operator.

"I'll enjoy it as much as I can."

Outside, the February weather was harsh. Snowcapped buildings, icy roads, and a windy atmosphere all met Terry's flushed face with a bitterness.

After viewing the chilly, winterly vistas, the stalking father saw Johnny—his arms outstretched with a welcoming posture—in the middle of the parking lot. And due to the extreme cold, no one else was outside the bar.

It was just the two of them now, alone and nose-to-nose.

"Here I am, Terry. You wanted me all these months? You wanted to settle this? Well now, you've got it. I'm not hiding any longer."

"I respect that…"

"Get some, then! Don't wait. I'm RIGHT HERE!!"

Terry stormed Johnny, tackling him to the ground as the young drunk's head smacked a mound of snow by the curb.

"Fucking shit!"

"You're going to die tonight, Johnny."

He's serious. He legitimately wants to kill me.

The two men—one relatively older than the other—were entangled in a rolling war on the white-as-dentures snow. Fighting as if their lives depended on it, they both struggled to get the upper hand—yet both gravel warriors continually failed to attain any sort of supremacy.

"GAH!" Johnny shrieked as Markéta's father achieved a full-on mount to gain control. "Lay off!!"

"Not until you're DEAD!" Terry barked with wide-eyed excitement. "Ya know…my daughter said that your dick wasn't even that big. She said it was pretty small, actually…what a shame that is…you were her first and it ended up being a massive disappointment!"

"THAT'S NOT WHAT YOUR WIFE HAD TO SAY ABOUT MY COCK AFTER IT WAS IN HER!" the blitzed male retaliated. "She *loved* it…and by the way, while your daughter slobbed on my knob, she nodded when I asked if she had sucked others off! Guess she's not that innocent, huh, Dad?!"

"You piece of shit! She was obviously just trying to impress you—my daughter hasn't done **anything** like that!!"

"She did with me!" Johnny corrected.

Terry reached inside his waistband.

"Is that…is that a…"

"It is!" Terry said in a kind of gone-ish giddiness.

The ongoing scuffle was about to take a turn. The despondent father had packed a weapon: a belt-concealed handgun.

A beautifully black SIG Pro semi-automatic pistol. As light as it was convenient, it had been heralded as a truly compact killer. Johnny recoiled, putting ten fingers up to his face—as if it would ward off the bullets.

The gun-toting father revealed the details of his dealings. "I'll tell ya somethin', man. Your mother's VERY good at giving blow jobs. Your shitty trucker dad has never given her the time of day, as he's always been a lot more concerned with alcohol; but she's an underrated head-giver. Just being honest."

Johnny spit in Terry's face. "Fuckin' liar! You're only saying that since I said what I said about your wife, which is actually TRUE. Even if my mom *wanted* to be with another man, she wouldn't ever go through with it because she fears my father more than death itself!!"

"And that's precisely why she did it! I threatened to stay there until he came home from his late-night shift to spill the beans about her baby boy raping a tween! She begged—but then caved after I dropped trow and told her to suck me to completion if she'd like me to leave. So that's what your still-hot mom did, as well as give me your location…all in an effort to protect you from him, which is ironic…don't you think?"

God, I hope he's lying about that…if he isn't, I'm mortified. Could my life get any worse?

Terry planted his gun right between Johnny's eyes, which were crossing to keep sight of the vengeful father's great equalizer. "But none of that matters now. Out here there's no judge, no jury, no *nothing*. Just you, me, and a glorious death…yours, specifically."

In a moment of clarity, Johnny Helks mentally succumbed to his wrongdoings. *Maybe this is what I deserve. Maybe this is my fate…maybe I'm just a horrible person who should be gunned down. I've caused so much grief for so many.*

And then, snapping him out of a personal beat-up session, Terry said some words that would hit a nerve—cutting words that'd stick to Johnny's craw more than anything else could.

"Look at you, giving in so easily…what a *worthless* life…no good for no one," the father observed, laughing in domineering confidence.

Johnny immediately thought of his dad, an abusive father who'd belittled him and beaten him any chance he got. A miserable man who had systematically ruined his life.

With demoralizing memories working wonders for his self-motivation, Johnny balled one fist inside a slushy sleet of snowfall and rabbit-punched Terry, briefly stunning the mounting father.

"What'd you just say about me?"

Arrogant that he was still in control of this witness-less battle, Terry bit. "I SAID…you're no good for no one, Johnny. No fucking good for *no one!*"

I'm not that, Daddy. I am not that, and I won't lie down! I won't let you hurt me or Mommy. Not ever again…

Blacking out from the previously dormant effects of a psychologically damaged childhood, Johnny overpowered Terry and wrestled the gun away from his cold, callous hands. "You're not gonna kill me, Daddy. And you're not gonna harm Mommy!"

"What are you *talking* about?!" Terry asked, confused, trying with all his strength to pry back the deadly pistol from the schizophrenic.

"I'm talking about how you've gone and hurt my mommy, how you've hurt me…socking me in the nose like you did! ALL I DID WAS GET IN YOUR BOX OF CORN POPS, DADDY! THAT SHOULDN'T HAVE STARTED IT! I WAS A GOOD BOY; I JUST WANTED THE TOY!!"

A twist of events resulted in Terry turning into the one who was insanely terrified. Thoroughly at a loss, he didn't know how to react to such a burst of unforeseen lunacy. "I…I'm not your daddy, Johnny. I'm Terry Janis, the father of the twelve-year-old daughter YOU took sexual liberties on!!"

"EW! That's ICKY! I've never even TOUCHED a girl! You know that, Daddy! Stop making stuff up; stop acting like someone else!!"

Terry, still in a wild tussle with the grown man who had just reverted to the mind of a child, knew that this scrap had deathly implications, and he knew that he had to finish the job. Markéta's father had to kill him.

"Just gimme the gun, son. I'm sorry I made up such a silly thing about you touching a girl. I was only kidding…" Terry said calmly, playing along to continue breathing.

"No flipping way! If I hand it over, you'll do something mean! I know how you are. I KNOW. Like Mommy says to me when she tucks me in: once a bad egg, *always* a bad egg!!"

"It's not like that, Johnny! Honest!!" the older man cried as the younger man gained the advantage while losing his marbles. "I'm a lot better now…I've become a good guy!"

Johnny scrunched his face in curiosity. "You're a good guy now?"

"Yes! Yes!! I am. So…just gimme the gun and this'll all go away…"

The twenty-eight-year-old schizo paused.

I dunno…Mommy's told me to be careful about what Daddy says. He's not too trustworthy. He hurts us, and constantly has us live in fear…

"NO! You're not going to fool me this time! I won't fall for it!!"

Believing that his time may be coming to an end, Terry made a move for the handgun. He tried to wrangle it away from Johnny's grip but was no match for his youthful power.

They continued to fight for the firearm, screaming at each other incoherently, as snowflakes covered both of their jerking bodies on the icy pavement.

Until a gunshot went off, ceasing the dramatic entanglement definitively and bringing an end to Johnny's personality disorder madness.

What the hell happened? Where am I? Why's there blood on my hands? Who is this underneath me?

But then it all came flooding back to him in picture-perfect detail.

The makeshift babysitting, the underage girl, the unauthorized sexual intercourse, and the father who was hell-bent on exacting revenge.

"Terry? Oh God, you still with me, man??"

The bloodied man's breath flickered up into the bitterly cold air, informing Johnny's worrying eyes that he was indeed still alive—although in serious need of medical care.

"Get…get help…go inside, please…" Terry barely muttered.

"I will…you just hold on here. Don't die, all right?!"

Ghost-white and bleeding, Terry nodded slowly.

Numb from the snow mounds seeping into his skin, Johnny shambled his way toward the bar he'd spent most of his intoxicated night in.

The door flew open as the twentysomething crashed to the floor in a fatigued disarray. "There's a man out there…and I just shot him directly in the gut. Call for help!"

"You did what, now?" the flustered bartender asked in disbelief.

"I *shot* someone, dammit! Please call nine-one-one!!"

Jason sighed as he picked up the phone. "Can't we ever have an uneventful night in this place?"

After the strapping barkeep had asked the rhetorical question to the slack-jawed patrons of his pub, a mentally shifting Johnny unpredictably switched back to his eight-year-old self. "Daddy has red all over his body. I did a bad thing…so don't tell my mommy…okay?"

<u>OUTSIDE: The Ragtag Group</u>

The smoky, gasoline-soaked atmosphere presented nothing but an apocalyptic wasteland every which way the freed prisoner and the girls went. Elements of fire and death hung above their heads with abysmal smells as well as charred flesh.

This isn't some game; this is real devastation, Johnny Helks thought.

A band of mismatched misfits by anyone's judgment, Johnny and his unmerry pack of teenagers—who'd just changed clothes without the freed prisoner's eyes undressing them even further—scavenged the vast land for any useful items they could find among the destruction swirling around them. Everywhere they went was the same song and dance—piles and piles of unrecognizable bodies mixed in with a generous amount of flames thrown in for kicks.

"How'd something like this happen? There's **no one** around. Alive, I mean. Where *are* we right now?" Lizzie Janis pondered. "I'm starving; we gotta get some more food."

Chelsea frowned. "This is worse than 9/11—from the pictures and videos I saw in school. Just look at all this soot!"

Johnny remained silent, adjusting to—and assessing—the open-house ruination that now seemed to be their new world, but he kept thinking. *Geographically, we should be in Ohio, since my prison's here…but if I blabbed about that, I'd be a damn dunce. And what difference does it make, anyway? Doesn't even matter if it's all in shambles.*

"It could be worse, ya know! We outta that damned bus, we outta them rope restraints, n' we sho' as hell alive!!" Tamika offered optimistically. "Or y'all in denial 'bout dat?"

"From the looks of it—I think we're dead. Don't quote me on that just yet, but this is honestly, like, some pretty grim stuff to take in," Riley admitted. "But I'm also starving, Liz. We gotta scrounge; stale tortilla chips and candy bars *aren't* going to cut it…but at least Johnny came through for us with that water break!"

They drank so many of those treasured Fijis. Have got to find more for me, Johnny reminded himself as he nodded civilly. *Maybe I should tell 'em about those pallets of pop to help ration out the waters? Nah, those teeth-killers are dehydrators…water is the only way to go in this thing. I'll be a nice guy and keep sharing.*

"I just wanna go back to when I was reading and eating blueberry muffins. I wanna go back to when things were completely normal! What have we ever done to deserve such a doomed scenario?? We're totally *screwed*!" Chelsea proclaimed, looking at the freed prisoner for guidance. "Should we go check that plane you mentioned seeing earlier?"

Johnny finally tried to rein it in, feeling almost as if he had to—since he was, by and large, the oldest and wiliest member of the burdened bunch. "That'd probably be a *bad* idea, as it's downed and destroyed. I saw the thing explode. Plus, you gotta take into consideration the toxicity circulating downtown right now. It'd be detrimental to go there and breathe all that in. We should hold off on that, 'cause who knows what effects it'd have on us. So let's not get ahead of ourselves here, girls. First we gotta take inventory. How'd we get here and where do we go next? Why have we been linked together? Who's behind these terrible attacks? We have to try and piece it all together."

Tamika agreed like an emotional churchgoer overstepping her boundaries during service. "AMEN! Preach it, my Caucasian!"

"Oh, I shall…raise the roof, sista!" Johnny said, laughing afterward in what came off as a hokey attempt to bond with the African-American teen.

"Ugh, that was too brutal…" Riley butted in. "Don't talk like that. Like…*ever* again. You're white, Johnny. Get a mirror!"

"I don't like you that much, Ry…but good looking out!" Tamika said, nodding as she pointed toward Riley in appreciation.

"Sorry about that…this isn't an excuse or anything, but I'm a bit off, you could say. I haven't slept in what feels like AGES."

Lizzie meddled in Johnny's business. "And just *where* were *you* when all of this went down, hmm? We still haven't heard your story."

"I'm gonna pretend that there was an entrusting tone there, Lizzie. Because to me, it sounded a little on the bitchy side."

The headstrong teen wasn't amused by his sidestepping. "It's merely a pedestrian question, is it not? I mean, *you're* the one who said that we should lay *everything* out on the table. Process the *how*s, the *why*s, the *what*s, and the *who*s to this hell-zone of a mess. So, that's what we should do. Right now. And I believe it's your turn, sir…"

Why's Lizzie pressing me…it's like she knows who I am…well, she does resemble that girl…that one girl who began the descent…that—

"Let's go, Johnny! We haven't got all day," Lizzie urged impatiently.

The rest of the girls—except for the literally attached invalids—looked on with anticipation etched on their collective faces. Chelsea, Riley, Tamika, and even the unsung leader of the teen team, Lizzie, waited silently as Johnny just stood there like he was in the middle of crafting a tall tale in his mind.

"Any time you want to start…" Riley pushed.

"'Fess up!" Tamika chimed in rudely.

Smiling innocently, Chelsea put her hand on the freed prisoner's right shoulder. "Don't be shy. You saved us. We're already biased toward you!"

Dammit, I wasn't prepared for this type of spotlight! How could you have been, dummy?! You were recently incarcerated. Never in your wildest dreams could you have imagined being interrogated by a mini-fleet of teens.

"We're WAITING!" Lizzie said aggressively.

What do I even make up? I can't tell them the truth! My hero status would be null and void so fast…

"Hello in there, Mr. Helks—who's here to help!" Riley teased.

Out of the blue, Johnny's inner bulb turned on. Running the far-fetched idea through his head, he started to stutter. "I—I…it's hard for me to talk about what happened…before—before this all came to be."

Unbelievably, the girls bought his woe-is-me act. An impressionable Chelsea held his shaky hands with both her warm, soft hands. "Johnny, it's *okay* to tell us. We wanna know. Whatever it is…it can't be as bad as what's going on out here!"

Shit on a stick, Lord knows full well that's patently false. What I've had to go through—my checkered past—they CAN'T know who I am! It'd flatline this unique partnership. And I can't have that happen. Can't be alone again—like I was in that horror show of a slammer.

"Come on, ya bald-headed saltine cracker. Out wit it already! Don't fret over some personal milk spilt; we gotcha on any evils n' ills you've had ta deal wit befo dis shit hit," Tamika encouraged.

Johnny gazed over to Lizzie, who was staring at him intently—and not in the provocative sort of way, but more of the *I'm-onto-you* sort of way.

Successfully eye-cornered by the blonde ringmaster of the victimized girls' brigade, Johnny proceeded to lie.

"My wife…or, I guess my *ex-wife*, I should say now…was driving our Honda Civic while I was riding shotgun—just nonchalantly peering out the car window—when it happened. She told me that—I, um, can we not talk about it for a little bit? It pains me to relive…"

Riley was the first to decline. "No, you're **not** getting a time-out, Johnny. We need to know."

"You can't *possibly* leave us hanging like dat! This ain't no loose-ends *LOST* ep, white boy!" Tamika added. "We gotta know what happened to you—n' yo woman too!"

"Hey, now! That show was awesome back in its heyday. Really revolutionary for its time. The lush cinematography, the amazing acting and writing—just *everything*. Even with quibble-causing plot holes and a lack of answers, it was all so well done. And don't get me started on that sweeping epic of a soundtrack! Mm, that composer, Michael Giacchino, is a *mastermind* when it comes to memorable melodies and arrangements."

"Trust us, we don't want to get you started on what seems like an obsessive love for *LOST* and its orchestral soundtrack or whatever. We wanna know what happened to *you*, silly! COME ON!!" Chelsea demanded.

"It sounds like you're stalling…" Lizzie said.

"Okay, okay. If you must know, my wife, Ericka…announced that she wanted to get a divorce. There; it's out in the open! The big mystery's solved: the woman I'd known and loved for about a decade and some change wanted to split up with me."

"Oh, Johnny! That's awful!! I'm so sorry," Chelsea consoled. "Were the two of you having troubles, or did this just come outta nowhere?"

The lying convict bit his lip on cue. "Was totally random."

Ericka? Wow, that's the first name to pop up? You're still not over her! And after all this time.

"No. I am…" Johnny mumbled, faint enough to be heard by the girls.

"Talking to yourself there?" Lizzie asked.

"Uh, yeah…sorry, I was just thinking about how tired I am. It's gotten to me badly. I could seriously crash on this here stash of human ash."

Lizzie cringed. "Don't joke about something like that. These people—these tragically blackened bodies—surely had families…loved ones, and…"

"And—they charbroiled n' dead now, girl! Don't you go thinkin' they feelins gon' get hurt from us talkin' 'bout 'em bein' burnt!" Tamika sneered.

"Harsh as T may be, she's right," Riley said.

"*Real* harsh…" Chelsea said, more to herself than anyone else.

Lizzie groaned in frustration. "We're getting way off track here! *Johnny*…keep telling your story. What else happened after Ericka said she wanted a divorce or do you not remember?"

Ugh, this girl will not let up…can't she be satisfied? Okay, so she wants more. Give her more, then. Dish it out!

"I remember only a little after that, but what I *do* remember probably ties to all of this—now that I think of it…" Johnny said mysteriously.

"Tell us what it is!" Riley cried.

"Yeah, you teasin' ass, we all gots ta know what went down…" Tamika followed quickly after.

Chelsea nodded at Johnny in a teacher-like fashion, imploring him to share his story with the rest of the group. "Take your time telling. And we'll listen to every bit of it…"

"C'mon, dude. Get on with it already!" Lizzie ordered, her intolerance toward him clearly building.

"So, once she laid that life-changing news on me…" the freed prisoner continued, as if he'd been detailing the story's narrative the entire time without starting and stopping, "…I felt a lump in my throat and an emptiness in my heart. I couldn't get over the fact that my wife could do such a thing to me. Sure, we didn't have the BEST marriage ever, but I was *good* to her. Or so I thought. See, she just never gave me any sign that this separation was even on the horizon.

Not at all…and, my God, if I'd known that something was up, I would've talked to her…I would've tried to save our sanctity…I would've given it my all to…to…"

The girls stood at full attention, their faces clinging to whatever was about to come next.

Wow, this is almost too easy! All right, keep on doling out your melodramatic divorced-male story! They are loving it. Make it good, make it good. Get in the mode. You've got them.

Johnny picked up where he had left off. "I would've given everything to have saved our crumbling marriage, you know? So that's what I did. I wouldn't give her an inch that whole car ride home; I talked her ear off. I went on a tangent about our relationship, stating how much we'd been through—like her serious battle with drug addiction—as well as going over the many years we'd spent together and all the aspirations and dreams that we'd had as a couple. We had always wanted to buy a nicer house, since we wanted to start a…we—we wanted to start…"

That's it right there…go for the kid angle now. Look at their watery eyes! I can get sappy and trail off, and they won't say anything! Not even Lizzie, Miss Judgmental herself! This is great stuff. I have 'em dying for whatever I'm about to say next!

"…anyway, it doesn't really matter anymore. Who cares if I had wanted to be a father? Who cares if I had pictured a white picket fence and a happy child swinging on our arms? Who cares about what I'd envisioned for our future? I thought we were forever secure. That's why I took those vows; that's why I held her hand at the altar with a tear in my eye. I—just…I wanted that life with her. And I *still* do, because I love her more than anything or anyone. I love Ericka with all my heart, even if she did say that she wanted a divorce and she's a recovering user. I **must** find her. Because I need to save my marriage."

I am such an asshole for doing this! But damn, is it fun!!

Chelsea gently squeezed Johnny's arm without saying a word.

"Anyway, back to the car ride—there we were, fighting and blaming one another for every single past squabble. Just doing whatever it is bickering married people do when they're pitted against each other. But to my credit, I kept calm during it. Even when she raised her voice at me, I wouldn't relent inside that automobile.

However, I got a bit carried away after a while…and I put my…AH, this is the hardest part to tell! Can we please drop it? It's too difficult to—"

"You can't stop now! What happened? What'd you do?" Riley asked.

So predictable. I LOVE this! I can take it as far as I want to take it. All right, swim to the deep end, Johnny. Go for broke!

"She said some stuff that triggered me—after I'd intentionally pushed her buttons for an honest response—so something different suddenly washed over me. It was almost like an out-of-body feeling. I put both my hands on her neck, and I shook her…not in a malicious way or anything, just in a *why-can't-you-get-this-through-your-thick-head* kinda way, if you know what I mean!"

Tamika grinned, signaling that she could relate. "I feel you. Sometimes ya gotta shake somebody like a piñata ta make 'em realize they ain't thinkin' straight! Did candy fall outta her?"

Lizzie rolled her eyes for about the tenth time, silently watching Johnny as he dug a deeper hole for himself.

"Please keep going! What'd she do? Did you stop or did it get worse from there??" Chelsea implored anxiously.

And here it is. Go in for the kill! Hopefully they'll buy what I'm selling…

"I didn't stop. But, well…something—or, actually, I should say some*one*—made me stop," Johnny trailed off for dramatic effect. "As Ericka yelled at me to let go of her, she wasn't keeping an eye on the road—she was too distracted by my grip—and when she turned back toward the windshield, there was a figure in the middle of the street. Somebody was standing in the road! By the time we saw the person, it was all a blur. She couldn't swerve quick enough to avoid hitting the guy. We were going way too fast, and he was way too close. Just couldn't register in time. What happened next is…even *more* of a blur to me. We struck the person head-on. And after that, I don't remember much of anything. I do recall screaming, putting my hands up, and my wife losing control of the vehicle, but that's it. Darkness. When light reintroduced itself to my beady eyes, I was alone in the passenger seat. No sign of my wife."

"Holy crap kittens," Chelsea said.

Riley stood slack-jawed. "Yeah, 'wow' isn't a word I throw around that much, but…uh, *wow*."

"That shit sounds like somethin' from a movie!" Tamika added.

Lizzie remained as stoic as ever. "So she was just gone? Like, no trace of her whatsoever? How's that even possible? If she were rescued, they would've gotten you out of there. And if she were injured and wanted to leave the car, she wouldn't have left you there to die! What gives?"

This is the most unbelievable thing I've ever had the pleasure of experiencing. I'm like some writer crafting fiction here!

"I truly wish that I could tell you why I was the only one in that vehicle, Lizzie! How do you think *I* felt upon waking? It was incredibly alienating—almost like something out of a horror story. This whole thing that we're in right now sounds like the premise of a madcap novel!"

At random, Chelsea hooted at the freed prisoner's out-loud thinking matching her own. "No kidding; that's what I was saying back at the bus! This'd make for a good book—your story *and* ours! Or maybe like a TV show; something for the small screen!! But it'd have to be a weekly series. No movie, though. Too much stuff to cover the canvas of an hour-and-a-half map. *Man*! Now I miss binging shows."

"Same here, girl…" Tamika said with sadness.

Lizzie, still wanting to know more of Johnny's falsified story, kept the conversation going. "So, you were saying…"

"There's not much more to say, really!" Johnny replied dismissively. "She was inexplicably gone—and I was alone in our compressed Civic. I got out of that glorified tin can; then I saw all the madness that we're now seeing together…"

"One problem with your sorry story; there's something that doesn't quite add up," Lizzie hinted, detective-like in her phrasing.

"And what's that?"

"Why are there no marks on your freakin' face? I mean, you were in a horrible crash. Right? Your wife hit a person, she lost control of the car, etcetera, so…again, what gives?"

"Losing control doesn't exactly equate to a wreck happening after that. I don't know what happened. Honestly. When I woke, our car was wedged in some shrubs off to the side of the road. And she was nowhere to be found. I know it sounds crazy to you, but it's *true*.

Check out these wobbly knees and refer to the back of my bloody head. It must've been from that…perhaps it was a crash. Besides, it's not as strange as what's going on around here. Look around us; there's death and carnage EVERYWHERE we turn. My story pales in comparison!"

"The man's right, guys…" Riley said. "With what we're in the middle of here, Johnny's tall tale almost comes off as a subplot…"

"Exactly! We shouldn't be so paranoid with each other. Why would this poor guy be against us? He's stuck—just like we are. That can't be a coincidence! Something's up. I believe there's a reason why only eight of us are alive. I just don't know what that reason is yet." Chelsea sighed.

"Yo, that's what we all wanna know. But how 'bout we keep on scanning through thangs? If we continue ta look 'round this bitch of a sitch, things gon' soon shore up on da proverbowl beach n' whatnot."

"Tamika…" Lizzie laughed as she spoke. "Did you really just attempt to say the word 'proverbial'? 'Cause I think that that word may be out of your wheelhouse."

"Yea! Proverbowl…that's what I was saying! What about it?"

"It's *proverbial.* There's no bowl at the end of prover. Never has been!"

"Oh, word; so I said it wrong, den?" Tamika clarified.

"Correct…not a big deal, it was just funny to hear you say it like that."

"My bad dare, Liz. I'll stick wit dem easier-to-say words."

Riley snorted back a laugh attack. "You're so dumb, Tamika!"

The girls then turned toward Johnny, waiting for him to say more.

"Ya know…we've all been through the ringer," the freed prisoner said, pausing as if he were pondering deep thoughts. "You girls were strapped to seats inside a shot-up bus and probably would've been stuck there for who knows how long if it weren't for me coming along! And as for me personally…yeah, waking up without my wife wasn't *as* mentally taxing, I'll give ya that. I simply blacked out when she hit some person in the street…"

"Sorry for being a little unsure of your story, Johnny," Lizzie said passively. "But you saw what we were trapped in; you plucked us out of it. In this crappy scenario, *yes*…we're all in it together, but a picture says a thousand words. That's the issue. With you, we only have your word to go on…'cause none of us actually saw what you went through."

"Well, isn't it a shame that the lot of you weren't packed into the backseat of our Civic?" Johnny joked, making light of his ambitious and fictitious story. "Then again, you girls wouldn't have liked that. Way too small—and a bunch of garbage lying around…like crinkled-up bags from fast-food restaurants and discarded Coke cans."

"Sounds like a man's car if there ever was one…" Riley said flatly.

"Ericka had kept it really clean, but whenever I'd drive it around, that common male dirtiness would take over!"

"Where's yo girl now, ya think? That's gotta be a big kick to da nuts!" Tamika lamented. "Not knowin' where she be n' everything…"

Johnny deflected humbly. "Believe me, I wanna know where she is. More than anything. But what's important now is that we don't harp on the past. We need to focus on the future—our fucked future…"

"He's got a good point there, girls!" Chelsea offered, standing in the middle of their circle. "And our first priority should be to find something or someone useful."

"Amen, sista…" Tamika said.

"So let's take a vote, then!" Riley suggested cheerfully.

"What? This isn't a democracy. We're just people who're in a crazy bad predicament," Lizzie said.

"Thank you for that update, queen of transparency," Johnny quipped.

Hmm, that may have been a bit too much. Can't be an ass; not now. And not to their supposed leader. As long as I don't tell them about my time spent in the pen, I'll be fine!

"I like dis guy…n' I usually think all white dudes are lame," Tamika informed the group, eyeballing Johnny with fondness.

"Yeah, Johnny…you're all right!" Riley smiled.

"Me three!" Chelsea exclaimed, joining in.

Lizzie bellyached. "Great; gang up on me, why don't you?"

"Come on, Lizzie. We don't mean anything by it. Or *I* don't, since I was the one who cracked the quip," Johnny said. "Truly sorry if it offended you."

"Let's just do this stupid voting thing…"

Riley explained their choices. "The options are as follows: either stay here—together—and continue to scour the area around us, or we spread out into teams…then meet back at some agreed-upon landmark in a little while."

"I kinda like the second idea," Chelsea admitted quickly.

"I'm in for dat as well. It's smart. We'll cover mo ground," Tamika said with confidence.

Johnny nodded slowly. "I like it; count me in on the team idea."

"So that leads to Lizzie," Riley remembered. "What's your vote?"

"I guess I'll go with the second one, too. Although it may be unsafe to separate, I don't see much progress being made if we sit around in one group for however long this thing lasts."

"Then we're all in agreement…" Johnny stated.

Various versions of *yes* sprinkled throughout the polluted air.

"If it weren't for this dry heat sapping my strength, I think I'd be more excited to explore! How I wish for rain right now…"

"Riley, everyone here wants raindrops. But rain's a funny thing. When you don't want it, it shows up…and when you *really* need it, it's nonexistent," Lizzie said.

I know I'd sure love to see this Liz chick wet…

"Peeps!" Tamika blurted out. "What about doze two girls who're attached to each other like paint to a wall??"

"Oh yeah! What in the world are we gonna do with them, anyway?" Chelsea wondered. "They'll slow us down big time. Not to be mean, but I don't know how they could even help."

Riley raised her hand eagerly, as if she were near the back of a classroom. "I've got it! It's perfect…you guys see those half-destroyed houses down by the caved-in road over there?" the brunette pointed as she asked. "Why don't we go into one of those homes and have 'em chill in there?"

"Eh, I dunno…they may freak out if we abandon them," Lizzie replied first.

Chelsea waved off the second-guessing. "But it'll kill two birds with one stone. We can search around the houses for survivors and stock up on supplies along the way…and whatever food and drink we find, we'll give a quarter of it to this human oddity."

"Hey, that's not nice; they can't help how they are! What if one day you have twins and they end up like this? Think before you speak," Johnny ridiculed in his most adult voice.

"Sorry; you're right. That was wrong of me," the shamed tween said. "I never should've said such a thing. It's honestly unlike me!"

Man, I just faked caring about those silent freaks 'cause it'd make me look good! This is great. I'm acquiring brownie points by the second!!

"Okay, then; so it's settled. How about I go looking around this smelly wasteland with Johnny, and the three of you take those stuck-together sisters—shirt five—and head to that neighborhood block—the section where the houses *aren't* burning. We'll then meet back up here at this beer billboard before dawn, okay? This can be our rendezvous point," Lizzie ordered kindly.

Johnny glanced at the blonde girl's face, curious about her specific pairings. "Just us?"

"What? Is that a problem?"

"Not really…but why do you wanna be on a two-person team?"

"I want to get to know you better. That's all," she said plainly.

"Shouldn't one of the other girls come with, though? Make it a bit more even?"

"Eh, I don't think so. Riley and Tamika look to me like they can handle themselves. And it'd be good for Chelsea to go with them—you know, to assist with the attached chicks," the headstrong teen answered. "It's not like we're gonna be away from each other forever."

You don't know that…not out here…

"Thanks, Lizzie! Appreciate the confidence in our abilities."

"No problem, Riley."

"We'll handle whateva comes our way!" Tamika added impulsively.

Chelsea scrunched her nose at the already-made decision. "But what about me? I don't have a say in it??"

"You don't wanna be with Ry and Tam?" Lizzie interrogated with a raised eyebrow.

"Oh…no, it's not that! I was just surprised by how easily I got lumped into something without having any input."

Riley gave the mild-mannered girl an assured smile. "It's no big thing, Chelsea. If you don't wanna go with us, you don't *have* to."

"No, no, no! It's not like that at all."

"If you have another idea you'd like to share with the group, share it," Riley continued. "Can't speak for everybody in this circle, but I'm thinking that we're open to ideas."

"It's okay; I didn't mean to sound like I was against it. After all, I did say I liked the idea. I'll gladly go with you guys!" Chelsea conceded happily.

"You gon' be super safe. No lies, four-eyes. Don't sweat," Tamika soothed.

Johnny gave a thumbs-up. "All right, then. We have our marching orders; so let's go…before we lose this daylight!"

Chelsea, Riley, and Tamika all agreed, waving and saying their goodbyes to the freed prisoner and the headstrong teen while Chelsea held the hand of the aforementioned human oddity.

"Looks like it's just the two of us now, Lizzie—the way you wanted it! How peaceful."

"Uh-huh; sure is, isn't it?"

"So, are you ready to scan this ravaged land with me?" Johnny asked with a weirdly playful disposition.

"I absolutely am. And I'm also ready to confront ya…"

"Is that right? Well, may I ask what about?"

Lizzie met his eyes with a cold glare. "I know exactly who you are."

<u>Search Party #1: Chelsea, Riley, Tamika (& the Human Oddity)</u>

After several minutes of a unified silence and observance, the consistent sound of eight legs crunching onto mounds of wreckage gave way to a deliberating twelve-year-old.

"Don't you guys kinda wish that we'd just stuck together? Maybe it would've been smarter to remain as one team," Chelsea speculated.

Tamika rejected the tween's second thoughts. "Nah; it's aiight. We good here…n' we strong, girl. Besides, Lizzie seemed like she had a bone to pick with Mr. Here Ta Help over somethin' or other…"

"Word. That was sorta weird, right? I was wondering why she formed a tag team with him so fast!" Riley said.

"Dunno…maybe our numba one wanted him all to herself so badly and so quickly 'cause she wants dat dick?"

"*Really*, Tamika?! It's gotta be a sexual thing??" Chelsea gasped.

"Jus sayin' da white boy's tight lookin'…he rough-n'-tumble handsome. Got that glisten to him. Naw what I mean?"

Riley disagreed. "He's too greasy for me. And kind of tattered-looking."

"But ya need 'em to be a little on da sloppy side…a bit tore up; shaved head, gruffness n' grit ta dat shit!"

"What're you even talking about right now?" Chelsea asked, chuckling. "You're a teen, Tamika. Stop acting like you have some experience with men, 'cause ya probably don't!"

"And who's ta say I don't?" the African-American girl implored.

"Well, she *just* said it, so…" Riley said, pointing at Chelsea.

"Whateva! I've had plenty o' guys on my backside. You don't know, yo!" Tamika crowed.

"Sure, sure. You were prolly a regular hussy on them streets."

"Shut da fuck up, Ry! We ain't friends no mo."

"I'm devastated…" Riley feigned disappointment, clutching her heart.

Chelsea tried to bring everything back down to a simmer instead of a boil. "Guys…can we all just take a deep breath and concentrate on our mission? Go to the homes, get whatever supplies are inside, and drop these conjoined girls off somewhere safe."

"Thanks for dat recap." Tamika snickered, her sarcasm shining. "Let's keep on rollin' 'long dis mess, den."

The group of girls continued trudging along the shredded setting with a genuine trepidation. Their youthful eyes squinted through the pounding sunlight bathing the obliteration as their restless minds wondered why the presumably nuke-polluted air hadn't caused any of them irreparable harm. Yellowish-greenish tints of a dazzling fume in an otherwise clear blue sky confused the already exhausted girls marching onward.

"Not even a nosebleed…" Riley mumbled as she looked up. "How is that?"

"Maybe whatever's in this chemical-warfare air is giving us an intestinal infection and we just don't realize it yet," Chelsea replied like some type of know-it-all.

"An intense what?!" Tamika asked loudly.

"No. Not intense. An int—you know what, forget it…"

"Chelsea. We really can't keep it a secret anymore! Tell her about the intense thing!!" Riley beseeched, laughing. "It's not fair to her."

"Er, you punks tryna play me?" the black teenager probed.

"Tamika, we wouldn't even *dream* of doing that!" Chelsea said in seriousness.

"Yeah…for real…we ain't playin' witcha!"

"Ya better not try ta be bold wit a bitch like me, Ry! I'll come over there n' whoop yo ass! Both your asses, ax willy! No dizoubt 'bout it."

"Did you just say *dizoubt?*" Riley asked in complete disbelief yet cracking a slight smile.

"And did you also say *ax willy* instead of what I think you meant to say—*actually?!*" Chelsea asked secondly, befuddled but suppressing laughter.

"Ah, I see what we gots right here…a few gram-knots! Nice, *real nice*—you white peeps are on some snooty shit," Tamika accused.

"Stunning, just stunning," Riley managed after nearly ten seconds.

"What?? Somethin' funny again?!"

"Nah, Tam. Not exactly. I'm simply blown away by you giving slang to even a thing like grammar Nazi. *Gram-knots*? Really now? That's too incredible!"

Bursting into a gaggle of giggles, Chelsea couldn't control her internal snickering any longer. "Oh, man; that is hilarious!!"

The African-American girl was about to let loose on a tirade, but a couple crashes up ahead startled her and the others.

"What was that?" Riley asked urgently.

"Don't know…but it didn't sound like a damned accident."

"Stop it, Tamika!" Chelsea insisted. "It was probably just a few dishes falling from a counter."

Both Riley and Tamika directed a death stare toward the tween.

"Sorry if you two disagree. But it's a possibility. Right, Ry?"

"*Anything* is possible around here…I think we've clearly seen that much," she answered gravely.

"You still wanna go 'round them houses?" Tamika asked in fear.

"Yeah…the plan hasn't changed. That's why we're by these places, anyway—to scope them out."

"All right, Ry. Let's go scope…"

"Let's," Riley said with a sparsity of uncertainty.

As the girls began to trek toward the mysterious crashes, another racket originated from the same house as before.

"I don't like this, guys. I don't like this at all," Chelsea stuttered.

"Well, *we're* gonna keep heading toward it," Riley declared, pointing to herself and Tamika with a sense of pride. "You wanna back out now?"

"No, okay? I *don't*. But what if this is like a plot device, something to lure us in for the bite? It's just that—you know, it's fine. I'm sorry. Keep on walking."

"A lure?!" Tamika snorted. "There could be peeps in need! And sittin' here stressin' won't help anything till we peek. Don't be so scurred!"

Riley halted unexpectedly, mere paces away from the block of half-destroyed homes—much to the chagrin of her at-times enemy, but much to the relief of one positively terrified Chelsea.

"Why're we brakin' all of a sudden?" the tween asked. "Callin' it off?"

"I'm just thinking of how to go about this. If those sounds were made by someone, we should be smart here. We need a weapon before heading into that house."

Tamika grinned from ear to ear. "Now *dat's* what I'm talkin' 'bout!! Why hadn't *I* thought uh dat yet?"

"I dunno…but I think I've found a pretty decent starter stick," Riley announced as she bent down to pick up a mint-condition Louisville Slugger.

"OOH, mama mia! A bat's where it's at!"

Chelsea gritted her teeth. "Are you sure that that's necessary?"

"Hell yeah it's ness sarry, bitch! If some fuck's in dat house n' he's fixin' ta get frosty, it's best we have some toppings for his ass!"

"Tam's totally right, Chels."

"I'm getting behind both of you as we head in there…" Chelsea said shakily. "Those sounds *were* ominous—I know that much!"

"Well, let's go see who caused those supposedly ominous sounds…" Riley said.

"After you, then. Please," the twelve-year-old girl urged apprehensively.

"Chill out already, will ya? I'm not gonna let anything happen to you—or *us*—and this here bat will make sure of that."

"Yes, yes; we got dependable protection now, so why don'tcha just stress less?" Tamika requested.

"Sorry; will do."

Riley patted Chelsea on the back. "Thank you!"

The girls proceeded toward the crumbling home, kicking away any wreckage that impeded them.

As they advanced closer to their destination, more glass-breaking sounds came from the suburban house lying ahead.

"Are you positive you guys wanna go in that place?" Chelsea asked.

Tamika grunted at the tween. "We've come this far; I ain't backing down now. We should feel safer since Ry's bat-strapping!"

An abandoned cluster of cars scattered across the neighborhood bureau introduced even more confusion and wonderment. Gas cans sat beside several vehicles with no sign of life in sight.

"Weird. I know we saw a couple of cars and trucks back by the bus earlier, but seeing a buncha rides wedged in like this—with all these cans to the side of 'em—it's spooky," Riley observed.

"Yeah. And no keys to be found anywhere. No people either, obviously. But if we can locate just *one* set of keys, maybe we could get outta this mess and see if this wasteland expands beyond where we currently are!" Chelsea said.

"Easier said than done…" Tamika rebutted. "'Specially in dis shit! We been stripped down ta nothin'!"

Chelsea, Riley, Tamika and the human oddity were only footsteps away from the front door of the beckoning household when they noticed a welcome mat on the porch with a mystifying message.

DO YOU DARE ENTER?

"Okay; *that's* a little unsettling…" Riley whispered.

"Could just be a stupid joke, like one of doze welcomin' mats dat try n' be funny or somethin'…y'all know what I'm talkin' 'bout?"

"No, we don't, Tamika. I don't think we ever really know what you're talking about, honestly."

"Shut it, Chelsea! That's some racist shit."

"Um…not quite…only stating a fact. Sorry!!" Chelsea backed off.

"The question on this mat certainly sounds direct. I doubt it's a novelty thing."

"Well, do we dare enter or what, Ry?!" Tamika asked.

"Yeah; we dare. I don't care what happens. I just want answers."

"Me too, Riley…but this seems uneasy to me."

"That's 'cause it *is* an uneasy situation! We gotta suck it up and go in, though; all right?" Riley encouraged Chelsea.

"Fine, fine. So sorry once again. You won't hear another word."

"We betta not!" Tamika said.

Riley nudged the spray-painted-in-black welcome mat to the left and after a deep inhale, she opened the front door swiftly—as if ripping a band-aid off a boo-boo.

Upon entering the house, the interior bewildered them even more than the outskirts of it.

The inside presented nothing mysterious at first. But the home was immaculate. Nothing was out of place; nothing had seemingly been looted. Not a single item had been destroyed or impacted in any way by whatever had affected the outer walls.

It was as if the exterior of the house was all a ruse: half-broken on the outside while the squeaky-clean interior was triumphantly tidy. On a rosewood console table near the front door, three peculiar things garnered their attention: an assorted basket of fruit from Shari's Berries, a baker's dozen of Cheryl's Cookies inside one cream-colored tin, and a case of unopened Fiji Water. The girls immediately went over to it, clawing at the contents and consuming it all like a pack of starved hyenas.

"This is a godsend! Apples, oranges, grapes, pears, kiwis, sugar cookies…AND bottled water!!" Riley exclaimed in between bites and gulps. "I was losing hope that we'd stumble upon something like this…"

Chelsea conceded. "Yes; me too. Buttercream frosting and even dipped strawberries? So happy right now!"

"Hope there ain't no poison in dis ish, doe!" Tamika said like a distrusting killjoy. "Don't really feel like croaking on a cookie!"

"I'm dying of hunger and thirst so bad that even if there *were* poison in this stuff, I wouldn't care!" Riley informed. "Just feels good going down the throat."

"Is that whatcha used ta say to yo' boyfriend?"

"Shut up, Tamika! Eat, drink, and be merry!"

"Yeah…what she said," Chelsea added, snickering.

Once done with most of the fruit and water, the quenched and stuffed girls entered the living room—which was found to be neatly organized, but with one alienating caveat. Three extremely lifelike mannequins were perched on an expensive-looking couch. Two were adult-designed—an attractive man and woman in summer attire—and the other was a little boy smiling mischievously.

Alienating them further, a white canvas that was nailed above the showroom dummies presented a slather of hair-raising words, dripping downward in what appeared to be a fresh coat of red paint.

LIKE WHAT YOU SEE?

SOON YOU WON'T. AT ALL!

"Oh my glob, this is so…SO…creepy." Chelsea shuddered.

"Glob? Don'tcha mean *God*??"

"Nope; it wasn't a slip. Ever see *Adventure Time*, Tamika?"

The black girl shook her head.

"Lumpy Space Princess? Finn and Jake? BMO? Nothing?"

"No! All right? I don't know it. Sounds stupid already!"

"Can we stop talking about a cartoon for *just* a sec and discuss what's in front of us right now? I know we've seen our fair share of crazy, but **what** in the hell's going on here? Am I really seeing what I'm seeing?"

Tamika sighed. "Yes, Ry…we see."

"Why in the world are there fucking mannequins propped up on the couch?!" Riley wondered, swiveling her head around the room as if spotting something would instantly answer such a bizarre question. "And what's with this damn sign? Who's doing this stuff to us and WHY are they doing it?!"

"That's the thing that is gooning me out the most," Chelsea revealed.

"But who knows fo' show if they doin' it to *us*, ya know?"

"Chels had a gut feeling that we were being lured to this ultra creeptastic house. And she was right! Get it through your head—those sounds weren't random!" Riley said to Tamika with conviction.

"We ain't sure of anythang anymo; dat's all I'm sayin' here!"

"I'm with Riley on this one…" the tween butted in kindly.

"'Course ya are! White stays wit white!!"

Riley groaned her objection, swinging her baseball bat onto the coffee table. "You're so bullheaded all around, you know that? We've established that you're black, okay? We got it. White's bad, black's good! Just give it a rest already, will you please?"

"Hey, you've got da bat…so, whatever you say, boss lady."

"*Thank you.* Finally. And you're right; I **do** have the bat."

At a bit of a standstill while quietly staring at the mysterious mannequins and the bemusing words above their heads, a glass window shattered in the kitchen, startling the girls. The shocking sound forced even the conjoined twins to perform an unnerved jump into the air.

"Yo, fuck dis noise. I ain't gonna go look in dat kitchen only ta get got like some punk! I'm outta dis bitch!!" Tamika declared.

"You and me both…" Riley agreed. "This is too messed up."

Chelsea shrugged her shoulders. "I'm confused. I thought we were gonna see it through no matter what?"

"Yeah; I mean, we *were*. Until we came into this funhouse of horror and were greeted by a three's company of mannequins, a freaky message, and—in case you're deaf all of a sudden—that massive crash that just happened!"

"Okay, then, Riley. Let's go to another home. I didn't even wanna come here anyway."

The weapon-wielding brunette nodded. "That's probably the smart thing to do now. I must admit, even equipped with this bat, I don't feel too tough at the moment."

Just then, another glass window broke in the kitchen, causing each girl's heart to race like a track-and-field athlete.

Before they could catch their collective breath, a grizzly male voice immediately complimented the shattering of kitchenette crystal, both repulsing and terrifying the teens. "Come to me; I want a *hug!*"

"OKAYYY! I'M OUTTA HERE!!" Tamika shouted, storming off.

Chelsea and Riley followed suit, running out of the house as fast as they could.

A slew of obscenities flew out of Riley's mouth. "What the fuck, what the *fuck*, what the FUCK?! I hope that weirdo doesn't try to come after us!"

"This is da scariest shit by far!!" Tamika added.

Tripping over the excess wreckage on the ground and falling directly onto her face, Chelsea screamed when she discovered just what she'd fallen into: a charred-up, burnt body, its eyes untouched by any flames. The deadened glare of the unrecognizable person's retinas would forever be preserved in the twelve-year-old's memory bank.

"Get up, girl; get up! We gotta get outta here!"

"I—I—can't move—I..." Chelsea could barely articulate. "Too much fear."

"WE'VE GOT TO MOVE! RIGHT NOW!!" Riley blared.

"Wait...*wait*. Where are those girls—the attached girls?" the tween asked frantically.

"Aw, damn; you must've let their hand go when we started ta bounce!" Tamika said.

"No! I am **not** gonna go back in there to retrieve them! And you aren't going to, either!!" Riley answered rudely before Chelsea could even ask the question.

"But they're in there with someone who's crazy! They're defenseless; we were going to try and protect them, place them somewhere safe!!"

"Chelsea, I'm sorry, but it's not our problem and it never was. Yeah...we were being PC with those twins and all, but let's face it: they were slowing us down. That's why we were figuring out a way to get rid of them!"

"*Word*. Ry's right! Cut our losses on da human oddity. We gotta go before dat freak—whoeva he is—decides ta come prowling!!" Tamika advised.

"So, you guys want me to forget about them like it's nothing? They were on the bus with us! Trapped and terrified—even if they couldn't verbally express it. You're heartless! Both of you!!" Chelsea yelled through tears.

Riley put her hands on her hips and tried to compromise. "Listen...we can talk about all of this later, but we *really* don't have the time to go int—"

Suddenly an otherworldly growling interrupted the consoling teen.

Earsplitting in its resounding roar, the girls instinctively cuffed their ears to avoid damaging their hearing. The sheer loudness of the bellows froze them in place, causing the group of girls to tuck into a standing half-ball.

"It's that thing from earlier! The thing that killed those dudes!"

"No duh, Ry!" Tamika screamed.

"I'd run right now, but I'm much too scared!" Chelsea admitted.

Unable to tear their eyes from the origin of the monstrous unknown's snarling, the girls felt their eyes widening by the second. At long last, they finally laid them upon the previously invisible creature. Like a hot knife cutting into a stick of butter, it bulldozed through the infamous house of mannequins with a graceful ease, tearing the roof from its foundation as though it had just been sucked up by an Oklahoma tornado.

"Holy God…what IS that?!" Riley asked in absolute awe.

The activated monstrous unknown, the length of a train with an oil-black casing, slithered like a snake around the penetrated house's midsection—entering and exiting at its leisure.

"That freaking thing's *huge*!!" Chelsea gasped, still immobilized by an abject terror from what she was witnessing and processing. "And its teeth alone…I swear, they're, like, *quadruple* the size of bear claws!"

"FUCK ME," Tamika said with an appreciation for the gargantuan gliding beast just a football field away from her.

"We have to—*we have to go*—we can't keep gawking at this unbelievably crazy thing! It'll murder us right where we stand if it sees us!!"

"Yeah, Riley…let's go…we can't save those poor girls; they're already in there, and it's too far away. So it's too late for them! And I *don't* want it to be too late for us…"

"Glad ta see you finally come 'round, Chelsea. ROLL OUT!" Tamika ordered.

Before they could move a muscle, the soul-shaking roaring magnified, thus creating an unparalleled gust of wind that sent the girls flying backward. Landing violently on a bed of steel ruination, they clutched their heads with concern. Pain shot through them almost equally as the bellowing continued to pierce the smoggy airways.

"Try to get up! We gotta go or else we're dead!"

"Don't ya think I'm tryin' to, Ry?! I'm in agony here, bitchness…"

"Help me, guys…*please*; I think I'm really hurt," Chelsea begged. "Something stabbed me when I hit the pile."

"Yikes! That looks pretty bad." Riley grimaced as she crawled over to the punctured twelve-year-old's position. "This blade got you good in the waist, but I think you'll live! We have to move, though."

"I can't; I can't get up and go! I'm scared, I'm injured, I'm—"

"*Chelsea*, listen to me! I'll carry you, all right? You're light enough. And I'll wrap up your wound soon!"

"Damn, that's dope, Ry! Talk about stepping up!!"

"I guess I am, huh? Chelsea, get ready. I'm about to lift you off the ground!"

"Okay; do it."

With one grunt and a bench press, Chelsea was hoisted up onto the back of Riley, the position resembling a soldier carrying a comrade.

"WHAT DA HELL?! IT HAS 'EM! IN ITS UNGODLY WIDE MOUTH!!"

Once the shouted words left Tamika's lips, Riley and Chelsea saw what she was talking about as their jaws dropped.

The monstrous unknown had snatched up the human oddity as its weak, vulnerable prey. In a wild display of unmatched power, it effortlessly chucked them out of its enlarged trap and high into the polluted air. The conjoined twins were in full flight now, appearing as some sort of soaring figurine to the aghast girls looking on.

Before the temporarily paralyzed teens could even process what they'd seen, the naturally mute human oddity had disappeared up and away into the contaminated heavens above.

Over a bed of roars and wreckage, Riley gripped her baseball bat tightly with just her right hand—as her left was already holding a weeping Chelsea—and heaved out a prolonged sigh. "I swear…this **has** to be some kind of alien invasion."

Chelsea continued to cry, sniffing through her words. "Whatever it is, we *need* to leave—like RIGHT now!!"

"Don't have ta tell me twice," Tamika said as she started to sprint.

Registering a piddling nod to show allegiance, Riley took off much like a horse in the Kentucky Derby as she handed Chelsea, who clung to her back for dear life, the beloved baseball bat for safekeeping. The three girls galloped as one in a frantic stride, running faster than they had ever run in their young lives. But the monstrous unknown spotted the terrified trifecta. Setting its sights on them with another bloodcurdling bellow and a final, thorough penetration of the mannequin house, it then drifted toward their nearby coordinates with a calculated menace.

Search Party #2: Johnny & Lizzie

Oh shit; she knows who I am? How's that even possible?!

"Whaddya mean, Lizzie? Stop being weird."

The headstrong teen laughed. "I'm not being weird. The jig is up...I **know** who you are, Johnny. You're the one who changed everything for me, for my parents, and most importantly—as well as most tragically—for my once-innocent sister."

Johnny acted indifferent and uninformed. "Look, kiddo. I haven't a clue as to what you're referring to, but I don't appreciate the accusatory tone. Not one bit. But I'll let it slide, since you must have me confused with some other guy. I've never done anything wrong to you OR your family."

Lies. All lies. You've committed so many misdeeds...who are you fooling?

"Enough. When you first came onto the bus, I thought you looked familiar; I just didn't wanna say anything until I was completely sure of it. But then you said your name and it clicked. Ten years is a long while, and you've aged a *lot* in that time."

"Gee, thanks!" Johnny spat back, offended.

"Stop pretending like you don't know what I'm talking about."

Play it cool and keep your composure...

"Honest to God, I don't."

"YES, YOU DO!!" Lizzie yelled with an ignited passion.

"Believe me, I'd truly *love* to know what or who has gotten you so wound up! But I'm not privy to it..."

"You babysat my sister. I was five years old, already in bed. And you...*you bastard*, you took advantage of her, got her drunk, and then had sex with her while she was passed out. You ruined her whole life—and pretty much mine, too!"

So that's why Lizzie reminded me so much of Markéta when I first saw her! They're related. Of course they are; the resemblance is uncanny...

Johnny decided to come clean with the emotionally charged teen. "Lizzie, listen. Ah, where to even *begin* with this? Okay." The freed prisoner took in a huge breath, letting it out slowly before speaking again. "I didn't mean to ruin anyone's life—especially your sister's.

And I didn't take advantage of her. She had asked me to be her first! Now I know that you don't wa—"

"Are you kidding me?! So lemme get this right, Johnny…by your insane logic, it was HER fault that you molested her while she was unconscious??"

You'd hate me all the more if ya knew that I drugged her drink as well, but that's neither here nor there! No one knows about that, and no one ever will. Only me.

"You don't know how it all happened. It's complicated to try and explain this to you, but we got along great that night. We gelled well. And yeah—all right, guilty as charged—I shouldn't have allowed her to drink so many of those ciders, but I felt bad for your sister! She was bummed she couldn't go to a party, some stupid thing where her crush was gonna be!"

"So you thought it was okay to have sex with her—an underage girl? Because you guys were just getting along *so* great?? You're messed up, Johnny. I didn't want to tell the other girls who you really were, since it may have caused a panic…"

"Man, I gotta say that I *did* notice how direct you were being with me at times!"

"You're lucky I haven't stabbed you in the heart yet," Lizzie grumbled, staring into his eyes with hatred.

"Why would you wanna do something like that?"

"WHAT?! 'Cause you're *dangerous*, that's why! You're a genuine sex offender, and forgive me for forgetting…also an attempted *murderer* who altered my entire family a decade ago!! By the way, I've always wondered, were there any others?"

"Others?!"

"Yeah, other *girls*. Were there others you messed with?"

Johnny shook his head in agitation. "*No*; no others at all, I swear. Just your sister; that's it. And I've served my time for it—some **very** hard time, I'll have you know. Due to my foolish actions, unspeakable things were put upon—and into—me within those walls. Vile, disgusting things that'd make you shudder. All just to *survive*. So, the way I look at it? I've paid the price for my two transgressions, PLUS INTEREST!"

"Foolish? That's how you're going to describe it; that's how you're gonna write it all off?" the teen asked breathlessly.

"Damn right I am. Truth be told, they were just two stupid mistakes on my part; I should've had better judgment at the time, but they're definitely not the worst things a person could ever do in this world! There are FAR more devious people out there! And I've seen a lot of them personally while incarcerated!!"

"You're actually justifying all of it in your head right now—right in front of me. Wow! I cannot believe this! Johnny, not only did you steal my sister's virginity much too early, you almost killed my dad! He was never the same after the two of you got into that near-fatal scuffle. And he never came back to be a father to me—or to my big sister. Nor a husband to my mom. They *both* quit on us; we were left in the dust. And it's all because of YOU!"

The freed prisoner rolled his eyes at such a pointed allegation. "At least you're lucky ya didn't have to see your dad put beatdowns on your mom like I did when I was a kid. And how's that even remotely my fault that your parents split?! I'd like to hear your reasoning!"

Appalled and astonished, Lizzie's jaw slunk. "You're subhuman, Helks. Are you so in denial that you can't see what you've done?"

Shut up, you bitch. You're no better than me.

"Listen…again, like I said to you a minute ago, I've paid for the past. I can't ever get that precious time of mine back—it's gone. Don't you understand that?"

"I do," the girl admitted softly. "But that doesn't take away from the fact that you've created so much destruction. **So much.**"

"Well, there's a *whole* lot more of it to go around now, isn't there? Like this dead zone, for example!" Johnny gestured to each and every corner of destruction. "Broken-down cars, no gas and no keys, all the burnt bodies…that's what we need to be focusing on—our predicament! I'm the *least* of your worries."

"What you did may have nothing to do with this, but you're almost as terrible as all of the death and famine in front of us!"

I wouldn't go that far. Something fishy is going on. Should I tell her about what recently happened to me?

Overcome with what had occurred inside his prison's walls, Johnny decided to reveal the truth to Lizzie. "Not so fast, my friend. There's some bizarre crap that I have to tell ya."

"Lemme make somethin' real clear here, Johnny. I'm not your friend in this predicament…and I'm certainly not gonna stan—"

The sweaty convict interrupted the impatient teen. "Before you go on the warpath yet again, just let me explain what kind of craziness went down on my side prior to running into you girls."

Lizzie sighed in such a way that signaled she wanted to know more but wouldn't admit her curiosity. "Go ahead, then. But don't lie this time—like you did with that overbearingly stupid car crash story."

"You didn't buy it? Not even for a second?"

"Not even for a second," the annoyed teen repeated. "Tell me what *really* happened. How'd you break outta prison?"

Time to let it all hang out…and not how you actually want to, either. Pervert.

"You might not believe it. It's an insane tale, but from what we've seen already to what you girls have gone through, I'm confident that my personal struggle is mere child's play."

"Lay it on me! I'm waiting. AGAIN!!" Lizzie said in frustration.

Johnny ignored her eagerness. "I guess the best place to start is at the beginning."

"Yeah, you think?!"

The freed prisoner recounted the events that had led him to the outside world. "I awoke in my cell suddenly, all because of this massive explosion startling me out of a sound sleep. When I came to, I realized that no one else was around. It was weird, ya know? Absolutely no other prisoners or guards were in the penitentiary. It was silent. It had me wondering if I was dead or something!"

"And perhaps you are; perhaps we *all* are…"

"So there I was," Johnny said, disregarding her two cents, "in a cold cell, freaked out to the fullest. I decided to try and escape after going delirious for a little while. But this is where it gets weirder…the door to my cell was unlocked! Straight up. The entire time, too. I accidentally discovered that when I placed my hand on the bars for balance."

"What the hell? You're right; that is crazy weird. So what'd you do?"

"What do you think, Einstein? I left my dingy cell, obviously!"

Lizzie shot Johnny a mean look. "Don't get snippy with me. I'm well aware that you left…I just wanna know how long you stayed in there—in the prison, I mean—and if you found anything compelling while looking around…like maybe some bodies of your cellmates?"

"I didn't find anything like that at all. Nothing. Every cell I checked was empty."

"That's…mysterious," the teen trailed off. "And it sounds made up."

"You don't have to believe what I'm saying, but it's the truth," Johnny snapped back. "I wouldn't make up something like this. Hell, I'm not bright enough to!"

"You seemed to have no problem concocting that ridiculous story about an imaginary wife."

"Just an on-the-fly imagination at work there; but honestly…that story of mine is no match for what I'm about to tell you. What happened in that prison's elaborate—way more elaborate than that one about the random person in the road. And it's *real*."

"It's not easy believing you, but go on…I'll try to keep an open mind."

"Thanks a ton," Johnny snarled.

"Proceed," Lizzie ordered.

"So…footnotes: no one around, and everywhere I looked? Completely empty. But some strange sounds started to pop off."

"Strange sounds?" the eyebrow-raising girl reiterated.

"Yes, strange sounds…"

Lizzie peered into Johnny's eyes suspiciously. "Continue."

"The pounding sounds kept happening—almost like those creepy crashes were meant to do one thing and one thing only: lure me right into a trap. And that's *exactly* what it was and what it successfully did!"

"Um, what do ya mean? What trap were you lured into??"

"There was a door, and somebody—or so I thought—was pounding on it from the other side. I consider myself to be mostly fearless, especially these days, but I was legitimately drenched in dread as I walked up to that door."

"Did some guy come sprawling out at you?!" Lizzie implored.

"Not exactly. But close. You're not that far off."

"UGH! TELL ME ALREADY!" the headstrong teen shrieked.

Johnny paused for a long moment, shaken from recalling the traumatic event. "When I opened the door, there was just a huge boombox on the ground. As strange as that sounds, that's what was there—the sound of knocks played through its speakers."

"Whoa…that's the weirdest thing I've ever heard."

"It was the weirdest thing I've ever experienced…and then somebody apprehended me from behind and plunged a needle into my neck!"

"Okay; come on, now! That did NOT happen."

"Oh no? You don't think so? Look at this," Johnny said, turning his neck to the left to unveil an injection mark.

"Why would someone wanna do that to you?"

"Beats me. I've been wondering constantly. Can't figure it out."

Lizzie nodded. "And where did all the other prisoners go?"

"The prison was spotless—it's like they were never even there to begin with. I don't understand it still…it's…I don't even know!"

"What happened after you got poked?"

"I woke up again—all alone like the last time. Only this time, I found myself at the front gate of the slammer. Freedom right at my fingertips."

"Shit…" the befuddled girl eked out.

Dammit; I forgot to mention being splashed in the face and the notebook in the hallway! Maybe I'll just keep that crap to myself. If I add things in now, she'll definitely think it's all made up.

"Yeah, *shit* is right!" Johnny exclaimed. "What do you think was going through my mind?"

"Can't even imagine," Lizzie said. "But I'm not sure I believe this."

"You can doubt what I've told you, but it is the truth. Besides, I really don't have the creativity to make up something like this. I'm no expert storyteller…no master at spinning a yarn. I'm no Stephen King…"

"Actually, your story *does* sound like something he'd write."

"Well, then…if we ever get outta this mess, I'll try to pitch this to him," Johnny joked, smiling.

"Dude's like eighty, though. Probably can't even think clearly nowadays. And by the way, you aren't going to get out of this—I won't let you. You'll have to kill me to physically get away. Seriously."

"Maybe I'll just have to do that," he said casually. "I have a gun on me, so don't you get any wild ideas."

"I don't see it. Show me the piece," Lizzie demanded.

"It's in my burlap sack," Johnny replied, tapping the bag slung over his right shoulder. "And I don't want to use it—'specially on a pretty girl like you. But I will if I *have* to…so don't test the waters!"

"I've got my eye on you."

"Like your sister did ten years ago?"

"You think this is all a joke, don't ya?! What you've done has had permanent repercussions. And for that, you deserve to go down."

"Whatever! You need me and you *know* it. I saved you and the others aboard that bullet-ridden bus; it'd be foolish for you to try and take me out in this perilous environment…I'm the **muscle** of this ragtag group!"

"We could fend for ourselves," Lizzie stated matter-of-factly.

"Could you really?"

"Yes, really."

"Well, I don't believe that to be true, so excuse me for thinking that I'm quite *valuable*," Johnny said.

"You're quite *unstable* is what you are."

"Hey, now; if it weren't for me bailing your butts outta that disturbing situation, I'm sure you'd all still be tied up…cryin' for your mamas!"

"And that right there is the only reason why I haven't tried to murder you yet, Johnny. You did save us, that much is true; but that's where it stops for me. I know the other girls aren't aware of who they're dealing with, but that's why I'm here—I plan on using you for your strength when needed to get around this wasteland. Then, when the timing's right, I'm gonna strike."

"You're bluffing. A cutesy teen like you doesn't have what it takes to get the job done. Hell, I bet you've never even gotten into a fight in all your life!"

A faint patch of roaring, along with the sound of some tearing architecture from afar, was heard in the background—and it was loud enough to be acknowledged and discussed.

"Did you hear that, too?" Lizzie asked a glancing-around Johnny.

"I heard it. And I hope to God that it isn't that *thing* again!"

"Me either. I've had enough surprises for the day. Plenty of them."

"Like I haven't?"

Really hope we don't get eaten. I just got outta prison, for God's sake!

After a few moments of their undivided attention, Johnny and Lizzie went on with their previous bickering back and forth, as no following roars were heard.

"Anyway, so about me being in an actual fight—yeah, perhaps I haven't been in one. But that doesn't mean I'll back down from seizing an opportunity…"

Johnny approached her with an aggression that she hadn't seen from him previously. His stern face was just inches away from hers. "Do you honestly think that *I'm* gonna back down from some prissy teen threatening me?"

This drastic change in Johnny's tone and stance threw Lizzie off, leaving her fumbling for words. "I—I don't think that you—"

"Just shut up! I don't even wanna hear it. Your babbling makes me SICK. You cannot possibly grasp what I've been through in prison for the last decade. I've been shanked, sodomized, beaten to a bloody pulp—among so many other things that could twist and turn your flat-as-a-board stomach into knots. So, whatever it is you may or may not have planned for me would be an *appetizer* to the entrée I've already had shoved down my damned throat."

Lizzie stood in silence, face-to-face with the man who'd so wrongly abused her passed-out sister ten years prior.

"You gonna say anything?!" the freed prisoner growled.

"What's there to say?" the scared girl uttered weakly.

"That's what I thought, then…oh, and whenever you intend to come at me with violence, I'll be ready for it."

"Good to know. I'll keep that in mind."

"Wise decision," Johnny quipped.

Making another wise decision off the top of her head, Lizzie changed the hostile-based subject. "Aren't we supposed to be looking for supplies instead of what we've been doing? You know, try and retrieve water and things that'll allow us to live for now—so that we can try and kill each other later?"

The convict eyed the puke-colored sky, coughed a couple of times, and then laughed at the teen's clever—yet topical—deflection. "You've got some wit, kiddo. And you're also right. Water's crucial to our survival, but for the time being, I think we're going to be straight on that aspect of this apocalypse."

"Oh yeah? Did you see more bottled water lying around?"

"Uh, sure did! And do you know what I did when I came across it?"

"What's that?"

"I left it alone, that's what I did, by God! Figured someone else may wanna take it for their own survival in this thing!"

"Okay, I get it. That was a dumb question to ask," Lizzie admitted.

"It was," Johnny agreed. "That's why I had to razz you."

"Gimme some of that Fiji."

"A *please* would come in mighty handy along with that rude order of yours, you know…"

"All right; please! I'm super thirsty…it's hot as hell out here."

"Ask and you shall receive. Here ya are!" the thirty-nine-year-old offered, reaching into his backpack and handing the in-need teen a water.

"Ah, thank you so much," Lizzie said as she emptied an entire bottle into her gullet within seconds.

"Don't mention it! You really *were* thirsty."

"I still hate you, though…so don't think this is a truce or anything like that."

"Of course not; how could I? You wanna kill me! Mere water wouldn't make a difference with that, would it?"

"No, it wouldn't and it *doesn't*. Hey…check this pile out," the snooping girl directed, leaning down to wade through wreckage. "Cell phones! We could turn them on, see if any of 'em work."

"I suppose it's worth a shot. Go for it. Doing something like that hadn't even crossed my mind…"

"Probably because you've been locked away for a decade. I don't think the warden would've signed off on prisoners using smartphones."

"Ah, once more, you're bringing the wit—much like your sister did during that rainy night oh, so long ago."

Lizzie pushed him as she got up from a kneeling position. "Don't talk about my sister or about that horrible night in my presence ever again unless I ask you to."

"*Don't* push me," Johnny warned.

"You deserved it, asshole!!" the heated teen said.

"Just check the fucking phones to see if there's a signal."

"On it. Don't tell me what to do. I was the one who found 'em!"

The sixteen-year-old fiddled with each smartphone for a few vexing moments, throwing down several of the electronic devices that wouldn't respond to her rabid, button-pressing commands.

"No dice?" the freed prisoner queried as Lizzie continued to fixate on each screen she picked from the pile.

"No damn dice! There're only a few left to check, but none of these have even turned on—not for one stinking second have any of 'em come to life. This shit sucks!!"

Ooh, she's so cute when she gets mad.

"I'm sorry. At least you tried; that has to count for something."

Lizzie chuckled at his dry reply. "What does it count for? None of them freaking work, man!"

"Except for that one you just flipped on…" Johnny observed, pointing for added effect as she jerked her head back toward a glowing, booting screen.

"AH! AH!!" the ecstatic teenager croaked. "Finally, something going *right* for once!"

"Don't get too excited. It may die as quickly as it came alive."

"Don't jinx it!!" Lizzie shouted.

When the blonde girl homed in on the brightly lit screen, her expression went from anticipation to mystification. "What the hell?"

"What is it?"

No response—just more staring into the phone with a look of consternation.

"HELLO, LIZZIE?!" Johnny pressed.

"This phone's wallpaper—the picture that's set on the homepage is that…that—" the confused teen stopped short, choosing to show instead of tell. "It's the bus."

The freed prisoner scoffed with skepticism, even as he surveyed the stumper of a pic. "No, it's not!"

"Dude, it is…*look* at it, the bullet holes…the broken-down couple of cars around it—it's the **exact** same bus we were in."

"But why in the world would someone make that a wallpaper??"

"To fuck with us, that's why. And they knew we'd come across it! None of this is a coincidence. You think we've been paired up randomly?"

Johnny groaned. "Man alive, this is hurting my brain badly—more and more as it goes along, in fact."

"'Course it says that it has no service. Oh, and just 2% battery left."

"Check to see if there are any text messages or emails—ANYTHING that could be useful. Maybe there's some clue on that thing!"

Lizzie checked the smartphone diligently for a minute. "Nope, there's *nothing*. Everything's been deleted, it seems—all cleared away."

"Nothing more? For real?"

"For real; that's it. What *is* this?" Lizzie asked out loud.

"Doesn't make any sense…how would they even know that we'd be observant enough to discover this phone?!"

"They wouldn't, really. Its purpose is for us to find and then get spooked from it, regardless of whether it works or not. I bet all these phones had the same wallpaper, and I bet there's a bunch of other weird crap awaiting us in this hellhole—it's all designed to fuck with us. That much is obvious."

"Even if that's the case, why? Why go to these lengths?!"

"How should I know, Johnny? I'm just as in the dark as you are!"

"I know you are; I know. Man…I almost wish I were back in my cell."

"Really?" Lizzie asked, somewhat shocked.

"At least I had a good enough idea of what to expect in there. Out here? I have no idea what's gonna happen next."

The blonde teen opened her mouth to say something but was interrupted by a herd of footsteps coming their way.

To the right of Johnny, a distraught-looking Chelsea, Riley, and Tamika appeared. All three girls were panting and gasping for air, as though they'd just participated in a 100-yard dash.

Riley tried to speak first over the loud heaving and hoeing within her party. While the wind had been taken out of her sails, the pale-faced teen mustered up some words. "That thing…we saw it…it's *massive*! It's the size of an imperial ship, I swear…and—"

"Slow your roll…you said you saw the *thing*? What thing? Are you talking about whatever it was that was hitting our bus??"

"YES! THAT THING!! WHAT THING DID YA THINK I WAS REFERRING TO?!" Riley shouted.

"All right; calm yourself. I was just making sure I knew what you were going on about. What is it??" Lizzie inquired excitedly.

"It's…I dunno how to describe it—to do it justice. Tam? You wanna take this while I catch my breath? Hauling Chelsea on my back was exhausting!"

"Absolutely, Ry."

"Thanks. Big ups…" Riley panted, raising her hand from her waist to pound knuckles with Tamika. "I need a few moments."

"So, Johnny…you know dat *LOST* show you like n' shit?"

"Uh, yeah; what about it?!" the freed prisoner asked in confusion.

"Da thing we laid eyes upon was a lot like dat Smoke Monster…except it wasn't a weak-ass whisk of black smoke…it was—"

Chelsea interjected. "You mean it wasn't a *wisp* of black smoke…"

"Yeah, that's what I was sayin', Chels! So anyway…it's like dat thing, except dis thing is like…*way* bigger n'…what's da word I'm lookin' fo'?" Tamika paused, deep in thought.

Riley recovered enough to contribute. "It's tangible, basically—looks like something you can actually touch. Unlike Smoky himself, there's a true body to it, a slimy-looking body. Black and alien-like."

"And it had TEETH, huge and horrible chompers!!" Chelsea added.

"What did it do? Were you able to see it do anything?"

"Oh…nothing too much, Johnny," Riley said calmly. "Just saw the scary monstrosity ravage its way through a house we were in mere seconds before destroying the foundation of it!"

"*Wow*," Lizzie blurted. "Chelsea…you okay?! Why're you holding a Louisville Slugger? And why does it look like you're bleeding through your shirt??"

"That's old blood. A flesh wound from falling on debris…I thought it was a lot worse than what it was! Here's the bat back, Riley." The tween tossed it over to her. "That's not mine; it's Ry's! She bandaged me up nicely with gauze after we stopped running. Discovered a fresh first aid kit and found that bat before things got crazy. But anyway, there were these freaky mannequins inside the home we looked in….and a freaky message above them! And some glass shattering led us there and we—"

"Whoa! Slow it down; tell us everything that happened to you guys from the very beginning. We have time to listen," Johnny said.

"If that thing's still on the prowl, I'm not so sure of that! It stopped chasing us after a while, almost like it was toying with us. But I wouldn't assume we're out of harm's way just yet."

"Smart girl you are, Ry…"

"Thank you, Tam."

"Hold on!" Lizzie yowled.

"What?!" Chelsea asked, surprised by her outburst.

"Where're those attached girls?" the headstrong teen questioned.

"That was the *craziest* part! That…enormous thing…took them in its wide-as-a-car mouth and chucked 'em straight up into the air like it was NOTHING!" Riley revealed, breathing with difficulty.

"Holy shit," Johnny whispered.

"*Holy shit fo' show*…da human oddity? She no mo," Tamika said.

"Number five's no longer alive," Riley confirmed.

"Tell us every single thing that happened," Lizzie insisted. "But before you do, let's head over to that beer billboard in the shrouded tree line. If we're gonna recap, we should be in hiding while we're at it."

"Safety first, right?"

Johnny nodded. "That's right, Ry…"

Imaginations were running wild as they walked toward a temporary concealment, and the worried group of five pushed onward in a depressed suppression—as their feet did all the talking.

A Billboard Blitz

With tall-to-taller trees concealing their whereabouts among a progressively dire landscape, Johnny and his clique of chicks sat Indian-style on a patch of unaltered ground. Sharing strands of small talk to pass the time and sipping water conservatively, they all wore a weathered look on their faces as the day gradually receded into dusk.

The freed prisoner looked up to the impure atmosphere in what must have been his thousandth gaze above with a wheeze and a lamentation. "We should get going soon. I don't think that ungodly monster's around anymore. Haven't heard its roar, so we're probably safe to trek about now."

"How do we know, though? *Whatever* that thing is, it's not dumb by any measure. It had deliberate movements in its attacks on that mannequin house and on the attached sisters—rest in peace, by the way. And it could EASILY have killed us if it wanted to."

"Yeah, totally! Ry's right; I thought we were toast. Then it just stopped chasing us all of a sudden…like it was called off of the hunt or something!" Chelsea said. "Maybe we should stay put for a while longer. You know, to remain unnoticed by anyone who could be prowling the area. We don't really know what we've been pitted against."

Lizzie pressed her hands on the freshly cut grass she had made into a seat for herself and rose up like only a spry teenager could. "What's the better idea, then? Stay here like a bunch of idiots? This air is tainted; the conditions out here aren't good at all. So if any of you care to know—*I* think we've got to find shelter before nightfall."

"If ya Ashley saw the thang we saw, you'd have a much different take…BET!" Tamika assured the blonde with a bevy of confidence.

"Did you just say Ashley instead of actual—you know what? Never mind. I should be used to it by this point," Riley muttered.

"There she go again! Always gotta put me on blast!! Sorry I don't speak all smart like you!"

"Girls, *girls*, **girls**…enough of this garbage. It doesn't get you—or us—anywhere. Lizzie's got the right idea. We should find a place to crash, as it's getting darker by the minute."

"Thank you for siding with me, Johnny."

That's it. Keep sucking up to her…she's bound to come around…

"You're very welcome, Lizzie!"

"Why we still here, anyway?? Let's bounce, bitches!"

Chelsea *tsk-tsked* at Tamika's colorful language. "Do you sincerely need to talk like that? It's not ladylike."

"Well, do you need ta talk like a stuck-up librarian? 'Cause to me, it ain't dat ladylike, either!"

"WHAT DID I JUST SAY, YOU TWO? STOP!!" Johnny screamed.

The four girls appeared shaken until Lizzie, being the least rattled of the group, eased the tension by coolly directing traffic elsewhere. "Okay. Let's collect ourselves for a moment. We're all on pins and needles; I get it. I get Johnny's outta-nowhere loss of control there, but we must calm down and head out. Like *now*."

"Agreed," Riley added promptly, rising up from the ground with the others. "This isn't a home any way you slice it. Chelsea…Tamika…you saw what that hideous thing did to the freaky-weird house…so imagine what it'd do to us with only these trees as our bodyguards."

"Don't have ta tell us again; we *know*. We seen dat nasty-ass thang…n' too much of it. Up close n' purse. And I show ain't down fo' seein' it one mo time, 'cause it'd be our LAST time breathin'!"

God in heaven, this chick's unbearable…whose idea was it to kidnap a wannabe thug like her in the first place? I'm ready to throttle her throat!

"Tamisha, I think y—"

"Say WHAT, my Caucasian?! My name ain't no **Tamisha**; it's *Tamika*, ya fucka!"

Perhaps it's a good thing the world's on its deathbed, because I don't think this unruly girl would've gotten that far in a civilized one—she either would've had to dabble in some drug-dealing, rapping, full-time prostitution—or all of the above.

"Sorry about that slight slip there, TAMIKA. I'll be sure to never confuse your name again," Johnny said insincerely.

"DANK YOU!" she hollered with ignorance.

As they began to tread through the forest of trees, there was a conspicuous rustling ahead, and the pattering about caused some concern.

Lizzie put her index finger up to her lips, signaling the group much like a natural-born leader would. "Don't move."

The other three girls obliged, but Johnny folded his arms rebelliously. "C'mon; it's probably just a deer frolicking around…" he semi-whispered. "Right?"

"*Wrong!*" a male's voice boomed from behind them.

Johnny and the girls turned to face the man who had sent chills up their spine.

"Easy, now; don't any of you try to be heroic here." The muscular man walked toward them as he smirked, his hands on a Glock. "We don't want no trouble—let me say that up front."

"Who's *we?*" Lizzie asked boldly. "And what DO you want?"

The man with a perfect five-o'clock shadow continued smirking, undaunted by the tense situation. "*We* is me…and my buddy in the bushes." He pointed to his left. "Greg, come on out!"

Another male appeared moments later, sifting his way through the rustled area. "How's it going, guys?" the lackey inquired flatly, smiling as big as the other man had been.

Tamika scrunched her face. "Da fuck is dis shit?"

The ringleader laughed. "Quite a mouth on this one!"

"I like it; I like it a lot. She should be the girl we take," the scruffy-looking male supposedly named Greg said. "Whaddaya say, Boss?"

"Neither of you are taking any one of us *anywhere,*" Johnny stated. "Not without a fight, you aren't."

Boss scoffed at the courageous speak. "We've got you outnumbered."

"No, you don't! There are five of us and only two of you!" Chelsea squawked hastily.

"Chels, shut up! Just shut up…" Riley insisted.

"Your friend's wise!" Greg said to Chelsea.

Lizzie stepped forward. "What's this all about? Have you guys come to poach our stuff? Is that it? We don't have much, really, but if we give ya everything we've got, will you go away? It's already awful out here. Let's try and be civil. Nobody needs to get hurt."

"But that's the thing, though; we don't want anything you have on you—we want *you*." The man known simply as Boss stuck his right hand out, bouncing his finger to each girl in the group as gray ash from a Cuban cigar he'd randomly began puffing fell to the ground beside their feet.

Johnny pushed Boss back, surprising the teens—and even himself. "I will NOT let you take any of these girls. Do you understand that? You'll have to fucking kill me to get one of them!"

"That can be arranged," Boss answered coolly. "Greg, this is getting boring; the macho grandstanding of this guy is nauseating. Take a girl—the black one!"

"Like hell you will!!" Tamika shouted as his henchman grabbed her.

"GET YOUR DAMN HANDS OFF OF HER!" Riley shouted even louder.

Chelsea cried like a baby, cupping her hands to her mouth as she pleaded to the two rogue strangers. "Stop! Just stop!! *Please…*"

"You muhfucka, get off me!" Tamika whined while thrashing her body every which way, looking for an escape route.

Sickened at the sight of this unkempt man imposing his will on the struggling teen, Lizzie charged the lackey.

Whoa…that's one fearless girl, Johnny thought.

Jumping onto his backside and tearing at his face like a girl possessed, Lizzie gave it her all. But Greg shoved her off, flicking her to the ground like a grody bug.

The headstrong teen then cowered on her hands and knees, nursing her tailbone as she moved in reverse.

That didn't work out so well for Liz. I should do something, and I should do it fast. WAIT. The gun. I've got it in my backpack. Of course!

Boss kept taking puffs of his cigar and tapping his firearm on his hip merrily, unaffected by the scuffle happening right in front of him. "Hoo boy, we got ourselves a live wire! Better stick the black beaut quick!!"

Upon hearing the suggestion of his superior, Greg reached into his pocket and pulled out a hospital-grade needle.

"What are you doing?!" Lizzie asked, bewildered.

Tamika continued to thrash around in Greg's arms, begging and yelling for mercy. But it was to no avail. The needle plunged into her neck—paralyzing the teen almost instantly.

"NO!!" Chelsea and Riley wailed at the same time.

I'm not going to let this stand. Fuck this.

Johnny unzipped his backpack and hoisted his own gun out, pointing it directly at Boss, then at Greg—who stood above a lifeless Tamika with pride, as if he'd just bagged a buck. Columns of thick smoke and pollution wafted across the darkening atmosphere. As everyone paused in place for a short moment, the only thing breaking the standstill silence was the swaying of the trees in a fiery breeze.

"Don't make me shoot you. 'Cause I will. I'll blow both your heads clean off your shoulders," the freed prisoner said.

"I don't believe that that's even possible, Mr. Helks…" Boss dropped his Cuban on the ground, grinding it into the grass with his steel-toed boot.

"Come again??" Johnny asked.

No answer. Only a yearbook smile to go with a cold-blooded stare.

Riley cleared her throat, tending to Lizzie on bended knee. "Hey, how do you know his last name?"

"You know something, little girl, I don't much care for your interrogative question. And come ta think of it, you're quite the looker. Almost like a young Rose McGowan—back when she was in *Scream*. I didn't notice it before…what with all that unbecoming fear etched on your face."

"Go fuck yourself, creepazoid."

"I'd prefer for **you** to do the fucking instead!" Boss said with a glower.

Okay, it's getting uglier now. Better step in…

"Why don't you let me do the talking, Riley? Just keep quiet and get behind me. I'm the one with the gun!"

"Yeah, that's right! He is!! So why don't you guys just back off, okay? Why don't we ALL back off and go our separate ways," Chelsea tested.

"That was never in the cards, sweetheart—and it certainly isn't going to be considered now!" Greg stated.

Johnny spit on the soil, his eyes locked and his gun cocked right on the forehead of his newfangled enemy. "Boss, is it? Am I right?"

"That's right," the well-built man answered cavalierly.

"If you don't walk away from this, I swear to you and your whore of a mother that I'll pull the trigger."

"Johnny boy, it's useless. And besides that important tidbit, it's not really smart to reply like that in such a heated standoff—such a pressure-cooker situation. Mom jokes? Should I stoop to that level as well and start slagging on your enabling mommy? Come on; you can do better than that, can't you?! I expected more…"

The freed prisoner didn't know how to respond. His grip on the firearm loosened as a mounting anxiety and fear began to shoot through his thumping heart and sweaty palms.

"What…got nothing to say? Man, I expected a *lot* more out of the INFAMOUS JOHNNY HELKS!" Boss suddenly screamed, holding his gun steadily on the balding convict. "I'm kinda disappointed."

"How the hell do you seem to know who I am?" Johnny asked.

"Now, if I told you all of that, it'd ruin the mystery, wouldn't it?"

Greg laughed like some scary clown at a kid's birthday party. "And everyone just *loves* a surprise!"

"In about two seconds, I'm pulling this trigger—unless you talk."

"Go on ahead. Make my day, big shot…" Boss permitted.

The three girls cowered behind Johnny while Tamika lay motionless at the feet of a smiling, taunting Greg.

It's hard to decipher if she's dead or alive in this chaos.

"DO IT, PUSSY! SHOOT US WHERE WE STAND!!"

Without another second of hesitation, Johnny fired.

After the gun recoiled and everything went breathtakingly still for one moment, Boss clapped in an annoyingly enthusiastic manner—coming off as more of a distracting theatergoer than an imposing mastermind to Johnny and the addled teens.

"Blanks, bitch!" Greg informed the confused group.

Boss proceeded to rub even more salt on the wound. "Correctamundo. You didn't think I'd just *allow* you to shoot me in the face, did you? How dumb do ya think I am? Or better yet, how dumb do ya think *you* are, Johnny? I'd imagine you feel pretty stupid in this moment."

"Why…why's this rigged? I don't understand."

"Oh, but you're not supposed to! You're the mark. It's for you to figure out and us to savor as things escalate," Boss boasted.

"Tell me what this all means. Right fuckin' now!"

"You're not in a position to be so demanding, jailbird!" Greg said.

"Jailbird??" Chelsea echoed the cocky lackey, stupefied by his choice of words.

Suddenly Riley ran toward Boss with her Slugger. "I'm gonna knock your block off!"

The brunette took a home run-worthy shot at the supposed man in charge, but Boss ducked the frenzied swing efficiently and strong-armed her down to the ground with just his right hand.

He then stared at the teen struggling to get back to her feet. "An admirable effort, Riley. *Really.*"

"HOW DO YOU KNOW MY NAME, TOO, YOU BARBARIAN?!"

Boss ignored Riley's scream for clarity. "Let it be known to this new world we live in: I didn't think that *any* of you girls would try to put up much of a fight. But you've proven me wrong. Hats off to the spunk; I respect it!"

"You crazy asshole," Riley said, clawing her way up to a standing position. "I won't miss on my next try."

"Don't! He'll kill you!!" Chelsea warned, hiding behind Johnny like a traumatized toddler.

What can I do here? My hands are tied. They've got us beat.

"Greg…I'd love to keep this going, but we've got a schedule to adhere to. You know what I'm talking about. Still lots of things to take care of."

"I'm aware of what's upcoming, Boss! Want me to subdue her like I did the black one?"

"It's like ya read my mind…"

Lizzie let out a guttural growl. "You're NOT taking her **or** Tamika!"

"Keep your mouth shut, blondie. Or else I'll open it for you…and you won't like what I'd *attempt* to put in it. Mm, well—maybe you would, actually. Are you into older men at all…like your sister was?"

"Fuck you!" she shouted.

How does he know about that?! Johnny thought, reeling from within.

For a second unexpected go-round, Riley stormed Boss with the bat and swung for the fences yet again.

Another wild swing and an even wilder miss.

An extra hard shove later and the persistent girl was square on her back, dazed and seeing stars.

"Stick her! I'm done with this impolite aggression!!"

"You got it, Boss," Greg obeyed as he lunged toward Riley. "One needle to the neck comin' right up!"

Who are these lunatics? Why're we in this hell?? Don't think; just do something about it. But I can't! I'm scared, so, so scared. Daddy doesn't like violence! He only likes when HE does it. My daddy isn—

"Do something! Stop them!!" Chelsea interrupted Johnny's inner-thought turmoil, tugging at his dirty white tee.

Boss pointed his finger in the most menacing way a human possibly could. "Don't you even **think** about it, Johnny boy. Unlike your limp-dick peashooter, I've got live ammunition in this here gun. And those bum knees of yours won't hold up if you decide to run toward me. So, I'd *strongly* advise you—and the two of you girls—to back the fuck up!"

"STOP THIS SHIT!!" Johnny yelled passionately, yet not moving an inch to protest since his knees still bothered him.

"Can't in good faith. The show must go on, my demented friend. GREG! Stick her already!!"

"Trying! She's a wiggly little worm, Boss!!" the lackey replied.

"No, no, no…" Chelsea whimpered, helpless and shaky.

Lizzie winced in pain as she crawled her way to safety. "Johnny? Try to do something; fix this…we can't lose them. We just…*can't*…they were on the bus with me and Chelsea. Please, man up for once in your life!"

In front of the pleading girls and a stoically silent Johnny, Riley squirmed in the arms of Greg, fighting with all she had to avoid the needle pricking her neck.

But the struggle against the brute of a stranger was too exhausting for her to keep up with…and after one misstep, the pale-faced teen was put on dream street.

"That's two down, baby! Anybody else wanna take a crack at me?" Boss challenged.

"Oh my God, oh my God," Chelsea kept repeating in shock.

"JOHNNY! FUCKING DO SOMETHING!" Lizzie ordered.

"I can't do *anything*, okay!! My knees are damn near shot and this whole thing is fucked. It's completely FUCKED!!"

"Cannot believe this; it's like you're no good now…" Lizzie said.

"Excuse me? What'd you say?!"

"I **said** it's like you're no good; no good for no one!"

Johnny changed entirely, switching personalities at the drop of a hat. "I am *too* good, Daddy. I'M A GOOD BOY! *You're* the one who's no good for no one now! And Mommy hates you—she's just too afraid to admit it!!"

Concerned by the swift changing of the guard, Boss and Greg looked at each other and then toward the nutso situation unfolding before their worry-laced eyes.

Johnny was, by all accounts from the onlookers, not himself.

"What is wrong with you, Johnny? You're *scaring* me…" Lizzie confessed.

"And me as well!!" Chelsea added bravely.

"I'M JUST SICK 'N TIRED OF ALWAYS GETTIN' BLAMED FOR EVERYTHING! I AM A GOOD KID! I CLEAN MY ROOM; I GET GOOD GRADES! I—I'M MAD, DADDY! MAD THAT YOU'RE STILL SO MEAN TO ME AND MOMMY!!"

"Dude," the blonde muttered. "What's happening here?"

Johnny seized the shoulders of Lizzie and shook her like a salt shaker. "YOU AREN'T EVEN LISTENING TO ME! WHY WON'T YOU EVER LISTEN?!"

"Please stop shaking her! This isn't like you!!" Chelsea squealed, poking the back of the freed prisoner as delicately as she could.

While Johnny disregarded the constant pleas to refrain from shaking Lizzie and instilling a vertigo overload into her petite, still-developing body, Boss fired off a couple of rounds up into the musky air. But it was of no use, as the shaking continued.

"He's lost it, man," Greg whispered in his superior's ear. "Any ideas?"

"Thinking! Don't hound me."

The lackey groaned. "I **told** you something like this could happen."

Boss brushed aside the backtalk of his accomplice. "I know what to do…without killing him."

"*Great.* Better do it fast, then!"

As Johnny incessantly scrambled Lizzie's brain, Boss speared him right in the ribs—sending him stumbling backward into a clearing, a good distance away from the startled Chelsea and the rattled Lizzie.

Johnny clutched his rib cage, apparently knocked back into a fractured adulthood instead of a blown-to-bits childhood. "Where am I? What's going on?!" were the only two questions the freed prisoner could prattle out before the butt-end of Boss's Glock met his temple.

The disheveled convict collapsed to the ground face-first, lifeless.

Boss turned his attention to the two conscious girls, making eye contact with the recently shaken Lizzie. "I'm *very* sorry we let it go that far. He's a dangerous person, and you shouldn't have had to experience his dissociative identity disorder live and direct like that."

"*He's* dangerous? What about you? What about your stooge?! He stuck a needle into both of our friends! They may be dead!!"

"Chelsea, I can assure you they're not dead. They'll be fine."

Lizzie screamed in frustration at the man's ambiguity. "How do you know her name, how do you know who Johnny is, and how do you know what happened to my sister?? Just what the FUCK'S going on here?!"

"I can't tell you, because I'd lose everything that I have ever worked for if I did. And so would he."

"Now I'm even more confused…" Chelsea sighed.

"Just go! Get out of here while you can, will ya…before the monster appears again," Greg cautioned.

"You know about that thing?" Lizzie asked with an apt investment.

The lackey laughed a tad. "How could we not? It's, like, the loudest entity anyone could possibly hear—or if you're unlucky enough, to see up close and personal."

Boss gave a throat-cutting signal to Greg. "Hush. We've said too much. Girls, like my thin-skinned partner here has said to you…just go."

"But what about Riley and Tamika? They're not mov—"

"Lizzie, GO NOW!" Boss yelled. "This zone isn't safe."

Chelsea got in front of the headstrong teen, looking the morose man right in the eye. "Promise me they're going to be okay and that they aren't dead."

"They really aren't dead, Chelsea. We *promise*." Greg looked directly in the worried tween's eyes with sincerity. "See, *we* aren't the bad guys in this—but that nutcase who's down on the ground, though? He most certainly is the bad one in this scenario."

"But why…**why** is Johnny bad?" the oblivious young girl asked.

"I'll tell you all about it, Chels. Let's just leave while we're able to."

"That'd be an intelligent decision," Boss said.

"You sure you want to trust these strangers, Lizzie?"

"Well, I know what Johnny's capable of. I'll tell you soon."

"Blah…all right. I'm not liking this, but I guess I'll blindly go with what you're saying," Chelsea grumbled.

"Thank you. Believe me, I know more about the guy than most…"

Boss nodded vehemently. "So we're good, then! Go find a safer section—and stay away from Johnny. We'll take care of the rest."

For a moment, Lizzie wanted to go against the grain and refuse to move, but she knew that it was best to fight another day.

The monster may be looming…

As Chelsea and Lizzie limped off, the headstrong teen couldn't help but look back in curiosity. And what she saw baffled her. Boss and Greg were placing the unresponsive bodies of Riley and Tamika onto separate blue tarps, covering their legs and torsos with wool blankets as though they were a pair of considerate EMTs.

"What…the…hell…" Lizzie whispered under distressed breath.

"What's wrong?"

"Nothing; nothing at all. Just keep walking."

Chelsea studied the blonde's face fixedly, becoming concerned all of a sudden. "You don't feel that yet?"

"Feel *what* yet?" the ticked off teenager snarled back.

"You're bleeding! Pretty profusely now, right from the nose. Could be the messed-up air!"

And the tween was right.

The spritzed sky had in fact been the culprit of Lizzie's crimson.

INSIDE: The Attackers

"If it's any consolation, I think you handled it well."

"I don't need any verbal consolation prize, Brent."

"Right. Man, that guy shouldn't be on the loose. He's an anomaly."

"We're too deep into the experiment."

"The powers that be have enough clout to stop it at any time."

"But they WON'T stop this; there's no reason to go down that road."

"Johnny's a danger to himself and to others, Simon."

"Don't you think I know that by now?!"

"You should've known that yesterday—when I pointed it out."

"God, it felt so *good* to whack him over the head with my gun."

"You just had to do it. He was gonna shake the life outta that girl."

"Sucks I let the cat out of the bag. An unusual moment of weakness shown there. I hate how I broke character."

"I disagree. I believe you kept it open-ended enough. While I see where you're coming from, they still have no clue as to who we are or what this is all about."

"True. I suppose it's not as terrible as I thought."

"Not at all. If I were you, I wouldn't even worry anymore. It didn't go as bad as it could have; he could've whipped out that knife instead of the gun."

"Or his dick!"

"Even scarier. Glad that didn't happen."

"Well…we haven't received any complaints from the brass yet. That's probably a good thing, yeah?"

"A very good thing, yes. I just don't know how long this'll go on for."

"They said to let it play out. Remember? No matter what."

"Oh yeah; I remember now. Sorry, it's easy to forget the four-one-one when you're in the trenches of this madness."

"Understandable. There's nothing quite like it, is there?"

"No, there's never been *anything* like this. Ever."

"How'd it go with the selected when they were dropped off?"

"All right, I guess. As I was leaving the post, they were coming to."

"Bet their grogginess hasn't gone away yet!"

"I can't help but feel like this entire project is morally wrong."

"And what if it is? Is that going to keep you from cashing the checks?"

"I'm risking my life here, Simon. I'd be a fool if I didn't cash them."

"Yes, you would. So what's the big deal, then? It's a job. That's all."

"With real stakes and real people, though."

"Ooh, you saying it like that makes it more exciting for me!"

"How do you not care about these teens? Are you *that* heartless?"

"Get over yourself, Gandhi. They're protected within this structure."

"Are you sure about that?"

"Completely. We've taken the necessary protocols. If that sick fuck puts his hands on them again, we will stop it."

"What if we aren't close by? What if they're in another jurisdiction?"

"You aren't seriously this stupid, are ya? There are other agents!!"

"Of course. How could I have let that slip my mind?"

"Because you're letting all this get to you; you're starting to think it's legit."

"It IS. You can't see that? Its realness—and the uncomfortable format of it—is the main reason why this is so revolutionary."

"I feel sorry for your brain, Brent. You're overworking it. Mine's already on a vacation; I'm just waiting for my body to catch up with it."

"Probably means I have a conscience."

"As long as neither girl is killed by that piece of shit, I'm at peace."

"You know, I thought of something kind of outside the box…"

"Oh, great; this oughta be good."

"What if this experiment messes with these girls' heads in such a way that it renders them basket cases…much like Johnny is from what he went through as a boy?"

"Are you Dr. Phil? You're going *far* too in-depth on this situation, and to be honest with you, it's getting REALLY annoying."

"Sorry that I care about their well-beings and you apparently don't."

"All I care about is seeing this craziness through and getting paid at the end of it."

"'Course that's all ya care about. Money's the motivator."

"It isn't for you as well? If this whole thing's so *immoral* to you, why don'tcha make a call to our boss and tell her you're done?"

"I've come this far; I can't. And you got me, okay? The money matters."

"You're damn right it does, so try and refrain from being lame. This is already a stressful enough job as is…I don't need you harping on the rights and wrongs of it. All right?"

"Yeah. All right. Won't happen again. I'll see it through with you."

"That's the spirit! Now, if you don't mind, I'm taking a break. This time for real."

"Cool. I won't hold you up like before."

"Thanks. Be ready to go to the next post in fifteen. It's gonna be a fun one."

"Absolutely. Wouldn't miss it for the world."

"Good; me either. I've missed seeing the monster."

OUTSIDE: The Monstrous Unknown

The scorched ground rumbled in its wake—one created creature, patrolling the widened perimeters of a chaotic aftermath. Unmatched and unreal. Unstoppable by design.

An air ripe with imposed impurities—hissing dirges alongside a sizzling overview as far as the human eye could see. A land once pristine now ruined.

But for what reason?

Its brooding nature, dedicated to a specific set of rules: detecting and destroying at will. At the push of a button. Indestructible by design.

Hundreds of miles an hour. Speed demon. Going full tilt. Nothing in the way to halt the awe-inspiring progress it made toward its guided area.

Black, oily—its enlarged fins contracting and then retracting with each dust-clearing swoop up and swoop down.

Always a spectacular sight…even at night. Unchallenged and undaunted. Impervious by design.

Cutting through buildings as if they were made of papier-mâché. Metal and wooden architecture reduced to rubble. All areas vacated, all families free of worry. Paid to stay away.

Staunch ramifications for the selected—not the ejected.

Wind rippled across a full frame in fluid motion as the monstrous unknown sported a beauty almost incomprehensible to its overall movement throughout a pulverized district.

A lucrative creation—and not of another world's, but of man's.

Firefighter life nets. High-end landing pads. Gymnastic crash mats. Designated protection. Closed off. Two girls, one body. Thrown into the heavens but arriving right back into a controlled hell.

Attached and afraid.

The blackened beast faced the conjoined twins, a pair of underprivileged teens who couldn't speak for themselves nor defend themselves but could only lie in wait—waiting to see whether this terrifying creature would either kill them or spare them.

Instead, it opened a side hatch on its mass. With manufactured intestines spread out, impeccable tendrils traveled to the target. Tightly wrapping its alien-like arms around the deformed girls' shared torso, it stored them safely in its chest cavity.

Once secured in place, the costly construction coasted away. And other than the sound of a whining wind, some muffled cries of the conjoined were all that could be heard over a questionable broadcast.

INSIDE: The Zebra

Chelsea and Lizzie had been walking for nearly half a day, their shoes dirtying while the toes inside them blistered with every step forward. The only good news was that Lizzie Janis's nosebleed had inexplicably stopped on a dime only a minute after pouring, as if someone had turned a lever.

But one tumultuous journey had been mapped ahead. And as the two scavenged for items and called out for help, there were no new threats to steer clear of. With youthful but exasperated minds, both girls were relieved to be in each other's company—and not in Johnny's.

"So…he was never really married?" the tween asked, clarifying for the last time.

Lizzie groaned, staring a hole into the clueless Chelsea. "Yeah, Chels, Johnny never had a wife. For ten years he was in prison. I told you all this already. And not that I wanna get into it AGAIN, but to drill it into your head for posterity, he molested my sister. Got her drunk and took advantage of her."

"Wow," Chelsea whispered in disbelief. "It's still hard to picture that…although his orange pants did make me wonder."

"Why's it hard to picture? Because he just seemed like such a nice guy to you?!"

"Uh, well…*yeah*…he did! Until he freaked!! Sorry if I'm coming off as insensitive or if I sound like I don't believe you or whatever. Trust me, I **do**. It's just that…"

"What? Johnny's a creep, all right?" Lizzie said, folding her arms defensively. "Sure, he saved us from the bus. But that's where it stops. He's a bad person—and a scary one."

"Fine, Lizzie. I'll take your word for it!"

"Really, Chelsea? You're gonna take my word for it? Is this some kinda infomercial? What he did—to my sister, to my father, and to me personally, when he shook the life outta me—was abhorrent…and repugnant…and—"

The tween suddenly gasped. "No freaking way!"

"What's wrong now?" the headstrong teen questioned.

"You used a couple of intricate words on me…"

Lizzie scoffed at being mocked. "Oh, so just because I have blonde hair and an hourglass figure, that should cause you to raise an eyebrow when I utilize supposedly intricate words?"

"Ah, lookie here…the debut solo album of Harry Styles!" Chelsea said excitedly, rummaging through a stack of burnt-to-a-crisp vinyl records. "I still love his song 'Sign of the Times' so much. Wait. What were we even talking about again?"

"Forget it." Lizzie kicked a pile of empty water bottles. "Hey…"

"Yeah?" the twelve-year-old perked up, still examining the records.

"You're the same age my sister was when Johnny did what he did."

"Er, yes…I put all that together on my own, Liz. Wasn't difficult."

"Just reminding you of the possible parallels between you and her."

Chelsea threw down the assorted vinyl collection and turned toward the older girl with a look of excitement on her face. "PARALLELS!"

"Ugh. Yeah. *Parallels.* Another intricate word."

The two continued to trod along for a while in silence.

"Lizzie, I'm so sorry to pry…and please know that you don't have to tell me if you don't want to, but…" Chelsea began. "Whatever became of your big sis?"

"She's pretty much a lost cause these days. I dunno."

"Why's she a lost cause? Sorry I'm prying even more!"

"The three *D*s: depression, drinking, and drugs. They all took over. She was straight-up damaged after that night with Johnny, but when she learned that she was pregnant with his baby, her life was instantly heaved into a hellish avalanche of soap-opera drama and trauma."

"WAIT A SECOND! A *baby*?! You omitted that tidbit…"

"And that was intentional on my part—since it's a sensitive subject."

"What happened? She kept it, right? Tell me she didn't abort!"

"No. Thankfully, *no*. But the second worst thing possible happened. My sister was forced to give the baby up due to her being wholly unable to handle the responsibilities of motherhood. And also because she was using and abusing hardcore at that time. It simply wasn't meant to be. The only good that came of it was the parents who adopted Markéta's baby girl—they were down-to-earth people. Super stable types. Great jobs, great marriage. I'm sure she's better off with them. **If** they're even still alive after what's happened out here…"

"That's terrible, Lizzie. I'm sorry about…*all* of that!"

"It's okay. I mean, it isn't really, but honestly, I just hope my sister's suffering has finally been put to rest. She deserves some peace."

"Hear hear to that," Chelsea said sweetly. "I think WE deserve some as well, wouldn't you say? My feet are killing me."

"Same. Walking long distances is overrated. We need to find a place."

"Shouldn't be too hard. We're surrounded by houses—and yeah, they may be partially wrecked…but all of 'em are now rent-free!"

"Yet not exactly carefree," Lizzie added cautiously.

"We'll have to lock every door of whichever home we decide to go into, and then do the zombie-lookout thing! One of us can sleep while the other stays awake on watch."

"I'm down for that."

Chelsea smiled, optimistic at the feminine prospects of a surreal sleepover. "What about that light-blue house right there?" The tween girl pointed to the left. "It doesn't seem to be *that* destroyed…it's like it almost looks presentable."

"That looks good, actually. Let's go check it out."

"You lead the way, Number One!"

"How 'bout we walk side-by-side, Girl Two?" Lizzie asked, smirking.

"An even better suggestion, leader."

"I'm no one's leader, Chels. Just stuck in this mess like you."

"Okay, then. I was sorta kidding with the leader stuff there, but all right…"

Lizzie shook her head, slightly embarrassed by her ego shown. "C'mon. Getting tired of looking at this disasterpiece."

"After you!" Chelsea motioned charismatically, as if she were one of those Botoxed, bosomed models presenting a brand-new vehicle on *The Price is Right*.

As they approached the home, nothing out of the ordinary was around the front yard. The three-level blue house seemed, for all intents and purposes, a non-threatening establishment at first glance—the porch was in pristine shape, the windows weren't shattered, and the roof was intact.

"Looks like this place went under the radar when hell swept over the rest of—" Lizzie stopped short, observing the destruction to the left and right of her. "…here. Is it weird that it's in such great shape?"

"Nope; not to me. There are far too many houses for that crazy monster mash thing…and *whatever* else it was that destroyed everything."

"Yeah…but whole skyscrapers were ruined, totally broken off from the top and on fire. Why is it that this one house is untouched?" Lizzie pondered. "It feels off."

"Maybe to you it does. Me, though? I don't expect every single place we come across to be destroyed."

"Not saying I expect that either; it's just weird."

Chelsea patted Lizzie on the shoulder. "Don't pop a vessel over it. Why don't we go see if the inside's as immaculate as the outside?"

"That's why we're here."

"Then you be the first to open the door—what with you being the *leader* and all."

"Nice, Chels. Good way of covering your cowardliness," Lizzie said.

"I'm not a coward! Just thought I'd be considerate and offer you dibs."

"Uh-huh; sure, that's what it is. Well…here goes nothing…you ready?" The headstrong teen looked at the tween sternly.

"Absolutely; open this bad boy up."

Already unlocked, the front door to the posh blue house swung open by Lizzie's push of a fading golden knob. The interior to the home had a conservative nature, while an assorted fruit basket from Shari's Berries, a baker's dozen of Cheryl's Cookies in a tin, and a pack of Fiji awaited them on an entryway table by the banister.

"*Another* fruit basket, even more sugar cookies, and bottled water!" Chelsea said with confusion. "Um…"

"'Another'? 'Even more'? What do ya mean?" Lizzie asked.

"It's an identical basket of fruit…and these frosted cookies are the exact batch as before. They're all the brands that Riley, Tamika, and I found back at that other house—you know, the one that'll cause me nightmares later!"

"Do you think that's just a coincidence?"

Chelsea cocked her head. "Who's into fruit baskets anymore? Two houses with the same setup? NOT a coincidence."

Should I tell Chels about the bus wallpaper Johnny and I found? No, that'd just freak her out even more…

"I agree. Definitely out of the ordinary. But if it's safe, we should eat and drink the stuff anyway…" Lizzie suggested.

"The last house's goodies were okay; I'm sure these are too."

"Cool! We'll chow down in a moment. Let's check the place first."

"Aye, aye, captain…"

Eyeing the cookie-cutter home with attentiveness, the girls saw that everything was perfectly in its place—like someone had decorated it painstakingly and then vanished.

"No mannequins," Chelsea pointed out in passing. "That's a huge plus."

"I suppose so." Lizzie laughed uneasily, on her toes. "But this pad…it's too neatly arranged, and that sorta gives me the willies."

"The *willies?*"

"Yeah, the willies! What? You've never heard that before?"

"I'm twelve, and it's 2028, so no…can't say that I have," Chelsea said, walking around the spacious living room.

"What about the heebie-jeebies?"

The tween cracked a quarter-smile, shaking her head.

"No? Gee whiz, I thought you read a lot of books…"

"UGH; I do!"

"And I also thought that you were super smart…"

"DOUBLE UGH; I *am*!"

Lizzie smiled at their playfulness, knowing that it may end up being short-lived. "Okay, my bad then."

"That's some really old terminology used to describe something so simple. Why can't you just say you're scared?"

"Now I have to simplify my vocabulary for a self-professed bookworm?"

"Argh…no!" Chelsea fumed, frustrated by being intellectually cornered. "Can we try to focus on what's at hand? Like checking every room in this house to see if we're *actually* alone?"

"For sure we can…"

"I'll go check upstairs, if that's okay with you."

"Fine by me. Scream bloody murder if you see something crazy," Lizzie replied, half joking.

"Oh; I was planning on not making a single sound."

"Whatever tickles your fancy, Chelsea…"

The two girls smiled at each other and parted ways. On the lower level, Lizzie found nothing out of place, nothing noteworthy. Just a kitchen meticulously clean and organized, a dining room that appeared to be ready for a lovely family gathering at a moment's notice, and a tech-packed living room that seemed ideal for hosting parties, yet none of the electronics had powered on when she tried.

No framed pictures. No children's toys. No trace of any man or woman who had lived there at all. A refrigerator empty. The kitchen cupboards—every which one—bare.

"So strange," Lizzie pronounced, opening drawer after drawer only to find nothing in them.

Steady footsteps creaking upstairs randomly startled a jittery Lizzie.

It's just Chelsea. Stop being on edge!

"You okay up there?"

No answer after a minute of waiting.

"CHELS! YOU OKAY UP THERE OR NOT??"

The tween ran down the stairs like she was being summoned for dinner by an impatient parent. "Yes, yes, yes! I was okay up there and now I'm okay down here. What's going on? Find anything?"

"No, I didn't. In fact, that's the weird thing about this place. There's nothing stocked in the fridge, the cupboards, or the drawers—*nothing*."

"Likewise," Chelsea said with a bit of sadness. "I didn't hear you the first time around 'cause I was in the bathroom messing around with the faucet and shower! Running water still…pretty cool!"

"That *is* cool. Odd that the water's working—and all the lights, too. Oh well…I'm not gonna complain!"

"Me either! So, what's the plan now?"

"Eat some of the fruit and cookies, maybe?"

Hopping ahead of her older trekker, Chelsea ripped the plastic off of their care package and chowed down. "Never thought I'd be salivating over apples and oranges!"

"*Hey*, leave some for me!"

"No way I could eat all this by myself!" the tween said as she squeezed the remaining juice from her organic orange. "Wanna camp out here for the night and make our next move in the morning?"

Lizzie nodded. "Sounds good to me. We've hoarded enough snacks in our pockets; we still have this fruit basket plus these sugar cookies; and we have enough bottled water to camp out for more than a night, if need be."

"OOH, perhaps this place could become, like, our home base!"

"Yeah, maybe…let's make sure the doors and windows are locked and then we can attempt to get some sleep. We'll take showers in the morning."

"I'm dying for sleep," Chelsea fawned. "But what about my lookout idea? Do you want to do it?"

"No; I can't keep my eyes open…and you look too tired to be on lookout duty! We'll be fine as long as we're all locked up…"

"Hope so! The last thing we need is some scary thievery."

Taking only a few minutes to spot-check each door and window, the two moved quickly, securing their position and hunkering down for the night, while Lizzie astutely unhooked a curtain rod from the living room—to use as a make-do weapon on any unwelcome trespassers. A cunning means of protection. Yet as they situated themselves for sleep, it was quiet and unassuming outside. Peaceful around the perimeter.

"Chels, you can have that nice sofa…I'll take the couch."

"Aw; are ya sure?"

"Positive." Lizzie smiled. "There may not be anything stored away and no working TV to watch, but at least there are blankets."

"So thankful for that. It's hard for me to fall asleep without one."

"Me too."

"Well…good night…"

"Chels?"

"Yeah?" the tween asked as she placed her glasses carefully on the carpet.

"What do you think's **really** going on here?"

"I was about to ask you the same thing."

"But you said good night to me!" Lizzie said.

"I *wanted* to get serious about stuff…I just didn't know how to go about it. So I'm glad you started."

"Can't stop thinking about Riley…Tamika…those twins…"

"Our backs were against the wall. We've already talked about what happened a bunch, but I still have no idea what this situation is…do you have any idea?"

"Haven't the foggiest notion, Chelsea. But I wanna find out."

"Same here! How are we going to, though?"

"We keep searching. Tomorrow will be a big day. I want to cover a lot of ground."

"Okay; I'm down. Just hope I stop seeping blood here! I thought the bandages Ry slapped on me would hold and I'd heal."

"Is it bad enough for me to be concerned? Or do ya think you'll be all right for the night?"

The tween shrugged it off. "I'll be fine! Let's rest; I'm bushed."

Lizzie brought a thin-threaded blanket up to her neck. "Already ahead of you…I'm a deep sleeper…" She then fake-snored loudly.

"You're goofy; you know that?"

"Sorry; I didn't hear you—I was too busy snoring."

"Night, Lizzie. I'm glad you're my wingwoman."

"As am I, Chels. See you in the a.m."

***

Lizzie awoke—as sleepy-eyed as anybody in the storied history of being groggy could—to the sight of a giant stuffed zebra in the middle of the living room.

That's just like the one I had when I was little…

"Chels, you up? You gotta see something!"

No answer.

"I know it's probably pretty early, but you *gotta* see this! There's a stuffed zebra by the TV!"

Still no answer. And no stirring.

"Stop playing around! I know you can hear me underneath those sheets, Chelsea."

The headstrong teen kicked at the side sofa connected to her couch, which resulted in a horrifying realization that the twelve-year-old girl was missing. Chelsea's now-crushed glasses were all that remained of her.

"Oh no. No, no, no, no…CHELS! WHERE ARE YOU?!"

All right; relax for a second. Maybe she went outside to chill on the porch…

Lizzie rubbed the sleep residue from her eyes, snagging her provisional mechanism for self-defense and sprinting awkwardly toward the front door of the showroom-like house. When she opened the door, a combined wave of disappointment and fear came over her. Chelsea wasn't out on the porch, chilling like Lizzie had hoped to discover her doing. Only fragments of dusted housing and a still-contaminated sky greeted the teen's downtrodden expression.

Not out here. So what? That doesn't mean anything. Keep calm. She could've gone upstairs to take her shower…I don't know; I'm checking up there before I spaz!

"YOU UPSTAIRS?!" Lizzie screamed, closing the front door behind her and locking it quickly. "HELLO!!"

Nothing. After every room in the home was checked, Lizzie officially determined that Chelsea was a ghost.

She wouldn't have just up and left on her own free will. Plus, her geeky glasses are totally destroyed; she needs to see! We should've done that stupid zombie-lookout thing! We really should have…

After several minutes of silence in an immaculate living room that had seemingly never been lived in, Lizzie dropped the rod and put her focus back on the zebra. With sleepiness and shock still coursing through her, she hadn't noticed a white envelope taped to the neck of the mysterious stuffed animal.

Whatever's written inside that envelope, I'm guessing it can't be good.

"Might as well open it. It's obviously been placed here for a reason."

*That's what they **want** you to do, though! How about you do the opposite? Just to see what happens…*

Obeying her rebellious thoughts, Lizzie stepped forward and tore the envelope to shreds. "There. All gone. I'll never know!"

But as Lizzie punched the zebra down to the ground, there was yet another white envelope appearing on the other side of its neck.

Interesting. I probably shouldn't destroy this one, since I'm betting it's important.

"But that first envelope was probably important, too!" the blonde replied crankily to herself. "Whatever; I'm finding out."

Lizzie opened it—with care this go-round—and saw a yellow piece of paper and a small glass vial. Inked in black marker, the words bled through its sheet.

YOUR YOUNG FRIEND, CHELSEA FIELDS, IS FINE. DON'T WORRY ABOUT HER ANYMORE— WORRY ABOUT JOHNNY. HE'S STILL OUT THERE. BUT YOU, LIZZIE JANIS, CAN PUT AN END TO HIM ONCE AND FOR ALL…AS YOU ARE NOW IN POSSESSION OF A VIAL OF FATAL POISON. ITS CONTENTS ARE ODORLESS AND TASTELESS, WHICH WILL MAKE THE DEATH PAINLESS. FIND

MR. HELKS IMMEDIATELY, POUR THE POISON INTO A BOTTLE OF WATER, AND…YOU GET THE IDEA…

IF YOU COOPERATE WITH THIS REQUEST, YOU'LL BE SET FREE FROM THIS CONTAINED TYRANNY. YOU WILL ALSO BE REUNITED WITH YOUR PARENTS. YES, MOM <u>AND</u> DAD: TOGETHER AGAIN. WE'VE MADE THAT HAPPEN!

SEE YOU SOON…IF YOU'RE SMART.

Dumbfounded, Lizzie stood there speechless, as only her heart and her thoughts raced on.

Who's behind all of this? How do they know Chelsea's name? How do they know MY name? I already wanted to kill Johnny, but why do they—whoever they even are—want me to do it as well? What's this about?! And how are my parents involved?

"I am so lost," she said. "I am so…"

While Lizzie read the foretelling note again to try and make some sense of it, the floorboards started to shake, and the blue house rattled like it was about to be ripped off its hinges.

Only one driving force was responsible for such awesome power: the monstrous unknown in all its glory.

Fiercely, it bellowed outside—deafening Lizzie's ears inside. Wreaking havoc on power lines and trees, the massive creature knocked them over with laser-point precision as if they were pins struck by a bowling ball barreling down a slick lane.

"That thing…" Lizzie whispered, on the verge of tears. "It's back."

Fuck.

OUTSIDE: The Hallucination

Facedown in a pile of wet dirt, Johnny Helks came to—lethargically and cautiously—by way of some loving licks. As he turned his head, he was surprised to see the same Siberian husky that had run up to him a day before.

This dog must really like me to keep visiting me…

Suddenly a drastic swivel of the furry animal's body occurred as his attention went elsewhere. The blue-and-brown-eyed husky looked off into the distance and then bolted for whatever—or whoever—was calling him over.

"NOT AGAIN! I thought for sure you'd stay this time…"

What's that hissing sound? A ringing in my ears? Tinnitus from the blast?

Once Johnny situated himself and his grimacing had subsided, he gazed upward to a divine, moonlit early evening. Its glow calmed him.

But only temporarily.

"What happened to me?" the freed prisoner wondered. "And why doesn't that damn dog stay in one place for very long?"

As he continued to gaze upon the sky, he noticed two airplanes crisscrossing directly above him, leaving slight trails of white exhaust behind them.

People? Alive?? Not crashing, either? Am I seeing things?!

Counting to ten, Johnny closed his eyes to rub the perceived delusion away. When he looked up once more, both planes had vanished.

Figures. Just a mind mirage.

Trees swayed around Johnny as an affected air seethed like a lion on the prowl for prey, traversing the ruined land with demonic constancy. Indistinguishable debris was now the chemically pelted environment's modernized tumbleweed—a foreboding visualization and a firm reminder of what little hope was left.

I can't remember anything. All I know is that the back of my head hurts.

"What…happened?" Johnny asked in pain.

Gone from his frail mind were the recent arguments and encounters that he'd had along the torrid way—yet not entirely forgotten.

Drug-induced amnesia—supplemented by lanky men in lab coats.

Come on; try to remember why you were sucking face with soil! It shouldn't be this hard!!

Hours later, after cross-examining himself with varied results, things began to trickle back.

"I was angry…and I was…" Johnny paused, collecting anything he could from his splintered memory bank. "…attacked?"

Yeah, yeah; I was. From behind! Some guy with a gun—he did it.

"And there was another man…standing over some girls…two girls…Riley and…uh, TAMIKA!"

The memories flooded back into his mind—the ominous men, the pair of teenagers falling to them, and even him falling to their command after strongly resisting it.

"Oh God, what're they gonna do to those girls?"

Why do you care? It's not like you're a choir boy when it comes to the taboo subject of underage females.

"Zip it, will ya?" Johnny yelled, smacking his cranium multiple times. "I've changed, and I *care*. Is that so unbelievable to you?"

Yes, actually; it is.

"There's no reason not to believe what I say."

Of course not! No reason whatsoever; only the fact that you're a psychotic man-child who is damaged beyond repair from some severe trauma suffered as an eight-year-old…

"I don't even know what you're referring to!"

All part of the mental illness; that's why. I mean, the…condition…

"I'm perfectly SANE—it's this world that's INSANE now!"

Absolutely. Forget I even thought anything.

"Johnny…oh, Johnny…" a feminine voice called out in the distance.

Before you ask, no…that's not me messing with you.

The confused convict started to sweat. "Who's there?"

"Johnny…oh, Johnny…" the unseen girl said once more, with the same teasing tone she'd articulated before.

"What do you **want**?! *Whoever* you are!"

"The name's Johnny Helks. And I'm here to HELP!" the young-sounding female mocked gleefully, duplicating what the freed prisoner had said to the girls on the bus. "Are you in need of some assistance?"

Okay, I'll admit that this is getting pretty freaky. But try to look tough.

"Stop this, dammit! Come out and face me!!"

On second thought, you may not want that…who knows who this is…

"Want to face your past?"

The directly personal question posed by her caused Johnny to involuntarily flash back to his sordid and tarnished past. He then sweat profusely, mirroring the appearance of a spent, headband-wearing basketball player—minus the headband.

"Leave me alone," the freed prisoner broke down, sloping his stubbled chin to his chest in shame. "Haven't you done *enough* already?"

"Haven't *you* done enough?" the girl asked hostilely.

"I'm sorry, all right? For God's sake, I've beaten myself up a billion times…and it's been brutal, so much more than what anyone else could ever do to me. Living in my head has been **hell** for the last ten years! So there's nothing that you—or *anybody* who still exists in this wrecked world—can do that could possibly be any WORSE!"

Amen to that; I should know. It has truly been difficult working with you throughout the many, many missteps.

"What if I took your whole life away from you, though? Like you did mine?" she casually pondered, walking out of the thick tree line.

"Who are you? You look…*exactly* like her…exactly like—"

"Markéta. That's because I *am* her; I'm the girl you ruined."

In the midnight light, the freckle-faced twelve-year-old brooded toward Johnny with ghostly resolve. With each purposeful step of hers taken, Johnny took a step back—buckling under the pressure of his own repressed memories, which were strangling his psyche.

"It's not possible. You're, like, twenty-two or twenty-three now; no…NO. This *isn't* real! I don't care if you look like her. There's no way you're real!!"

*This is all just one big hallucination…I'm not in the right state of mind. After everything experienced, I'd be surprised if I **didn't** hallucinate every once in a while!*

"I am real, Johnny Helks. I'm all the clutter that you've tried to hide under your bed."

The girl stopped walking toward Johnny, and before he could respond to her shoddy metaphor, she let out a banshee-like shrill that reverberated in the freed prisoner's skull.

Hunched over while covering his ears for the duration of her earth-shaking shriek, Johnny slowly rose back up moments after she fell silent.

When he opened his eyes, the girl was plastered in blood—bright red, coagulating, and pouring rapidly all at once. As the freed prisoner looked on in unmitigated terror, the twelve-year-old laughed maniacally. Backpedaling until tripping onto his behind, Johnny felt his eyes nearly bulge out of their sockets at the sight of her.

Have you considered running for your life? Because I think that now would be the appropriate time to do so. Run like hell!

Not wasting another moment, Johnny Helks got right back up and ran as fast—and as far—as his hurting feet could physically take him.

And the bloodied girl kept on laughing as the troubled man kept on running.

THIRD STRIKE

Sometime in 2028 & 2029…

FULLY OPERATIONAL: The Drop-Off

An industrial-sized ceiling fan was the first thing Tamika saw as she regained consciousness. The second thing seen by her glassy eyes was the place itself—a sprawling warehouse, with perfectly made beds in perfectly made rows.

And all of them appeared to be vacant, except for one down the right-side row.

"Ry? That you, girl?" she asked woozily.

"Tamika??" Riley asked back in a haze, yawning.

"Where we at now? You know?"

The fair-skinned brunette yawned again. "I'm in the same boat—or bed—as you, sister. I have no idea what this depressing-ass warehouse is, but it's already a **whole** lot better than the bus we woke up in."

"True, true. But you didn't see nothin'? Nothin' at all??"

"I was unconscious. Just like you were. How the hell would I have seen *anything*?"

"Sorry 'bout askin'…got my clock cleaned firsthand, so I'm fuzzy as fu—"

Riley promptly interrupted the teen's needless exposition. "I know, Tam. I was there; I saw it…and I tried to stop them. But obviously, it didn't all go as planned."

"Hopefully Johnny n' da others are okay, whereva they at."

"Maybe they were able to get away, but that's just my stupid optimism. Don't mind it."

"Are we da only ones here, ya think?"

"Sure seems so to me. This place is about as drab as a dentist's sense of humor…"

"But you could prolly eat off deeze flows!" Tamika exclaimed. "Dem super clean."

"It *is* spotlessly sterile."

"Some toothbrush treatment, yo."

"'Scuse me; what was that?" Riley furrowed her brow. "Are you sayin' people must've gleamed these grounds with itty-bitty bristles?"

"Yup; why not? I can almost see my refection in 'em!"

Riley's hand slapped her knee. "REFECTION?! My, what a difference *one* letter makes…"

"Shut it. So, what we gon' do now? Wanna look 'round wit me?"

"I do…once this headache of mine calms down," the seventeen-year-old replied. "I got a crazy rush to the nog the moment I woke."

"Me too; just didn't wanna say so immediate-like, 'cause I ain't a whiny little bitch."

"Suck it, Tamika."

"Aw snap, you gots a dick? I woulda never guessed…"

"Nope, all female over here, my antagonizing friend."

"Damn; k den. But if imma be honest, you *did* look a bit butch someti—"

Suddenly a steel-plated door opened by the front end of the largely empty warehouse, bringing their conversation to a complete stop.

Walking methodically—and mechanically—toward the two teens still beached in their beds, the Automated Service Replicant raised its robotic branch of an arm as the towering figure stalked forward.

"Uh, what? It's a motherfucking ASR?!" Tamika stammered.

Unable to stop herself from staring, Riley couldn't manage anything other than a timid whisper. "I thought those damned things were outlawed."

"Least we ain't in a movie theater; we may be coo…"

The shiny black automaton spoke from a preset greeting. "Hello! Welcome to Exit Stage Left of Operation Offender, a burgeoning and groundbreaking program set to air worldwide in the first quarter of next year. Your services are no longer required at this point in time, young citizens. So after some paperwork is taken care of, you'll both be free to go."

"WHAT?!" Riley and Tamika shouted collectively.

"You didn't hear my vocalized speech pattern? How can that possibly be? Is the programmed volume not at an acceptable level for your humanoid ears, or are the two of you suffering from a form of impaired hearing?"

"WE HEA—we heard you…" Riley yelled again prematurely, lowering her hostile tone as she thought of the several ASRs that had demolished so many poor souls in an amphitheater nearly three years before. "Heard ya quite clearly. But what is this? *Why* are we in a huge warehouse?!"

"YEAH; n' why da fuck are we in dis shit when we were just needled?! Almost seems like we safe now…" Tamika followed up.

"I am not computing your slang rhetoric. But yes, if you are believing to be completely exempt from harm, that much is affirmative. You aren't in any physical duress—and your vital signs are stabilizing."

"We're definitely in a lot of *emotional* duress, though, you monotone toaster!" Riley stated combatively.

"Young female, I advise you to calm yourself before your heart rate elevates. It is unnecessary. The taxing time you've put into this aspiring venture is genuinely appreciated by everyone at CDN. But now you must leave these premises—preferably in peace and not in protest."

"Or else what?! You gonna step to us or somethin'?" Tamika questioned.

"Again, I am not entirely computing your slang rhetoric. However, getting back to your pending departures, I can inform you both that to the right of this building, a fresh pair of clothes is stored inside a locker for each of you. Furthermore, you are both expected to be fully ready and fully cooperative to traverse toward the drop-off box outside and sign some highly important release papers within fifteen minutes. No acceptable excuses. After formalities are discussed with your assigned coordinators, you're then officially free to leave."

Riley scratched her head. "You mentioned CDN…isn't that like a TV network?"

"Correct," the sleekly designed ASR responded.

"What is dis shit?! This was all a GAME??" Tamika screamed.

"Incorrect. It is, in fact, by all definitions hardwired into my reasoning, a show. But one that is steeped in endless ambition, one that has come with real dangers, and one that's going to change—and greatly expand—an archaic medium's veneration forever."

"YOU'VE GOTTA BE KIDDING ME!" Riley bellowed with pent-up rage. "WE WERE TERRIFIED OUT THERE!! TIED UP IN THAT BUS, CREEPY MEN TAKING US DOWN, AND DEALING WITH WHATEVER THAT MONSTROUS **THING** WAS…THAT—" Riley ran out of steam, unable to continue at such an accelerated pace of wailing.

Tamika screamed alongside her agitated friend. "THIS IS BULLSHIT!"

"While I am programmed to sympathize with your predictable reactions regarding this mind-melting revelation that I have just delivered, the two of you—and the other participants selected—were and *are* technically safe. Always. There were precautionary measures in the proper places for any conceivable variable to be concerned about. Nobody has died. It was all implied. Death never does fail to up the stakes."

Riley caught her breath, determined to get some much-needed clarity from the advanced artificial intelligence. "What's all this supposed to accomplish? Other than the long-lasting traumatic effects that this experiment is gonna have on us, I don't see the point to it!!"

"You are not meant to, either. That's the precise hook. For the near-obsolete human mind to concoct something of this magnitude, to create such a resplendence within the constrictions of a controlled bleakness, well…it is to be applauded. The visionary of this influential undertaking is a true forward thinker and is also my actual god. Without her, I would not be functioning—or standing—in front of you today. Without Miss Drake's financial backing, I'd still be but a distant dream in a broke developer's regime."

"This thing…it wasn't *real*…ANY OF IT?!" Riley shrieked.

"False. That is where you're mistaken. In the broadest terms, it was—and is—real. To the lot of you, it was a very real scenario, playing out naturally. To Johnny Helks, who's unfortunately still down in some muck, it is playing out naturally for him. Right now as I speak, in fact!"

"But who else is left? Chelsea and Lizzie? Fending for themselves in your bunk plastic apocalypse?! And if we're all safe—as you so calmly say we are—whatever became of those mute twin sisters? They were flung up into the air; we all saw it! WHAT EVEN IS THIS?!" Riley demanded, balling her fists.

"They—the twin sisters you have referred to—are presently safe, much like you are in this air-conditioned building. Regarding your concern for their frightful flight, there is no need to be alarmed. They landed on a bed of sophisticated crash mats, and it went off without a hitch. Their parents have signed their release forms. Now they're being shuttled away to a more livable environment—their home. As for Chelsea and her specific fate, she was taken off of the grid about an hour ago because of an unexpected injury sustained. A fellow ASR is currently communicating the details to her in the same way that I am with you. At this time, Lizzie and Johnny are the only ones who remain, but if you'd like some behind-the-scenes knowledge to process—from the outset, it was pragmatically designed for that to occur all along. Hence the reasoning for your numbered shirts; they were meant to emphasize each participant's value and order of elimination, with number five being the first selected to go, four being the second, and so forth."

"I bet your net execs were upset we didn't wear them that long."

"Not so, Riley Parker. They were happy to watch the peerless progression..." their ASR lipped monotonically.

"So that's it, then? Endeavor over?"

Creaking, the machine nodded. "For you it is."

"Ry 'n I just 'sposed to roll out...no more questions ta put on ya?" Tamika asked. "We're really bein' set free?"

"Yes. The show's now over for both of you. My work here is done. I would suggest not being dour and/or malignant citizens about this matter. Accept your setting and move forward."

"But I don't...*wait*, don't go! INFODUMP US!" Riley said, elevating her voice to the tune of desperation. "There's so much more we have to ask!! You can't just **leave**..."

"I **can** leave, as I've given all the pertinent instructions for your next step. You may have many more questions, but I do not have the clearance to answer them. Goodbye." The magnificent, towering structure turned around and headed toward the front exit, leaving loudly in the wake of a shared silence as its stainless steel frame clinked and clanked on the gray concrete flooring.

"Back to square one, I guess," Riley said as she started to make her way over to the lockers.

"HEY! That's my line!" Tamika claimed, following closely behind. "Anything else in dem locks or not?"

The clothes inside the unlocked metal cubbies were free of wrinkles and smelled like they'd been recently washed and dried.

"Nope, just some crappy clothes: standard white tees and blue jeans for you and me. Here, slap 'em on...get outta those dirty dungarees n' that mucky blouse. I won't look—if you don't look, either."

"SO...we ain't gonna talk 'bout dis?"

"What's there to talk about, Tamika?" Riley asked while putting her head through the top of the crisp, clean tee and discarding her muddy green V-neck. "You heard the super-shiny ASR."

"Yeah, I did. But, like, what if dis strange shit's a trap? We seen some wacked stuff out dare, Ry, so you wanna take an android's word as bond...n' open dat door to see what's up?"

"That's *exactly* what I want to do. What's our other choice...stay in this bleak-looking warehouse and dawdle for no good reason?! Face it, it's our only move—we have to leave. Even if we wanted to stay in here, that robot warned us that it wouldn't be in our best interests...so I'm sure it'd come back soon."

"You right; you right. I'm just sayin' it's shady. This whole deal. But no doubt, we haveta make a move or else dat machine's gon come back 'round. N' you can bet he'd be pissed. I don't wanna end up like doze peeps at The Noni."

"Me either, Tam. That's why I'm gonna comply with his—*its*—orders that were laid down so systematically. Because if not, I'm sure it wouldn't be a fun experience for us."

"No...I can't see it being a chill sitch at all. Again, you right. I just...man, I'm a bit shook still. Don't even know what's outside or who's waitin' fo' us."

"Well, why don't we go and find out what's what right now?" Riley urged.

"Oh, you ready?"

"About as ready as any other traumatized victim could be..."

Tamika laughed to cope, remembering all the previous struggles they'd shared. "Let's do it, den. I'm witcha...open da door n' let's see what's what..."

"All right…*well*, here we go. Another new adventure to embark upon…" Riley began to turn the knob clockwise until she paused dramatically. "Did you grab everything you'd like to take along? You know, before we head out and leave this place behind…it's always smart to get the essentials."

"Ry, you a funny bitch. You know damn well we ain't got nothing ta take!"

"Just checking. Better safe than sorry!" The brunette grinned warily. "Time to face the music…whatever that music may be…"

The door to the spacious warehouse opened, revealing yet another large-scale warehouse—trumping the one that they'd awoken in by far. Luxury sedans, black and white, were parked to the left side of the closed-off area. To their right was a fleet of well-equipped and well-armed ASRs with a big neon-lit sign above their eight-foot frames stating:

Contestant Coordinators

"What the…still no human interaction? All bots and that's it?" Riley asked.

"WHERE ARE SOME REAL-ASS PEOPLE?!" Tamika wondered aloud angrily.

As they stood together by the smaller warehouse that they had just come out of, Riley spotted a tiny tween—none other than Chelsea.

"My God; look over to your right, Tam!"

"Holy shit. Dat ASR wasn't playin' wit us…"

The two teenagers were thunderstruck, saying nothing more to each other as they witnessed the bubbly twelve-year-old walk away from the coordination station, then jump up and down in happiness when a cherry-red Jeep drove toward her.

"DAD!!" Chelsea shouted with pep and relief. "IT'S REALLY YOU! SO THEY WEREN'T LYING TO ME AFTER ALL! YES! YES! YES!!" The tween ran into her father's arms the moment he set foot outside his vehicle.

"My little girl! It's so good to see you again. I'm sorry that your mother and I signed off on something this crazy, I truly am…but—"

Chelsea, full of boundless energy, interrupted her father's apology. "It's all right! *Really*; it is. They told me everything. And ya know, it makes total sense to me now! So I don't blame you. And I'm not upset at the decision you made on my behalf—not one bit!!"

"Isn't that a balm for my restless soul. Thank you, honey. I hope you realize that we did it for you. *All* of it."

"I do; I do! With the type of money that we're gonna receive from agreeing to participate, you won't ever have to worry about paying for my college tuition…or that pesky new Internet system that's been put in place…or just about *anything* else! Probably for the rest of our lives!!"

"Honey, you are wise beyond your years. Do you grasp that?" The father embraced his daughter tightly, as if he hadn't seen her in an eternity.

"Thanks, Dad. I appreciate that and I know you guys wouldn't have dared to incorporate me into something that was *actually* dangerous—even though I DID get stabbed by some shrapnel on set. I'm still shocked by the things I've seen; when those stealthy handlers grabbed me late at night like a pair of freakin' ninjas, my heart almost stopped! Lizzie really **was** a deep sleeper!! Or maybe they were just that quiet; I dunno. Even though they clumsily crushed my glasses in the process…"

"But look at your new specs! Way better!"

"Oh, I know!!" The tween beamed. "They've definitely taken care of me. This whole thing's been confusing, honestly, but those ASRs explained stuff in an understandable manner—enough to satisfy me, anyway. So now I'm okay with it. Seems like it'll be a super intense show to watch."

"That's good you're okay with it, and I'm glad they've lit the logs for you; but on the drive home, I'll toast the marshmallows, so to say. How's that sound?"

"It sounds great! I'd love to know how this all came about…I also would *love* to get back to my books! I've SO missed reading."

"'Course. We'll cover everything on the drive."

Chelsea perked up even more. "Where's Mom? I thought she'd be here…"

"Well, honey, she wanted to come today, but she's currently cooking a special dinner for you! Wait, did I just ruin the surprise?" the father pondered, smiling.

The tween jumped for joy. "OOH! Fresh food! **Finally**!!"

Still smiling, Chelsea's dad ushered his daughter into the Jeep, with his right hand on her back. "Watch your step as you get in; I know you may be woozy from the sedatives and sore from the set mishap! If ya wanna sleep and talk later, I understand."

"No freaking way…I'll be fine! My coordinator gave me eight Good Day Chocolates for an energy boost—freaking *delicious*! I'm completely awake and ready to discuss all of it!"

"Very well, then. Hey, a couple of girls are lookin' at us by those crew cars…" The father pointed as he started the engine. "Were they also a part of the selected?"

"OH! Yeah!! Riley and Tamika: number three and four in our group! They were nice to me—most of the time! I was just *so* happy when I found out that they were safe!" Chelsea said, patting her father's knee urgently. "Dad, could you lower my window? I wanna say bye to 'em!"

The father obliged immediately. "Absolutely; why the heck not?"

"RILEY! TAMIKA!! DON'T EVEN WORRY…IT'S ACTUALLY A REALLY COOL THING. TRUST ME…YOU'RE SET FOR **LIFE** NOW! I'M HAPPY TO HAVE MET YOU! TAKE CARE! BYEEE!!" the tween wailed.

As she waved to the cheery and hyper girl departing, Riley glanced at Tamika to see if she looked as perplexed as Riley felt.

"Set fo' life? What's going on up in here, Ry?"

"I don't know; I sincerely don't. But I do know this much: the only way we're gonna find out is by going over to those coordinating hunks of junk. And…I dunno who *you* have waiting and worrying back at home, but I'd like to see my boyfriend, as I'm sure he's been worried sick. Our ticket outta here is through there. So what do ya say? Ready to see what's what once and for all?"

"*Hell yeah* am I ready to see what's what!"

As the cherry-red Jeep drove off, the two unsure entrants walked hand-in-hand—while fears rose to their throats—toward an elaborate coordination station, and toward an affluent future.

ON-LOCATION: The Malfunctioning

Lizzie kept running—rodless—through the incalculable wreckage but could not get away from the enigmatic monster roaring hot on her trail. Destroying houses closely behind, the monstrous unknown and its wrath loomed large. Its drive to rip apart anything standing in its way was evident—and by hook or by crook, the massive, oily black creature wouldn't stop until its appetite could be satisfactorily satiated.

As diversified things continued to be catapulted up and over Lizzie's head from all directions, eviscerated portions of housing sprinkled the greenish-tinted sky like cheapo fireworks on the Fourth of July.

"Why's the sky more eerie-looking than usual??" Lizzie asked gaspingly, dashing and darting away from the many objects cascading down around her.

Can't this thing find something else to annihilate?!

The teen's feet were miserably sore, and with her constant stomping on a ground ripe with debris, such force could easily have broken an ankle at any moment. As she ran like a sketchy criminal, her legs were faltering and unable to hold up to the wear and tear of fleeing frantically from an entity hell-bent on inflicting pulverization.

Just go away. PLEASE. I don't wanna die. I want to grow old…

Her perilous thoughts ran as rampant as her cramping legs across the unpredictable wasteland. Wanting to give up after sprinting nonstop for what seemed like a lifetime, Lizzie surprisingly didn't call it quits, but instead tripped over a bungee-corded computer chair left lying on its side. A jolt of pain rushed down her right shin. The tumble had left her powerless—a wounded animal for a much larger hunter to bag and tag.

Get up; GET UP!! That thing's right on your heels; you can't let it win.

Moving even an inch proved to be excruciating for the prone girl as she tried to mobilize herself. Her legs had been damaged, and they were exhausted—cramped up and giving out. Her will to push forward in the sea of depravity hadn't been entirely broken, but it'd been severely crippled. And just what would her fate be if the monstrous unknown were to clamp its razor-blade teeth onto her torso? It was a visual that she didn't enjoy picturing, and one that she'd do everything in her admittedly limited power to stop from becoming a cataclysmic reality.

God, don't let it end like this. Get me out of this insane situation and I'll be eternally grateful. I refuse to be eaten by some gross brute, some weird alien shredding every single thing in its damn path! I need a miracle, and you can make that happen…

"AH!" the panic-stricken teen yelped. "THAT NOISE!!"

Deafening sirens began to blare across the affected airways, startling the scared-as-hell Lizzie into contemplating submission.

These sounds…that doesn't mean that…no…the cloudy sky…its greenish-bluish hue…oh my God…anything but that…on top of what's already happening??

The sirens screamed, coming to the forefront of Lizzie's full-on fear.

"It can't be. It just can't." The blonde gazed up to the strangely green sky, its calming aesthetics increasing her worries the longer she looked at it. With the monstrous unknown swirling around nearby—as if it were playing with her much like a cat would a bouncy toy—a raging calamity appeared to be on deck as heavy rainfall started to pelt her flinching face.

Rain?! Of course it would rain now. Things couldn't be any bleaker.

"Help me, God…" Lizzie whispered, while the slithering creature bellowed and bulldozed its way through architectural setups with an enthralling nonchalance.

Lizzie Janis resorted to one final gesture and request. She pressed her shaky, slippery hands together and closed her eyes—praying for an outright end to whatever outrageousness was about to commence upon her unlucky soul.

A gray, ring-wrapped tornado that was more than a mile wide barged into the tarnished territory at over 100 miles an hour, tearing the roofs off homes with an ease akin to only the monstrous unknown. Fragments of foundation spun around and around as Lizzie looked on, utterly helpless to do anything but watch it all develop. Bug-eyed at such a wonder of nature, the terrified teen shielded her head and curled up into a ball—hysterically crying and praying and trembling. Hoping for light, hoping for peace, hoping for anything positive in her time of burden. The shrieking sounds of the mysterious entity and the cyclone drilled into the canals of Lizzie's covered ears.

Draining; torturous. A fierce apocalypse atop an even fiercer one.

Kill me from above, God, if this is how it's going to end. All I ask is that you make it quick. Please? Impale me with a sharp object; have this twister shoot my body up into the air and drop me back down to Earth. Snap my neck. ANYTHING quick!

A whirlpool of devastation rotating. An unrestrained destructor circulating. With no idea when it'd desist, Lizzie cried like a crib-imprisoned infant. It was all she could do—cry and hope—wish it away by some grace of a greater being.

"What's gonna get me first?" she asked herself, wiping tears mixed with raindrops onto her dirt-ridden sleeve. "The monster or the weather?"

As if the monstrous unknown could understand the English language, it swooped down onto her vulnerable position—uncomfortably close and unbearably horrific—snarling by Lizzie's puffy, reddening face with malice as the girl's unsteady fingers sunk into the marshy ground. Its bulbous head and fang-like teeth dripped with a disgusting gunk, and its breath was so rancid that it caused the teen to nearly faint.

The dripping creature, ominous and frightening in its legless, protracted build, deployed numerous tentacles toward her. Blanketing the ransacked area around Lizzie, black and purple limbs pulsated and retracted like finely tuned machinery as her date with death was nearing.

Well, this is it for me. At least go out like a badass before you die…

"WHAT THE FUCK ARE YOU?!" the cornered teen screamed as loudly as possible. **"WHAT PLANET ARE YOU FROM, HUH?!"**

When Lizzie's screaming stopped, the monstrous unknown screamed back—much, much louder in its otherworldly retort—permanently damaging her left ear.

Delirious and prepared to be killed, Lizzie barked out to the slimy destroyer. **"SO YOU AREN'T GONNA TELL ME? WHY DON'T YOU JUST GO AHEAD AND FUCKING KILL ME, THEN!!"**

Alien-like appendages cut Lizzie's newfound bravery right off, wrapping stably around her narrow neck as her bulging veins appeared to be on the brink of popping. The teenager's precious airway had become constricted from the tentacles' tightening grip.

This really is it. Now I wish that that tornado had been the thing to do me in.

While the monstrous unknown strangled her, Lizzie Janis writhed about on the ground like a fly caught in a spider's web. Her juddering hands were muddied and weak. As she attempted to yell in defiance, her pleas came out like squeaks while entangled within the monster's sticky limbs, and all she could do was gasp musty patches of defeat. No words—only strained air exiting with a death entering.

"STOP, YOU UGLY BASTARD!" some harried man ordered from afar. "LET HER GO!!"

Lizzie could faintly hear the urgency in the male's voice due largely in part to the precipitation, but her consciousness was gradually slipping away in the clutches of such a colossal invader.

Who'd have the guts to confront this thing overtaking me…you'd have to be completely insane to…to…

"Johnny?" the drifting teen managed to say before going limp.

Once her dainty body lay dormant, gunshots fired off at a rapid clip—inaudible due to the racket now being made by the twister tearing into trees. With pandemonium all around, the monstrous unknown was sent reeling backward—and not from the planted blanks firing toward it, but from the commanding fury of Mother Nature herself. The unyielding tornado trounced the imposing figure, yanking its mile-long chassis off of Lizzie and hurling it into the torn sky with no effort exerted.

"Unbelievable," the freed convict said from a safe distance, stunned by seeing their personal tormentor dominated and upended. Johnny Helks ran over to the fallen teenager and knelt down by her side.

Her face was pale on sight, cold to the touch. But Lizzie's wetted body lured his spotty thoughts into a smutty realm.

This red shirt of hers…hugging that perky chest…my goodness…stop…there're more important things to focus on right now!

"Lizzie, wake up! We gotta go. It's probably not that smart to be hanging around here. I dunno about you, but I for one do **not** wanna see whatever else they have in store for their war!"

The unrelenting sirens blared in the background while the whirling tornado continued to handle the monstrous unknown with total supremacy, treating it like a Frisbee tossed from left to right.

"HEY! YOU GOTTA GET UP!!" Johnny insisted, slapping the unresponsive girl. "COME ON! WE GOTTA JET!!"

The panicked man looked up from his kneeling position beside Lizzie to see the black mass valiantly resisting the twister's push-and-pull—until finally succumbing to it. The creature was thrown violently into a water tower, the contents of which hurriedly spilled out.

Showering rain droplets added to the visual flair as the monster's extended body was engulfed in a million gallons of water spewing from the repository like a vicious tidal wave. Doused by the constant stream of water pumping out from the upheaved tank, the monstrous unknown short-circuited and flailed in an ocean that the relentless tornado had just created. Blue sparks of light began to set off like bottle rockets from its malfunctioning, mastodon frame.

The beast that had once been presumed impervious and infernal had been thoroughly electrocuted—and much to the surprise of Johnny, it'd been tamed by way of a water reservoir. Thrashing about uncontrollably and glitching in its many presets, it spiraled out like a shot-down aircraft. Its massive build then lay still on a bed of trees that had buckled underneath the two-ton weight of one cryptic enormity.

Defunct and demystified, the monstrous unknown had been dethroned.

What a scene I'm seeing…if there was ever any doubt, this sure feels like the apocalypse now, the mesmerized male thought. *But why's that oily monstrosity electric? I thought it was an alien! This just keeps getting weirder and weirder.*

"So was it a man-made type of deal or what?" Johnny pondered aloud. "Nah; there's no way a thing like that could be assembled in a factory! Not possible. And aliens have electricity, too; I'm certain of that…I think…"

Before leisurely theorizing other avenues about the monstrous unknown's origins of creation, Johnny observed that the still-spinning tornado had not brought its demolition to a close just yet.

We've gotta get outta here, or else we'll both end up like that black behemoth. Dead and discarded…

"Lizzie, come on. Wake the hell up! It's coming back around now…God, it's coming RIGHT toward us!"

The blonde teenager remained unconscious—amidst the continuing sirens and rumbling twister on its erratic warpath—as the convict showed concern over her previously compromised throat and shallow-breathing chest marked by brown glop and minor lacerations. The foul smell emitting from her slender physique gave Johnny's gag reflexes a bit of a workout. Even so, the nauseous man was determined to lift Lizzie over his shoulder and carry on.

We're leaving this disaster behind for good, if at all achievable.

"I'm picking ya up!! We can't stay here…"

Since she weighed no more than a hundred pounds, it was altogether easy for Johnny to lift the out-of-it girl and find higher ground.

Power-walking away with a lifeless teen bobbing on his shoulder blades, he eyed possible safehouses.

There's one just over the horizon…and it's not obliterated!

Stepping it up a notch, Johnny sauntered briskly toward the suitably placed home—a dreary, *Last House on the Left* type—in an otherwise destroyed suburban neighborhood.

"Executive decision time, but please feel free to disagree: I believe that the home in front of us should be our lodging. What do you think?" The freed prisoner repositioned the waterlogged teen from his shoulder to his arms as if he were a groom carrying a bride over the threshold.

"You really wanna know my opinion about the place?" he asked a sleeping Lizzie, pretending she'd conversed with him. "I think it looks exceptionally…*acceptable*. And it'll do! It's ours."

The girl was gone in his arms as he ogled her features.

She's soaking through those clothes…yum…

"Shall we head in?"

Johnny stepped forward and slammed his forehead into something hard but invisible. With the shock surpassing the pain stemming from it, he set a still-sleeping and soggy Lizzie down—carefully—by the house's flight of stairs.

The hell?!

Clutching his head with his left hand, the freed prisoner reached out with his right in the hopes of feeling whatever it was that had hit him.

Nothing but this modified air.

"What *was* that?" Johnny kept panning his hands and arms across the drafty mist of pollution obsessively.

Yet the rotund object he'd rammed into had disappeared.

I swear I hit something! Heard an errant buzzing, too…just like back in the prison…

"Forget whatever that was…right? We've got a house to reside in tonight! And I think that that's cause enough for celebration. Don't you think??" Johnny brushed the blonde's bangs from her shut eyes as he smiled but then frowned at the obvious lack of improvement.

He picked Lizzie's limp body back up, cradling her frail neck in the process, and proceeded to their destination. Checking behind him as he walked toward the front door, Johnny saw the daunting, screaming tornado heading east—further away from them—and vanishing as a whole after minutes of staring at its magnetic luster.

"Great; it's out of range and the rain's finally halting…now if only those damned sirens would shut up!" he said while turning the knob of an unlocked door. "Jackpot."

The moment it opened, the sirens came to a stop.

Nice. Silence is golden.

As they entered, the door easily took down a life-sized cardboard cutout of one mature and manicured Justin Timberlake. The businesslike—yet smiling—fake face of J. Timberlake amazed Johnny in all the worst ways.

What in the holy hell is this doing in here? Now I am really freaked!

After Johnny's bearings were gathered and he heatedly pulled apart the cardboard caricature completely, he scanned their discreetly dissimilar surroundings. "A home in perfection condition, with cookies and a fruit basket on the table to eat and more Fiji water to drink. Imagine that."

The house was spotless—with beautiful décor, hotel towels supplied on metal racks, and scented candles lit, filling the living room with a sense-pleasing aroma.

Smells like salted caramel and…what's that other one? Pumpkin pie? Ah, that takes me back! I loved munching on some caramel candies and pumpkin pie when I was a kid…but hey, wait…

"Why're there candles burning? That means there may be people somewhere around…or they *were* around!" Johnny laid Lizzie down onto a beige sectional sofa. Tucking her in as if he were her father, he rested his right palm on the teen's cheek, stroking the outline of her plump, soft lips with his left index finger. Beside her head on a coffee table adjacent to the sofa were some CDs, a cylindrical bottle of water, and a sealed bag of Trader Joe's Nacho Cheese Tortilla Chips.

"Hardcore albums, VOSS, n' nacho cheese chips?!"

Oddly specific items to place on a table…it's almost like someone knows what I used to be into…and those convenient towels on the wall…is all this just a happenstance?

"But it was raining…and who puts towel racks in their living room?"

Disregarding his preordained paranoia, Johnny grabbed the fat stack of discs and looked them over with a tinge of nostalgia.

"Some of these are true classics…"

Alesana - *The Emptiness*, As Cities Burn - *Son, I Loved You at Your Darkest*, Breather Resist - *Charmer*, Converge - *You Fail Me*, Counterparts - *Tragedy Will Find Us*, Every Time I Die - *Low Teens*, Exalt - *Pale Light*, Fear Before the March of Flames - *Art Damage*, From Another Planet - *An Ever-Changing Perspective*, Genghis Tron - *Board Up the House*, HORSE the Band - *Desperate Living*, Knocked Loose - *Laugh Tracks*, Minus - *Jesus Christ Bobby*, Norma Jean - *Redeemer*, Poison the Well - *You Come Before You*, Taken - *Between Two Unseens*, The Chariot - *Wars and Rumors Of Wars*, This Day Forward - *In Response*, Trap Them - *Crown Feral*, and Within the Ruins - *Creature*.

If only there was a boombox lying around, and not that oversized one that tricked me inside the prison…I'd play all these right now!

After reliving many past concerts and even more rounds of car-ride karaoke, Johnny Helks stared back into the peaceful face of Lizzie Janis.

"You're more beautiful than your sister."

Stop it at once, you idiot! This is like last time—she's passed out. And she's underage. Ringing any bells? Don't take advantage of yet another helpless girl. It's wrong. So, so wrong!

"I'm not doing anything wrong. I care for her, all right? Is that such a crime?!"

No…but what you're thinking of doing is. She can't even say if she wants you or not, for heaven's sake. Are you against trying your hand at nabbing a conscious, same-aged woman?

"My intentions are pure with her. How can you not see that? With what we've been through, saving Lizzie from the bus and the beast—I really think that should land me some goodwill!"

You've always been quite a master at justifying all of your twisted, lustful actions.

"I'm not justifying anything. Look…I know this girl probably hates my guts for what I did to her older sister—and if I'm being honest with myself, rightfully so—but this stranger-than-strange experience has us conjoined at the hip. Kind of like those twin sisters! This isn't like the last time; that was a *way* different time for me. I've changed; I've grown. And I have fully accepted my past transgressions."

Sure you have. You're almost like a normal person now, right?

"I mean, **maybe**. But I wouldn't necessarily go that far."

Yeah, me either. Don't kid yourself. You're an atom bomb, waiting to be detonated—and I feel sorry for whoever's around when it eventually happens.

"I'm ignoring you from here on out…since I don't have the patience to deal with your backtalk anymore. Or back thoughts, I guess."

Be my guest. I'll happily take a vacation from your schizo ass. Good luck on your own!

"Okay, Lizzie. Back to you and me. Sorry about that! My thoughts have a way of creeping into the forefront at times," Johnny said, wiping a pond of rain and sweat from the side of his neck. "I hope you don't hate me for what I've done to your sis, to your family—and I suppose to you as well, in a roundabout kind of way."

With her eyes closed and a steady, faint breathing at the helm, Lizzie lay on the off-white couch in tranquility, as if she were entombed in amber.

"Why are you such an attractive girl? It makes it hard to resist you!" Johnny trailed his fingers across her lukewarm cheekbones, sighing as he continued to glide across Lizzie's soft-as-silk yet sopping foundation. "OH, I gotta dry you off! Almost forgot to do that…forgive my forgetfulness! One moment; I'll be back."

Walking over toward the provided towels, he weighed his options. "I could just take her soaked shirt off instead…probably *would* make it easier for drying."

The freed prisoner counter-argued himself. "But when she wakes up and sees me looking at her—in only a bra—how would I explain myself? That wouldn't go over well. I'm trying not to be creepy; I'm trying to be caring."

Once the towels were collected from the accommodating racks, Johnny settled three of them onto Lizzie's legs, torso, and upper body.

"There; that should warm you up," he said, rubbing the sides of her shoulders like she'd just gotten out of a shower. "I want to kiss you. I wanna kiss you so *badly* right now. Would that be okay? Have I earned your trust?"

No response, no movement.

"It'll be a lot different this time around…" he assured the sleeping teen. "For one thing, we're the only two in this home. So I believe that we'll be safe. I've locked all the doors. Bolted and chained! Nobody's coming in tonight, unless they want to fight for it. And if something like that *does* happen, I'll gladly fight them right back. For you, Lizzie. 'Cause we've gotta stick together."

Gazing longingly into the blonde's blank face, Johnny went in for a delicate kiss on the lips. Unwrapping her from a towel-concocted cocoon and supporting the base of her wiry nape, the freed prisoner closed his eyes to mimic Lizzie's and softly connected his lips to hers. Locked as one for nearly a minute, Johnny felt a surge in his testosterone levels as he caressed Lizzie's uncovered waist. Her luscious lips increased his deepest desires with each peck and touch given, driving him to the point of irrationality regarding his elevated libido.

"This is wonderful, tasting your sweet, wet lips in an apocalypse. I couldn't possibly be any happier than I am in this moment."

Alarming Johnny out of a serene state, someone at the front door began rabidly trying to get into the house.

"NO, NO, NO!!" the agitated convict shouted, as the knob kept turning in frantic bouts of an obvious determination. "DAMMIT TO HELL, FIND YOUR OWN HOME!"

The deadbolt mechanism turned, informing Johnny that the unseen person outside had the proper keys to come inside. Freezing in place beside an unconscious Lizzie, the registered sex offender hoped that the door's chain would be dependable enough to hold and ultimately discourage the person from entering.

Johnny stood protectively by the girl, with one hand on her dampened head and the other clasping the handle of a knife that he had found earlier by the bus. Suddenly the rattling at the door ceased, and an uneasy silence heightened his senses.

"I'm warning you. Don't attempt to break in! We don't want any trouble, whoever you are, but I am *not* afraid to defend what I've found here. So if you wanna try me, fucking TRY ME! I'm holding my ground—you can count on that."

As soon as he defiantly challenged the lurking outsider to try and make his way inside, the front door blasted open—its chain lock flying off and clattering onto the stairwell banister, vaulting Johnny's heart from its chambers. Once the door crashed down to the carpeted floor, Johnny raised the hunting knife up to defend and protect Lizzie, yet he quickly found himself dismayed to see that there wasn't just one man to contend with but *two*. The two men leered in the doorway—the very same men who had knocked Johnny Helks out and had taken Riley Parker and Tamika Wilson against their will.

"You guys again…WHY…what do you want?! Can't you just leave us alone?"

"It all ends now, Johnny. We're calling this in. It's gone way too far," the well-built male known as Boss said authoritatively. "The game is over."

RE-EDIT: The Unsafe

"GAME?! What game?? Listen, I've already warned you—before I even fucking saw you—stay back! Or else I *promise* you'll get hurt!!" the freed prisoner threatened, shaking his knife at the pair of armed men entering the living room guardedly.

"No, Helks; you listen. This bullshit has gone on for far too long. And we're both tired of it. It's too dangerous now. Sure, we were instructed to let it all go…no matter what. But between the tornado taking out our monster—which none of us were prepared for—and you putting your dirty hands and lewd lips onto that unconscious girl, well…morality's setting in at last."

"It's true," the other male previously known as Greg agreed. "We don't even care if we've ruined the proceedings. If what we're doing right now spoils the series, then that's fine with us. It just HAS to stop. And no one else who's involved in this crazy thing has the *compassion* to do it. That's why we're ending it."

"I **really** don't understand what you're saying to me!" Johnny said.

"We wholly understand your confusion; we do. But see, the thing is that you're a risk to yourself, Johnny, and to all the others enmeshed in this mess…to put it as plainly as possible," the leader of the men said bluntly.

"Forgive me for not listening to you with an open mind. I suppose that I don't put much trust in hostile captors! For God's sake, *you* took those girls, Riley and Tamika…*you* injected them both! And *you* knocked me out from behind…like damned COWARDS!! Hell, and if I took a moment to put two and two together, I'd say that you were probably the ones who ambushed me back at the prison!"

"We were," the pair of armed men admitted.

"You even splashed me with water and ran off! Why?!"

"If ya wanna get technical about it, *we* didn't splash you—a bucket from above did." The leader laughed. "As for why, it was meant to wake you up—keep everything moving along…"

"WHO ARE YOU?! AND WHAT IS THIS??" Johnny screamed angrily.

"My name's Simon," the man who had once called himself Boss stated.

"And I'm Brent," the other man added.

Johnny waved his jagged knife toward them, successfully fending off any forward advancement and keeping the two men at bay. "I don't give a single fuck what your names are, you bastards! What I want are the *answers*…answers to why all this has happened to me and to them!! **WHAT** WAS THAT EXPLOSION OUTSIDE? **WHY** WAS I ABLE TO LEAVE MY CELL SO EASILY? **HOW** DID YOU GET THOSE GIRLS DRUGGED AND INTO A BUS? **WHERE** IN THE WORLD—OR WHAT PLANET—DID THAT INSANELY ENORMOUS MONSTER COME FROM? AND JUST **WHO** IS IN CHARGE…WHO'S CONTROLLING WHATEVER THIS SHIT IS??"

"All your pressing questions are exactly the ones that are going to fuel this entire experiment—for millions upon millions of viewers," Simon revealed.

Brent nodded. "That's the whole point of this thing in a nutshell. Money, ratings, and more money. *Bringing TV back to a revered prominence with unequivocal shock*—those were her opening words at the pitch meeting. It was a vision from our spunky showrunner to reach a golden age of television again—and with such an ambitiously risky project caked in reality, it's bound to succeed."

Johnny smacked his head repeatedly, as if trying to wake himself from a nonsensical nightmare. "What…in the…*fuck*…are you even talking about? Ratings? TV? An ambitious project?"

"*Ambitiously risky* is what he said, actually…" Simon corrected the on-edge Johnny. "Although I guess *ambitious* works, too."

"But what does that have to do with anything? No way do I believe that everything that's happened to me—and to those poor girls—over the last couple of days could've been staged!"

"You'd be surprised what financial backers can accomplish when incredibly motivated. They went all out with production values on this venture," Brent informed a doubtful Johnny. "It was a risky project for investors to take on, but its scope and layout were just too promising to turn down."

"Now, that twister wasn't in the cards. That was unplanned!" Simon clarified. "We aren't on a set per se. We're out in the middle of nowhere…in the great state of Montana."

"Yeah, Simon's right…that wicked twister wasn't even *expected* to happen. I mean, Montana isn't a place known for natural disasters; it's known for…being mundane?"

Simon expounded on the situation. "The original plan illustrated in storyboard—which made its way into the final shooting script—was to have the bloodthirsty monster grab hold of Lizzie, giving off the illusion that it was choking her to death, when in truth, its rubberized tentacles safely wrapped around her throat were dipped in chloroform. Then you'd come in and save her after a choreographed struggle with our monster. But that tornado changed a lot of plans around."

Johnny blew a gasket. "SO THIS ENTIRE TIME…YOU'VE BEEN THE REAL MONSTERS…IT'S ALL A SHOW! AN ELABORATE, DEMENTED HUMAN EXPERIMENT PARADING AROUND LIKE IT'S SOME TYPE OF GROUNDBREAKING TV SERIES! YOU HAVE BEEN TOYING WITH LIVES, POKING TEENS WITH NEEDLES AND CHLOROFORMING AN INNOCENT GIRL FOR THE SAKE OF ENTERTAINMENT?! FOR THE SAKE OF MONEY? IF YOU DIDN'T HAVE THOSE GUNS POINTED AT ME, I'D RIP YOUR FUCKING HEADS OFF RIGHT NOW!"

"Ease up there, jailbird. Every one of those teens are much better off for it. Financially speaking, they're going to be taken care of. Granted, they never knew what their strapped-for-cash parents had signed off on before being seized, but that's what made it so captivating, so intriguing. And now as the dust settles? Well, now they won't *ever* have to worry about money for as long as they live. So there's a bit of that clarity you seek. But just one last heads-up for ya…you need to calm down."

"And it was a *checked* dosage, by the way! I made absolutely certain that it wouldn't be lethal," Brent said sincerely. "I've always been the considerate one of this duo."

"When ya say it like that, you make me seem like such an asshole." Simon glared at Brent for a second. "But you're right; you did care more than I did. Which I do regret now, looking back at the big picture."

"Somebody give these men a medal! Bravo!!" The freed prisoner clapped, his right hand still firmly gripping the knife. "They have real remorse toward willingly participating in the abduction and the poisoning of minors! All for a fat paycheck? You're tyrants. Damned TYRANTS."

"Johnny, what you've just said right there…that's precisely why we're here today—the sheer madness of it all. That's why we'd like to put an end to it…and hopefully, with your cooperation, it'll come to a *peaceful* end. For your information, this thing wasn't supposed to conclude for, like, another three weeks, give or take. It's only been three days! Can you fathom the torment that was in store for you and them? Simon and I can, since we've seen some of it. So, knowing what we know, we can't see it trudge on any further. It's too hazardous, too deadly…"

"Sadly, the powers that be are gung-ho about the grit that's been tracked so far, which means that we can't stop what's already been shot. It's going to air with or without us. They'll find a way to make it work. Renowned editors can perform miracles, and I guarantee you they'll trim the fat. Somehow, some way, they WILL be able to. But here's what *we* can do, and it'd be a pretty difficult thing to edit out: we can conclude this craziness with a composed surrender."

Johnny Helks laughed. "From *me*, you mean?"

"From you; yes." Simon stepped forward with caution.

"And then what? Where do I go from here? Back to prison?"

Brent took a cautious step forward as well. "Then it'll be over, Johnny. It can be over. And no, you aren't going to be transported back to the penitentiary…that's not the next step planned. It's much grander than that."

"Is it as grand as you dousing highly sophisticated prosthetics with chloroform, rendering a sixteen-year-old unconscious?"

"Even grander; when it comes to humanizing things," Simon answered dryly. "In time you'll understand. So, how about you drop that knife and come with us…"

"You'd be smart to do so," Brent spurred on.

"Guns or no guns, I don't give a damn…'cause if the two of you honestly think that I'll just drop this knife and knuckle under your orders, you're a whole lot crazier than me. And that's pretty crazy, as I'm sure you know by my rap sheet."

Simon took a few more steps toward Johnny, confident in his ability to defuse the standoff with rationale. "Johnny boy, you're trapped. There's nowhere to go. But let's hypothesize for a second, all right? Even if you were to *escape* this current quandary by some off chance, what would you do? Go ahead and tell me your plan; I'll wait."

Johnny stuttered his way through a sentence. "I—I'd—go somewhere—I don't know where, but I'd try to find an area tha—"

"No, you wouldn't. It's undeniably an understatement to say that we're quite mindful of your many misconceptions by now—what with all your head trips and personality flips—but like my in-field partner has said to you: there is nowhere to go. Nowhere at all."

"WHY DON'T YOU COME OVER HERE, THEN?! WHY DON'T YOU TRY YOUR HAND AT TAKING ME DOWN??" The convict raised his arms outward, as if he were Christ on the cross. "I'M BEGGING YOU TO SHOOT."

"We *can't* shoot you; that's the thing. We had to sign several contracts before being deployed, and they explicitly state that we cannot shoot you anywhere on the body under any circumstances. Believe me, I've wanted to so many times."

"I can vouch for that," Brent quipped. "He doesn't shut up about it."

"All these damned rules, all this posturing…and for what…some stupid reality series? So many people hired on to meddle in the lives of others…" Johnny spoke aloud to no one in particular. "The hell we've been through…the anguish! Just greedy producers pursuing amusement for consumers? What a fucking HOAX!!"

"Hoaxes are usually meant to deceive maliciously or stir up interest for recreational reasons. This lofty experiment was meant to educate—as well as entertain, sure—but it's mainly about the fascinating human condition. With real people in real predicaments…while being in a *real* location," Simon said in a matter-of-fact manner. "A lot of thought's been put into it…and even though we don't agree with the overall vision, the endgame—still—is unlike anything else that's out there."

Brent scoffed a bit. "Man, you are kinda sounding like a walking, talking advertisement for this project. For me, it's a little too much

Kool-Aid drinking. Yeah, there was a lot of thought put into this, but let's not mince words on what it truly is: an intricate money grab."

"Fair enough; it is that." Simon inched closer to Johnny. "Come on, buddy…let's attempt to end this easily. It doesn't have to get violent."

Buying time in a ploy to stall the men out, the freed prisoner shot off questions with rapid-fire precision. "I still have a load of things to ask! Like…why'd you guys have a plane crash into that burning skyline? Did you have some crazy kamikaze do it?! And just *what* was that invisible object I knocked my head into before entering this house? Also, who was that bloodied girl saying my name and laughing maniacally outside?? All those crashes inside the joint…those notes left for me to read—were those just done to lead me wherever you wanted me to go? Answer and then I'll leave with you—with no problems."

Simon let out a groan, sighing as he started to speak. "Since you seem to hate mysteries so much, I'll be the one to answer quickly. Brent would take too long. Numero uno, that was a remote-controlled aircraft. You think they'd have hired a kamikaze for a stunt like that?! No; just no. Dos, that invisible object you hit—and the ones you heard buzzing about in prison—are called Cloak Drones. They're our filmers! No humanized camera crews. State-of-the-art stuff…the public has had things like the DroPho and whatever, but CloDros are only available to the richest of the rich— like Claire Drake, inventor of the ArmLarm…and all of *this*."

"Whoa…Claire Drake? You mean…the former President of the United States??" Johnny asked, surprised at hearing such a powerful woman's name.

"Don't act so shocked. A lesser person wouldn't have been able to pull off something this extensive—and expensive!" Brent shared.

"Anyway…" Simon proceeded to fill in the blanks. "Tres, that bloodied girl was an actress—really good for her age too, considering the pressure. And that blood spring-loaded onto her face and body from a latch mark in the ground was legitimate blood; it just wasn't human plasma. It was a cow's! No theatrical blood was used at all; the makeup department went for the utmost realism, following the pattern of how forensic scientists make use of cow blood for training new investigators!"

"That's insane. It looked so real. Her face…and every single one of those bodies, strewn about the landscape…all mangled and bathed in blood," Johnny reminisced. "Mind-melting!"

Simon ignored the freed prisoner's input. "And…oh yeah, CUATRO! Those noises and notes were all meant to direct—with intentions to usher you toward our next checkpoint. The boombox, the messages, many things. Predetermined, like pro wrestling. But we've also had a good amount of creative control throughout. Ready to go now?"

"Not quite. What about Lizzie? What happens to her after this ends? That's important to me."

"She'll be taken into custody, examined thoroughly by the best medical personnel around, and then she'll be sent over to the drop-off warehouse—where she'll be released and picked up by her grandmother once all pertinent forms are completed."

"Wow; this operation's real regulated, isn't it?" Johnny cross-examined. "Must be a pricey payroll for Ms. Drake to oversee."

"The priciest!" Simon confirmed, mere feet away from the freed prisoner. "Okay, well, there are your answers, Johnny; so come on already."

"Seriously, the exposition egg timer has run out…" Brent said.

Abruptly, Lizzie arose to consciousness, inhaling deeply and sitting up. "Johnny? What's going on? Did you save me from that monster? Last thing I remember I was being strangled by tentacles." The teen looked around groggily. "OH GOD, it's them…"

Johnny patted her on the shoulder soothingly. "It's okay; I am not going to let them have you."

"Are you kidding me right now?" Simon asked with repulsion. "You've agreed to comply with us, ya delusional psycho! There's no escape route for you."

Brent appeared confused. "We don't want any trouble with you or Lizzie here, as we've both stated so openly to your ignorant ass. Miss Janis, it's all right to come with us. And you *should*…since you're liable to catch a cold or worse, due to how…watery you look. Bottom line, *we're* the good guys in this—*not* Johnny."

"But you already know about his deficient character, don't you? The things that he did to your sister, and to your father—his actions have led to this huge showdown, and **all** of it was by design…" Simon educated the still-woozy teen. "You realized long ago who the real evil is: him."

Lizzie said nothing back, knowing full well that the armed man wasn't wrong; yet at the same time, she was conflicted, hectically reliving the memories of being saved by a person she'd vilified for years.

"Get up slowly and steadily…the effects of your dosage are starting to wear off. Your head must be swimming; sorry about that…" Brent apologized awkwardly.

"You can't just tell her what to do—like you've had nothing to do with how she's feeling?! YOU'RE THE ONES WHO DOSED HER!" Johnny yelled.

"All right; *calm down*. This is ending before it gets outta hand," Simon said firmly.

Brent concurred with his partner. "We only want this to wrap in peace—so no hostilities or complications are needed. It can all be avoided."

"NO HOSTILITIES, NO COMPLICATIONS?! THAT'S ALL YOU'VE GIVEN TO ME AND TO THEM!"

Lizzie grabbed hold of Johnny's elbow. "Relax; don't scream. My head…"

"Oh, right. Sorry…" Johnny turned toward the blonde girl seated on the couch. "I didn't mean to—"

Suddenly Simon stormed toward the distracted freed prisoner and performed a double leg takedown on him, sending Johnny crashing to the living room floor.

As the men struggled for supremacy against one another—and while Lizzie pleaded for them to stop—Brent apprehended the flapping and shouting teen, moving her away from the apish scrap.

"LEMME GO!" she demanded. "BREAK THEM UP!"

"Simon's able to handle himself," Brent said, backing away from the fracas. "What's vital is that we get you out of here and into some fresh clothes at the warehouse right now!"

"But what about them?! There's a gun and a knife involved! NEVER GOOD!!"

"Whatever happens happens…that gun's genuine, but that knife? Fake as plastic surgery. Just like the contents in that vial we planted on your stuffed zebra. So I think Simon'll be all right. And besides, what do you care? Johnny's a total piece of crap…lest we not forget what *he*'s done!"

"I know, asshole. But he saved me—and the others—and that *has* to mean something."

Brent shook his head, still clutching and dragging the blonde away. "Yeah, he saved you. And he saved them—but by *design*. It was ALL by design, Lizzie!"

"You guys may have set up paths for him, but he chose to save us. That was *his* decision. He could've been a horrible person…he could've done something awful to us instead."

"Something awful like touching you without your permission and kissing you on the lips while you were unconscious?!"

"He did that?!" Lizzie asked, letting up on her valiant resistance.

"Yes. And once this is all over, we'll show you that footage—the proof of it happening."

The fight became ear-piercing, drowning out Brent and Lizzie's dialogue.

"OW, YOU SON OF A BITCH!" Johnny barked beneath the body of Simon.

"Just SURRENDER, basket case…this doesn't have to get any messier!"

Johnny Helks squirmed below Simon's forceful control, straining to spread his arms out just enough to snag his knife.

Only inches from the freed prisoner's fingertips, Johnny grunted and groaned his way toward the blade—a simple but effective weapon that could sway things back in his favor.

Closer and closer.

Inch by inch.

Scream after scream.

Until he finally got hold of the resin-coated aluminum handle.

In possession of the knife without his mounted initiator even knowing, Johnny stopped grunting but kept maneuvering, trying to find any opportunity that would present itself to stab his bigger and stronger adversary.

"Don't make me pistol-whip you! I may not be able to shoot you, but I can sure as shit sock you right in the skull! Things like that were *nowhere* in the fine print. Stop struggling, dammit!!"

"FUCK YOU!" Johnny defied his mounter.

Simon snapped, whipping the pistol into the convict's nose three times. "STOP…FUCKING…STRUGGLING!"

"**FUCK**…**YOU**!!" Johnny repeated, bleeding copiously but still clutching the blade.

Another crushing blow.

And another.

"That's five now!" Lizzie pointed out urgently. "PLEASE; he's done some unforgivable things in the past, but surely Johnny doesn't deserve to *die*!! This could KILL him here!!"

"Cool it; he's only teaching him a lesson…and didn't *you* threaten to kill the guy yourself? He should've listened to us…" Brent said with no emotion whatsoever. "C'mon, we have to get you outta here!"

"And let your butt buddy do more damage?? NO; this isn't right!!"

Lizzie kicked Brent's shin hard with her heel, and once she was free from the man's grasp due to his newly appointed pain, the petite teen swiveled around and kneed him in the nuts, breaking away.

"SHIT, BITCH! GET BACK HERE!!" Brent shouted while on his knees in agony.

By the time the man's pained words were said, Lizzie was already halfway across the room and halfway to where she wanted to be: a combat zone containing only two combatants, a beleaguered Johnny and a conquering Simon.

She leaped onto Simon's hulking shoulders, only to be swung off effortlessly with a backhand. Seeing the blonde backhanded so recklessly infuriated a pancaked Johnny, causing his anger to boil over.

Lizzie shrieked in surprise, four on the floor. "You maniac! Stop hurting him!!"

"Don't fuckin' interfere!" Simon barked back. "Just step away. If you know what's good for ya…you *will* abide…"

The freed prisoner gripped the knife tighter—a specific blade that was thought by Brent to be just a prop—and concealed it for a little while longer in order to find a fatal opening.

Rapidly losing patience, Simon pressed his thumbs into Johnny's eyes. "SUBMIT!"

Blinded by Simon's stubs for thumbs, Johnny thrust his knife up toward the aggressor's throat.

One last-ditch effort.

After the wild swing of the blade, there was a puncturing of flesh—but it wasn't the flesh of Simon's, it was Lizzie's. The headstrong teen had heedlessly attacked from the side instead of from the back like before. As if exiting a water cannon, her neck shot out a high-velocity stream of blood, lavishly spilling onto Johnny's face and Simon's shoulder.

Palming her own plasma-plastered scruff, Lizzie fell to the floor as all hell broke loose.

"NO, NO!!" Simon yelled, getting off of Johnny straightaway to tend to the bleeding teen.

"Oh, God…oh, Jesus…" Brent said in total shock. "Why wasn't that a fake blade?!"

"LIZZIE??" Johnny called out, attempting to get up.

"*Brent!* Don't just clutch your crotch and stand there all stoic like some Queen's Guard!! Keep the bastard down while I call this in…" Simon put his right index finger to an earpiece, spouting off a mayday code. "One-zero-eight-one-zero-eight. I repeat…One-zero-eight-one-zero-eight. Hello? Come in! Agent Number One on standby inside sector twenty-three, awaiting your immediate assistance."

"Please hurry, man. She's bleeding pretty badly," Brent worried.

"Doing my best! I can't help it if they're not coming in quickly. Don't freak." Simon kept focused on his earpiece, listening intently to whoever had arrived on the other end. "Yeah, it's a code duress, level ten. Bring the chopper down, bring the med crew, just…make the effort to get here ASAP! Okay; all right. Thank you."

Johnny's facial contusions prevented him from seeing things clearly, yet he could tell that a scowling Brent was above him—with a size-twelve boot pressed up against his hyperventilating chest, making it difficult to get any kind of decent look. A wave of guilt washed over the convict, even though he knew it was an accident. "I'm sorry; I'm sorry. I am so...*so*...sorry!" the pinned man cried, looking up to Brent with an amalgamation of distance and shiftlessness.

"Save it. We *know* you are. But you'd better hope that this girl makes it through what you've just done."

"IT WAS AN ACCIDENT! I DIDN'T MEAN TO DO THAT!! YOU HAVE TO KNOW THAT."

"Shut the fuck up, Johnny...keep him held down over there, Brent."

"Already am! So what's the word? How long until they reach our coordinates?!"

Simon sighed, applying taut pressure to Lizzie's leaking nape as he answered his in-field partner. "Not that long. Maybe three minutes at the most? They are constantly monitoring, so they saw it. They're near us."

"In one of those underground bunkers?"

"Yeah; where else?"

"IS SHE GONNA DIE?!" Johnny asked, scared out of his mind. "IS SHE GOING TO MAKE IT??"

"Well...if she *doesn't* make it through this, it'll all be on you..." Simon replied, aloof to the held convict's impassioned questions. "So stay quiet and pray, Johnny boy—pray that this scenario doesn't get a whole lot worse for your ass."

"I thought that that knife was a damn prop, man! Chad switched 'em out when we took two of the selected and that freak was asleep. This wasn't supposed to happen."

"Somehow he must've flubbed the blade exchange. And I'm aware of what was *supposed* to occur. Our prop master will be in deep shit for this snafu!"

"This is bad, Simon. This is **such** a bad situation!"

"Stating the obvious...as always...listen, if we're lucky, they'll be on the scene within a few."

I have to get up. I've gotta get away from this man holding me down. I have to help her…since this is my fault. God Almighty, this is all my fault! So I must make it right! I MUST!!

Johnny powered up to his feet, obtaining any intestinal fortitude and strength he had left in his body to overcome his subduer. The freed prisoner pushed a distracted Brent down to the ground, causing the agent to crush the corner of a coffee table upon impact. With Simon shouting orders to his collapsed partner, the back of Brent's head gushed blood, severely cut from the tabletop glass panel.

Brent was out cold, lying motionless on the carpeted floor as Johnny's eyes locked onto Simon's.

"You crazy idiot…you're seriously gonna try and injure me too? In case you can't see what's going on right now, I'm tryin' to keep this girl ALIVE!! She's **bleeding out**. So if you try to stop me from applying pressure to this here neck, we just may lose a life, ya erratic maniac! And then *that* means I won't get paid!!" Simon said, condemning Johnny with his selfish words. "For me, her death would mean debt…"

"All you care about is money? A teen's bleeding on your hands; she's dying in your arms, and the only thing that's going through your mind is a contract stipulation?!"

"Goddammit, I didn't go through *all* of this just to end up with NOTHING!!"

Think. Weapon. Where. What. Grab something! Look around. Quick!

Motivated by the self-absorbed man's indifference toward Lizzie's life hanging in the balance, Johnny swiped the cylindrical, 1.5-pint bottle of Voss still sitting atop the half-destroyed coffee table, unfazed by Brent's head smashing into the corner of it.

"Stay right where you are, Helks," Simon warned firmly, with one hand on Lizzie's slippery neck and the other with his gun aimed right at Johnny's head. "Unless you want this girl to die right here on set!" The well-built man became distracted by his earpiece, placing the gun that had been pointed at Johnny to the side of his temple. "Yes? Okay, great. See you soon!"

And that was all the freed prisoner needed as an opening to make his move.

Johnny raced over to Simon, tackling him off of a fading Lizzie.

"CRAZY FUCKER!" Simon shouted as he tumbled to the ground. "STOP! SHE'LL DIE!!"

Now in a favorable mount position instead of being the one underneath, Johnny clutched the bottled water like a murder weapon and rained down shot after shot with the glass instrument. With no mercy shown, Johnny proceeded to pulverize Simon's face into oblivion as shards of jagged glass broke off and into the pores of the apprehended man after each blow delivered.

"Die, Daddy…*die*…**die**…DIE, DADDY…*DIE*…**DIE!**" an entirely hollow Johnny repeated over and over, reverting back to his childhood trauma in an instant as he inflicted more damage on Simon.

As the former prisoner continued to hail down strikes at a feverish rate, paramedics, producers, and muscular guards rushed into the living room.

"Get him off of Simon before it's too late; go, go, go!" one of the sharp-dressed producers said pressingly to the huge guards close behind.

A pair of stocky handlers strong-armed the displaced Johnny off an annihilated, quivering Simon. As handcuffs were slapped painfully onto his wrists, the convict cried out and pleaded to go over to where Lizzie was. The once-headstrong teen was now relegated to a weak shell of her former self. Bleeding freely onto the white carpet, she stained the fibers under her with a vibrant red claret.

"MOMMY! AGH, SHE'S REALLY HURT! DADDY HURT HER!!" Johnny screamed inconsolably.

"GET THAT MENTAL PATIENT OUTTA HERE!" a tending paramedic ordered to the handlers. "Put him in the psych van—make sure he's secure, and then *leave* this area!!"

"Right away…" one of the handlers said.

"No problem; we've got this under control," another handler added, shoving Johnny forward.

Forcibly leaving the home that had actually been an intricately made set, a coming-down-to-earth Johnny Helks looked up to the sky in sudden admiration, as its normal purple hue of pollution had all but vanished. In its place was a pristine blue sky—an atmosphere teasing him with a cleanliness that he would never again be able to gaze upon.

"Watch your head as you go in, loon!" the biggest and burliest of the handlers instructed.

Johnny obliged the direct order, mentally whitewashed and physically weakened. "Okay." He could hardly breathe. Cowering backward as two van doors slammed shut in his void of a blotted face, the crying convict saw a futuristic—to his sheltered eyes— helicopter landing beside the house he'd just exited. Dirt flew up as the chopper's rotor blades spun around and around lightning-quick, while three gurneys were sent into the house by crew members.

Why has all this happened? Why can't I simply go back to how it used to be—back to when I was asleep in my cell? This is worse than being stuck in prison.

The van with no license plates sped off, leaving the contrived destruction of uninhibited homes—or rather, the mass-produced set pieces—far behind as Johnny's jumbled thoughts couldn't cease for even a nanosecond.

WRAP-UP: The Handlers

"Hey, buddy, how's your head?"

"It's all right, I guess. A lot better than what it was earlier."

"That was quite the spill you took there."

"Tell me something I don't know!"

"Be grateful that you survived. Why you guys didn't just storm Johnny immediately is beyond me."

"I told you; I meant what I said. We *really* wanted it to end peacefully…and we also wanted to keep Lizzie Janis as safe as possible."

"And how'd that work out for ya?"

"CAN IT! Where's Simon now? Still in critical condition?"

"Your partner, well…"

"What? He didn't actually, no…he didn't re—"

"Sorry to tell ya this, but yeah, he wasn't so lucky."

"Man…I can't fucking believe…"

"Believe it. Detached retinas, swelling of the brain—among other things—all led to his end."

"So, what does this mean, exactly? Who am I reporting to, then?"

"You're not to report to anyone anymore, Brent. Your duties are hereby terminated."

"Why? The next phase is coming up! I was assigned to that."

"There's no show to man. Not for you, anyway. You broke protocol. So many of them."

"That's it? This is what I get for all my time given to the experiment?"

"Be appreciative that you're walking away from this thing uncharged."

"I busted my hump for you, for them, for HER! Getting legs under the table of this monolithic outfit was a hard sell for some, but I stayed. With reservations, I remained. While we had a cast and most didn't last!! Now I'm supposed to just suck it up and leave?"

"Yes. Take your severance pay at the main gate and leave within fifteen."

"Do you realize how much time I've spent working out there…in the field…planning and prepping?! Before it even began?"

"Brent. I do realize and recognize the time you've put in. But your time's up here. Don't you get it? Your services are no longer needed."

"All the beta testing, the worrying, the prowling…manning my way through a simulated storm, even!"

"Simulated? No; that was a legitimate twister. It threw us for a loop, too…"

"You kidding? Simon and I thought it was just a really well-done simulation."

"Then why in the *world* did you talk about it like it was real to Johnny?"

"Because we were still—somewhat—trying to go with the flow! We thought it was an added bonus to the series!!"

"Absolutely not; it was an unexpected occurrence…one that almost ruined everything."

"Oh, well, it seemed to ruin the monster—an amazing monster that I had thought to be indestructible."

"Wasn't in the forecast for us to ever test a million gallons of water against our oily beast."

"Manufactured or not, that mile-long monstrosity was a sight to see."

"I can't disagree."

"That tornado, though…it was damn near *Wizard of Oz*-like…looked kind of real but not **too** real."

"Okay; enough dicking around now. Gather your things, Mr. Douglas. It's time to close out your tab."

"A year invested. Down the drain. I don't even know why I took this job in the first place."

"There'll be a black car near the front of the warehouse, and it's waiting for you."

"I brought my own transportation; thanks."

"Plans have changed, Brent. I suggest that you follow protocol."

"Why's there a car awaiting me outside?"

"Because that's your ride."

"I didn't sign on *any* dotted line to be escorted outta here like some schmuck!"

"And *I* didn't sign on the dotted line to get lathered in blood makeup and have prosthetic pieces applied to my face and body, now, did I? But guess what? I did it all when asked—for the good of the program."

"It's different, though! That was an off-the-cuff addition to the bus battle scene; and besides…you sounded like you were totally into it!"

"Well, I **was** into it before I had to be anchored down in a chair for hours. *The Void* boys have a strong preference for practical effects. Found out the hard way."

"Hey…Jeremy and Steven are dope directors. They know what they're doing, so it was worth it."

"Getting made up in believable gore just saps one's patience. I STILL have a bunch of red stains on my skin!"

"At least your gold necklace didn't get stained. That's some silver lining to your memorably bloody contribution to the show. You guys were real good, too. *Jack and Gil?* Cheesy name choices, but funny…"

"I'll admit…it was great seeing my bunkmate fire shots off around the bus. He earned his salary. Really brought it."

"Yeah, he definitely did. Except for that one flub. If I'd been in charge, I would've docked him for losing control of his husky—TWICE!"

"And that's why there are leash laws—to prevent crap like that from happening! Good thing Walt had a dog whistle on him, or else I think Cisco would never have left Johnny's side."

"Indeed. So…should I presume that I'm gonna be charged with insubordination soon?"

"Don't presume anything. You're not being pressed with charges. I've already told you that you aren't! You're getting off scot-free."

"You mean to tell me that there're really no repercussions for tipping our hand to that human hairball Helks?"

"None that I know of. And I can understand why there wouldn't be…it'll spike ratings."

"How come?"

"'Cause it adds even more intrigue and mystery to the overall arc of this large-scale project. Ya gotta admit, we've had a phenomenally fertile field to work with…"

"That we did. What about the reparations? Are those girls and their parents truly going to be taken care of?"

"Yes. They are. With all their cooperation, it's been an easy process."

"I wish Simon would've made it. I was going to buy him some cigarettes after we got out of this."

"A loner-type guy like him, with the military background that he had coming into this…"

"He probably would've wanted to go out the way he did."

"Took the words right outta my mouth."

"I just…I cannot *believe* it's all over."

"Try to, though. You should get going. Don't want to keep them waiting. Claire's on her way."

"Miss Drake herself?"

"Yeah; so you shouldn't be around for much longer. I've been too lenient, too forgiving."

"Just one question before I go."

"Fine. What's on your mind?"

"The selected…I know they've made it back home safely, but Lizzie…she was stabbed, so—"

"She's okay now. It was a little touch-and-go for a while, but Blondie made it."

"All right, well—that certainly calms the nerves."

"Good; glad to hear it. So, I suppose this is goodbye forever?"

"Suppose so. Sorry that it got pretty messy during filming."

"It's cool, my friend. Don't worry about it. You're leaving. Out of the equation now."

"Well, take it easy. It was a pleasure getting to know you throughout this unusual process."

"Likewise. Honestly."

"Ha, this is embarrassing. But where do I exit? That door to the left or the one down to the right?"

"One to the right."

"Okay; sounds good. See ya in another life, then!"

"Maybe…or maybe not…"

"HEY! GET YOUR HANDS OFF ME!! WHAT IS THIS, SEAN?!"

"It's a course correction—a cleaning of the gutter."

"You said that I wasn't in trouble, that I wasn't being charged!"

"Eh, I guess I only told you half of the truth. While you're not being charged with anything, you ar—"

"ASSHOLES! ALL OF YOU!!"

"…*are* in a tank of trouble. Load him into the car, boys. Handle this fourth-wall breaker."

"Not a prob. We'll dump his body later tonight, tidy as can be—erased from existence!"

"WHAT? YOU'RE GOING TO KILL ME??"

"Affirmative. As per the former president's request. And what she orders, we cook up."

"My wife…my unborn child…please…you can't do this…I'm sorry we went off-script!!"

"Don't you worry about the future of your wife and child; they'll be financially stable. In a year from now, Josie will probably remarry—all because she'll still be so saddened over your unexplained, random abandonment—and your baby will grow to know another father."

"I—no—just please—hold on—"

"Take him away already! I'm not in the mood to hear another sob story."

"Will do. Right away."

"Refrain from dragging feet. It only prolongs the inevitable."

"Get in the back of the car, Brent."

"HOW 'BOUT YOU GET IN FIRST?!"

"Push him in. Can't be haggling with a dead man."

"She's gonna be here soon. We should get a move on. I don't wanna be fired."

"*PLEASE*…**WAIT**!"

"Well, me either! All right; cool. He's in there now. Let's go settle this."

"Yeah, we gotta. The *woman* behind the curtain is about to make her grand entrance…"

PRE-SCREENING: The Jailed

Detained for days inside a four-walled, padded space, Markéta Janis had been an unwitting subject in a binge-watching experiment. All for a polarizing new reality series that was about to be released. Cut off from any kind of amiable companionship or communication, the wearied woman gave in to the program after many resistant outbursts. Broadcasting a total of thirteen episodes with each one ending in a riling cliffhanger, the too-close-to-home show took up most of the mystified woman's thoughts.

Forty-five minutes in length per episode—stripping away the commercial breaks that would air on the national broadcasts—*The Last Offender* had recently overridden the twenty-three-year-old's wayfaring attention with its daring directions and tantalizing twists. Due to having an integral connection to the driving plot, her emotional investment was off the charts, and with the wide-ranging scenarios that had unfolded, it inflicted echoes of a resounding trauma more times than she could count.

My sweet little sister…why would anyone have gone to these lengths to create something this real? How depraved are these people? And WHO are they?! What is this sick study?

"Why am I here? Why am I trapped in this chalky-white room?!" Markéta asked aloud with desolation and desperation in her cracking voice. "What do they—YOU—want from me?"

Such basic questions, yet such tangled answers. She had asked them in various ways, repeatedly and constantly, while imprisoned. But the only response that Markéta had ever received was that of food and water being delivered through a plexiglass slot at irregular intervals. The deliverer—if it were a man or a machine, she could never be sure—always went sight unseen. Every time. Even so, her door-within-a-door had become an event to anticipate. A brief, nonreciprocal means to communicate. A recurring glimmer of hope that whoever was on the other side of that door would eventually buckle and demonstrate a dot of compassion. That's what she banked on.

Where, oh where is the HUMANITY?

Nothing that the entrapped woman could constructively think, verbally plead, or physically heave could be construed as productive activities. Whether it be through stomping, screaming, or throwing expendable TV sets against her padded walls…

Absolutely nothing that she ever did had resulted in anything other than silence.

If one television was destroyed, another emerged in its place right after she awoke the next day. It was a cyclical counter to her subversive behavior. Concealed, controlled, contained.

Exact replicas. I've probably smashed about ten of 'em…and it never fails…it never changes…

"A brand-new set after every box I lay to waste…each time…so it doesn't matter, does it?" the hemmed-in, track-mark-infested woman speculated. "I could keep wrecking these TVs…keep delaying whatever this SHIT is, and it wouldn't matter at all! So maybe I'll just let this show play out. I mean, that's the point of this repetitive exercise, right? Watch and wait for whoever's watching **me**." She looked up to the clear glass ceiling. "Whenever you're willing to manifest, Mr. Mystery, I'm ready for you to divulge! I am right here."

Lashing out toward the sleek, contoured screens had caught up to the confined female. And now, all she wanted to do was sit back and relax on the stiff futon that had been bolted down in her cramped room. A bare, joyless space that could defeat any psyche.

Time to roll with the punches…even if I do feel like I've been continually KO'd…

Markéta wanted to see how the personally distressing series would end—if it even *did* have an ending. More than anything else, she needed resolution—to this alleged reality presented, this episodic offering of an apocalyptic suffering. But most importantly, she yearned for some communicable acknowledgment of her own precarious position. She craved and ached for conclusive answers. Her weeks-long entrapment had epitomized a clear-cut secrecy. It encapsulated intrigue. And the twenty-three-year-old desired to be indulged.

Settling in to the slickly produced show, as unholy and unpredictable as it was throughout its run, episode twelve—the penultimate episode—was wrapping up with tensions rising and discomfort building. Markéta's virginity-taker, Johnny Helks, had been carrying a soaked Lizzie—her unconscious sister—over his shoulder and into a modest-looking home. Successfully fleeing the monster as well as the tornado that had been pursuing them, they were seemingly safe from both dangers.

The older sibling looked on as *The Last Offender* unraveled before her eyes, fully invested in whatever would develop next between the man who'd taken advantage of her a decade earlier and the sister she'd never really gotten to know. With negligence enacted and poor choices made after giving up her baby, Markéta had detached herself from family and friends—to attach herself to drugs and thugs.

And so there she was—detoxing and deliberating in a closed-off room with not a clue. Far away from any known civilization, she watched Lizzie—utterly helpless in her current state thanks to a bundle of otherworldly tentacles—on an ordinary couch with an impulsive person who should still have been locked up. As the freed prisoner pet the teen's dampened hair, making Markéta more uncomfortable by the second, the show did a jarring smash cut to the upstairs bathroom. Through the steamy glass doorway, a shower blasted streams of water onto the face of a human figure.

"There's somebody else in the house!" the fidgety woman declared to the minimal room, as if she were in the house herself. "Get outta there and help my sister!!"

The Last Offender jumped back to the downstairs area with a pan-and-scan shot of the living room, where Johnny knelt beside a sleeping Lizzie. A quick succession of smash cuts was then shown: the upstairs bathroom from an outside angle, where some shadowy figure stood under a showerhead, and to the living room set—viewed from a panoramic fisheye lens that had been strategically tucked into a hoity-toity Venetian chandelier.

An extreme long shot showed a man who resembled Johnny rising to his feet, noticing the faint noise coming from up above. "Hello? Who's there?"

Oh no, he's gonna go investigate! Yup, there he goes! Ah...I can't bear to watch...but I HAVE to!

"I'll be right back, sweet pea. Don't you go anywhere, ya hear?" the indistinguishable male requested sardonically from yet another artsy-fartsy, top-down angle.

"What's **wrong** with you? That's not even funny!" Markéta said to her curved QLED monitor, annoyed and offended. But she was glued to the tube attentively.

The only thing giving me company is this fucking screen. That's my reality. And my sister's reality is…

Cutting to the flight of stairs from the top, Johnny Helks made his way up to the bathroom. Tentatively. Once his dimly lit face came somewhat into focus on the hidden camera embedded inside one plain frame of a family photo, the show smoothly transitioned to the shower stall. Abruptly off-putting visually, the tracking closeup revealed a life-sized dummy with painted-on eyes. Dripping wet, the stationary model's matted black hair hung over its feminine facial features, covering its manufactured face entirely—resembling the spine-chilling girl who had crawled out of a TV in *The Ring*.

A freakin' mannequin in the shower? Really? Just…WHY? This is even weirder than when the girls found those three mannequins in the mid-season finale. Or when that bucket of water splashed Johnny from a cell's ceiling in the second episode. At least that was amusing, though!

While the ensnared woman racked her brain over what this could possibly mean, Johnny opened the shower door at high alert. Appearing about as shocked as Markéta was when she first saw the mannequin, the freed prisoner knocked the drenched dummy down, and it lay as still as ever on the tub's acrylic flooring. The irate man began to scream and fling the idle thing from pillar to post as the camera caught everything from its fixed top-down angle.

Yeah, that's it. Let all that aggression out on something lifeless. Better to do that than to unleash whatever demons you have on my little sister, who's unfortunately at your mercy.

"I just wonder whose mercy I'm at inside here…" the woman pondered. "Ugh, this shaky cam freakout is making me queasy."

The stale filming technique—one that's utilized to try and heighten the intensity of action scenes—recorded Johnny's vulgar display of brutality put forth onto an articulated body.

But it had brought up a conundrum.

If this thing's filmed so surrealistically—and with such voyeurism—why's there even a shaky cam at all? That'd mean that someone's there, holding it in their hand to capture it all…

"Right?" Markéta asked herself. "I don't get what's going on here, or over there…" She pointed at the glowing screen flippantly. "HEY UP THERE! IS ANYONE WATCHING ME LIKE I'M WATCHING THIS?!" The frustrated woman looked around her white padded cell. "JUST ANSWER ME; PLEASE."

As she'd expected, no one answered her pleas, so the narcotics abuser kept watching, choosing to keep quiet and keep ingesting the show. With the shaky camera steadying on an overhead shot of Johnny, his rage toward the shower mannequin tapered off while the once-nauseating scene faded away. Blackness remained on the TV for just enough time to make the captive female think that the episode was over.

When are they gonna drop off more food and water? It's been like eight hours since the last one!

"How many episodes are left? And WHY am I being forced to watch, anyway?"

It's your sister, obviously. And it's the man with her. You're meant to see what happens. You're meant to see how it ends…there's meaning in this test screening.

"But why?? Where do **I** fit into this?"

She was stumped as to what the endgame would entail.

A new scene materialized, establishing the beginning of the next episode.

Markéta had been right; the penultimate installment was history. The downtime in between episodes—whenever she'd allow them to actually complete—was approximately sixty seconds, which she could keep track of via a countdown clock. And since her lockup, it had taken two workweeks to see the series, thanks to the older sibling's outbursts.

Viewing keenly from a secluded spot, the bright display showed that Johnny had returned to the living room to be beside Lizzie. In lieu of nonstop internal conjecturing, Markéta's attention reverted back to the screen.

Moments went by where nothing really happened—a tepid kickoff. The freed prisoner knelt down by Lizzie Janis. He didn't move much; he remained docile by the sleeping teen's side.

"Johnny seems to be relaxed now—more than he was upstairs, at least, back when he was mauling a mannequin!" Markéta noticed, becoming nervous regarding his gliding presence with her sister, yet giving him the benefit of the doubt.

To my surprise, the guy's been shockingly gentlemanly by not tearing her clothes off.

"But don't you get any ideas, slimebag…I know what you're capable of!"

And much to her horror, Johnny moved in for a soft kiss on Lizzie—and a lot more, judging by his hand placements.

Stop doing what you're doing! She's asleep!! It's like last time…with me…

Unnerved, the captive woman scrunched her face and begged for someone—anyone at all—to break in and interrupt him. As Markéta's forlorn praying continued, she watched the disgusting scene unfurl with fingers up to her eyes.

The show then cut over to the front door of whichever house Johnny had holed up in with Lizzie—and from the other side of the brown door, two men were trying to get in. Both armed males had been seen regularly by the twenty-three-year-old addict throughout *The Last Offender,* so she knew all too well the bad blood between the freed prisoner and the dastardly duo.

This probably isn't going to be pleasant once they make their way in…oh, Lizzie, why are you caught in this mess?! Why am I caught in this mess? I just want it to be done. I just want my sis to be safe.

"Please," the older sibling groveled. "I don't wanna see any more."

Silence.

"TURN IT OFF!"

Again, silence.

"Do you hear me up there?" She struck the futon. "This is WRONG, and I'd like for it all to END."

Still no answer.

Not taking her eyes away from the TV's glimmering rays despite a tenable declaration of having had enough, Markéta watched the persistent men break the chain that had temporarily been holding them off. Johnny Helks raised a knife in defense, standing right beside Lizzie Janis as he did.

Markéta's heart raced as she watched the cleverly edited, well-produced spectacle go down.

Johnny was sweating buckets during the intense standoff. "You guys again…WHY…what do you want?! Can't you just leave us alone?"

"It all ends now, Johnny. It's gone way too far," the man known throughout the show as Boss said.

The Ultra HD cam did a 360° pan across the room, intensifying the delayed response from Johnny.

"Listen, I've already warned you—before I even fucking saw you— stay back! Or else I *promise* you'll get hurt!!" the convict threatened.

A closeup on Boss now. "No, Helks; you listen. This bullshit has gone on for far too long. And we're both tired of it."

"It just HAS to stop. That's why we're ending it," Greg, the smaller man, announced calmly.

"I **really** don't understand what you're saying to me!"

"You're a risk to yourself, Johnny, and to all the others enmeshed in this mess…" Boss added.

"For God's sake, *you* took those girls, Riley and Tamika…*you* injected them both! And *you* knocked me out from behind…like damned COWARDS!! Hell, you were probably the ones who ambushed me back at the prison!"

"We were," both of the men admitted.

"WHO ARE YOU?!"

Elegantly, a swell of orchestral music came into the mix, complementing the culmination to perfection after an otherwise isolated score—save for some motifs peppered into certain sections.

"My name's Simon."

"And I'm Brent."

There was a seamless transition into a medium-range shot of Johnny, now more hostile than ever.

"I don't give a single fuck what your names are, you bastards! What I want are the *answers*…answers to why all this has happened to me and to them!! IF YOU DIDN'T HAVE THOSE GUNS

POINTED AT ME, I'D RIP YOUR FUCKING HEADS OFF RIGHT NOW!"

Who's the antagonist here? They're all crazy to me, Markéta thought while watching.

The burly-looking leader stepped forward. "Ease up there, jailbird. You need to calm down."

"You're tyrants. Damned TYRANTS."

"We can conclude this craziness with a composed surrender," Simon said.

Johnny laughed. "From *me*, you mean?"

"From you; yes." He nodded.

"It can be over," Brent added.

"Guns or no guns, I don't give a damn…'cause if the two of you honestly think that I'll just drop this knife and knuckle under your orders, you're a whole lot crazier than me."

Lizzie suddenly came to as the camerawork kept ratcheting up suspense with interweaving shots of the armed men and the woozy, waking teen. "Johnny? What's going on? OH GOD, it's them…"

Oh, no; oh, no…please don't let anything happen to her…please let this end peacefully…

"Get up slowly and steadily…" Brent motioned nicely. "We only want this to wrap in peace—so no hostilities or complications are needed. It can all be avoided."

"NO HOSTILITIES, NO COMPLICATIONS?! THAT'S ALL YOU'VE GIVEN TO ME AND TO THEM!" the freed prisoner yelled disruptively.

He's outta control, dammit! Stop him before he ruins another life!! You have the guns; use them!

Lizzie placed her hand on Johnny's elbow. "Relax; don't scream. My head…"

"Oh, right. Sorry…" the frazzled convict apologized, turning around to face the groggy teen. "I didn't mean to—"

Another closeup of Simon's face now, running toward Johnny and tackling him to the ground.

Markéta, absolutely transfixed as to what was transpiring on-screen, stood up again. With both fists balled to her lips, she rooted for her sister to find the strength to escape. "Get out of there, Liz; get out of there now…" the captive woman whispered anxiously.

The Last Offender relied on more shaky cam to capture the brutal scrap as both of the men at odds struggled on the carpeted floor, while the orchestral music, which was composed by the lauded Bear McCreary, shifted into a stress-inducing cacophony. Strings and snares punched in and out as the soundtrack accompanying the grisly fight swelled to a breaking point.

This is giving me motion sickness…nix that handheld shit.

After the hectic tussle went on for a while, Simon gained control of Johnny, mounting him as if he were fighting inside an octagon.

"OW, YOU SON OF A BITCH!" the freed prisoner wailed below the stocky man.

"STOP…FUCKING…STRUGGLING!"

Listen to him, you maniac. You're going to lose no matter what…you're outmatched!

"**FUCK**…**YOU**!!" Johnny replied disobediently.

Bad choice of words there. Not smart.

Switching frenziedly from Brent and Lizzie standing on the sidelines to Johnny and Simon scuffling on the ground was almost too much for Markéta to digest.

Unending shaky cam reigned supreme during the full-blown chaos as Markéta's eyes darted all over the screen to keep up with everything. In a frightening moment, Lizzie ran over to the two grounded men and bit off way more than she could chew. When Johnny went to stab the throat of Simon, he stabbed the throat of the sixteen-year-old girl instead. Blood shot out everywhere. Uncensored, unreal, and unscripted.

"SIS!" the older sister hollered. "No, no, no, no, no. GOD…don't let me see her die on TV—don't allow this to happen! Please, please, please."

"NO, NO!!" Simon yelled, immediately jumping off of Johnny to tend to the bleeding teen.

"Oh, God…oh, Jesus…" Brent muttered.

"IT WAS AN ACCIDENT! I DIDN'T MEAN TO DO THAT!!"

Markéta sobbed. "Who cares if it was or not? You still *stabbed* her!!"

"Shut the fuck up, Johnny…" Simon ordered as he applied pressure to Lizzie's gaping neck.

"IS SHE GONNA DIE?!" Johnny asked with fright. "IS SHE GOING TO MAKE IT??"

"This is bad, Simon. This is **such** a bad situation!"

Without a moment's notice, Johnny attacked a stricken Brent out of the blue. One heavy shove to the chest later and the freed prisoner sent Brent crashing into the corner of the living room coffee table.

Busted open and out cold, the camera zoomed in on the unconscious male in a lingering shot.

"WOW," the entrapped woman said, still standing.

The stinging music that had been swirling over the program then died, with Markéta riveted by the deadlock. Nothing but immense suspense.

Only two conscious people remained, staring at each other. Simon broke the nail-biting tension with a dose of realism for the dissociated man to hear.

"In case you can't see what's going on right now, I'm tryin' to keep this girl ALIVE!! She's **bleeding out**." Simon stood his ground, not moving away from Lizzie's gushing neck, even though his in-field partner was as limp as a bonefish.

Smash cut over to the knife-wielding Johnny, and back to the firmer-than-firm Simon.

A standstill: two men who just wouldn't budge in their respective beliefs.

The orchestral soundtrack began to swell.

"C'mon…someone *say* or *do* something!" Markéta whined as she watched on. "And save my sister…PLEASE…she's gotta be dying…"

"Stay right where you are, Helks."

Who's going to make the first move? And where's some help?? Lizzie needs medical attention!

Johnny—crazier and braver than Simon could've anticipated in the moment—recklessly stormed the broad-shouldered man who'd been doing his best to nurse Lizzie's substantial laceration. The element of surprise had worked, and Johnny was now the one dominating instead of the one being dominated.

"CRAZY FUCKER! STOP!!" Simon howled.

"Die, Daddy…*die*…**die**…DIE, DADDY…*DIE*…**DIE!**" the unhinged male responded incessantly as he rained down blow after blow to Simon's nose.

Holy shit, that psychopath has reverted back to his child persona…this is scary…

A cutaway shot of the half-demolished homes planted outside hastily postponed the exasperation happening inside the centerpiece home.

"Why in God's name would it cut away NOW?! Get back to showing what's going on in the house! I've seen enough of the outside crap to last a lifetime. Get back to what matters!!" Markéta demanded, on pins and needles.

When *The Last Offender* finally cut back into the home, Johnny was handcuffed and roughed up—apprehended by a pair of musclebound freaks. All while Simon, a bloody mess, snail-crawled on the floor.

What happened?? How'd they stop him from pounding that guy into submission? Why'd they not show that?!

"GET THAT MENTAL PATIENT OUTTA HERE!" a green scrub-shirted paramedic yelled over to the enormous men.

"Right away…" one of them said obediently.

This is insane! Who are these new people?? Was this all just a facade?

Markéta's head was spinning. "Where are they taking Johnny? What're they gonna do with my sister?! What does all of this mean, for the love of God? Somebody please **tell** me!!"

The off-center program—now taking place outside—shifted to a top-down drone shot as a violin-based motif played over a montage of everything that had led up to the dramatic conclusion.

Blood-soaked and bawling, Johnny was shoved into a white van with total disregard for his safety.

"WHAT ABOUT LIZZIE? SHOW HER AGAIN!!" the older sibling screamed in her padded cell.

Suddenly coming into view, a modern-looking helicopter landed nearby the crazy scene as a trio of gurneys was briskly taken into the house by the chopper's crew. No wasted motions.

"Thank you; thank you *so much*. Go save her!" Markéta clapped.

As a superbly ostentatious symphony swept over the speakers, Lizzie was carefully cinched into her temporary bed by an EMT. *The Last Offender* then cut to black.

No; wait. What? Why's it ending? This can't be the end…

Several seconds of complete darkness passed until credits rolled—echoing the much-talked-about and much-maligned series finale of *The Sopranos*.

Markéta Janis was quite the livid captive.

Is that it, then? A lack of finality…after all those episodes, after all those cliffhangers?! No closure, no answers??

The older sibling looked around her white-walled prison, a frequent action of hers while being confined. "What have you done with my little sister?! She better be okay…is anyone even *listening* to me?! I KNOW you're watching my every move, you shitheads!"

A conked Johnny Helks surfaced precipitously on her screen for a post-credits scene. Strapped in by leather constraints on a hospital cot with IVs hooked into his right arm, the freed prisoner was all alone. Just like he'd been at the outset of the pilot.

Markéta stopped breathing momentarily and watched him with a grain of empathy, as well as a marginal hope—for some strange reason—that his eyes would open.

And after an uncomfortable closeup, Johnny woke. Sedated and sore, the restrained man mouthed just two words: "I'm sorry."

Again, the sleek display darkened. But unlike before, when the confounding program had stayed blank for an insufferable minute, it immediately switched to a bird's-eye-view—of Markéta's padded enclosure itself.

What in the hell's this?!

Text sprang onto the black-mirrored monitor, reading: **-TO BE CONTINUED…SOON…VERY SOON…STAND BY-**

"Oh…mind games, huh? Okay. I can do it right back!" the imprisoned woman said.

With the tug of a few cords, Markéta hoisted the near-weightless TV above her head and chucked it toward one of the white walls.

"That's easily eleven now!!" The feisty female folded her arms and waited.

Notwithstanding cracked glass and a flickering screen, the closed-circuit television remained squarely focused on the twitchy twenty-three-year-old, who was now completely ready—more than ready—to meet her captor.

And she would.

Soon.

Very soon.

Stand by? I HAVE BEEN.

POST-PRODUCTION: The Visionary

"Hot damn; another one destroyed! She's such a renegade," the editor surveyed.

A production assistant clicked the end of a red ballpoint pen compulsively. "Should we alienate her some more? Sprinkle opiates in the next food drop? Looks to me like she's on edge and needs it."

The reviser disagreed with his colleague. "No. That wouldn't do any good. Besides, we've beaten that procedure into the ground! The druggie has already had enough trauma thrown her way, and above all else, she's seen the ending."

"She read the text, too…"

"Exactly! So it wouldn't have much of a point, would it?" the celluloid cleanser probed.

"Suppose not; and she's been made aware—however slightly—of the phase that's to come. But not of the mind-scrambling vapors that are about to…"

"Right you are; I forgot about those! We don't have much time to kill today; it's flying by…" The middle-aged bespectacled man checked his Fitbit Ionic. "Miss Drake's about to arrive and take a look at the most recent cut; that should be stimulating. Hopefully it's up to her high standards."

"You've put your best work into this project, Donald. You have really condensed the complexity into an easy-to-follow trajectory. I wouldn't panic if I were you."

"Thanks a lot, Harrison. I guess I shouldn't be too worried…Claire used to be pretty demanding and intimidating, but she's softened up."

"She *definitely* has; and she'd come in to see the dailies, which wasn't expected by any of us," Harrison added superfluously. "Claire's cool now."

"What's this I hear as I enter the monitor room? I'm cool *now*? What about BEFORE?" the former commander in chief asked, closing the biometric, fingerprint-coded door behind her.

"Oh! What a pleasant surprise. Morning, Miss Drake. We didn't mean to offend you…Donald and I were just talking about how great you've been through this whole process!"

Claire Drake waved off the alarmed explanation. "It's fine, guys. Your blood pressure can lower…I'm not here to headhunt. We've got too much to do today."

"We absolutely do! You look lovely, by the way," Donald buttered up the determined lady. "Would you like to do a run-through of the rough?"

"Isn't necessary; I know we've got gold and I trust your cut judgment. I've watched most of it already, anyway. So where are we here? She's done watching, I see…" Claire said.

"That she is; that she is. None too happy about the text blurb, though."

Harrison chuckled. "Would *you* be happy reading that *stand by* line, Donald? I think the woman can receive a pass for being mad. She's been trapped in a nondescript cell and forced to watch a show that's harshly exploited her past life and endangered her sister's present one!"

The main editor lightly shook his head at his truth-telling associate.

"Why're you bug-eyeing me, man?"

"Are you **questioning** my ambitious, soon-to-be imitated program, Harrison?" Claire asked pointedly. "Because I'd say that if you feel so strongly about Markéta's predicament—about this elaborate examination of a real, comprehensive story with only raw reactions—then maybe you should hand over your access badge to me right now, yes?"

"Oh, no; with apologies to you, I didn't mean it like that, Miss Drake. I only meant to bring recognition to the girl's ongoing situation." The production assistant gulped. "I mean, it has been a *tad* exploitative from start to finish. Don't you agree?"

"Exploitative? Let's talk about what that word means. To me, it means *money*. This show will be a cash cow for everyone involved: for EVERYONE who's here in this bunker and stationed in the seven others spread about this arranged terrain of factory-made pain; for EVERYONE who's still out in the field cleaning up the mess; and for EVERY SINGLE ONE of the sponsors that have made all this possible. Regardless of whether they were fortunate enough to receive screen time in the show or not—mark my educated words, they knew what they were getting into…"

Both Donald and Harrison nodded like the biggest pair of douchebag yes-men to ever live.

"And you know why I'm so confident in that bold prediction?" Claire continued. "Do you?"

The well-paid employees stammered, creating answers that their boss would like to hear. "Uh, 'cause there's nothing else like it?" Donald guessed nervously.

"Yes…uh-huh…go on…" the former president said.

Harrison piggybacked off of his colleague's hollow, programmed words. "And it's actually real?"

"That too!" Claire concurred. "But the most vital thing about it will be the viewership. The large demographic we've been researching over the past month has been wonderful! You know what all has gone into this: scouts going to low-income suburbs, talking to families desperate enough to sign off on their kids participating in our entertainment event—lots of legwork. But we went out of our way to keep the selected safe. Houses stocked with goods…EVERY house was, for that matter. And comfortable beds or couches for them to sleep on. It was all mapped out."

Both diffident men nodded again.

"Fellas, *The Last Offender's* only been in the can for, what, like a couple of months? The length of the damn thing was only three days and two nights, and although I had really wanted it to go on for much longer—as did all our paying sponsors and those overpriced trauma victim actors by our undiscovered plane crash site—you and the crew have managed to squeeze a whopping thirteen installments outta this juicy orange!" She smiled tenderly. "Yeah, so it's not picture locked just yet, but it's incredibly close to being complete. And if you'll humor me for a second, lemme get back to that misleading word Harrison has brought up: *exploitative*, and all the variations that come with it…"

"Go right ahead," Donald said tepidly. "Floor's yours."

"Our ethnically diverse research groups have experienced a mutual elation during the exploitation of what I have gone out of my way to create and fund…so I take it as an affront, Harrison, that you'd throw that word around like it was some sort of damning thing. This show of mine, this big-league brainchild, has done record numbers when it pertains to its across-the-board approval ratings. RECORD NUMBERS! Those two things you've both mentioned: unparalleled originality, there's nothing else like it, yadda yadda yadda, as well as the mysterious realness presented within the format—of course they've played a role."

"Sure…and I never had any doubt abou—"

Claire brazenly cut Harrison off to parley more corporate speak. "But where others have failed, I have succeeded in this saturated market. I have taken the reality television bull by its horns and I haven't let go. I've stayed right on its back. An illusion is important to maintain. Viewers *want* to suspend their disbelief; they *want* to be taken on a remarkable ride, and they even like to be confused! I've always believed that to be true, which is clear by the way I've had this series butchered by you; right, Donald?! Enhancing a grounded reality with a lifted pageantry—and padding when need be with reshoot dramatizations, such as that mannequin add-in that didn't *actually* happen to Johnny—all makes for a better product. And while the on-location filming done here in Montana wasn't that difficult for me to acquire a thirty-five-hundred-acre land grant for, funding for the gaudy, expensive monster actually *was*…since it was the most advanced prosthetic robotic ever assembled. The bioengineered sky above is another great example of the limitless depths we've gone to in molding the clay that is *The Last Offender*…"

Donald shut off the fifty-inch display monitors inside their operations control room and looked right into the eyes of his effeminate boss. "Well, I for one have never disagreed with any of that. And what about the song that plays during our opening credits? I love it…as it's **perfect** for the show, and everybody knows in this biz that having a memorable theme—a signature tune—is half the battle. Granted, there were potholes for me to pass over. I didn't think amassing a set that's quadruple the size of Central Park was necessary. Witnessing the selected having to contend with so much was indeed disturbing. And I may have had a *minor* issue with chemtrails being distributed in the atmosphere aboveground—which our scarred star saw only because that damned dog woke him up way too early—but my picky gripes have since passed."

"They're only contrails, my good man. Contrails!" Claire winked, grinning deviously. "And I'm glad Johnny saw all that; I'm actually *glad* he was awakened by that dog and then saw our two planes. Both of those things weren't meant to happen, but it's unscripted moments like that that have all played a part in adding even more intrigue to the proceedings! Damn, now I've got Longwave stuck in my head…"

"It's certainly been an unforgettable series to be a part of, and I also love our theme music! Longwave's a great band; their album is excellent from front to back. Donald's been playing it a bunch while editing…as well as some of the others that were in the primary pile Johnny perused—our apocalyptic playlist!"

"But Harrison hates hardcore! He's into indie and indie only. Anyway, many good songs are on *Secrets are Sinister.* Happy we were able to put it up there. 'Life is Wrong' has gotta be my fave, but 'No Direction' is just so lyrically fitting, and it easily established the mood we were shooting for when piecing the trailer together."

"Our licensing department did a heck of a job landing that track, and that trailer's ending where our monster is RIGHT up to Lizzie's face with the tornado vortex behind them? That final shot gives me goose bumps every time!" Claire said proudly. "Not all of this show's process has been mired in controversy."

"Controversial avenues aside, I've had fun working on *Offender*," Harrison appeased. "I worked on several other so-called reality shows in my younger years. Like take *Bar Rescue,* for one—that restaurant-renovating show's so fake. They'd do multiple takes for every little thing, even when the braggart host talked to the chef and staff."

"I remember that chintzy show; I'm not surprised whatsoever by that revelation there!" Donald said. "Not all reality shows are terrible, however. Without a show like *Face/Off* and our decent connections made there years ago, we wouldn't have been able to nab Neville Page, our brilliant concept designer."

Claire saluted the selfless recognition to one of their affiliates. "Wholeheartedly agree. Why do you think I had the movies *Cloverfield* and *Oblivion* littered in the wreckage outside? Shout-out to Half Price Books, by the way, for giving us great bulk deals on all the media that we plastered around our homemade landscape! But ya know, if not for Neville, there'd really be no monster to fear, no destruction to gasp at. And on a smaller scale, this scar on my face—the one that I got from a disgruntled ex-employee—would be a LOT more noticeable if it weren't for his talents with concealer…even after my surgery!"

"I forgot that you even *had* a scar!!" Donald lied.

"Thank you; that's kind of you to say. My new daily talk show that just launched, *Unscarred*, has been doing well in its time slot, partly because that girl was my first guest…so I guess I shouldn't be too mad at her for scarring me with coffee."

"Was just another opportunity to build your brand…"

"Absolutely, Harrison! That debut episode received rave reviews. But gentlemen, getting right back to why we're doing this…we had a motto at our *Offender* pitch sessions: stop at no expense for suspense. Everybody else in the game is treading water while we're scuba diving. You realize that? We are scuba divers, and with this resourceful undertaking, we have discovered deep-sea treasures together."

"I feel like we're copulating over ourselves too much here!" Donald larked.

"Copulation is key…because when you've gone to these galaxy-sized lengths, why not showboat a bit? Look at the drop-off warehouse as another example: we used ASR employees only. No humans handling the selected discharges so as to avoid any unnecessary conflict or long-winded exposition. Just black-and-white instructions given. I can't stress it enough; all the focus and sacrifice that has been put into this collective effort is unprecedented. And I'm the proud creator of a contained universe with its world-building brilliance. Up there…" Claire Drake pointed to the crystal-clear glass ceiling. "Above this bonkers bunker, an undesirable post that you two have resided in for the duration of this covert program, lies a masterpiece—full of authentic cadavers that were flown in from overseas and believable structures that were built by hundreds of competent hands. Facilitating a new texture to pop culture; that's what we've achieved. Gentlemen, this is *truly* one masterpiece that shan't be overlooked."

"I'll give ya that…it most definitely won't be ignored. I know that for a fact!" Harrison intimated. "Way too much intrigue. On all levels."

"Personally speaking, what I found to be so ingenious about *Offender*…" Donald chimed in, "…was that…like, no matter WHAT they did up there, they weren't going to get far. You know what I mean? It was totally futile. They'd be cut off at every turn, either by Tar or by our main agents, Simon and Brent. It was perfect all around. That's what I found so clever about it."

Claire giggled like a schoolgirl. "You guys named the monster Tar?"

Both the badge-wearing men shrugged innocently as Harrison said, "It's fitting! That one set he roamed where he breathtakingly destroyed so many houses during the chase scene with Lizzie—we coined that area *Tar's Yard*…oh, how we're gonna miss him and his menace…"

Donald conceded with his live-in bunkmate. "It was sad to see Tar systematically shut down. We loved that weighty monstrosity…"

"Me too; me too. And ya know somethin', I like that name you gave him. It's suitable! Just a shame he had to be put to sleep. That towering water tank fried its electrical components. We thought that the thing was waterproof, since it was extensively tested in a downpour simulator before launch. But that amount was simply too much for it to take all at once. Never in a million years did I ever expect an ass-kicking twister to hit our stretch of land, let alone defeat our beloved beast! We didn't think to simulate something like that…"

"There was nothing you could do to save Tar?" Harrison asked in seriousness. "Nothing at all?"

"Sadly, no. But it was a blessing in disguise, 'cause that massive thing was wide and hard to house!" Claire divulged. "For me, it'll be more of a relief than a grief to move on from its passing. Or **Tar's** passing, rather; sorry." She sheened, showcasing her pearly whites to the two rapt employees, then grew somber. "I'm just bummed that I've lost my investment to Mother Nature. The budget for Tar was lucrative—equivalent to a *Star Wars* feature-length film. Oh well; it was quite the visual when its death took place, was it not?!"

"Sure was. We thought it was so magnificent…that it *had* to have been predetermined!" Donald said.

"I wish that that were the case! Isn't it amusing…you go and hire yourself a dozen or more writers to craft possible set pieces, and none of them can come close to hatching something that visually dazzling, that naturally spectacular…"

"Even Simon and Brent thought it was planned! They didn't buy the tornado as a real entity at first."

"Very true, Harrison; they did not. That's why editing exists, though. We really had to cut that fat off the bone. When they went blabbing about all the inner workings, I was halfway tempted to pull the plug. I didn't know where it was going to go. But luckily, my man Donald here was able to salvage the show and scrub off their immersion-breaking reveals. He kept it pure, steady—and rich with escapism."

Donald smiled, hesitant to ask about the agents' whereabouts. "Are they all right now? Simon's face was a mess; it didn't look too promising for the guy after Johnny was through with him. And while Brent wasn't worse for wear, he *was* knocked out by Helks. Any update on them, Miss Drake?"

"They've been…handled," she said flatly.

"Handled?" Harrison repeated with some unease in his voice.

"Yes. They broke protocol by breaking the fourth-wall guidelines, so they were relieved."

"I see…" Donald mused, pausing. "So I guess it's safe to say that they're not in one of the bunks?"

"No; they are not. And they won't ever be again."

An uncomfortable moment passed before Claire genially changed the subject. "On a lighter note, you gentlemen have done a fine job here and will not be *handled* anytime soon. Not in the way that they were, at least!" the vivaciously confident woman joked. "I thank you for all of your hard work throughout! But pardon me—as you know, today is THE day, and I must be going…Markéta Janis awaits my presence…"

"We'll be watching," Harrison assured. "If she gets disorderly, we will step in."

"I'm sure you would! But I'm convinced it'll be okay. We're set to pump the vapors of hydrogen into her quarters, so a narcosis should be ripened by the time I go in. But thank you for having my back."

"Thank *you*, Madam President. It's been a wonderful experience!" Donald said.

"Yes, yes; it certainly has," Harrison simpered, biting his tongue and shaking the soft hand of his imperious paycheck-giver. "I was just about to make the call to Bunker Five and tell them to release the gases in Markéta's cell."

"Good man. Wish me luck, guys."

"You've got a whole lot more than luck on your side; it's not like you even need it!" Donald boasted as both employees smiled at their superior. "We've got you covered either way, though."

Claire smiled back at the two men and exited the operations room. As she did, an approaching advisor of hers—a dapper, blue-suited man in his early thirties—greeted the secretly nervous woman with a powdered Danish donut and a LIVE Kombucha in tow.

"Hello, hello, Miss Drake. Mega big day today. I believe you need a sweet and a healthy drink."

"For me, Elijah?"

"Who else? Nobody else around here deserves such deliciousness; only you!"

"Thank you. I *have* needed some sinful sweets and organic probiotics in my system."

"Figured you did," Elijah said knowingly, taking a Bai beverage out of his jacket pocket to drink. "Good thing we have loads of that zestful kombucha and this antioxidant infusion of excellence still in stock. The products didn't get a second on-air…too bad, so sad. But now we've got boxes of it!"

"I was just discussing our backers and their crapshoot deals with Donald and Harrison. Many were left out in the cold since the show ran so depressingly short. Perhaps I'll be nice and give a few of the unaired products exclusive screen time during our next venture— half-off their original agreements, even—to show I'm sincere AND sorry!"

"That'd be graciously accepted by them, I would think."

"Oh, I know it would be. Make the calls; see what they say. We'll place these drinks front and center, right on the table…with their labels facing the camera *American Idol*-style, and maybe a box of Wheat Thins or somethin' to snack on. Let's go ahead and do that."

"Will contact those companies as soon as we're done speaking here!"

"Good; very good. So how's our fabled antihero doing down the hall? Any problems?" Claire questioned as she ate her freshly made pastry.

"Not too many. But he is crankier than a disturbed hornet's nest."

"Up his dosage, then. We didn't strap Johnny into a bed and hook an IV into his arm for nothing. She has to feel at ease in there—**has** to—for all of this to pan out. That's absolutely the highest priority."

Elijah smiled accordingly. "Couldn't agree with you more, even if I tried to! But what if *she* doesn't agree to go along with what's planned?"

"She will. I'm not concerned about that. I can come from lots of angles to coax her into doing it. She's ours now. Don't doubt me, my handsome, overpaid aide. I've got this."

"Not doubting you or your prowess! I'm sure you'll take care of it quite handily."

"Yes; you can count on that. All right, well…it's nearing go time. See you soon, hopefully. Do not forget that extra dosage. We need him to be obedient."

"You've got it! Ah, I wish we never had to depart. Ciao for now!"

"Ciao."

After her dreamboat of an assistant rounded the corner of the underground corridor, Claire took a deep breath and exhaled.

This is going to be amusing.

With her index finger on the intercom button beside Markéta's padded cell door, she knew that what she had to initiate couldn't be adjourned any longer.

It had to be taken care of. The next phase relied on it.

No time like the present. You can do this. You've done harder things.

"Like when I stood up to that homeless would-be rapist with a kick to the nuts…" Claire refreshed herself cockily. "I've got this in the bag. After all, I'm the one in control."

The hydrogen vapors shot into the cell loudly, hissing like a rattlesnake.

That was fast.

"Press the button. It's time."

Why am I even worrying about this? She's gonna be disoriented! Wait for a minute. Okay. Go…

"Ms. Janis? This is Claire Drake, former President of the United States. Please do not be startled by the fumes infiltrating your chamber, and don't get testy once you see me. Need I remind you that you are being watched, and every single move of yours is being documented. I'm coming in now; keep a safe distance as I enter. You'll be slightly mixed up by a hydrogen narcosis, and your psychotropic cocktail may contain some hallucinogens. Simply precautionary measures. I'm entering…"

Claire placed her palm on the access terminal, and after a chirpy-sounding beep and a green light shone bright, a blast-proof door opened.

As envisioned, the confined female—who was near tears—looked to be dumbfounded by her well-known visitor, squinting her eyes at the first real sight of incandescent light.

"It's okay; just breathe for me. Soon you'll be steady. It's a small dose—since I'd like you coherent enough to speak, but not strong enough to strike. Can you breathe, please?"

"Yeah…yeah, I'll try…" Markéta eked out, gaining courage to speak more freely as she breathed. "Why have you, *you* of *all* people, done something like this? What do you want from me; what do you want from my sister? Where is she?? What is this bullshit?!"

"I had a feeling you'd be a question machine." Claire Drake smiled at the alienated Markéta Janis, trying to soothe the drug-addled woman. "I've come here today to offer you a new lease on life."

"Please tell me why," the twenty-three-year-old requested. "*Why* have you created this?"

"Markéta, dear, the *why* of it all is multifaceted. But let me start from the ground up…"

Staring into Claire's energized eyes with her tired and astray ones, Markéta discomforted the wealthy woman with gravitas.

This is becoming clumsy. Begin the process.

"Once upon a time when consumer options were limited, you didn't have to be as inspired creatively to receive attention. Back then, it was a lot easier to get noticed if you had something good. But today, there're **so** many kinds of content creators vying for relevancy. Everyone has a voice, an opinion, and a need to speak their journey. Yet it's tough—very tough—to come across worthwhile ones."

"What's your POINT?!" the unbalanced female yelled. "Where's my sis, you fucking witch??"

Claire put her hand up as if she were directing traffic. "First off, I'm going to remind you once again about what I said a minute ago: don't get testy with me. Or else this'll go a lot differently, okay? I'm in control here—not you. Second thing, you're going to want to listen to me. So no outbursts. And I'll get to your sister in a moment, but not if you keep nagging me about it."

"All right; just get through your spiel. Whatever it takes to be enlightened…if I *ever* am!"

The former president continued on as if she hadn't even stopped. "Life's fleeting, unpredictable. We honestly have no idea when something great—or something bad—is gonna happen to us. So you have to leave a mark before time expires. Especially in this attention-deficit, flavor-of-the-week world we've helped cultivate today. Understand?"

Markéta barely got a nod in, waving her hands in front of her bloodshot eyes, stupefied by the ghost-fingered trails.

"Since other TV shows can't quite compare to my own, the Internet is my only competition for what I have set out to do. But those government-issued phones are like conduits—digital bridges to advertise on. Two years ago, I had a vision to construct something that would transcend ALL platforms. That's what this is, the wild show you just watched—that's something that'll get people talking. During these crazy distraction-filled times, you've got to stand out in an intensely crowded market, and that was my main motivation to create *The Last Offender*…"

Markéta continued to stare a hole into Claire's eyes.

Keep going…she'll learn…

"*Offender* was about choices, about destiny. Steering through the rights and wrongs. What I'm getting at is this: we all have our stories. Mine's been well-documented, and I've made something of myself from it. But your story…and your sister's story? They aren't known at all, and I think they *should* be. So that's basically why I've done this costly experiment."

"Because of my real anguish and trauma suffered that night with Johnny over a decade ago, you've decided to package it into some tidy presentation? For ATTENTION, for PROFIT? I hope this show of yours bombs and bombs hard."

"*The Last Offender* bombing? Pfft. Highly unlikely! The show's already tracking **well** above our lofty projections. Even the damned doubters said they'll hate-watch it in toxic comments sections, since it seems so expertly engaging! Their words, not mine…though I do agree. Plus! Its theme song is about to become number one on every online music service that's left, and the show isn't even out yet; its teaser trailer has been watched over twenty million times in just its first week of release alone! Also, it caused a fatal car accident after going viral!!"

"THAT'S NOTHING TO BE PROUD OF! And that No Direction song *was* kinda catchy, until I had to hear it over and over again!!"

"Wasn't our fault you chose to keep destroying those television sets. You could've just heard it thirteen times, but no…ya had to go and be a rebel."

"I HATE YOU FOR WHAT YOU'VE DONE!"

"Last warning: *don't* raise your voice to me, Markéta. I'm serious. I will be respected."

"I know you're a master at faking honesty since you were the president for a term, but surely even you can see just how mental this all is."

Claire Drake whooped in amusement. "It's not mental whatsoever, my dear girl! It's **sane**. Creating a world like this…one cannot be crazy, one must only be *cunning*. And that's what I am. Above us, out there…what you saw on the series wasn't just a huge set that I had to have constructed; it was an actual place. We're in Montana right now! Thirty-five hundred acres of booby traps, funhouses, and mind freaks. Faux homes built with state loans. Anything you could imagine, we gave a thought to at some point. Subtle nods throughout—to Johnny's past and even your sister's, with lots of scattered product placement and nostalgia-nurturing. I won't bore you with the details, because I'm positive that you'd like me to move forward faster…but I also had to have an entire penitentiary recreated from *scratch*. We went to that level of real. We even retri—"

"WHY WAS I ABDUCTED? WHERE'S LIZZIE?? SHE WAS STABBED…ALL BECAUSE OF YOUR DAMN SHOW! AND HOW'D YOU MANAGE TO CONVINCE FIVE FUCKING FAMILIES TO PUT THEIR KIDS INTO SOMETHING LIKE THIS ANYWAY, INCLUDING MY OWN?!"

"You know what; we've already come this far in the social niceties, and I know that I've given you a last warning, but I'll let that be a freebie. As long as you don't touch me, we are good. Just don't interrupt again. Regarding the five families, I didn't really have to do a lot of convincing. You'll be surprised to learn that your grandmother was the easiest one to nail down with an agreement, as she'd burned through her life savings on getting back that new 'Net for her and your sister! Shootin' fish in a barrel easy, I swear. And those conjoined girls' parents were the second easiest. Special needs children require an incredible amount of financial help, so I'm glad I could assist them there. As for Tamika, do I even need to say anything? She was our token black girl from the ghetto; diversity equals ratings! Her penniless mom was tickled pink when we selected her. Only snag in the road was Riley; her mom wanted the money badly but didn't want to do the drugging. So I got Riley's boyfriend to slip her the secret sauce at a movie theater. Had to pay him off too, though. But I've made all their lives fruitful and bountiful. Oh…and your sis is safe and sound; she has recovered completely…and she's in dry clothes now!"

"Thank God."

"I'm not Satan, sweetie. When things spiraled out of control at the end with your sister, I was the one lobbying in the editing booth to fix it…censoring some of the bloodshed by cutting away was the right call all in all. Rest assured that our prop guy—the one who botched the blade switch—has been properly dealt with. I give you my word Lizzie's living. But this, right now, isn't about her—it's about you."

"It's unimaginable, what you've gone and done…but keep talking," the older sibling said with little energy after expending so much of it. "I do wanna know your justification for this framed hell."

"So, where was I before ya cut me off? Oh yeah; the jail blueprint! The finest architects were hired, since I had to make Johnny think that he woke up in his very own prison—in fact, it was of utmost importance that it'd be such a defined replica once he came to consciousness that Mr. Helks wouldn't even THINK that something was off about the high-priced structure. We also retrieved the makeshift tools that he'd been hiding inside his legit cell!"

"What about the people—the other cellmates? Where'd they all go?"

"Wow, you are really woozy! Perhaps our pharmaceutical distributors went too high on your dosage."

"Perhaps…" Markéta said, slumping her head to the side.

"In any case, the question that you've asked me should be put in reverse. You should've asked where *Johnny* went…and, well, you'd already know just where he went if you were actively listening! Mr. Helks was drugged and then choppered out here—the great state of Montana! In the middle of NOWHERE!"

"But that blast at the beginning…it sounded like it actually happened. Was that not real too? And how'd the prison that he was *originally* in allow you to just poach him outta incarceration?!"

"The explosion was real. We wanted him to wake up with true shock, so we opted to demolish a building close by the constructed correctional institution. The downside was that my architectural unit had to erect the physical structure first, only to then destroy it. I gave them a sympathy raise for that. As for his prison situation, it was a payoff. The penitentiary he was in was struggling; their walls were crumbling. So I threw money at 'em, and we made a mutually beneficial deal. They didn't care one iota about the guy; I was surprised by how easy it was! I'm now the sole owner—or warden, you could say—of Johnny Allen Helks."

"What if he'd gotten into a car—something around the area with working wheels—and then sped off? If we're in a state and not a contained place, how could you have been so sure that any of them wouldn't have found a way to escape the game?"

"Every single car on our lot was already broken down; there were NO working wheels. They were junkyard fetches. Engines were extracted, stripped clean to appear usable, and that's it. But I'm glad you've asked about escape routes! We gave a lot of thought to the series and had many discussions about it. Have you ever seen *The Truman Show*?"

"With Jim Carrey? Yeah, I've seen that movie."

"Then you know that by the end of the movie, when Truman was sailing on his boat…trying to flee the bogus town, he slammed right into a wall. A painted backdrop—like the ones done up in old cinema, before CGI was a thing. Its blue-skied fence had been placed there as the cutoff point—a seemingly real restriction up close. Except for the door that he eventually found and opened, of course. My point is that it was an artificial world at its core. To a great degree, it was a small space. So I wanted to do something more cutting-edge than that. I wanted a REAL location, where there were no walls, no cutoffs, and no sound stages anywhere. Only obstacles. And if Johnny—or the selected—had strayed too far from our checkpoints, we'd then dispatch agents like Simon and Brent. Or on special occasions, we would call in the big dog if any of them were resting on their laurels, or if it was beginning to become a little boring and we had to spice things up…"

"Who? Oh; you mean that hideous monster?"

"Tar. Yes, him!" Claire Drake grinned, liking the oily beast's name more and more as time passed.

"What *was* that thing, anyway?" the woozy woman inquired.

"An expensive headache. That's what it was!"

"Why did it always chase after the girls?! Why not Johnny? HE deserved to be eaten!"

Claire rolled her eyes. "Thought this would go without saying, but all of those teens reaped sympathy…unlike Johnny. And at the end of the day, we had a show to craft. If our monster's motive had been to pursue Johnny instead, that wouldn't have elicited any danger, fear, or empathy within our focus groups! He is—for the most part—an unsympathetic character. Irredeemable, even. So that's why the monster was programmed to only go after the girls. But let's not talk about Tar's background right now. It's altogether inconsequential to what lies ahead. I'd like to talk about *you* and your future…"

"My future? What about it? I'd honestly just like to see my sister. I want answers. Where is she right now? I **need** to see her."

"Well, if you sign this contract in my hand, you'll receive every answer you could ever want. And your future will be bright. That I can guarantee."

"*How*? After torturing my little sis, having my ass kidnapped at a bar by some guy spiking my drinks, and forcing me to watch that awful experiment…you wanna make it right all of a sudden? How would you go about doing that, exactly? With money? Is that what it'd be?"

Claire clasped her hands together and sighed. "Markéta, you can either play ball with me, or take the ball and go home—it's your choice, needless to say…but if I'm not mistaken, that home of yours is a roach-infested, bottom-feeding hellhole. But! Like I've stated, it is *your* choice to make."

"You can't do this; you CANNOT get away with something that is this wrong!" the captive woman cried.

"I already *have* gotten away with it. Look at it like this…even if you leave and run to the liberal media with the truth, it'd just sound implausible; so who're they gonna believe? A down-on-her-luck junkie or the former POTUS? I think I like my chances and dislike yours…"

"But…what you've done is a crime. It's *several* of them!"

The former president nodded her confirmation. "It would be; yes, it would. IF the selected—and their parents, who signed them up for it—threatened to sue for mistreatment and defamation. But do you think I worry about all that? I'm a president; I'm protected. And I have a fleet of lawyers. Regardless. Those kids aren't pissed; they're going to be celebrities! They are signed. It's a done deal."

"This is a living nightmare," Markéta said.

"No; it's a dream coming true for you, Ms. Janis. If you sign on the dotted line, that is. Think of the drugs you could score with unlimited funds! If you're not cool with that, feel free to retrieve your things at the drop-off, and we'll just see who wins in court."

The twenty-three-year-old mulled it over, lolling her overwrought thinker from side to side as her withdrawal symptoms screamed from within. "I—I—"

"What'll it be?" Claire Drake interrupted the captive's stuttering. "My time is of the essence. What does Markéta Janis want the *most* in this moment?"

"I want…I need…the money…so tell me how I'll be able to get it…" The drug-dependent female deferred to the high-powered woman in charge. "Tell me how you'll brighten my future."

"Right, then! Well, after signing this contract, I'll whisk you away to where Johnny is now. We will go into his room. As per the contract's wording, you'll be agreeing to us filming your first confrontation with him in over ten years. *The Last Offender* wasn't ever intended to be the end, as we have SO much more to document. For instance, do you even know why your parents got divorced?"

"Of course I do; they separated because of what happened to me and what I'd become!"

"My dear, how little you know. That's the reason your family told you, but it isn't the reality of the situation. While Johnny *did* have a part in breaking them up, it had nothing to do with you—it had more to do with your mother…"

"What?! Tell me exactly what you mean by that right now!"

Claire wagged her right index finger like a windshield wiper. "Nope; that was just a sneak preview. A teaser, if you will. Always leave 'em wanting—that's the mark of great storytelling."

"And what if I don't agree to go along with this madness…this…"

"**Miniseries**…sorry for not clarifying what it is. It's going to be called *Victim Versus Villain*. Good title, yeah? We're gonna air it right after *Offender's* done with its run in the spring. We're still negotiating with three major networks who are in a bidding war for TLO's sanctioned home, but if I don't like their final offers, I'll just put it on my own network as a fallback! Hmm…that'd probably be better!! Cut out the middleman and release it all at once, so mindless morons can binge on it! One way or another, it's airing. Exciting, isn't it?"

Markéta became irritated by Claire's glorification of her traumatization. "Sure; whatever."

"But to clarify all the more: if you don't agree to our arrangement, you won't get paid. And I suppose I'd be seeing you in court, since I know that you'd fight this kidnapping tooth and nail!"

"What's this purported series even trying to accomplish? You didn't fill me in…"

"Oh, right! It'll be a lot more stripped down than the previous one with your sister. A *Dateline* or *60 Minutes* sorta thing. Remember those shows? Probing, personal material that a variety of viewers will be invested in. It'll be you and him. One-on-one. In a room, with cameras rolling and Johnny detained, securely strapped to a hospital bed. Over the period of a three-day weekend that'll be jam-packed with surprises and intense guests, we're going to explore both ends of the spectrum. Your family; his family. Really…this is just a huge, HUGE onion that has layers upon layers. You have no earthly idea how **connected** you all are. And guess what? I'm gonna be the one who conducts the interview! How's that sound to you?"

"Sounds…terrifying…unsettling…" Markéta Janis answered candidly.

"You think so? Nah; I think that for you, it'll be a scrubbing of the soul. A purification. An opportunity to dispense the demons of your past; a once-in-a-lifetime chance to rid yourself of what's gutted you."

Markéta broke into a waterfall of tears, her face reddening and her arms quaking. "I can't."

"Hon, it's okay. You can do this. It'll make you so much stronger—all just by talking to him. Confront the man who violated you—who made you forfeit motherhood—and say whatever you wanna say to him. Sign the contract and take my hand; I'll be with you every step of the way…"

"I can go in there and get everything out? And I'll be taken care of financially?"

"Yes; you can. Say and do everything you need. We'll record it all. And *yes*, you will," Claire said.

"Then I'll sign. Gimme the papers."

When you're broke, you break, bitch.

"Delightful! I knew you'd make the right decision. But remember: play ball. There can be absolutely *no* mention of being detained or references to any of this…or else we'll have to stop rolling and reprimand you. The same goes for Johnny, but way worse. We've put electrodes on his hips and nips! Talk about your strict discipline; am I right or what?!"

The light-headed, weak-kneed woman nodded and scribbled her name onto multiple lines of the contract as if she were signing to buy a house. Ocean-blue ink imprinted the thin white sheets as the former president smiled victoriously, pleased to know that she was about to make the most money of her illustrious career by continuing to create controversial content that many people would discuss over wonky watercoolers at their cubicle-plagued workplaces.

"Markéta Erin Janis, you've just made the greatest decision of your life!"

"Doesn't feel like it…" The frail girl wiped salty tears from her face. "Feels like I've sold out."

"You've bought in. BIG difference!" Claire Drake reassured the young woman. "So now that everything's explained away, I'm sure you're wanting to leave this confined space. Me too. Let's move on to the next stage!"

Alongside a wobbly Markéta, Claire exited the padded, vanilla-colored room and they walked down the immaculate corridor in one silent stride. Some paces down the hall, cameramen, makeup artists, and personal assistants—including Elijah—joined the mobile women. Boom mics, lighting fixtures, macchiatos, and skin foundations were all presented—the quintessentials for on-air professionalism.

Gotta look and sound perfect. The whole country's going to be watching these crazy things, the former president thought.

Upon arriving outside Johnny's room, the women started to get their faces powdered and their hair styled while having mics clipped onto their collars as they sat in two cushy booths. Thirty minutes of primping and pre-producing later, Claire asked the chemically altered female—whose effects were wearing off enough to be camera-ready—a couple questions before proceeding inside.

"So this is it. Showtime. Are you sure you'd like to continue? Ready to deal with your damaging past?"

"It's now or never."

"I like that go-getter attitude of yours! Reminds me of…me!!"

Markéta exhibited an expression of conformity, of defeat, of despondency.

"Head on in…"

Claire Drake opened the door for the twenty-three-year-old to finally see the thirty-nine-year-old—an emotionally breakable man who'd ruined all of her innocence in but one evening, and a physically unable man who'd never sincerely apologized for causing her and her family so much pain, so much turmoil.

A tied-down and doped-up Johnny Helks turned his shaved head toward his new visitors and blinked his baggy eyes like he'd just laid them upon a silver-spooned UFO hovering in the night sky. "Markéta?"

"Johnny."

At full volume, the central videographer announced to all personnel standing by, "Quiet on the set! *Victim Versus Villain* goes **live** in three, two, one…"

Acknowledgments

The two years it took to create this story were extremely exhausting but fun. With that being typed, I have some people to personally thank for their words of encouragement as well as their helpful suggestions. Firstly, Tamara Beach. You rock (and roll). Thank you for editing me; thank you for everything. Without your incomparable input and support, *The Last Offender* wouldn't be where it is today. So thanks! Secondly, the beta readers who read the novel in its first-draft stages when many others couldn't find the time to: Derek Mills, Justin Bauer, Luke Carroll, Misty Mount, Jenna Rae Montes, and Caroline Brantley. Lastly, much appreciation to Josh Bennett for making all of this novel's absolutely awesome artwork. You're an amazing artist. We did it, dude. Thank you.

Other books by Noah Nichols (me):

Cat Incarcerated

No Net